P9-CZV-075

BONES OF THE EARTH

ALSO BY ELIOT PATTISON

THE INSPECTOR SHAN NOVELS

Skeleton God

Soul of the Fire

Mandarin Gate

The Lord of Death

Prayer of the Dragon

Beautiful Ghosts

Bone Mountain

Water Touching Stone

The Skull Mantra

ALSO

Bone Rattler

Eye of the Raven

Original Death

Blood of the Oak

Savage Liberty

Ashes of the Earth

BONES OF THE EARTH

ELIOT PATTISON

MINOTAUR BOOKS ☙ NEW YORK

BONES OF THE EARTH. Copyright © 2019 by Eliot Pattison. All rights reserved. Printed in the United States of America. For information, address St. Martin's Press, 175 Fifth Avenue, New York, N.Y. 10010.

www.minotaurbooks.com

The Library of Congress Cataloging-in-Publication Data is available upon request.

ISBN 978-1-250-16968-6 (hardcover)
ISBN 978-1-250-16969-3 (ebook)

Our books may be purchased in bulk for promotional, educational, or business use. Please contact your local bookseller or the Macmillan Corporate and Premium Sales Department at 1-800-221-7945, extension 5442, or by email at MacmillanSpecialMarkets@macmillan.com.

First Edition: March 2019

10 9 8 7 6 5 4 3 2 1

To the unsung heroes
and saints of Tibet,
bastion of the human spirit

BONES OF THE EARTH

CHAPTER ONE

The devout in Tibet wear their altars on their necks, an old lama had explained to Shan years earlier, during his early days in prison. Shan had soon learned that nearly every inmate in his gulag barracks wore a prayer amulet, a *gau*, hung with string or a shoelace, most of them makeshift devices of folded cloth or cardboard with a prayer sewn inside. More than a few of the imprisoned monks would point to their flimsy, makeshift altar and say, only half joking, that their lives hung by a thread. When danger lurked nearby or tormented memories overtook them they would clasp a hand around their gaus and stare toward the distant snowcapped mountains. Their long, unfocused stares had unnerved Shan at first, thinking they were seeing their deaths, but a lama in his fortieth year of imprisonment had said no, they were just consulting a higher plain of existence.

Shan found himself locked in a similarly sightless stare each time he parked at the sprawling complex before him, his hand clasped around his own little copper gau and his eyes tilted toward the square of paper draped over his steering wheel on which an intricate mandala had been drawn. At first he had cajoled himself into thinking he was engaged in meditation but eventually he had come to realize that it was more a trance that let him deny, however briefly, where he was and what he had become.

He jerked back to awareness at the sound of something striking the door of the truck he had driven from Yangkar, and he looked up into the sneering face of Major Xun Wengli, who weeks earlier had discovered Shan's ritual and learned to respond with his own rite, loudly drumming his baton on the truck.

Shan carefully refolded the paper mandala, returned it to the glove box, and climbed out. Xun pointed with his baton at the gau that still hung exposed on Shan's chest, laughing at Shan's embarrassment. Shan ignored him, stuffing the prayer amulet back inside his shirt then walking around to the passenger door to retrieve the uniform tunic that hung there. Xun looked disappointed as Shan fastened the top button of the new constable's tunic, then gestured him toward the three-story concrete building in front of them.

Colonel Tan, governor of Lhadrung County, had not indicated why he wanted Shan in Lhadrung town, seat of the county government, but Shan had assumed he had sent Xun, his senior adjutant, to make certain Shan attended still another briefing on the latest People's Congress or one more lecture on the new, ever-stricter law enforcement initiatives in Tibet.

To his surprise the form he was given to sign by the receptionist in the new government center had his name printed beside the signature line, and the list held fewer than twenty other names, most of which he recognized. It was to be a very private propaganda session. He hesitated when they reached the auditorium door, looking for Colonel Tan, then Xun pushed him past the door, down an unfamiliar corridor. With a chill he saw he was being taken into the new office complex for the Public Security Bureau, which was rapidly expanding its presence in the county. His mind raced as he tried to recall the other names on the registry he had signed. Some were other constables, some senior military officers under Tan—including the wardens of three of his infamous prisons—and two were names that often appeared prominently at the bottom of directives issued by the Public Security headquarters in Lhasa. One of those recent directives had announced a campaign in which officials would be required to swear new loyalty oaths to Beijing while connected to lie detectors. Is that where the gloating

Xun was taking him? Shan found himself slowing, his feet leaden. If he had been summoned to be tested by a lie detector, then he would likely be back in a prison cell before nightfall, or at least unemployed and homeless.

"Quickly, Constable!" came Xun's impatient urging. "Can't be late!" The major motioned Shan through a pair of double doors into a large two-level chamber that had incorporated a natural rock wall on the far side. A shiver ran down his spine as he saw the faded images of a lotus flower on the whitewashed stone, and he recalled that the new government center, like many others in Tibet, had been deliberately built on the site of a former temple. The lower half of the room had been part of a chapel, no doubt one of the subterranean *gonkangs* where fierce, sometimes hideous, protector demons would have been worshipped.

Two rows of seats were arranged to overlook the lower, stagelike level, and Major Xun directed Shan to the only one that was still empty, the last chair in the first row. All the other chairs seemed to be occupied by the others who had signed the registry. One of the gray-uniformed Public Security officers, which the Tibetans called knobs, stepped to a podium at the edge of the little balcony they sat in, nodding to someone out of sight below. As the officer began to read in a rapid, singsong voice from a file before him, Shan studied the lower chamber. Long ago, shelves had been chiseled into the stone face where figurines of lesser deities would have been arranged. The whitewash on the back wall did not entirely conceal the soot stains that started halfway up the wall, where for decades, probably centuries, butter lamps would have burned on an altar, tended night and day by novice monks. Through the whitewash Shan could now make out dim ghostly images of demons which had been painted over the altar. Some of the old Tibetans believed that the demons actually resided in the old gonkangs. One of the protector demons was being crushed by the concrete wall of the new construction. The central figure showed through only faintly, but as Shan studied it he made out a feminine shape with four arms, two of which held a bow and arrow.

When the knob finished droning about some criminal enforcement matter, a door could be heard opening below him and a Tibetan janitor appeared. The gallery watched with a strange fascination as he uncoiled a hose then leaned a mop in the corner where the ledge met the concrete wall before disappearing and returning with a metal armchair. A murmur of nervous laughter rippled through the audience as he stumbled on the hose before placing the chair near the back wall.

Shan looked again for Colonel Tan, governor of the county, who had ordered him to the compound, but saw neither the colonel nor his steadfast matronly assistant Amah Jiejie. Xun caught his gaze with a thin, expectant grin. A Public Security sergeant appeared below, leading a middle-aged Tibetan with thinning hair whose face seemed empty, devoid of expression. The Tibetan shook off the knob's hand, then straightened his clothing, marched to the chair and sat. He looked up at his audience, briefly fixing his intelligent, piercing gaze on each of the men and women in the chairs. Shan was last, and the man's gaze lingered on him, with a hint of curiosity in it now. As he looked at Shan he loosely curled the fingers of one hand and held them briefly over his chest. Another, younger, Public Security officer appeared, a lieutenant whose hair had unusal tinges of auburn in it. He bowed his head to the spectators before turning to the Tibetan. The young knob's thin lips were set in stern determination, but Shan thought he detected a hint of amusement in his eyes.

"Chou Folan?" the lieutenant asked.

The prisoner ignored him. A Chinese name had been assigned to him but he refused to acknowledge it.

The lieutenant glanced up at the officer at the podium, who gave an impatient nod.

"Metok Rentzig," the lieutenant stated. "Yes," the Tibetan replied in a melancholy tone. Then he suddenly twisted toward the ghostly demon on the wall behind him. "*Om Kurukulla hrih hum svaha!*" he called out, defiance in his voice now.

Shan's heart wrenched as he saw the weapon in the young officer's hand. With a quick upward motion, the knob leveled the pistol and shot Metok in the head.

Shan had no idea how long he remained sitting, staring down into the sacred chapel that had been converted into an execution chamber. The other witnesses had quickly filed out the door after the man at the podium had declared the ceremony adjourned. Major Xun had been the last of them to leave, closing the door with a cackling laugh aimed at Shan. Two attendants appeared with a gurney and hauled the body away. Shan watched, numbed, as the old Tibetan janitor limped in and hosed down the floor. When the water was not running Shan could hear him whispering a mournful mantra. The janitor hesitated as he saw the blood and gray tissue spattered on the back wall, then moved a few steps back and sprayed it away. He missed a spatter higher up the wall below the eye of the faded goddess. She seemed to be weeping blood.

The janitor was nearly finished mopping up the pink-tinged water when a hand clamped around Shan's shoulder. He looked up into the icy eyes of the county governor.

"This was not my idea, Shan," Colonel Tan said. "I didn't know until Amah Jiejie told me where you were. I came as soon as I heard."

"You invited me."

"To my office, not to this. This was Major Xun's doing. It was a case run out of Lhasa, but they asked him for a quiet place for the execution. He heard you were coming and had her tell you to come here, then added an extra chair to the official witness gallery. He seemed to think it a good joke."

"I wasn't laughing."

"No. I don't suppose you were. I'm sorry. Major Xun is the most efficient adjutant I've ever had but he can be overzealous at times."

Shan did not reply, but as he walked silently, a step behind Tan, he realized that in all their time together he could not recall ever hearing the colonel apologize to him. Tan led him outside toward his waiting car, a worn, boxy Red Flag limousine that should have been retired twenty years earlier. Once Tan got in beside Shan, the driver sped onto the paved road that led out of the expanding government compound and into a landscape of barley fields and grazing sheep.

Tan stared out the window and did not turn when he finally spoke. "I need you, Shan."

Shan heard the unexpected worry in the colonel's voice and realized Tan had sensed his desolation. Had he sensed the words that had been on Shan's tongue since the moment Tan touched his shoulder in the execution chamber? *I resign*, Shan silently mouthed, then swallowed down the rest. *I can no longer be a gear in Beijing's monstrous machine. I can no longer be a law enforcement official in your soulless empire.* He had practiced such speeches several times in recent months, but each time the words choked away with the grim realization that he could not walk away from Tan. He hated Tan for being the tyrant who ran the most infamous camps in the Tibetan gulag, but he owed the man his freedom, his job, his housing, his life. He would never be able to find another job, another place where he could legally reside or, most importantly, ensure the safety of his son Ko, an inmate in one of Tan's brutal prisons.

"His name was Metok Rentzig," Shan said at last. "I didn't understand what the assembly was for. I thought it was just going to be one of those testimonials from a rehabilitated Tibetan. Charges must have been read. I wasn't listening."

"Metok was a senior official at the new hydroelectric project. He took bribes. It was in the papers."

Shan searched his memory, recalling now that he had seen mention of corruption at the Five Claws Dam, the huge project in the far north of the county, thirty miles from his station at Yangkar. "I remember reports at the time of his arrest. Nothing since then."

"Corruption at such a high level is an embarrassment to Beijing. Public Security is told to handle such things quietly."

"You mean a hidden trial," Shan suggested. "Then a hidden execution."

"What I mean," Tan shot back, "is proceedings that appropriately protected the interests of the motherland. The Party took jurisdiction and the investigation was conducted out of Lhasa. We weren't involved."

Shan spoke toward the window. "Corruption isn't a solitary crime. Yet only one man is charged and executed. A Tibetan."

A rumbling sound of irritation came from Tan, but he vented his anger by tearing open a pack of cigarettes and lighting one. After having a lung removed he had been under strict orders to stop smoking. A few months earlier he had broken the nose of a nurse who had tried to wrestle a cigarette from his hand.

They drove in uneasy silence for several minutes, then Shan saw the towers of the compound they were approaching and stiffened. "I have seen enough of the 'People's Justice' today," he said in a tight voice.

"Not like this," Tan muttered, then flicked the stub of his cigarette out the window as they slowed at the security gate. The guards offered nervous salutes to the military governor then darted to open the gate of heavy timber and barbed wire.

A freshly painted sign by the entrance declared they were entering Camp New Awakening. Shan had always known the facility as the 105th Reeducation Brigade, although most inmates called it the Shoe Factory. Its residents were all prisoners, but they were considered salvageable and split their days between memorizing Party dogma in classrooms and manufacturing footwear for the People's Liberation Army.

They parked in front of the main administration building and for the second time that day Shan was escorted to a small reviewing stand, this one just a modest foot-high temporary platform with ten chairs. A military march erupted from the public address system as junior officers took seats in the back row. Shan and the colonel were directed to seats beside an overweight, nervous officer whom Shan recognized as the warden. As they sat the gate in the inner fence of razor wire was opened, and prisoners began filing through under the watchful eyes of armed guards, forming in barracks companies a hundred feet in front of the little reviewing stand. For the most part, these were not the long-term prisoners found in Tan's hard labor brigades, located in more remote sections of the county, but only the nuisance makers sentenced to forced reeducation. A Public Security officer could sentence a man to up to a year of such servitude with just his signature, and the power was applied liberally whenever a gathering of Tibetans even hinted at political protest. Scattered among them, however, would be a few hard labor prisoners in transition, who were near the end of their sentences or sometimes just the end of their lives.

Once a month at the Shoe Factory the prisoners were assembled for what the camp administration called its graduation ceremony. Shan braced himself for the usual patronizing speeches by the warden and leading pupils, who would read a prepared speech to express their collective gratitude to the motherland for correcting the wayward paths of their lives. The music faded, and a young officer rose with a megaphone to announce awards, praising one unit for the cleanest barracks, another for the best scores on Chinese history exams. Half a dozen such announcements were made, then a list was handed to the officer and he began reading the names of those to be released. Eight names were called and the prisoners warily marched forward, each accepting a rolled paper that would be proof of completing the Party's curriculum and one of the little red books of Mao's quotations that were ubiquitous in reeducation camps. The books were all in Mandarin, which Shan doubted any of the graduates could read. Each man gave a respectful bow to the warden then was escorted to a van waiting by the administration building, where duffel bags sat on the ground, no doubt holding the belongings they had arrived with.

The officer with the megaphone cast an anxious glance at the warden, who nodded, and one more name was called. "Yankay Namdol," the officer stated over his megaphone. "Come and be recognized."

At first Shan thought the old man who broke out of the ranks was one of the transferred hard labor inmates, for he hobbled as if lame, one shoulder seemed strangely crooked, his unruly hair was mostly gray, and his face was lined with age. But as he approached the platform he grew more erect and his limp became less noticeable, as if he were growing younger before their eyes. He cast a long glance at the gate, where a young Tibetan woman had appeared, holding the reins of two horses.

The warden seemed oddly relieved as the man named Yankay Namdol obediently bowed his head, as if he had feared the graduate would behave disrespectfully in front of Tan. A soldier dropped a soiled drawstring bag at his feet, then the warden handed him his diploma and little red book. Yankay bowed his head to the gathered officers then backed away as he extended a hand into his bag, extracting a tattered coat, one of the sheepskin *chubas* favored by herders. The scores of witnesses watched with a strange, silent fascination as he put it on over his pajama-like prison tunic. He turned toward the brigade of prisoners, held the book over his head and made a deeper bow to them, raising a murmur of amusement in the ranks. Then he waved toward the woman at the gate and began walking in her direction, then paused to watch as several dogs ran out of the storage sheds behind the office building and began barking. A team of mules hitched to a cart of night soil bolted, their teamster running down the road after them. Shan saw the hint of a smile on the old man's face, and when he continued toward the gate his limp had nearly disappeared.

Shan did not fully understand the little drama he was watching. He bent toward Tan. "What was his crime?" he asked.

"He killed two soldiers."

Shan stared at the colonel in disbelief. A Tibetan who killed two soldiers would not even be alive a year later, let alone be walking out of a light duty education camp.

Tan frowned. "There were complications," he added.

But Shan only half-listened, for he was now watching the strange motions of the Tibetan. Thirty paces from the gate he paused and pulled from his bag a bundle of dried sticks. He extended the bundle to each of the four directions then dragged his heel in the dirt, inscribing

first a six-foot-wide circle then a series of short lines like tangents along
its edge, before continuing on. The warden cursed under his breath and
leaned toward a subordinate, pointing toward the circle in the earth
and sending him to erase it. But at a sharp command from Colonel
Tan, the young officer halted.

Every man in the compound watched in silence as the gate opened
and Yankay climbed onto one of the horses as the young woman
mounted the other. No one moved until they began trotting away.

"Return to assigned duties," the warden said with obvious relief,
and the young officer conveyed the order through the megaphone.
The prisoners had begun to file back behind the inner wire when
several shouted and pointed. Some were indicating the released prisoner, who had dismounted on a nearby hill and was doing a strange
dance along its summit, again waving the bundle of twigs over his
head. Others were pointing to the tall wooden flagpole in the center
of the wide yard. The pole had started to sway.

As Shan watched in confusion, the pole snapped and the Chinese
flag fell into the dirt. Then the ground itself swayed.

It was not a large earthquake, only one of the minor tremblers that
struck parts of Tibet every few weeks, but prison staff began running
in panic out of the administration building. One of the junior officers
gasped and ran frantically toward a guard tower. Two soldiers leapt
off the tower stairs as the support struts split with a loud crack. The
tower toppled onto its side, followed by another loud crack behind
the stand. Shan turned to see that the posts holding up the short roof
over the entranceway to the administration building had snapped,
slamming the stubby roof into the door, blocking the entry. Then the
earthquake ended as abruptly as it began.

The prisoners, filing back toward their barracks, began to sing.
The song had the rhythm of one of the work songs used when prisoners were digging ditches or breaking rocks in roadbeds. But after a
few verses Shan realized it had been adapted to sound like such a
chant to please the guards. The words were those of an old song that
gave thanks to protector demons.

He became aware that the warden, standing in front of them now, was speaking. Tan was still staring in the direction of the now-empty hill where the released prisoner had danced. "Sir?" the warden repeated.

Shan touched Tan's elbow and the colonel turned toward the warden, then looked past him at the toppled guard tower. To Shan's surprise, the look on his gaunt face was not anger but rather fascination. "Carry on, Major," he said to the worried warden, then added, "Have the flag back up before nightfall."

Tan had the driver stop his car a hundred yards past the gate. Without a word he opened his door and began climbing up the hill where the prisoner had danced. Shan paused as he opened his own door. "Who was that prisoner who was released?" he asked the driver, an old sergeant who had served Tan for most of his career.

The sergeant gestured to the fallen tower. "A sorcerer," he replied in a worried voice. Shan remembered how when they had first met years earlier, the driver had always spoken of Tibetans in dismissive, deprecating tones, as Tan himself had. Neither did anymore.

Shan caught up with the colonel at the summit of the hill, where he was sitting on a large flat boulder, smoking another cigarette. There was no sign of the Tibetan sorcerer other than a dust cloud in the direction of the northern mountains.

Tan inhaled deeply on his cigarette then emitted twin streams of smoke from his nostrils. "There's going to be trouble," he declared.

Shan sat beside him. "What kind of trouble?" he asked, gazing at the cloud of dust. To the north lay his own remote jurisdiction, the town of Yangkar and its surrounding township, and he saw with relief that the track of the horses was veering east, out of his domain, toward the tallest of the distant snowcapped peaks.

"Your kind of trouble."

Shan watched the dust cloud for several breaths. "You forget, Colonel," he said. "These days I specialize in finding stray yaks and settling disputes in the farmers' market. Last week I had to decide whether a chicken was worth ten heads of cabbage or fifteen."

Tan gave a grunt that may have been a laugh. Then he set his own eyes on the receding dust cloud and sobered. "A small convoy was coming through to Lhadrung from Sichuan Province, just two army trucks and two Public Security vehicles in escort."

"You mean some very special prisoners were being transferred to one of your establishments." In all of China, Tan was reputed to have the best prisons for making inmates disappear forever. It had been the reason Shan had been sentenced to the 404th People's Construction Brigade years earlier.

Tan didn't disagree. "Only six prisoners, three in each truck, with two guards in the back of each, Public Security cars in front and back. The Public Security officer in charge, who had just been assigned to Lhadrung, decided to take one of the old roads through the high mountains, though damned if I know why. If they had bothered to ask, I would have told them those roads are too unreliable, subject to landslides and worse." He drew on his cigarette again. "An old man appeared on the road as they rounded a curve, waving and doing a strange dance. He stopped every few moments and shook his bundle of twigs toward the sky, which rapidly grew darker.

"The Public Security officers in the front car and two of the escorting soldiers got out, shouting at the man to move, but he seemed not to hear them. They fired pistols in the air, but his only reaction was to laugh and point toward the sky. As they approached him hail began to fall. Not little pea-sized balls, but huge balls of ice, the size of apples. Windows shattered. The escorts ran. The two Public Security men made it back into their vehicle, one with a broken collarbone. But the two soldiers had farther to run to get into their trucks. Too far. They only wore soft fatigue caps and their skulls were quickly shattered. They died instantly. By the time it stopped their bodies looked as if they had been pounded with hammers."

"And the old man?"

"You just saw him ride away on a horse. One of the escorts said he disappeared as the hail began but was back on the road as soon as it stopped, then went to the dead and began chanting something before he was arrested."

"Arrested?"

"Lieutenant Huan, the chief Public Security officer, insisted the man had directed the hail onto them and charged the man with murder. But not even the tame judges used by Public Security would buy that story. How could the government formally acknowledge that there are Tibetan sorcerers, the judge asked the officer. I was there, Huan replied, and Yankay Namdol killed them as surely as if he had aimed a gun at them. The judge cited a report that said the road Huan had taken was so well known for hail that the local people called it Ice Ball Alley. He dismissed the case, and the officer was deemed responsible for negligently causing the deaths. I saw to it that he was taken off the promotion lists for three years and transferred out of Lhadrung before he even settled into a job here. Before he left he had the last word, by assigning the old Tibetan to administrative detention. One year at the Shoe Factory."

"Which expired today."

Tan turned and looked back at the camp, where prisoners were hauling away the wreckage of the tower. "Expired rather dramatically." He pulled out another cigarette. His doctor, resigned to Tan's stubbornness, had insisted that he at least buy filtered cigarettes. Tan broke the filter off and threw it into the brush before lighting the cigarette. "How the hell could he cause an earthquake?" he growled.

In his mind's eye, Shan replayed the scene of the prisoner marching to the warden and receiving his belongings. His old chuba had been tattered, its fleece lining soiled. On the back and sleeves there had been faded images, some of them complex geometric designs and others depictions of deities, too small and too faint for Shan to recognize. On his march to the gate Yankay had drawn another design. Shan bent and in the sandy soil in front of him he drew a smaller version with his finger, a circle with four equally spaced short tangent lines. "He's a hail chaser," Shan said.

"A hail assassin, according to Public Security," Tan said.

"In old Tibet there were such men," Shan explained, "usually senior monks who had moved on from their monasteries to roam the countryside and tap the power of the earth deities, the ones who control land and sky. They were paid by farmers to influence the weather. Mostly it was to chase away hail, which could destroy a year's crop in minutes, but the best ones were said to be able to call in hail as well. Some were even said to be able to summon the deities in the earth as readily as those in the sky."

"The earth gods who make earthquakes," Tan suggested.

Shan looked at him in surprise. "They're only old tales, Colonel. Folklore, really."

"Of course they are, damn it!" Tan's temper could instantly flare and cool just as quickly. "It doesn't matter what I think. The man has a following. It's like they found a loophole in the law."

"By using gods?"

Tan's face tightened again. "Don't play the fool with me! It doesn't matter if the gods aren't real to you or me. What matters is that so many believe they are!"

"I'm not sure what we're talking about," Shan confessed.

Tan motioned with his cigarette toward the fading cloud of dust. "He's on a line toward the project."

"The project?"

"That damned hydroelectric project. The Five Claws Dam, they call it. Biggest investment the government has ever made in this region. Two more years to complete and they already have its dedication on the Chairman's schedule. Five miles farther north and it would have been out of my county," he spat. "They're following a new model. Fast track, where national strategic interests are involved. Keep the approval process quiet, start construction before the public even knows about it. Which means they started without even talking with me, let alone asking my permission." Shan glanced at Tan. Corruption was a minor sin compared to slighting the colonel's authority.

"Started. Meaning what?" Shan asked.

"Reshaping the valley. Leveling some old ruins."

Suddenly the earlier events of the morning came back to Shan. He had watched the execution of a man who worked at the hydroelectric project. "A few miles farther west and it would be in my township," Shan whispered, relieved that the strange Tibetan was not riding into his little piece of the county. But why had Tan even invited him that morning? Why had he been made to get up in the middle of the night and drive the long hours to Lhadrung town?

He inwardly shuddered at the thin smile that appeared on Tan's face. "Right," Tan said. "As the constable of Yangkar you need not worry. But—" he reached into his tunic and extracted an envelope, extending it to Shan.

The letter was simply addressed to *Shan Tao Yun, Yangkar Township*. Shan accepted it with a knot in his stomach. As he read Tan produced a small black leather folder and set it on the rock beside him. Shan stared intensely at the letter, as if he could will the words to disappear.

"You'll still be constable, still have your station, but I'm bumping your pay by fifty percent."

Shan read the title Tan was bestowing on him. "Special Inspector for the County Governor's Office. There's no such thing."

"There is if I say so."

"I would have no authority."

"Amah Jiejie composed a decree for the file. The governor has the same police powers as Public Security within the scope of his jurisdiction. And my own jurisdiction has been expanded to matters related to supply of army materiel, consistent with Lhadrung becoming the regional depot for the military." He pushed the wallet toward Shan. "Open it. It was her idea. She said it would help you."

The leather folder contained a brass badge mounted on one side and a laminated card on the other. The card, signed by Tan, said *Shan Tao Yun, Special Inspector* then, underneath, *By Appointment of the Governor, Lhadrung County.*

"I don't accept," Shan said.

"You have no choice."

"Why?" The question was unnecessary. They both knew the reasons why. Shan, the disgraced renegade investigator from Beijing, had been released years earlier from the gulag prison where he had been sent to die. His sentence had been indeterminate, which for those in disfavor with the State Council meant life in prison, preferably a sharply curtailed life. But five years into his sentence he had done Tan a favor and the colonel had released him, on his own authority, without the approval of any official in Beijing. Shan also had no permission to live outside Tan's county, and no employment except that which Tan gave him. But the most important reason was his son Ko, who was an inmate in Shan's former prison. The warden and guards had hated Shan, and Ko would be in grave danger without the protection of Tan and Amah Jiejie, who visited Ko so regularly the staff referred to her as Ko's aunt.

But Tan surprised Shan. "I need you, Shan," he said for the second time that day. Theirs had been a complex relationship through the years, starting as bitter enemies then slowly evolving toward a grudging mutual respect. Shan had saved Tan more than once from disgrace, and once from execution for a crime he had not committed. Tan had protected Shan from the merciless, often ruthless hand of Beijing. In the last year, after he had learned from Shan that a revered general, a godlike Hero of the People, was a corrupt murderer, Tan had begun showing signs that he, like Shan, no longer trusted his government. He had killed the general in front of Shan, creating a new bond between them.

"The Five Claws Dam is a national project, run by Beijing. Metok was prosecuted out of Lhasa," Shan reminded Tan.

"It's *my* county, damn it!" There was a reason why some people referred to Tan as the warlord of Lhadrung. He had been the governor of the huge county, larger than some eastern provinces, for so long, ruling with an iron fist, that it had become more like his personal kingdom.

They sat in silence. The clouds cleared over the distant mountains and the sun lit their white snowcaps. On the lower slopes of the nearest peaks Shan could make out several points of white, as brilliant as the snow above. They were *chortens*, structures consisting of a dome on a block with a spire on top, ancient shrines that the local Tibetans had been secretly restoring. The line of chortens stood like sentinels against the prison camps in the valley. There were still very old, very hidden secrets in the mountains.

Tan gestured toward the diminishing cloud of dust and spoke in the grim, knowing tone of an old warrior. "Metok's execution was not an ending, it was a beginning. There's a reason the hail chaser is riding toward the Five Claws."

Shan realized that Tan had expected the Tibetan to go north. "I don't quite understand, Colonel," he said. "Are you asking me to start investigating crimes that have not yet been committed?"

He expected an angry reply, but Tan considered his words for several long breaths. "Tibet is a land of broken places and broken people," he said in a contemplative voice. "And you, Shan, are better at fitting those pieces together than any person I know." Without another word the colonel rose and began walking back to his car.

A young officer from the camp awaited them. "The warden said you should be aware. The earthquake ruptured our cisterns," he reported to Tan. "We have no water. We'll need tankers. And the new mural of the Chairman on the wall of the instruction hall has cracked, split down his face."

Tan cast another pointed glance at Shan. Camp New Awakening had become one more broken place.

CHAPTER TWO

Shan pulled onto the shoulder of the road as Yangkar came into view at the far side of the valley before him. When he had been forced by Tan to move there he had considered the dusty wind-battered town to be little more than a forlorn exile, but it had come to feel more like home to him than any place he had known since childhood. He had grown fond of many of its Tibetan residents, who greeted him with tired smiles and did what they could to shield him from those few who would always hate any Chinese constable. The town harbored deep secrets, and bitter memories, like Shan himself, but it endured as a scarred, weary survivor, also like Shan. Perhaps the reason he treasured it the most was his discovery that beneath its surface, Tibetan traditions still ran deep because its remoteness and inhospitable weather meant that it had been largely ignored by the zealots who ran Beijing's Bureau of Religious Affairs, the agency dedicated to eliminating religion in the People's Paradise. Since the Bureau had helped annihilate the ancient monastery of Yangkar decades earlier, it had almost never been seen in the town again.

As three sheep bounded out of the late-day shadows to cross the road in front of him, Shan groaned with sudden recollection, then put the truck in gear and sped toward town. Ten minutes later he skidded to a stop on the gravel drive of the schoolhouse, and the young Tibetan woman sitting on the steps stood and slung a backpack onto her shoulder.

"I'm sorry, Yara," Shan said as he climbed out. "I had to drive to Lhadrung. I should have called you from there." He extended the keys to the Tibetan teacher, whose forgiving smile burnt away his guilt.

"Just as well," Yara replied as she tossed her pack onto the seat and climbed behind the wheel. "The headmistress gives me suspicious looks whenever I get a call from the constable." She glanced up at the steep slopes above the town, which had begun to show the long shadows of sunset. "It's just that my grandmother won't want to sit in the back in the dark." Yara was taking the old woman up to her grandfather's camp, where he was watching over their tiny herd of sheep and yaks, waiting for the passes below the summer pastures to clear of snow.

"Of course, she can sit with you in the cab," Shan said. "Just ask her not to use the siren this time."

"But you know she'll smoke her cigar all the way. You'll smell it for a week."

Shan acknowledged her warning with a small bow of his head. "My penance for being late."

Yara smiled again then extracted a folded paper from her shirt pocket and handed it to Shan. "While I was waiting I wrote a letter," she said. "I'll leave the truck behind the station as usual," she added and then sped off to the rug factory where her grandmother worked.

As he walked the five blocks from the cinder block school to the town square, Shan studied the squat, windblown houses on either side of the street. Nearly all had lotuses, conchs, fish, or other auspicious symbols painted by their entries. One, that of the new Chinese barber, had a poster of the Chairman tacked to its door. An old man on a bicycle, a terrier in his handlebar basket, gave Shan a nearly toothless grin as he sped by. A woman kneeling at the small chorten shrine at the edge of the square nodded in his direction. A pigeon landed on the oversized bust of Mao the Great Helmsman at the opposite side of the square. As he turned toward the police station, a goat ran out the door, encouraged by a boot flung in its direction.

Shan sagged for a moment, then straightened his uniform and walked across the dusty street into the station. Two Tibetans were in the outer office, locked in brisk argument. As Shan loudly pushed the door closed behind him, they abruptly stopped and gasped in surprise. The older man darted through the adjoining door. The younger man, in his early thirties, stood up straight and tapped his forehead in a gesture that may have been a salute.

"Constable Shan," his deputy ventured, with a nervous glance at the goat droppings on the office floor.

"Deputy Choden," Shan coolly acknowledged. "Is that your boot out on the street?"

"A winter boot, I am taking them home," Choden said uneasily.

"But what will you wear when I assign you to the sheep counting station in the high passes? The snow may be deep up there."

The young deputy's face turned pale. "I will fetch it, sir, at once."

Shan stood at the window and watched his assistant as he darted outside, wondering if he should send the form he had completed requesting Choden's transfer. His prior deputy had proven to be a ruthless murderer, had even killed Shan's predecessor, so Colonel Tan had paid special attention to his replacement. Choden had had the highest exam score of any Tibetan in his class on the law enforcement exam but he seemed incapable of asserting the authority of his office.

"I told Lhakpa the goat had to go an hour ago," Choden groused as he returned with his boot.

"You mean because you knew I would be returning later."

"Yes," Choden replied, then hesitated, as if sensing a trap. "I told him family can only visit for an hour a day. Rules of the jail."

"It's a goat," Shan pointed out.

"Well . . ." Choden began in a tentative tone, as if about to argue the point. He had been raised only a few miles away in one of the many families who not only fervently believed in reincarnation but also knew that most of the prior generation had died with terrible burdens on their everlasting spirits, meaning they had come back as lower life-forms. Nearly all of the traditional households in the township included animals who were believed to be relatives. "He's convinced she's his young niece, who took a terrible fall off a mountain last year. He says that's why she came back as a goat, to learn to pay better attention on the trails." Choden fixed Shan with a hopeful gaze, as if he believed he was winning the argument. "I tied her in a stable on the far side of town this morning. But she always finds him, no matter where he is. Very clever, that girl. He says she has his niece's eyes," he added uncertainly.

Shan sat at his desk and stifled a yawn. "No animals in the jail," he said, then noticed the short typed report on the center of his desk. He read it out loud. "Incident One. A yak was reported to be knocking down road signs near milepost 200 on the highway." It was an event that occurred nearly weekly somewhere in the township. "Incident Two," he continued. "Mrs. Lu reported that three onions were stolen from her windowsill. Incident Three. Mr. Xing reported that a vandal chalked a sun and moon symbol on his back wall." Shan cocked his head at his deputy.

Choden shrugged. "I told him it was intended as a protection, a good luck charm, really, and that it would help keep mice away from his grain." The Chinese residents represented perhaps five percent of the town's population but accounted for ninety percent of the complaints.

"Incident Four," Shan continued. "A van with four scientists from the Institute stopped and had lunch at the noodle shop." He looked up. "What scientists? What Institute?"

His deputy shrugged. "Four Beijing people." The description had become the Tibetans' code for any Chinese, after several insistent propaganda campaigns that declared that all Tibetans must call themselves

Chinese. "Marpa served them lunch," Choden said, referring to the owner of the noodle shop. "They told him they were passing through, studying mountains."

Shan and Choden both knew no one just passed through Yang-kar. It was at the end of a long spur off the highway. "What kind of scientists?"

Choden shrugged again. It was his defining characteristic. "Mountain scientists, I guess."

Shan read the final item on the page, and a shiver ran down his spine. "What do you mean, Public Security in Lhasa wants me?"

"A Public Security officer called from Lhasa. She asked if Shan Tao Yun was the constable here."

"You had to write that up as an incident?"

"It sounded important, sir. I can't remember the last time Public Security headquarters called us. She asked, 'Did Constable Shan speak Tibetan and wear a prayer amulet?'" Choden looked down into his folded hands. "I'm sorry. I had to tell her the truth."

Shan replayed in his mind the gathering of witnesses at Metok's execution. There had been the senior officer who read the findings against the engineer and the arrogant, oily younger officer who had smiled as he pulled the trigger. There had been no female officer there, at least not in uniform. But Tan had said the case had been handled by Public Security in Lhasa.

He rose and poured himself a cup of tea from the thermos in the narrow alcove that served as their makeshift kitchen, then found that it was cold. "Patrol for half an hour then go home," he said to Choden, who greeted the orders with a grateful nod then frowned as Shan pointed to the goat droppings.

The deputy dutifully cleaned the floor then paused as he opened the door. "Is there really such a place in the passes?" he asked. "A sheep counting station, I mean."

Shan emptied the cup in the sink. "You'll find out if you persist in treating our station like a stable," he replied and waved his deputy out the door.

He brewed a fresh pot of tea, poured two mugs, and carried them through the door at the back of the office. He set one on the table in front of the two cells then opened the unlocked door of the first cell and set the second on the stool by the cell wall before sitting at the table.

"I saw early flowers along the high mountain road today," he declared after a few sips.

Lhakpa, the old man who sat meditating by the stool, gradually stirred to consciousness. His eyes opened, and he slowly turned his head toward Shan then lifted the steaming mug with an appreciative nod. "Spring's slow to come in the high country," he observed. "But I'll start climbing in a few days."

"I found an extra blanket you can take," Shan offered, "and I'll give you as much barley as you can carry."

Lhakpa had appeared weeks earlier, sleeping in unused stables after Shan had explained that he could not camp beside the chorten in the town square. Several of the Chinese residents, represented by their self-styled Committee of Leading Citizens, had complained that the homeless man was an affront to socialist society, as if Lhakpa had chosen not to have a permanent home as a political protest. More than one had asked if Shan had checked his residency permit. Like the Tibetans who lived in the town, Shan knew Lhakpa had no such permit, and several of them had started sharing provisions with him that they could ill afford to lose. After finding the old man sitting against a tree one morning, shivering and covered with snow, his only source of warmth the goat in his lap, Shan had found the solution. He had arrested Lhakpa, satisfying the committee, and kept him in a warm, dry, and unlocked cell for the remainder of the winter. Shan had not anticipated, however, the devotion of the goat that followed Lhakpa everywhere. "She has to stay outside, my friend," he said now.

A low, dry laugh escaped Lhakpa's throat. "I wish you could have met my niece Tara, Shan. Sharp as a blade, and quite beautiful. Her eyes were deep pools of intelligence and so full of life. For years she avoided those who tried to take her away to one of those boarding schools, but they finally caught her when she was fifteen. I made her promise she would do her best, and they said she showed great promise, was going to be nominated to attend one of the universities in the east."

Shan leaned closer. This was the most Lhakpa had spoken about the goat to Shan. The Tibetan was a man of many secrets, but that was true of every wanderer in Tibet, and Shan was loath to pry. Such Tibetans had many reasons not to trust law enforcement officials.

"But she hated it," Lhakpa continued, "and ran away every two or three months to come back to us. Then her parents died. She had no one left but me and my brother. The next time she escaped and came back I told her it was her destiny to go to the Chinese university, that there was nothing else left for her. It was her chance to make a new life, away from the suffering in Tibet. She got angry, yelled at me for the first time ever, said she knew who she was and she was not a Chinese puppet. Then she left in a rage. It was the last time I ever saw her. She sent a letter saying she was sorry, that she was coming home to give me a proper apology, asking if I could just try to consider that she and I might make some kind of new Tibetan life for our family, maybe start a farm. It was a five-day trip over the mountains to reach our village. An ice storm struck on the third day." Lhakpa sipped at his tea again then spoke in a whisper. "A herder found her body, where she had fallen off a slippery trail and over a cliff."

"I'm sorry," was all Shan could say.

"It's one of the reasons I decided to become a snow monk," Lhakpa explained. The Tibetan had made it clear weeks earlier that he was preparing to become a hermit monk but he never told Shan why. "After she died, I needed to get away, to confront the world in solitude for a year or two," Lhakpa said, referring to one of the Tibetans who chose to be unregistered monks or nuns, living a solitary life high up in mountain hideaways. "Six months after she died I was walking down a road and heard this urgent bleating. This young goat came trotting up to me. There was no herder, no farm nearby, though I kept trying to make it turn around since I was certain it must have escaped from somewhere nearby. But she stuck close, and that night when I camped she sat in front of me and stared at me. And at last I really saw those eyes, those deep, energetic eyes that I had only ever seen on my niece's face." Lhakpa drank again and shrugged. "I told Tara to stay outside. Deputy Choden took her all the way across town this morning. But an hour later here she was, butting her head against the back door."

"I'm surprised she hasn't wound up in someone's stewpot."

"No, no. No one would do such a thing. Tserung at the garage tied the red on her last month." To the Tibetans the red yarn tied around the goat's neck meant she had been ransomed, that someone had gained significant spiritual merit by paying money to keep her from ever being butchered.

Shan recalled the first day he had encountered Lhakpa and the goat. She had worn a red yarn then too. "Tell me, old man, how many times have you sold her life?"

A low wheezing laugh came from his prisoner. "It makes people feel good. I never keep the money. Last time I bought some grain for her, gave some to the woman who maintains the shrines and the rest to that Tibetan circuit nurse who rides in the mountains, to buy medicines."

Shan dipped his mug in salute, then sat in silence for several moments before rising to bring a candle from the office. He lit it then switched off the overhead lights, knowing the meditative Tibetan preferred the soft flame to the glare of the naked light bulbs.

"I watched the execution of a man today," he confessed to Lhakpa, who was the closest thing to a real monk in the town.

"I'm sorry," Lhakpa said, gesturing to the worn *mala*, his rosary, that lay on the stool. "Tell me his name and I will say a thousand beads for him tonight."

"They made me an official witness," Shan recounted. His heart felt like a cold stone as he explained what he had been forced to do. "It felt like I was pulling the trigger myself."

Lhakpa silently stared into his steaming mug. "Then I will say a thousand beads for you as well, Constable."

Shan sipped at his tea. "Did you work in the square at all today?"

On days when the weather was fair Lhakpa usually helped maintain the public square, officially on work release. "Did you see the visitors?"

"Those Chinese? Most people fled the square when they appeared. Mrs. Lu stood in front of her house and waved a little Chinese flag at them. She seems lonely."

"Deputy Choden says they ate lunch and left."

"Not before shooting the mountains."

"I'm sorry?"

"They took an instrument out of the truck and put it on a tripod, up on the old gate tower. Sort of like a telescope but not exactly. Sort of like a camera but not exactly. I think it was one of those devices that shoots laser beams for measurements." Not for the first time, Shan wondered about Lhakpa's background. Not many Tibetans, and certainly almost no snow monks, would know about such devices. "One man aimed it at each mountain surrounding the valley then read out numbers as another wrote them down on a clipboard. Then another man who did have a camera took photographs from the top of the gate tower, many photos, turning a little every few seconds until he completed a circle of the town. When he came down, he saw Tara and me watching and laughed, then took our photo too."

Shan remembered the letter Yara had given him. He had to write a letter of his own to his son Ko to go with it as a cover, for Tan had seen to it that Shan's letters to Ko would not be opened by the prison staff. He drained his cup and stood.

"The dead man's name?" Lhakpa asked. "For my prayers."

Shan hesitated. He felt a strange bond with the man who had been executed. "Chou Folan," he said, using the man's Chinese name. He instantly felt a pang of guilt, yet he sensed that he had secret, unfinished business with Metok Rentzig and was not ready to share that business with others.

"I shall pray that his soul finds harmony," the snow monk declared. Although he had said he would pray for Shan as well, it seemed he did not have much hope that Shan would find harmony.

. . .

Shan awoke before dawn and sat on the edge of his bed, looking at his scattered belongings in the dim light that streamed in from the pole lamp in the courtyard behind the station. He, like Lhakpa, had taken winter quarters, moving into the apartment that was set aside for Yangkar's constable, but he longed for the solitude of his little farmhouse above the town. The cracks in the walls of the long-abandoned building made it impossible to keep the frigid winds at bay, however, and the roof leaked in heavy rainstorms, but still it was his home. In the sterile quarters of the building behind the station compound, he felt like an intruder, just as he increasingly felt like an intruder in the constable's uniform.

He washed then stepped outside. Tara, Lhakpa's goat, was lying on the step to the back door of the jail. Shan filled a bucket of water for her then sat and rubbed her back as she looked up with her moist, strangely beseeching eyes. After several minutes he walked around the building and onto the town square. It had once been the courtyard of the huge monastery that had dominated the town, and in the grayness before dawn he often fancied he could hear the morning prayers from ranks of chanting monks echoing across the empty square.

The kitchen of the noodle shop was already filled with the steam of boiling pots and the scent of the cardamom Marpa used in his spiced *momos*, Tibetan dumplings. Shan poured himself a cup of tea and sat at the little table along the back wall where the proprietor usually took his own meals. Marpa left his young nephew to watch the pots and brought two bowls of porridge to the table.

"The snow monk still with you?" Marpa asked as he lifted a spoonful of porridge.

Shan hesitated. His duty, they all knew, was to turn an unregistered monk over to Public Security. "Why wouldn't he be?"

"After what happened yesterday, I thought they were going to haul him away."

Shan lowered his spoon. "The visitors took some photographs and left."

Marpa gave a tentative nod. "Mostly took some photographs and measurements of the mountains, of the square, of your station."

"My station?"

"Yes, and then the man who took the photos ran over to the oldest member of the team and they had a long discussion, with the photographer pointing at Lhakpa. They started to approach him, but then he made a *mudra* in their direction and they halted," Marpa explained, referring to the symbolic hand positions used sometimes in Buddhist worship. "It was like they thought it was some kind of dark magic. While they stood there, staring at him, as if summoning the courage to approach him, Choden ran out of the station and put handcuffs on Lhakpa then marched him back to the jail."

Choden and Lhakpa had both been very selective in reporting on what had happened that afternoon. "You saw all this? Who were they?"

"Served them lunch and watched through the window when they left." He shrugged. "Officials from outside."

"But they had instruments."

Marpa, eating again, nodded. "There was one of those symbols, a logo they call it, on the door of their van." He dipped a finger in his tea and drew three inverted, interlocked V shapes. "Three mountains. Mapmakers is my guess. The government's never really had proper maps of this area." He paused as a look of chagrin crossed his face. "Too bad, but it was always going to happen. Once it happens in Lhasa, folks say, it's bound to catch up with Yangkar in thirty or forty years." He saw the query in Shan's eyes. "Once you have good maps, civilization isn't far behind," he explained in a doleful voice. They were both aware of what Beijing's notion of civilization meant for Tibetans. More roads. More boarding schools for Tibetan children who would be assigned new Chinese names. More factories and mines where Tibetan workers would be overseen by Chinese managers. More patrols by Religious Affairs, to snatch up photographs of the

Dalai Lama and ensure no unauthorized monks or nuns roamed the countryside.

Marpa raised his mug of tea then paused, cocking his head upward. Ice seemed to materialize in Shan's belly as he heard the increasingly loud *thump-thump-thump* from the sky. The proprietor's expression turned grim. "They work fast," he murmured.

CHAPTER THREE

One of Colonel Tan's young staff officers, Lieutenant Zhu, was leaning against a boulder as Shan rode up on his bicycle. Zhu greeted him
with a disappointed expression. "Your truck is broken?" he asked as
he motioned Shan toward the waiting helicopter.

"My deputy may need it today. Where are we going?"

Zhu did not reply, gesturing to his ears as the engine began to
whine and the long rotor turned. Even when Shan repeated the question after they had buckled in and donned their headphones, Zhu only
motioned toward the southwest. Ten minutes later they began to follow the Lhasa highway.

Shan found himself watching for the Potala Palace, and as it came
into view, a dark ruby against the distant snows, he found himself
grinning. Despite Beijing's relentless efforts to turn Lhasa into a Chinese city, the old Tibetan fortress still dominated the landscape, the
rest of the city just a gray smudge below it. He turned away as the
expanse of Western-style buildings grew more distinct and watched
the outline of the Himalayas on the horizon until the helicopter banked,
crossing over the Lhasa River before it began its descent.

The Lhasa Railway Station was only a few years old, built as a
temple to Beijing's ambitions. The huge stone and concrete structure
was the terminus of the railway from Qinghai Province in the north,
where it connected with trains to the eastern cities. As he studied the

squat, heavy building, it looked not so much like a proud public work as another fortress. Construction of the railway, highest on the planet, had been one of the most controversial projects ever undertaken by Beijing. It had sliced into pristine wilderness, cut off ancient migration routes for the wildlife of the high plateau, and most importantly for its Beijing planners, provided fast, easy access into central Tibet for both Chinese immigrants and soldiers.

The parking lot outside the station looked as if it had been built as a vast staging area. Another helicopter already sat in a corner of the massive paved lot. Half a dozen police cars, some with lights flashing, were lined up by the station entrance, the kind of reception usually reserved for visiting dignitaries. At the end of the station half a dozen army trucks waited.

Zhu hurried Shan into the cavernous hall and toward a train which had been isolated at the rearmost platform by an outer cordon of police and an inner cordon of armed soldiers. Colonel Tan was standing by the sleek, green American-made locomotive, an impatient frown on his face, as a man in a business suit harangued him. A second man in an unfamiliar uniform, probably the engineer, listened nervously a step behind the stranger.

The colonel brightened as he spotted Shan and his escort. "Comrade, I commend you to the able hands of my brightest staff officer, Lieutenant Zhu," he declared, and pulled Zhu in front of the irate man. "I have been explaining to the stationmaster," Tan said to his lieutenant, "that his train may not leave on the return service until we give him permission. Please," he added with a hint of amusement, "continue the dialogue, Lieutenant Zhu." Shan saw now that a soldier with a submachine gun hanging from his shoulder blocked the entrance to the locomotive cab. Tan sobered, and unexpectedly touched his open hand to his temple. "We salute the Chairman's wisdom," he said. It was a slogan from one of Beijing's newest posters and had become a warning to anyone who would challenge the government.

The stationmaster, suddenly looking worried, promptly repeated the slogan.

Tan led Shan down the platform. "You can get on this train and in two days be in Beijing," he said. For a moment Shan wondered if he should take the words as a threat. "It shouldn't be so easy. My first time it took me three months to get to Lhasa."

"Battle tanks do tend to travel more slowly," Shan observed. Tan's first experience in Tibet, he knew, had been as commander of one of the armored brigades that had invaded Tibet. His words brought a nostalgic gleam to Tan's countenance, and they spoke no more until they reached the line of soldiers that blocked off the last car of the train, the only car without a line of windows along its side.

"They call it the utility car," Tan explained, "mostly used for freight and supplies for the train."

Shan saw now the angry men, some in Public Security uniforms, some in blue police tunics, who were being kept away by Tan's commandos. A knob officer and a police officer were having two separate, heated arguments with Tan's deputies.

"It is possible that there are differing perspectives on jurisdiction here," Shan suggested.

"Nonsense. The first Lhasa detective who arrived got a broken lip from one of my sergeants," Tan said as he returned the salute of the soldier who admitted them through the line of guards. "That ended any dispute. They're just expressing their disappointment now."

Shan had never been on one of the trains, had only watched in chagrin with crestfallen herders as one had sped over their ancient pastures. Consistent with the boasting in countless newspaper and magazine articles, the car was the epitome of modernity, everything made of shiny metal and plastic. Tan made a point of showing Shan the two chambers for train staff, each with a narrow upper and lower berth, and the tiny washroom they shared, then entered four digits on a wall keypad and with a hiss the door to the rest of the car opened. It was sharply colder in the cargo compartment. Shan could see his breath.

Tan pointed to an electronic control panel on the wall inside the door that had been smashed. "Door controls, temperature controls, oxygen controls all inoperable from this side," he explained.

Oxygen. Shan remembered reading how oxygen was pumped into the train compartments to ease the altitude sickness many passengers suffered, in addition to the individual oxygen access at every passenger seat. It was why advertisements for the train sometimes claimed the train was pressurized.

They passed racks of food supplies in cartons and large cans, two of which were bulging after enduring the railway's huge changes in elevation and air pressure, then reached stacks of wooden crates marked prominently with the insignia of the People's Liberation Army and the words "Munitions, Lhadrung Depot."

"Most of these are special fuses for the new generation of howitzer shell," Tan stated in a tight voice. "I keep telling them we should move them in military convoys, but some clerk always comes back with proof of the great savings to be had by rail transport. Just a way to make up some of the train's operating losses."

"Surely no one would try to steal your munitions," Shan stated.

The colonel did not reply. He continued to a space where a single large crate had been packed between the higher stacks, creating a little alcove. Quilted packing pads, used to cushion cargo, had been piled in a heap on the solitary, four-foot-high crate. Tan lifted the pads and tossed them in the aisle. Shan froze, then stepped back.

"My men were on board for the cargo as soon as the train stopped. They called me immediately."

The dead man sitting on the crate was Chinese, in his forties. His arms were wrapped around his knees. His fingertips were dark blue, his fingers a lighter shade. His face, contorted in pain, had a distinctly bluish tint. His eyes stared out in silent anguish.

"He's blue," Tan observed.

"Cyanosis," Shan said. "Pulmonary edema."

"Meaning?"

"His body couldn't adapt to the low oxygen at the high elevation. Fluid built up in his lungs. Although with the heat off in here he may have frozen to death before the fluid killed him. Was he an escort to your cargo?"

"No. The cargo was checked and the gate locked in Xining. Nearly twenty-four hours ago. The entry can be opened only by entering the code on that keypad."

"Did he carry identification?" Shan asked.

"No one wanted to touch him. One of my soldiers said he had been possessed by one of those blue-faced demons you see in old Tibetan temples. No one went near after that."

"Public Security will have procedures they will want to follow."

"To hell with them. It's not the first time someone has died on these trains. They will just reprint the usual press release, lamenting another accident caused by the ill health of the passenger and issue a reminder to the public to consult the doctor on board when they travel. I don't need that. I need the truth. You're my Special Investigator. What are your procedures?"

"There's a doctor?"

"Every train from Xining has one." Tan anticipated Shan's next question and turned to the officer who was waiting down the aisle. "Find the doctor," he called out.

Shan clenched his jaw and reached out. The dead man's limbs would not move, though he could not be sure if it was from rigor mortis or from being frozen. If he was going to find a wallet, he would need help moving the body. He pulled back the man's heavy sweater and explored his shirt pocket, extracting a worn identity card and two business cards.

"Sun Lunshi," he read from the official identification, then confirmed that the same name was on the topmost business card. "From the Institute of Applied Geophysics." He stared at the logo of three interlocked mountains on the card, exactly as Marpa had described it from the van in Yangkar.

Tan took it from his hand and cursed as he read it.

"You know them?" Shan asked as he glanced at the second card. *Dakini Delights*, it said, over the legend *Exotic drinks, exotic dancers, exotic adventures.*

"I know the Institute. They show up at every big infrastructure project."

"Infrastructure," Shan repeated. "Like the Five Claws project."

Tan frowned. "Half the Institute's people are real scientists and engineers, the other half politicos who make sure the scientists plan their projects in a manner that achieves Party goals."

"Which was he?" Shan asked.

"No idea."

"Four of his colleagues were in Yangkar yesterday."

Tan's anger was instant. For a moment Shan actually thought he was going to slap the dead man. "They're supposed to clear travel in Lhadrung with me," he growled. "What the hell were they doing?"

"If you recall, Colonel, I was with you, watching a Tibetan hail chaser. They apparently took fixes on nearby mountains and photographed much of the town, including my station." Shan looked back at the crate the man sat on. It did not have the army markings. "Were they shipping something with your munitions?"

"Of course not!" Tan snapped, then cursed as Shan pointed to a label on the crate bearing the Institute's logo. The colonel summoned another staff officer, and as the officer received his orders and stepped away, Shan stopped him with one more request.

Tan remained in front of the dead man, fixing the body with a baleful stare, as Shan explored the cargo compartment. Tan was, Shan suspected, furious that the man had not survived to receive the colonel's wrath. The quilted pads yielded nothing but a few bloodstains. The stacked crates were heavy, but two near the rear door had been knocked askew. On the small window of the rear door, beyond which soldiers waited with hand trucks, Shan discovered a smear of blood, six feet from the floor.

The doctor and the conductor both looked like they would try to flee at any moment were it not for the two fierce-looking soldiers who herded them toward Tan. The uniformed conductor was angry, and the tall, thin doctor clearly frightened.

"You have no authority over the railway company!" the conductor growled as he approached. "Our schedules are set by Beijing! They may not be disrupted! Our sky train is a national treasure! The stationmaster is calling a general in Lhasa this very minute!"

Tan smiled and stepped aside, revealing the frozen corpse. The conductor gasped and staggered backward, colliding with the crates behind him. The doctor clutched his belly, ran to the rear door and opened it in enough time so that most of the contents of his stomach made it on the tracks outside. The waiting soldiers erupted with laughter.

"Do you recognize him?" Tan asked the conductor. "A passenger? Or perhaps a stowaway?"

"Look at him!" the conductor sputtered. "How could I—" his words choked away.

"Imagine him less blue," Tan suggested.

"Sun Lunshi," Shan offered. "His name was Sun Lunshi. Search your manifest."

The conductor still stared, so transfixed that Shan was not sure he had heard. Then he extracted an electronic device from his tunic pocket.

The doctor summoned enough courage to bend over the dead man, muttering under his breath. "I can't be responsible for someone who hides!" he protested. He looked up at the colonel. "You must make it clear this one did not seek any assistance!" The physician was clearly not as concerned about the death as he was about his own reputation.

"How many deaths have you had on board the trains?" Shan asked.

The doctor shrugged. "Several each year. They usually just stop breathing in their seats. Older people mostly, out for a little adventure in Tibet. They don't bother to read our literature that points out that Beijing has an elevation of one hundred forty feet and the train takes them to sixteen thousand feet. We very clearly recommend in our brochures that they spend two or three days acclimatizing in Xining but almost no one does." He lifted one of the man's hands, which seemed to be thawing. "Look at the cyanosis!" He grew more eager. "Can I take photographs?"

"When the army is done," Shan said.

"Coach B, Seat 21A," the conductor announced behind Shan. "One-way ticket."

The doctor bent to examine the dead man's eyes. "One-way is right," he murmured.

"So he was a paying passenger," Shan said, glancing at Tan. "One of the lieutenants will go with you to collect any luggage and belongings at his seat." Tan nodded his approval.

"Of course," the conductor said, with obvious relief. By now it was not clear if he was more uncomfortable with the dead man or with the colonel.

Shan turned to the doctor. "It was pulmonary edema then?"

"Yes, of course. Look at the fingers." He pointed to the mouth, where a pink crust was melting. "Look at the color of that sputum. A textbook case."

"Which makes it natural causes," Tan said to the doctor, though he was pointedly looking at Shan, warning him not to argue.

"Yes, yes. The autopsy will find his lungs full of fluid."

"Thank you, Doctor. You may share your conclusion with the detectives waiting outside so they understand no crime was committed. The body may be removed as soon as we clear out my cargo."

"They will want to see the scene just as he was discovered," the doctor said.

Tan gestured toward the crates that bore the insignia of the People's Liberation Army, then leaned toward the doctor and lowered his voice. "National security, comrade," he stated. "National security." The doctor's eyes went round, and he vigorously nodded. "When Public Security asks, it was natural causes, an accident."

"His employer had cargo here," Shan inserted, pointing to the large crate. "He came to check on it. He didn't recognize the onset of his altitude sickness. He became dizzy and fell against the control panel after the door behind him closed. Unfortunately, there was no way for him to get out, no way for him to alert someone to save him. He couldn't go out the rear door with the train speeding through the mountains. He sat and piled blankets around him, thinking he would just ride that way to Lhasa. But to be complete, you will have the usual tests done and report back to Colonel Tan with the results."

The doctor began backing away. He looked frightened again. "Of course," he agreed. "Very straightforward."

"Excellent," Tan observed to Shan as the doctor hurried down the corridor. "The simplest stories are always the best."

"Just so long as you don't confuse it with the truth. Two people were in here. They fought, probably just with their hands. Crates were pushed about. Someone hit the back window, probably with his head, leaving a smear of blood. It wasn't Sun. His head shows no such mark, and he wasn't tall enough to leave a smear so high on the window."

"Another passenger, you mean."

"The train is essentially sealed. It's like a spaceship for the last twelve hundred miles. Yes, another passenger, though I have no idea how the second man escaped with the inner door jammed and the train racing through the night."

"The other passengers are all gone."

"Your cargo is intact. It's the Institute's loss, not yours. Do you really want to push harder?"

"The Institute invaded my county, and my military transport. Now they're probing your town. Yes, I want the truth."

"Then I want to know exactly why Metok Rentzig was executed and who prosecuted his case."

While the soldiers unloaded the cargo and Tan called his office, Shan wandered around the station. It wasn't only passengers who used the station. Tourists would come just to see the famous sky train, and a few now stood beyond the cordons of soldiers, taking photographs of the sleek machine. Some monks, probably staged there by the travel service, rang little *tingsha* cymbals and greeted people with mantras at the entrance. A group of Japanese travelers took their photographs, followed closely by a crowd of Chinese senior citizens. A Western couple wandered around the kiosks of tourist merchandise, where stuffed snow lions and mugs with the Chairman's picture were prominently displayed. Another Westerner sat at a booth that sold tea and soft drinks, snapping photographs of the monks, the trains, the policemen, and the soldiers. Shan glanced around for the Public Security patrol that should be warning him not to take images of the Chinese military or police. Too much interest in soldiers or knobs could get foreigners ejected from Tibet.

An ambulance, lights flashing, pulled up at the entrance and attendants hurried in with a stretcher. Shan lingered in the shadows, watching the brief commotion at the end of the platform before the attendants, now escorted by soldiers, carried a lumpy burden under a blanket toward the ambulance. The station patrol appeared, shouting at the Westerner and other tourists to stop photographing the events. The stretcher passed Shan, a few bluish fingers dangling out of the blanket. Public Security knobs began pushing back observers, ordering tourists onto their buses. Shan glanced at the tea stand. The Westerner had disappeared. Tan was marching toward Shan, ready to leave.

Shan made his way to a lingering group of Chinese tourists and picked out an affluent-looking man with an expensive Japanese camera. He flashed his badge. "I need to see the photographs you were just taking," he announced.

The man paled. "Officer, I never meant—"

"Quickly!"

The frightened tourist fumbled with his camera, then a picture of the stretcher emerged on the screen at the back of the device. "Earlier," Shan said, and the man began scrolling through photos. He stopped the man on the fifth image. At the edge of the photo he could see the lean Westerner with short-cropped graying hair at the tea stand.

"Can you enlarge that part?" he asked, pointing at the Westerner. The tourist complied, until the man filled half the screen. Clearly visible on his forehead was a red-tinged bruise.

There was no sign of the Westerner anywhere when Shan rushed outside. Buses were pulling away. Tan was waiting. "You're coming back with me," the colonel declared. "The file on Metok will be waiting for you."

At the top of the tired old building where Tan still kept his office in Lhadrung, the colonel's steadfast assistant Amah Jiejie greeted Shan with a cup of tea then took him into a conference room where a foot-high stack of papers awaited him. The matronly, ever-cheerful administrator opened the curtains and pulled a notepad and pencils out of the cabinet along the wall. "The colonel said it was better to ask for all corruption cases in the past five years than single out just one."

"The colonel is a chess player," Shan observed.

She extended a finger to a thin file not on the stack. "Not much there I'm afraid."

The dossier contained fewer than a dozen pages of evidence and a two-page case summary prepared by the lead investigator, Lieutenant Huan Yi of Public Security in Lhasa. Metok Rentzig had been a member of the Party—otherwise he would never have been eligible for his post as deputy engineer at the Five Claws project—so he was subject to the jurisdiction of the relentless Central Commission for Discipline. The data sheet affixed to the inside cover of the file showed that the defendant grew up in central Tibet, had been a star pupil, and received an engineering degree from the university in Chengdu, under the name Chou Folan. His residence was in Lhasa, where his wife and teenage daughter lived. He had been working on a highway project west of Lhasa when he had been reassigned to a special projects team, and weeks later was transferred to the Five Claws site. That Metok had received high praise for his work performance was mentioned only briefly in the case summary, which focused on four key pieces of evidence. First, and central to the case, was a copy of a Hong Kong bank account in Metok's name with a sum exceeding two hundred thousand American dollars—foreign currency being mentioned since it always gave an unpatriotic flavor to a crime. The rest consisted of three affidavits. One was from a Public Security officer in Hong Kong named Daoli who certified that the money had been put in Metok's account by a contractor on the hydro project. The second was from Lieutenant Huan himself, stating that he had discovered evidence that the contractor had provided substandard work that had been approved by Metok. The last was an extraordinary statement by the same officer Daoli, dated after his first statement, that he actually recalled seeing Metok in Hong Kong on the very date that the illicit bank account had been opened and had confirmed it by locating a hotel reservation for Metok on that date—although the hotel documentation was conveniently not provided.

It was the flimsiest of cases. The trial had been conducted in secret due to its political sensitivities, and Metok's request for an appeal had been denied. He had been executed a week after the verdict. Shan read the file a second time, then examined the front of the file and the personal data sheet taped inside it. He peeled away the top of the sheet. Something had been stapled there, and removed, replaced by the taped sheet. He braced his head in his hands as the scene of the Tibetan's execution returned, unbidden, to his mind's eye. Every instinct inside Shan told him Metok had not been guilty of corruption but had been urgently eliminated for another reason. If that was the case, Shan had not witnessed an execution. He had witnessed a murder.

Metok had made a gesture with his hand before his death, then offered a mantra. Shan recalled the scene in his mind's eye, focusing on Metok's hand and his words. Shan had mistakenly thought the engineer had made a mudra, a Buddhist sign of devotion, when he had curled his fingers. But he had been imitating claws with his fingers and thumb. He had been signaling the Five Claws Dam. His words, moreover, had been a very special, very old mantra directed at the central deity on the wall of the former chapel. He had summoned the fierce red protector goddess.

Shan stood at the window gazing toward the government complex at the edge of town. Once there had been a temple there. His gaze drifted toward the northern mountains, toward the hydro project, then toward Yangkar.

Shan returned to the ever-attentive Amah Jiejie and asked if that morning's security video footage from the station could be electronically sent to her computer, and whether she had the file on Yankay Namdol, the Tibetan recently released from the Shoe Factory.

"The sorcerer?" she asked with a mischievous smile. "Of course. I can't tell you how many times the colonel has read it." She disappeared into Tan's office and moments later put the file in Shan's hand, then picked up the phone for the call to Lhasa.

The file on the soft labor prisoner Yankay Namdol was much thicker than that of the executed engineer. It held the service records of the two dead soldiers from the convoy in the mountains, a lengthy statement by the Public Security officer in charge which read like a prosecutor's opening in a trial, an investigative report into the hail chaser's background, and even a bizarre statement that the officer had obtained from Bureau of Religious Affairs saying that, based on historical records, it seemed there were individuals in Tibet who knew secrets for controlling the weather and the Bureau had no way to prove that they could not. Shan paused over the conclusion of the Public Security officer, who stated that he had witnessed murder by "remote means." The officer, Shan recalled, had been taken off the promotion lists for three years and transferred to a desk job in Lhasa, both at Tan's insistence. Lieutenant Huan Yi had effectively been demoted and exiled from Lhadrung.

Shan hesitated, looking at the name again, and then searched the Metok file for the name of the Public Security officer who had supported the engineer's prosecution. Huan Yi. The same officer who had been disciplined for his handling of the deaths in the northern mountains had later assembled the case that caused Metok's execution. Amah Jiejie was on the phone, speaking with uncharacteristic impatience, as Shan walked past her to Tan's office. "You never told me why you took me to see the hail chaser released," he pointed out to the colonel. "You said there was trouble coming. It could only be because you had already found trouble. You meant more trouble."

Tan rose from his desk and closed the door, then stood at his window, staring in the direction of his prison camps for several breaths before turning to Shan. "Six weeks ago I was at a meeting at the new supply depot. My driver waited in the car. It was cold so he kept the engine running. When I returned to the car he was unconscious." The colonel opened a drawer in his deck and tossed a wad of cloth at Shan. "This had been stuffed in the exhaust."

Shan straightened the cloth. It was a Tibetan prayer flag.

"Three weeks later I came to the office not long after dawn. Amah Jiejie wasn't here yet. I went to look for something at her desk. This had been left in her chair" Tan said. He extracted another object and dropped it on his desk. Shan studied it, confused, then picked it up. It was a bundle of sticks wrapped with a vine. Inserted in the sticks was the cutout image of a skull. Pasted to the back side of the skull was a small photograph of the Dalai Lama.

"You saw the hail chaser," Tan said. "He had a bundle of sticks like this. It was recorded in the crime report."

"A bundle of dried juniper, yes. The fragrance attracts the deities. But this isn't juniper." Shan pulled out the image of the skull. "It would have been blasphemous to do this. No Tibetan left this on the chair."

"My driver would have died if I had returned a few minutes later."

"Not Tibetans," Shan said again.

"So I was made to understand." Tan returned the objects to his drawer. "Don't tell her."

"Who led you to understand it wasn't Tibetans?" Shan asked. But then Amah Jiejie opened the door and motioned Shan back to the conference room.

Tan's assistant, showing no sign of her argument with someone in Lhasa, sat Shan in front of a computer screen and showed him how to view the video sent by the Lhasa railway security office. When he fumbled with the controls she pulled a chair beside him and asked what they were looking for. Shan had her freeze a frame and pointed to the Westerner sitting at the tea shop. "Where did he come from and where did he go?" Shan answered.

She played the images in reverse, until the lean Westerner with the smear of blood on his forehead rose and walked backward from the platform. "He came off the train," she said. "The same train, though he carries only one small knapsack for luggage." She played the image forward at triple speed, putting her fingertip below the man sitting with his tea, taking photographs. Shan could see his own shadowy image at the edge of the screen. Amah Jiejie traced the man as he rose and blended into the crowd of tourists being ushered outside and onto waiting buses. The stranger boarded a city bus, not one of those chartered to tour groups.

"What can you do about getting the names and nationalities of the passengers on that train?" he asked.

"The travel service will always have the—" she began, then looked over Shan's shoulder. Behind Shan, Tan was standing with an obviously frightened Tibetan man in tattered denim clothing. The colonel's face was even more gaunt than usual. "Jampa has information," Tan tersely declared, then motioned the Tibetan into the chamber.

"Tell Inspector Shan exactly what you told me," Tan ordered the gray-haired man as soon as he sat at the table. Jampa had difficulty speaking. His hands were shaking. He was sitting, defenseless, before the dreaded warlord of Lhadrung. He opened his mouth once, then again, but no words came out.

"He's shy," Tan said, and ignored Shan's confused glance. Tan seemed to know the old Tibetan.

Amah Jiejie brought in a thermos of tea with a tray of biscuits and spoke comforting words as she poured the tea. When Jampa just stared at his cup, Tan rose, appearing more embarrassed than impatient, and disappeared into his inner office. He returned moments later with three bottles of beer, which only added to Shan's puzzlement.

Then he glimpsed Amah Jiejie standing in the shadow just outside the door, gazing at the man with a sad smile. Suddenly he recalled how she had confided to him months earlier that Tan had befriended the Tibetan janitor who cleaned his office.

Jampa took a long swallow from the bottle Tan pushed in front of him, then spoke in a whisper. "He was a good man, I could tell." He looked up at Shan. "You're the constable who used to be in prison." Shan nodded. "You were there. I saw you in the front row."

With a sudden chill Shan realized he had seen Jampa before, washing gobbets of Metok's brain off the wall.

"He gave me a note two days before, when I was cleaning in front of his cell." The old Tibetan wiped moisture from his eyes. "I'm sorry. Maybe I could have saved him. I was so scared. Last year they sent the prior janitor to the Shoe Factory just for talking with a prisoner. They said it showed reactionary sympathies." A sob wracked the old man's body and he burst into tears. Tan put a hand on Jampa's shoulder. When he collected himself, he reached into his pocket and produced an envelope which was stained with what looked like blue-green soap. Inside was a ragged piece of toilet paper with a hastily scrawled note.

I am not here because of what they say, it said. *I am here because the American woman and the archaeologist were killed in front of me and not where they said they died. Find someone who lives by the truth. Warn Sun Lunshi. Metok.*

Shan's spine turned to ice. He exchanged an anguished glance with Tan.

"They can't know I came here," Jampa said.

Tan stared at his bottle. He understood the bitter irony of making such a statement to the county governor and his chief inspector. Shan studied him, suddenly as interested in the colonel as Jampa. The old janitor had come to Tan when he wanted to find someone who lived by the truth. "No," the colonel said. "They can't know." He looked at the tormented Tibetan. "You couldn't have stopped his killing, Jampa," the colonel offered in comfort.

"I pray for his forgiveness every night," Jampa said.

"There's nothing to forgive," Shan said.

Jampa said nothing but seemed to be weighing Shan's words. He scrubbed at an eye again. "Then I will pray for his eternal soul, and of the other two who were murdered, the American and the archaeologist."

"What American?" Shan asked. "What archaeologist?"

"I didn't know. My nephew has a computer. He searched some newspaper reports," Jampa explained. His voice was growing hoarse. "There was an American student and an archaeologist from Chengdu who died in an automobile accident an hour west of Lhasa. You know the kind of story. Sudden storm, a high cliff, and a sharp turn. Their names were Natalie Pike and Professor Gangfen." He shrugged. "It's all I know. Please, I have to get to work."

"Did the other name mean anything to you?" Shan asked the janitor. He pulled out the second business card he had taken from the body on the train, then decided not to ask the old Tibetan about the exotic bar in Lhasa. He had examined the card on the helicopter ride to Lhadrung. On its back was scrawled *75 curry 2* above the word *gymnast*. He looked up and saw Jampa was staring at him. "Sun Lunshi. Did that mean anything to you?"

"Nothing. But I thought you would find him and give him the warning. Perhaps he is in danger too." Tan and Shan exchanged a troubled glance. Sun Lunshi was beyond warning.

Tan took out a cigarette and pushed the pack to the old man, who gratefully extracted one and accepted a light from Tan. They sat in silence, drinking and smoking, until Jampa drained his bottle and rose.

Ten minutes after the distraught janitor left, Shan found the article and printed a copy for Tan to read. An American graduate student from Maryland named Natalie Pike had been driving in the mountains with Professor Gangfen when their car had encountered an unexpected patch of ice and went off a cliff-face road. Pike had been on a special research project, assisting the professor with an excavation of a Chinese army camp dating back to a campaign in the early eighteenth century which, the government-owned paper emphasized, was demonstrating the lengthy and historic presence of the Chinese government in Tibet.

When Shan finally spoke, it was in a whisper. "Metok witnessed their deaths. He was at the hydro project."

Tan replied in the same low, tight voice. "Why would they be at the Five Claws? Their archaeology work was over a hundred miles away."

Amah Jiejie, sensing Tan's dark mood, said nothing as she laid a sheet of paper on the table. It was the list of passengers from the train. Shan ran a finger along the column of nationalities. There had been six Westerners on board. Three were German women traveling together. The other three had been a Canadian couple and a solitary American. He stared at the American's name, then circled it and pushed the paper to Tan.

"There was an American who traveled on the train but stayed in the station and took a great interest in that body," Shan declared.

Tan's eyes narrowed as he stared at the name. He cursed under his breath.

"I saw him," Shan said. "He had a bloody bruise on his head. He is the one who fought in the cargo car with Sun Lunshi. Cato Pike is his name. He has to be the father of the dead American woman."

CHAPTER FOUR

Shan was so intensely examining the other corruption case files to be certain none involved the Five Claws project that he was not aware when Tan left the conference room. When he rose and walked into the outer office, Amah Jiejie pointed to a small box by the door. "The colonel said you didn't have lunch," she said. "You can eat on the way home."

He offered a dim smile. "Except I don't have a way home," he pointed out.

She lifted a set of keys and tossed them to him. "It's the utility vehicle parked out back beside the colonel's car. The colonel says it's yours so long as you keep the new badge."

He added an hour to the drive home with a detour on the rough gravel road that led him to a familiar overlook. He parked the car Tan had given him, sturdy despite being several years old, and walked to the edge of the cliff where he had built a small cairn months earlier. Below him was the 404th People's Construction Brigade, where he had been an inmate. A line of dust marked the closely guarded convoy that was returning prisoners from their daily ordeal of building another road in the mountains. Memories of being on the trucks still ambushed him at unexpected moments, the spasm in his heart sometimes so severe it would paralyze him for a minute or two. The prisoners would have been worked brutally, beaten if they did not keep up the pace, and many of the younger inmates and Chinese prisoners would be slumped against each other, sleeping. But the old ones never slept, just whispered their mantras during the long drive back, quietly working malas, their prayer beads. Their original malas, some centuries old, would have been confiscated decades earlier, so they used makeshift rosaries composed of buttons, little cardboard discs, or even fingernail clippings. Those same battered lamas had saved him, had filled the crushed, hopeless shell that had been Shan with new life and new meaning. Shan did everything within his power to help his son Ko, who was now on one of those trucks, but he knew that the strength and determination he had seen growing in his son was owed much more to the old monks than to Shan. In the last few months much had also been owed to Yara, who had abandoned her life as a feral, defiant, unregistered Tibetan, to get her papers and her teaching job so she could visit Ko every few weeks.

Shan watched as the trucks slowed and entered the gate, thinking now of Metok, who had been a prisoner himself for a few weeks before being executed. When Shan had left the prison, he had said to one of the aged lamas that he owed them everything. "No," the old man had replied with a serene smile, "you owe us only the truth."

It was early evening when he parked in front of the station. Choden met him at the door. "You have a new car?" he asked, visibly excited. "It can't be more than three or four years old!"

Shan shrugged as he walked inside. "Heater works. But I don't think it has a siren."

"And it's green," Choden observed. "I don't think law enforcement has green cars."

"So much the better," Shan replied, then noticed the map laid out over Choden's desk. Someone had been writing on it.

Choden answered his question before he could ask. "Lhakpa," the deputy explained. "This morning he went out and climbed the gate tower, like those scientists did yesterday, even seemed to study each mountain like they did. Then he came back in and asked if we had a map of the northern sector of the county. He studied it for nearly an hour, muttering 'wrong, wrong, wrong,' again and again. Then he took out a pencil and began making corrections."

As Marpa had indicated the day before, existing maps, including those issued to mere constables, were grossly inaccurate. Lhakpa had been making corrections along the northern border. He had slightly shifted several peaks, even highlighted a remote valley and written a name on it, Gekho's Roost, and then drawn little chortens in a ring surrounding the valley.

"I don't understand," Shan said. "Why did he do that?"

Choden shrugged. "He's a snow monk," he said, as if such men were never expected to act rationally.

"Gekho?" Shan asked. The word seemed vaguely familiar, and Shan suspected he had seen it in the archives hidden under the streets of Yangkar.

Choden looked nervously about, and his voice dropped to a near whisper. "An ancient one. A very fierce protector god. The first of the earth deities, the old ones say, from before the days of Buddha," he added, meaning Gekho was a god of Bon, the animist religion that had dominated Tibet before Buddhist missionaries had arrived from India.

"But why?" Shan asked. "You should ask Lhakpa."

"I can't."

Shan saw the awkward, worried expression on his deputy's face and opened the door to the cell block. Lhakpa was gone. He had packed his belongings and departed.

"You criticized him yesterday," Choden said, a hint of accusation in his tone. "You made it impossible for him to spend time here with his niece."

Somehow Shan suspected his departure had more to do with the visit of the Institute team than the rules of his jail. "Check the stables for him," he said.

"He won't be in anyone's stable. He and Tara left on the north-eastern pilgrim's trail, up into the high mountains. We won't see him for months. It's what snow monks do: bless us then disappear."

Shan looked back at the map. Why had Lhakpa gone to the trouble of marking the map then just left it? It had been a message of some kind, Shan realized, left for him. Why would the snow monk be frightened away from Yangkar by a visiting team of scientists? Why would the Chinese scientists seem to recognize the unassuming, contemplative Tibetan?

He went out to his car and returned with an army map he had found in the glove box and laid it beside Lhakpa's map, locating the valley Lhakpa had marked to the northeast of Yangkar. The army map too had a recently penciled annotation, on the same valley. The army map identified the valley as simply Five Claws.

Shan left at dawn for the forty-mile drive to the hydro project and crested the slope leading down into the valley as the work crews were filing out of a large prefabricated building that he took to be a mess hall. He pulled over and trained his binoculars on distant figures as they climbed into dump trucks, tractors, pickups, and even bulldozers then dispersed toward work sites spread throughout the long valley. Before the mess hall, closer to the main road, was a building with a circular drive in front of it centered around a tall flagpole flying the red flag of the People's Republic. Beyond the mess hall were rows of modular units, hauled in by truck, that he assumed were mostly dormitories. The project was massive. He counted the number of modular units. Even if some were used for storage or offices, there had to be scores of workers. Near the mess hall was a concrete mixing plant, where trucks were lined up to receive their loads. With his binoculars he studied the work at the southern end, the deep, narrow pass where huge forms were being constructed for the footers of the dam itself.

The ground shook beneath his feet as a heavy truck crested the ridge and roared past him. Its license plate explained why he had not seen more signs of the project. The truck was from Sichuan, meaning supplies and equipment were coming in on the road from the east, bypassing most of Lhadrung County.

The valley, as depicted in Lhakpa's map, was surrounded by a double ring of mountains, the first a series of rugged ridges that enveloped the valley on all sides, then a series of much steeper snowcapped mountains that stood like sentinels guarding the fertile valley. At the northern end, the two highest peaks funneled a tall waterfall onto the floor of the valley, into a small lake that was an intensely turquoise color. From there a narrow river flowed through the valley into the gap at the southern end where the dam would be built. That vital gap, which made the entire project possible, was a narrow split in the tallest of the surrounding mountains, a magnificent snowcapped peak with a descending series of flats that resembled steps, large enough for a giant. It was what Tibetans would call a grandfather mountain, and what Lhakpa had labeled Gekho's Roost. Huge juniper trees grew around the lake and along the river, and probably had grown all the way to the far end of the valley before the work crews had begun cutting them down and scraping the ground bare.

The Tibetans believed there were spiritual power places created by the earth deities, typically small areas shielded on the north side by natural formations, open to the east for the benefit of the sunrise, and preferably near water and juniper trees. The valley was a power place on a massive scale, the biggest Shan had ever seen. At least it had been before Beijing had overtaken it with bulldozers and dump trucks.

Amah Jiejie had called ahead to make sure Shan was expected as Colonel Tan's envoy at the project headquarters. The director, Dr. Ren Yatsen, an overeager man with a vacuous smile, enthusiastically welcomed Shan, and had his assistant serve tea as he presented a short slide show depicting the valley as it would look in the future. The placid lake in the artist's rendering was framed by concrete structures. In a second perspective from the land below, beaming Tibetans stood before massive turbines as they received outflow waters into fields of golden barley. It would become, Ren assured him, a great source of pride for Tibetans, who could boast that their once useless valley was powering the motherland. When Shan raised a questioning eyebrow, the director explained that the transmission lines would go directly into Sichuan Province, from where power would be distributed into the heart of China.

Ren insisted on taking Shan on a tour of the construction, and as he climbed into Ren's car, Shan caught the director eyeing his constable's uniform.

"I am not on the colonel's military staff, if that's what you are wondering," Shan said.

"No, no. I confess I was confused when the colonel's office said he was sending his inspector."

"I live in Yangkar," Shan said, "the closest county office." Ren seemed somehow relieved by the explanation and resumed his pitch about the wonders of his project as he drove along the valley floor, passing by piles of smoldering trees and huge mounds of fill dirt being brought from the slopes to smooth out the bottom of the valley. Ren stopped at the head of the little lake and pointed to a wide stripe of yellow paint halfway up the cliff face that towered over them.

"Our projected water level," Ren explained with pride. It meant, Shan saw, that the beautiful valley would be entirely submerged.

The director noticed that Shan's gaze lingered on a pile of lumber, many of the boards cracked and broken, that a bulldozer was compacting to burn.

"Construction debris," the director said.

But Shan could see the broken wall frames and sections of roof. It wasn't debris left from building, it was the ruins of a new structure.

The creation of the huge hydro facility was really a combination of projects. The director eagerly pointed out the teams busily scouring the bottom of the valley, making sure nothing was left that might later foul the turbines. Then he showed Shan the massive foundations being prepared at the base of the narrow high-walled pass, the cement plant, and the rows of worker housing beside the equipment yard. When Shan's gaze fixed on the fence being erected around the equipment yard, Ren touched his shoulder and indicated the work being conducted high up the slope near the road, where the control rooms would be built.

"What was the conclusion of the assessment done by Religious Affairs?" Shan asked as Ren pulled up by Shan's own car.

The unexpected question raised a wince to Ren's face, which he quickly forced into a smile. "I assure you all required assessments were properly completed, Inspector. There were a few odd artifacts discovered in a cave that we hauled away for recycling."

Shan paused as he opened his door. "A cave. You mean a cavern temple?"

"Just a hole in the mountain with some rusty junk abandoned ages ago," a new voice inserted. A well-dressed man in his thirties had appeared by Shan's door, blocking his exit. "The engineers consider such things impediments to clean water flow."

Ren gave a small wince before making the introduction. "My deputy director, Jiao Wonzhou," Ren told Shan. "Inspector Shan is representing the governor today," he added to Jiao.

"I didn't notice a cave," Shan said.

"Gone," Jiao proudly explained. "We blasted it, caved it in. Who knows what other trash might have been inside it. Can't have debris drifting out into the turbines. Those machines cost millions each."

"No doubt the antiquities were given the customary evaluation by Religious Affairs," Shan suggested.

Jiao's face hardened. His eyes flared at Shan, then his anger was gone, and he shrugged. "Petty bureaucrats have to learn there is no role for them here. The Bureau of Religious Affairs does not appreciate the challenges of hydroelectric construction."

It was clearly not the first time Jiao had used the words. Religious Affairs had been trespassing on what Jiao considered to be his territory.

Jiao leaned closer. "A few rusty gods in a cave aren't meaningful to the motherland. And a handful of blurry photos sent by a convicted criminal cannot be relied on. If you wish to help us, Comrade Inspector, you can tell them to purge their files."

Shan turned away, trying not to show his reaction to the discovery that Metok had sent photos to Religious Affairs. "But no doubt you explained how some old figurines hidden in a cave could foul your huge dam." He cocked his head at Jiao. "It does sound a bit supernatural, just their thing."

Jiao studied him with a simmering eye, taking in the frayed cuffs of his uniform and scuffed boots. "I'm sorry, Comrade Shan. I didn't realize you were an engineer as well as an inspector. Why exactly did you come?"

"Comrade Shan is Lhadrung's closest senior official," Ren quickly explained. The director seemed to be unsettled by Jiao's intervention. "He reports directly to the county governor."

"Colonel Tan thinks that since his resources are being utilized by the Five Claws team we should have some knowledge of the project," Shan added.

Jiao's thin smile did not fade. "Resources?"

"Our jail in Lhadrung. Our new execution chamber. The secure compartment used for his military cargo that yielded a dead Institute worker. The Institute is a partner in your glorious project, I understand."

Jiao's gaze grew more intense. "So, you are here as constable of some farm town."

Shan shrugged. "Constable, special inspector for the governor, roaming goodwill ambassador. Sometimes I get my hats mixed up."

"We pride ourselves on our autonomy, comrade," Jiao said, an edge of warning in his voice now. "If the colonel wants us to pay for using his cells, he can send us a bill. And that man Sun was not affiliated with the Five Claws. Just a cartographer on a day off."

"I didn't mention the dead man's name," Shan pointed out.

"The Institute is creating a master development plan. They are one of our valued partners in advancing the interests of the motherland."

"Master development plan?" Shan asked. "I fear you have Lhadrung County confused with the suburbs of some eastern city."

Jiao took a step back to let Shan out of the truck. "The motherland has a responsibility to all her children," he replied. "And we are well aware that your Yangkar is the closest town to our project," he added with a gloating expression, then raised a hand in farewell. "Please send Colonel Tan our deepest respects. We look forward to paying him the homage he deserves some day."

The director seemed relieved as Jiao walked away. "Glad the colonel is finally showing an interest," he offered in parting. "Tell him to come visit us personally sometime. He's never bothered to show up. We are going to transform his county."

Shan drove a mile down the road then waited until a dump truck passed and returned to the compound in its dust cloud, parking at the mess hall. He removed his tunic jacket and donned the old work shirt and wool cap he had thrown in the back seat before leaving Yangkar that morning, then ventured into the dining hall. There would be different shifts for eating, he knew, and a few dozen workers were already in the early lunch line. He took a tray and stood behind them, accepting a bowl of rice and vegetables, then filled a mug with tea and found a seat by a group of men his own age. As he approached he stuffed his left arm into his shirt as if it were immobilized.

He ate in silence, listening to good-natured banter about the weather, equipment breakdowns, and news from distant families. Seeing him struggle to reach a bottle of soy sauce, the man beside Shan pushed it closer. "Flying on one wing, eh?" the worker said.

"Tripped when I fled as that building came down," Shan ventured. "Could have been worse."

"Hell, just good fortune that no one died," the man replied. "No way that big garage should have collapsed like that. A freak wind they said. We can put a new one up easy enough but it'll take weeks to replace the equipment lost that day."

"Lucky no one has died anywhere yet," the burly man across from them put in.

"There's been other accidents?" Shan asked.

"More than I've ever seen on a job," his neighbor said. "Engines seize up. A sinkhole opened overnight and swallowed a bulldozer. Cement don't cure right and walls collapse when the forms are pulled away. The cold weather some say, the elevation others claim. Twice they began to cut trees and a wind comes out of nowhere and topples 'em in the wrong direction, taking out a dump truck each time. Some of the Chinese foremen are even suggesting gravity works differently here, 'cause it's the top of the world. Others say burning all those juniper trees makes smoke that attracts the Tibetan demons. Should never have leveled that graveyard of dead gods, that's what I say."

"Graveyard of gods?" Shan asked.

"Rows of squared stones so covered with lichen they seemd older than time itself. Gave me the shivers just walking by them. All gone now, no trace left, and not a prayer spoken."

"Messages started coming from the sky," a man down the table volunteered.

"The sky?" Shan asked.

The man nodded. "Prayers drift down out of the clouds."

"Shouldn't have blasted that god's hole," muttered the burly worker across from Shan.

"God's hole?" Shan asked.

"An old cave with strange markings all over its walls and an old painting of some blue demon in the entrance, like he lived there." The man lowered his voice and grew solemn. "As if he were the last of the old gods, watching over those graves of his friends. Some of those close by the blast said they heard the god screaming inside as the cave collapsed."

Half an hour later Shan parked behind a boulder just below the highest point on the access road, then pulled out his binoculars and began walking. He found a flat ledge overlooking the valley, then sat in the wind-shielded place between two boulders and began scanning the slopes, looking for where the god cave had been. He paused to focus on unusual piles of rocks and loose earth then finally discovered a line of tall *lhatse*, rock cairns, a third of the way down the tall ridge near the mouth of the valley where the dam was being constructed. Tibetans built such cairns as markers but often also to hold *mani*, stones inscribed with prayers along pilgrim routes or paths to temples. He could see eight cairns, four at an equal distance from each other, then a large gap in the line followed by four more that were evenly spaced.

When Shan was young, Shan's father and uncle had taught him the verses of the *Tao te Ching*, and he still sometimes threw the old yarrow sticks that were used in Taoist meditation rituals to randomly select a verse for contemplation. He knelt for a moment, bypassing the ritual, and with a stick drew a tetragram in the dirt near his feet, a solid line over a broken line of two segments, a solid line and another broken line of two parts. It signified Chapter Eleven, one of his favorites. Using the emptiness, his uncle called it. *Clay is shaped to form a vessel*, one verse said. *What is not there gives it meaning.* He had long ago discovered its use as an investigation technique. The cairns were guideposts on either side of a destination. The shadowed gap was what gave them meaning. It was the mouth of the god's hole. Was that where the American woman and the Chinese professor had died? Workers had heard screaming from inside.

If two archaeologists had come to the valley, it would have been to that cave that held old rusty artifacts and strange markings on the walls. They might even have been caught inside inadvertently in the explosion. Except Metok's message had stated "*They knew.*" He could only have meant that the ones who had detonated the explosives had known the archaeologists were inside, meaning two more murders had been committed.

At the corner of his vision a flock of birds fluttered, frightened no doubt by one of the blasts that regularly rocked the valley. But then he glanced upward and saw the brilliant colors. It was not birds but a long line of prayer flags, quickly gaining elevation as they soared toward the center of the construction. Lifting his binoculars, he discovered that the flags were arranged as the tail of a kite, a kite that was nearly invisible because its color matched that of the sky. He rose and began hurrying toward the anchor of the long line.

Ten minutes later he steadied himself on a huge boulder, gasping for breath, knowing he never should have run so hard in the high elevation. The kite flyer was a young woman clad in a gray chuba that matched the color of the ledge rocks around her. She was laughing as she played out the line, then cocked her head as if gauging the wind and cut the line.

Shan was strangely entranced as he watched the flags drift downward, and he remembered now how he had seen one of the red-helmeted foremen directing bulldozers toward trees with colored cloth caught in the branches. This was not the first string of prayer flags launched over the valley. *Prayers drift down out of the clouds*, Shan's messmate had said.

Suddenly Shan looked back at the woman, realizing he had seen her before. She was already hurrying toward a field of tall outcroppings when he began running after her. By the time he reached the spot where she had been standing she had disappeared into the rocks. He bent to retrieve the short length of kite string she had left behind, and then gazed in the direction of the rock outcroppings. He had seen the woman at the gate of the Shoe Factory, waiting for the hail chaser.

When Shan reached the gap in the rocks where she had disappeared, his head was throbbing and he knew he had to rest. He spotted what he thought was the woman's gray chuba on the ground in the shadows and stepped into the gap, then dropped to his knees in surprised exhaustion.

It wasn't a sheepskin coat he had seen. A different young Tibetan female was lying in the rocks. Shan would have recognized the deep, inquisitive eyes anywhere. Tara the goat cocked her head at him, then rose and gave a short bleat before butting Shan onto his back and disappearing into the shadows.

• • •

It was late afternoon when Shan arrived back in Yangkar. At the
school he found Yara sitting with a young Tibetan student, helping
with his homework. Shan handed her a one-word note, "*Garage*," and
drove on to park behind the station. Entering the rear door, he discovered Choden sleeping on a cell cot. He shoved the cell door shut
with a loud clang and continued into the office.

With his usual diligence, Choden had left his report on Shan's
desk. His deputy had frequently reminded him that auditors would
come some day and demand to see proof of the station's efficiency.
He constantly suggested ways that would assure they would receive
passing marks in an audit. Today he had created a new form, titled
Yangkar Station Complaint, Incidents, and Action Log. Listed under
the column for Incidents was a brief description of how a customer
of the astrologer Shiva had grown angry with her for advising that he
must delay his trip planned for the first of the month and threw mud
on her door. Shiva had laughed but Mrs. Lu, ever vigilant for antisocial behavior, had brought the news to the station. *Action*: Choden
and the customer had scrubbed away the mud, the man had profusely
apologized to Shiva, accepting Choden's warning that it was perilous
to offend an astrologer, and Shiva had given him a charm for protection against lightning, at no charge.

Next the new Chinese barber had complained that someone had
stolen his cherished poster of the Chairman right off his front door.
Action: Deputy Choden had explained that the wind had ripped off
the poster and closed the case by pointing out the shreds that were
stuck in the top of a tree in the square.

Incident Three: a young Chinese girl of perhaps five years, traveling
with a middle-aged Chinese woman, had tipped over the trash cans
in the square then run up the stairs of the old gate tower and laughed
as the woman picked up the litter. Choden had gone out to help. The
deputy had explained to the child that he would not lock her up for
this first offense.

Shan's grin faded as he read the final report. A Public Security officer had come looking for Shan. When told the constable was away on duties, she indicated she had to return to Lhasa but she would be back.

Choden understood the cause for Shan's frown. "A frigid one. She was most unhappy when I told her you were gone for the day. A tough character, a real ballbuster."

"From Lhasa," Shan said. "The one who called."

"Must be."

Shan heard the question in Choden's tone. He extracted the leather folder from his pocket and dropped it in front of his deputy. "I will have more reason to go to the city now," he announced.

Choden's eyes went round as he opened the folder. "You?" he blurted in disbelief, then reconsidered. "I mean congratulations." He hesitated. "But you want to work with Colonel Tan? You know the stories. The hellhound, the iron fist, the tormentor, they call him."

"Colonel Tan wants to work with me," Shan said.

Choden offered a grim, sympathetic nod. "So, you are moving to Lhadrung?" he asked, unable to keep the hope out of his voice.

"No. I will work out of this station, and I will remain the constable here. I will only work on special cases." Shan did not miss the disappointment in Choden's eyes. It wasn't that his deputy yearned for a promotion, he simply wanted a superior with more spit and polish. "But I will be away more often," Shan offered in consolation. "You'll be in charge when I am gone and you'll have full use of the old truck."

Choden brightened. "Can I use it to haul sheep for my cousin?"

Shan rolled his eyes. "Just clean out the back afterward and don't let the Committee of Leading Citizens spot you with livestock in the constable's truck."

Yara awaited him at the back of the town's only garage, sitting on an old car seat. Surprisingly, she greeted him with a quick embrace. "I can make the trip this weekend," she said with a smile that lifted her dimples. "My grandmother's coming to watch my son."

"I have a new car," Shan announced, returning the smile. "A better heater and no smell of tobacco." She laughed, and he warmed at the prospect of another long drive with Yara for a visitors' day at Ko's prison. They would share stories of their very different childhoods. Sometimes, after silently gazing up at the high mountain pastures, she would break out in one of the old herder's songs.

"I'll try to keep my grandmother and her cigars away from it," Yara said with a grin, and led him into the junkyard.

The entrance to the path they took was concealed between two overlapping truck wrecks, and when they entered the junkyard Shan had to take out his flashlight to guide them through the many twists and turns that the owner had designed to throw off anyone trying to follow. Finally, they reached a deep shadow between the five-foot-high copper head of a Buddha and a pair of giant clasped hands, both salvaged from old temple statues. Shan followed Yara down the set of narrow stairs.

The librarian's clothes were invariably soiled from his days spent in his garage, but Tserung always fastidiously washed his hands before arriving at his second job. He sat at a table between two bright lanterns in the first of a half dozen stone-walled chambers. Every room was lined with shelves, and every shelf was filled with *peche*, the loose-leafed books of Tibetan tradition that had, at mortal risk, been secretly hidden in the former subterranean chapels while the army and the Red Guard had been demolishing the huge monastery that had sat above.

Tserung had a small bottled gas burner with a pot of tea on it that he now shared with Shan and Yara. "Nearly two rooms done," the mechanic reported with a proud grin, showing two missing teeth. He had been the firstborn son of a traditional Tibetan family and as such had been destined to become a monk at the monastery. But Beijing had crushed the hopes of such traditions. The mechanic had told Shan that down here, serving as the guardian and librarian for the clandestine, illegal collection, was the closest he would ever come to feeling like a real monk. He had enthusiastically embraced Shan's suggestion that he catalog every one of the thousands of peche on the shelves. Tibetan books were all hand-printed, their carved wooden printing plates carefully guarded and treasured by generations of monks. Religious Affairs had not only destroyed millions of such books but also scores of thousands of printing plates, making bonfires of the often centuries-old carvings, which meant that there were probably books on Tserung's shelves that were the only one of their kind surviving, never to be printed again. Scattered among them, moreover, were hand-scribed chronicles and journals kept by the administrators of the big monastery, which had been the economic, cultural, and religious center in the region for centuries.

"There's a large valley to the northeast, just outside the township," Shan said. "I think some call it Gekho's Roost."

"You mean where the Chinese are reshaping the earth," Tserung said in a tight voice. "The Five Claws."

"Yes, the hydro project. But there was something else there, from a long time ago."

"Gekho's Roost, yes. But the old ones also called it the Valley of the Gods, because it's where the land gods first came out of the earth."

"Yangkar was the main monastery of the region. Families living in the valley would have sent their sons to Yangkar. Have you come across mention of it?"

Tserung fixed Shan with a contemplative gaze, looking more like a monk than Shan had ever seen him. "No one was living there," he said, correcting Shan. "Only hermit monks. It was the holiest of ground. People went there to pray, as pilgrims, since before time itself. My grandfather always just called it the original valley, like it was there before everything else. I remember once my grandmother argued when he said that, and he told her don't be silly, there had to be a first place, from which all creation flowed. He said it was the foundation place, that all the bones of the earth were anchored there. If that anchor were broken, then those bones would disconnect."

Strangely, the words shook Shan. After a moment he nodded. "A place of great spiritual power. I was hoping to find references to it here, to help me understand it better."

Tserung kept staring at Shan. "Are you going to stop what they are doing?" he asked in a hopeful tone.

"I want to understand it," Shan said again. "No one can stop it."

"Because the gods of Beijing are more powerful than the gods of Tibet," Yara inserted.

Tserung weighed her words and cocked his head. "Or the gods of Tibet are just sleeping so soundly they haven't awakened yet to what Beijing is doing." He shrugged and ran his fingers through his long black hair. "I've seen passages about monks going to the valley to collect medicinal herbs, and monks going on summer retreat there, two or three hundred years ago. And many references to pilgrims traveling to the sanctuary of Gekho's Roost. It was very important for pilgrims. They would stop in Yangkar to rest up for the long trek into the high mountains. Left handers, mostly, because the chronicles mention that they camped around the little chapel outside the walls."

Shan chewed on the mechanic's words. "You mean they were Bonpo pilgrims," he said, referring to the practitioners of the old animistic religion that had prevailed in Tibet for millenia prior to the arrival of Buddhism from India. Bon and Buddhist practices had blended to create Tibet's unique form of Buddhism, but some embraced the old traditions more than the new. Among those practices was the walking of pilgrim circuits, or *koras,* in a counterclockwise or left-handed direction, instead of the clockwise path of Buddhist pilgrims. Bon pilgrims would have been welcomed at the monastery, but they often had their own priests and their own chapels.

"I can look in earlier volumes," Tserung volunteered.

"Yara and I can help for an hour or two," Shan said. Tserung lifted a lantern and guided them back to the farthest chamber, where the oldest books lay.

As was often the case, Shan got lost in the reports of daily life from centuries earlier. He became quickly absorbed in an account of sculptors who had arrived from India to begin work on new statues of dancing *dakini* goddesses that would adorn the walls of the main sanctuary. Then he lingered over a three-hundred-year-old passage describing a trek into the northern mountains to pay homage to a white yak that had been spotted by herders.

Yara and Tserung were so immersed in their own reading that they took little notice when, stifling a yawn, he bid them good night so he could return to his quarters for a predawn departure in the morning. If Public Security from Lhasa was looking for him, the best place to avoid them would be Lhasa itself.

CHAPTER fIVE

Shan had just descended the mountains and turned onto the north-south highway when a bell began chiming in the glove box. He pulled over and discovered a cell phone under the maps in the box. The call was from a number in Lhadrung.

"You finally found it," came Tan's gruff voice. "You never answered yesterday."

"I think you are aware, Colonel, that outside of Lhadrung town there is no cell coverage in most of your county."

"Yet we are talking."

"Because I am on the highway to Lhasa," Shan said. He then explained that after visiting the Five Claws project, he suspected the archaeologists had been deliberately killed by the implosion of the cavern they were studying. He chose not to speak of earth deities, Tara the goat, or the hail chaser and his companion.

Tan asked him what his business was in Lhasa. "The American Cato Pike is in Lhasa," Shan explained. "Unlikely he has friends there. All he knows is what the public reports say. I will search hotels and guesthouses. I want to speak to Metok's family, if Amah Jiejie can send that address from the file."

"Watch for a message and watch your back," Tan said and hung up.

By the time Shan reached the outskirts of the capital city, there were two messages on his phone: one listing an apartment address, the second simply stating Lotus Garden Hotel. He approached the hotel warily, parking blocks away and watching for the tall American, who would have a hard time blending into any crowd in the city. In the lobby he stayed behind a row of potted plants and watched Western tourists come and go.

"There you are," came a loud voice behind Shan. He turned to face Tan's youngest staff officer.

"Lieutenant Zhu," Shan said in surprise.

The lieutenant gave an uncertain grin. "Inspector."

"I'm working. And please keep your voice down."

"Yes. The records going back six months show that no one named Pike has stayed here." Zhu saw the confusion on Shan's face. "It's my assignment. I am to assist you until the colonel says otherwise. He told me the first task." Zhu produced a slip of paper with a list of hotels. "I checked half a dozen already. I can cover the rest by 1500."

Shan frowned. Tan's message had just been intended for Zhu to connect with Shan. He looked away for a moment, fighting the temptation to order Zhu back to Lhadrung. Tan knew Shan worked alone.

"This isn't a military operation, Lieutenant."

The young officer weighed his words then brightened. "I have civilian clothes in my car. I can change in the hotel washroom."

"What exactly did the colonel say about your assignment?"

"He said you were an insubordinate son of a bitch," Zhu said, then hastily added, "Sir. An insubordinate son of a bitch, sir. And to do whatever you said, unless I might go to jail for it."

"Those were his words?"

Zhu thought a moment. "His exact words were unless Public Security might catch me at it."

Shan tried to suppress a smile. "What do you do for the colonel?"

"I left college to go to officers' school. I was trained to lead missions in the mountains," Zhu explained, meaning he was trained as a mountain commando, the toughest of Tan's troops. "But right now, I mostly write reports that sit on some clerk's desk and summarize reports that come in from other clerks. Sometimes I drive the colonel when the sergeant isn't on duty."

As innocuous as it sounded, Shan knew it meant the colonel placed his trust in the officer. "Doing anything for the colonel requires a certain degree of bravery," Shan observed.

Zhu grinned again. "Should I go change then?"

"Yes. Finish checking the hotels for any stay by the American. And I don't want the Lhasa police or Public Security to know you are asking."

Zhu began to salute then reconsidered and dropped his hand. "Evasive reconnaissance. My favorite kind of mission." He took a step away and turned back, reaching into a pocket. "Almost forgot. She said to give it to you. Your eyes only," the lieutenant added in an inquiring tone. Shan took the envelope, confirmed that it was addressed in Amah Jiejie's elegant hand, and then to Zhu's obvious disappointment, put it in his own pocket. "There's a tea shop with a big red door on the north side of Barkhor Square," Shan said. "See you there in four hours."

On the waiting room wall of the drab building that sat behind Lhasa's temple complex a plaque proclaimed that the Bureau of Religious Affairs was the "lifeblood of cultural responsibililty in Tibet." Shan sat for nearly half an hour, contemplating the many ways the words might be interpreted, before he was ushered into a surprisingly elegant meeting room.

The two men waiting for him seemed almost excited to see Shan. "Welcome, Comrade Inspector. We are so grateful to at last receive some recognition from the government of Lhadrung County," declared the older man, who introduced himself as the regional director. He pushed a porcelain cup of tea across the table to Shan.

"I just had some questions about a criminal case," Shan said, unable to disguise his confusion.

"Yes, yes, so the note you sent up explained. Religious Affairs is a pillar of cooperation."

"A man named Metok Rentzig sent you some photographs."

The regional director looked down into his folded hands, then glanced at his companion. "That case is closed, we hear," the younger man offered.

"Just tidying up the file," Shan said. "Did Rentzig send any explanation, perhaps a description of the subjects of his photos? Perhaps a detailed location or even some suggestion why he, as an engineer, would be sending them to you directly?"

The two men exchanged wary glances. "The photos from the Five Claws are safe in our warehouse on Kunming Road. We are willing to make a compromise."

His hosts seemed to think Shan came to negotiate. "A compromise?"

"Surely that is why you came, to resolve things with Deputy Director Jiao."

Shan took a deep breath. "There's much to resolve."

"But still two years before the Chairman comes for his glorious visit."

"To visit the Five Claws, you mean."

"Exactly. Surely Jiao must understand our claim to jurisdiction is well-founded."

"I am here about Rentzig."

"Yes, well, we are willing to say the photos came from Jiao himself," the regional director suggested. "We can be practical. The involvement of a criminal was just coincidental. We will, of course, support development of the project, even postdate the report if he prefers."

"I would have to understand what Metok said."

"But there is no need to include his name anywhere, I assure you. We were already asserting jurisdiction."

Shan's mind raced. "So you can have a place at the table when the Chairman visits," he said.

"Astutely put, comrade. You have pierced the essential point. And, of course, Colonel Tan will be there. We can add his name to our report if he wishes. We just want Jiao to provide some reciprocity. Where would he be if we had not already tamed the Tibetan reactionaries?"

Shan had to swallow his bile. "You did assess the photos from Metok, but your report will dismiss the artifacts as unnoteworthy."

"Not exactly," the younger official replied. "Better to indicate that they presented a challenge which we were able to overcome through painstaking and expert evaluation to minimize their importance. We call it mitigation. We will say we mitigated the problem to advance the interests of the motherland."

Metok's apartment was in one of the new blocks of apartment buildings on the south side of the city. Shan knocked for a long time and was about to give up when a weary woman in her mid-thirties opened the door, took in his uniform, and fixed him with an accusatory stare.

"I am from Lhadrung," Shan said. Metok's wife wore her hair in a tight bun at the back of her head. She wore a dirty sweatshirt, and her eyes appeared puffy from crying.

"I think," the woman replied in a surprisingly sharp voice, "that we are finished with Lhadrung."

Shan cursed himself for not rehearsing a better opening.

"Could there be anything left for you to do to us?" the woman snapped. "Evict us today instead of in a month? Maybe you're here to reclaim his work clothes—I might be able to find some mud-caked shoes you can take back as trophies."

"My name is Shan. I am just a constable. I want to try to set things right."

Metok's wife gave a bitter laugh. "A bit late for that, isn't it, Constable Shan? Perhaps you came to collect the cost of the bullet that killed my husband? I hear Public Security does that sometimes."

"I am not Public Security. They would be furious if they knew I was here." Shan cast a nervous glance down the hall, where an elderly woman carrying a bag of cabbages had paused to gawk at him. "Please, may I come in?"

"You people always do what you want," she said as she stepped aside for him to enter. "No point in saying no." She turned her back on Shan and called toward the kitchen. "Dolma," she said to the teenaged girl who emerged. "Go to your room," she instructed, then sat in one of the two worn armchairs in the modest sitting room.

Shan admired the shelves of books that lined two of the walls of Metok's apartment. It was a well-read household. Instead of the usual framed quotes of Mao that were often hung in rooms that visitors might frequent, there were two quotes from Buddhist scripture. Another wall held several photographs of Metok standing by bridges, tunnels, and a highway—no doubt souvenirs from past projects for the civil engineer. The shelves on the remaining wall were stripped empty, with cardboard cartons stacked below.

Metok's wife stared at the carpet as he sat. Her voice cracked as she spoke. "You killed him for no reason," she said, pressing a hand to her mouth to stifle a sob.

Public Security had been careful to keep Metok's trial and execution a closely guarded secret. How could she have known he was dead? "A note was smuggled out of his cell," Shan said. "Your husband asked that the messenger deliver it to someone who lives by the truth." He realized after he spoke that he had answered his own question. The old janitor Jampa could easily have smuggled out more than one note.

She scrubbed at her eyes then studied Shan with a confused expression, which gradually turned sour. "And that's supposed to be you? You, in your scuffed shoes and tattered constable's uniform? You don't strike me as anyone's savior."

"I was there," he said, switching to Tibetan. She looked up in surprise. "In the official witness gallery. I was forced to watch. He looked at me only for an instant, but it was long enough. In his note your husband said he was being silenced because he saw something, because he knew about a crime at the Five Claws. If that's true, then what I witnessed wasn't an execution. It was a carefully orchestrated murder."

The words triggered a new flood of tears. She picked up one of the photos of Metok and fixed it with a forlorn stare as she spoke. "My husband was a good man. He worked hard, for his family. For the . . ." she seemed to force herself to say the word, "the motherland."

"Did he ever say anything to you about archaeologists working at his project? A foreigner and a professor from Chengdu?"

Metok's widow spoke to the floor again. "Someone who knew about such things could suffer the same punishment as my husband. My daughter has only one parent left. I can't afford more trouble."

"I am not Public Security," he said again. "I am not the military. I can see things that are sometimes not so visible to others."

"And what are you doing here?" the Tibetan woman asked.

"Following a little spark that might brighten into a spotlight. No one knows I am here. No one need know."

"They've taken our apartment away on one month's notice. If they suspected I was talking about this, they would take away my job too."

"Your job?"

"I am an English translator for the travel service. Which means I am mostly a tour guide for Westerners. They watch us closely. Any hint of disloyalty and I would be finished."

"No one will know," Shan assured her.

She frowned but gave a curt nod. "My name is Lekshay," she said, then wiped at a new tear that streamed down her cheek. "You mean my husband died because he knew something that more powerful men couldn't have him reveal."

"I think so."

"Surely that's impossible. Do you know how many would have to be involved in such a conspiracy? Public Security, the Ministry of Justice, judges, Party officials, not to mention people at the project."

"Not as many as you would think. Only those who falsified the evidence. No more than a handful. I saw your husband's file. He was shot for corruption."

"Which is ridiculous. Our salaries are modest but they suffice." She cast her gaze around the apartment. "I probably couldn't afford to keep this place anyway. And I'll never have enough on my own for my daughter's education." She stifled another sob.

"The case was based on a Hong Kong account with two hundred thousand American dollars in it."

"Never! He never took a bribe. He never even went to Hong Kong!"

"The officer who signed the report about the bank account also signed a statement that he had seen Metok in Hong Kong. Then there would have been someone in Public Security here in Lhasa who assembled the file. Probably three or four people were likely involved in conspiring against your husband, no more."

Lekshay wrung her hands then looked up at the altar in the middle of the central bookshelf, where a little ceramic Buddha sat beside a flickering battery-powered candle. "It's impossible. No one could hope to punish such men."

"I don't think your husband was looking for revenge. Just the truth."

She stood and went to the Buddha, as if consulting it. When she turned back to Shan, there was a glint of determination in her eyes. "I don't know how I could possibly help, Constable."

"Just talk with me," Shan said. "I want to hear about Metok, about his job, about Director Ren and Deputy Director Jiao at the Five Claws."

"And I would like to know about that message," she said. "Maybe if I could meet with that messenger from the jail, if I could hear about my husband's final hours, I think it would ease the pain somehow."

"Just an old man who works at the jail. Did your husband ever speak about Director Ren and Deputy Director Jiao from the Five Claws?"

They spoke for nearly an hour about Metok and the hydro project. Metok had not been getting along with the director, who in fact had no experience building dams, but had been selected because he had been successful building new highways in Manchuria and, more importantly, had recently attained membership in the Party. Jiao, she had heard, had successfully completed an important project in Sichuan Province. The deputy director had been furious when he had discovered Metok had made a makeshift Buddhist altar in a supply shed where Tibetans could go in their time off and had threatened to report him to Religious Affairs.

"Your husband had a friend named Sun Lunshi," Shan said as the widow gave him her phone number in case he had follow-up questions. "He died on the sky train the day after your husband was executed."

"It has been a season for sorrow," Lekshay said. "I didn't know Sun, except for what my husband spoke of him. A tragic accident. I saw it in the newspaper. That train is more dangerous than people think."

"He was accompanying cargo for the Five Claws."

"Then he died performing his duties. A hero."

"A season of sorrow indeed. An American student and her Chinese professor died as well."

Lekshay looked confused. "I think I read something in the paper about an American dying."

"Natalie Pike and Professor Gangfen. Did your husband perhaps know them?"

"Of course not. I recall they died near their archaeology project, west of here. Far from the Five Claws. One of those terrible road accidents in the mountains, I recollect."

"Your husband was arrested the day after they died."

She shrugged. "Metok may not have shared all his secrets, to protect me, but he could not have possibly known them."

"Sun died the day after your husband was executed," Shan reminded her.

She shrugged again.

Shan himself did not think the deaths could all be related. But Metok had sent an urgent message while he waited for his execution, asking for Sun to be warned, as if those who wanted Metok dead would soon be pursuing Sun. Sun had died before he could be warned, with no other clue to his fate than the card of an exotic bar in Lhasa.

Jamalinka Island, though located within the traditional boundaries of old Lhasa, did not seem part of Tibet. Shan had seen it from afar several times but had always avoided it, for it was the center of the predominantly Chinese nightlife district. He had left his uniform tunic in his car and bought a cheap sweater to pull over his uniform shirt but still felt conspicuous as he walked across the bridge and reached the first strip of karaoke bars. Small groups of tourists, mostly Japanese and Western men, were wandering through what looked like a neon labyrinth. There was almost no sign of anything Tibetan except for a remarkably lifelike mannequin in the doorway of the bar he was seeking, made up to look like a naked dakini goddess.

Some of the tired-looking women sitting outside the bar glanced up at him and quickly looked away. Most were Chinese, and he recalled stories of how, after train service began, entire brothels had relocated from eastern cities to serve the burgeoning Lhasa tourist traffic. He was surprised, however, at the number of Tibetan women he saw, and he recalled other tales of how for centuries practices of polyandry had deprived many country women of husbands, and they had gravitated to night work in Lhasa. Early chronicles had even reported that the short-lived Sixth Dalai Lama had been so obsessed with the brothels of seventeenth-century Lhasa that he had never taken his final monastic vows.

He fought a sudden impulse to flee and stepped into the alley to summon the courage to go inside. As two patrolling Public Security officers walked by on the street, he reminded himself that a female knob officer from Lhasa had been seeking him.

A teenage boy on a delivery bicycle approached the building from the shadows, and Shan stopped him. For a handful of coins, he bought

the boy's cap, then on impulse he showed the boy the card. "Gymnast,"
the boy said. "Sure, everyone knows her. It's because she can bend in
amazing ways. She works here sometimes as a dancer. That's what
people call her, the gymnast."

"And this?" Shan asked, pointing to the handwritten line that
said: *75 curry 2.*

The boy shook his head. "No Curry Road, if that's what you
mean."

"What about a name from India?" Shan asked.

The boy laughed. "You mean like it was someone's idea of a joke,
or one of those codes." He threw a thumb over his shoulder, gesturing
behind him, then pointed to an alley leading to another street beyond
the neon-lit corridor. "Bombay Road, back there, or Delhi Pass, the
block ahead of us. Maybe Number Seventy-Five, second floor?"

Shan found an empty cardboard box marked *Adult Toys* in four
languages, hoisted it on his shoulder, and ventured back into the
brightly lit street. Delhi Pass proved to be a utility road lined with
small warehouses and the loading docks for the bars and clubs that
faced busier streets. Bombay Road, though a narrow cobblestone
track that was little wider than an alley, proved more promising. Its
old tenements were in various states of disrepair but many appeared
to be occupied. Shan found a shadowed alcove and watched Number
Seventy-Five for a quarter-hour, until a blond woman in a miniskirt
raced past him and up the stairs of the building. As she put a key in
the door of the second-floor apartment, he darted up the stairs then
stepped in behind her and pushed the door shut behind them. As she
turned with a surprised gasp, he saw that she was not a Westerner but
a Chinese woman trying to look Western, with blond hair and a tight
silk blouse.

"I'm sorry," he said, and began reaching for his badge.

She grinned. "I'm sorry," she echoed, just as something slammed
into Shan's skull.

. . .

When he regained consciousness, he was in a metal armchair, his fore-arms bound to the chair with duct tape. He blinked away the pain in his forehead and saw a thin, athletic-looking woman with short black hair in a kitchen alcove preparing a meal.

"Tink will share some noodles with you, before you go," came a deep baritone voice from the shadows along the wall, "just to show no hard feelings. First timers sometimes get smitten and don't always understand it's hands off. She's a dancer, and sometimes a masseuse, but that's all." It was a Western voice, but it spoke perfect Mandarin.

"Tink?" Shan asked. The fog in his head was slowly clearing, and he turned toward the speaker, who now approached. The American had a strong, lean face. Its small scars from close-in fighting had not shown on the grainy security video.

"When I lived in Beijing, I was surprised to see images of Peter Pan," the man said. "I realized that the yearning for eternal youth is universal. That's why places like Jamalinka exist, little pockets of Nev-erland to capture an instant of youth. It took me a lot longer to real-ize that just a smile from a beautiful young woman often does the job as well as an hour in her bed. Tink has a magical smile. I told her she should charge for her smiles. Tinker Bell, the fairy of eternal youth. And she cooks!"

"I've never met a Chinese woman named after Tinker Bell."

"My invention, but she likes it."

"Being knocked unconscious seems to dilute some of the magic," Shan observed.

The American gave a short laugh and pointed to a club on the table, with a towel wrapped around it fastened with duct tape. "We soften the blow so there's no permanent damge. You need to learn that there are rules in places like Jamalinka. A lot of rules. Don't fol-low a girl home, that's one of the important ones. Don't trespass into her apartment. Don't trespass and start taking off your clothes. I helped you avoid greater unpleasantries. It was a light tap, in just the right spot to take you out for five minutes. I'll find you an aspirin. Tink's noodles are first rate."

"I wasn't taking off my clothes," Shan explained. "I was reaching into my pocket, Mr. Pike."

The American stiffened and muttered a low curse in English. Shan did not resist as he reached into Shan's pocket and opened the leather folder. He stared at Shan for several long breaths. "This can get complicated, Inspector," he said. "How about if I just leave and Tink gives you a rubdown?"

"I am very sorry about your daughter," Shan said.

He didn't see the blow coming, just felt the explosion of pain as Pike slapped him. It felt like he had been hit by a piece of lumber. "And I'm very sorry about all your damned lies," the American said in a defiant tone. "Is that why you are here? Scared I'm going to rewrite the story? This isn't over. And you've got nothing on me."

Shan tried to rub the numbness from his cheek with his shoulder. "There's the matter of the dead man on the train," he suggested.

Pike's eyes sparked, then he went very quiet. "Not on me. The fool attacked me. He smashed the controls on that cargo chamber door. He could have gotten out the rear door when the train stopped up in the mountains and run back on board the same as me if he wanted. I even called out to him to come with me. I'm sorry his bad judgment killed him. I only wanted to speak with him."

"Somewhat urgently, I take it, considering that you flew from Lhasa just to take a train back to Lhasa."

"I don't talk with Chinese police," Pike growled. "Chinese police are the problem, not the cure."

"You have me confused with Public Security," Shan said.

"Right. Special investigator for the governor of Lhadrung, who must be a Party boss. Which makes you worse than Public Security. You can operate totally in the dark. One of those secret watchers who throws citizens into prison for just muttering the Chairman's name in a cynical tone."

"The Chairman is a tyrant who is turning my country into a massive internment camp."

The words stopped Pike for a moment. A bitter smile crossed his face. "That's what happens when you install security cameras every fifty feet. What was the number I heard recently? The People's frigging Republic has five hundred million cameras, with more every day. Boggles the mind." He turned toward the woman. "I have to pack," he said to her in a disappointed tone. "I can't come back now."

The woman wasn't listening. She stepped toward Shan and picked up the table lamp. Shan tensed, thinking she was going to hit him with it, but she just leaned in with the lamp, looking at the top of his wrist then his neck. "A convict," she declared.

"No way, kiddo," Pike said. "Not with that badge."

She was good, and experienced with life in Chinese prisons. The little pairs of discolored spots on his hands and neck had faded. No one had noticed them for years. "Here, here, and there," she said, pointing to three of the pairs. "From where a guard turns a cattle prod to maximum charge and presses it into your skin." She pulled up the sleeve of her T-shirt and pointed to similar pairs of dots near her shoulder. "On women they usually apply it to places that don't show."

Shan shuddered as Pike produced a pocketknife and unfolded its long blade. He sliced the duct tape on his arm and turned it over. "Jesus bloody Christ," he muttered as he saw the tattooed numbers, then pushed the blade close to Shan's throat. "Recite that number," he ordered Shan, then cursed again as Shan did so without hesitation. "What's your game?" he asked. "You're no cop."

"I keep telling my boss that, but he won't listen," Shan said. "I'm from Lhadrung. Colonel Tan, the governor of Lhadrung, makes his own rules."

Pike seemed to recognize the county name. "Not even in that gulag wilderness do convicts get badges."

"I was an inspector in Beijing. I investigated the wrong people and they sent me to a prison in Lhadrung because the death rate is so high there. But the governor had a problem. I helped him, unofficially, and to show his gratitude he pulled me out of the hard labor camp. Some days I wish I were still in that prison."

The American laughed. "If you think that I would believe that—"

The Chinese woman held up a hand to silence the American. She rose, stepped into the kitchen, and returned with a bottle of grain alcohol and a cloth. Shan watched in puzzlement as she soaked a corner of the cloth in the alcohol. Then she gazed at him in challenge and he understood. He extended his arm. First, she stretched his skin around the tattoo then rubbed the cloth vigorously over the numbers. If the tattoo were recently done, the skin would be reddened around the numbers. If, on the other hand, it was temporary, the numbers would smear.

"It's real," she announced in surprise.

The American studied Shan in silence for several breaths. "Which makes you the strangest Chinese I've ever met."

"You have no idea."

Pike hesitated, then pressed the blade to the squarish lump on Shan's chest. "A gau?"

"It wasn't really Colonel Tan who saved me. It was some old lamas. And I'm trying to avoid Public Security as much as you are."

"Why?"

"Because they don't want me looking into the deaths of Natalie Pike and Professor Gangfen."

Pike studied him in silence again. Shan had never seen eyes like his. The intelligence that burned in them was as deep as their sadness, but there was also something fierce and untamed. He had a strange sense that he was looking at a reincarnation of one of the warrior priests who once roamed Tibet, accountable only to Buddha.

With a quick motion, the American cut Shan's other arm free. "Now I insist that you have some noodles with us."

Shan did not mention that an army lieutenant was expecting him, and when he asked Pike why he was using the apartment the American just motioned to the table and said, "Eat."

The Chinese bar dancer was surprisingly adept in the kitchen, where she worked with an athletic energy, and served her noodles with a stir-fry of vegetables. It was the best meal Shan had had in weeks. As he finished his bowl he realized Pike was staring at him again.

"Why is an investigator from faraway Lhadrung interested in my train ride?"

"Colonel Tan is responsible for the regional military depot in Lhadrung. The cargo on that train was bound for his depot."

"Not everything. I have enough sense not to interfere with the People's Liberation Army."

"You were there because of Sun Lunshi."

"He was a friend of a friend of my daughter's. I needed to have a quiet conversation with him. I located his office but when I started to go in, Public Security arrived. He suddenly took off for Golmud, like he was fleeing. I decided to find out why."

"Did he know who you were?"

"When I caught up with him and told him, I didn't expect him to get so upset. That's when he ran into that cargo car. He smashed the controls to keep me out, but I slipped through just as the door closed. He trapped us both in there, which suited my purposes just fine."

"What was in the crate?"

"I don't know. I was just there to talk. And I don't think he was going to check any cargo. When I caught up with him, he was looking in the staff berths, calling out for the doctor. Guess he was already feeling sick. I would have helped, but he wasn't inclined to talk. Just laid into me like a banshee." Pike fell silent then repeated his own question. "Why is an investigator from faraway Lhadrung interested in my train ride?"

"Be grateful that I am, and only me. The Lhasa police would have called it a homicide if we had given them jurisdiction. Witnesses would have recalled you chasing Sun through the train, making you their prime suspect. You don't exactly blend in here. It wouldn't take them long to find you."

"Again, you don't answer my question, Inspector Shan."

"I am not investigating what happened on your train ride. I am investigating the execution of a Tibetan named Metok Rentzig."

Pike's eyes narrowed. "He's dead?" The American's knuckles

wrapped around his teacup and began to turn white. "I had the impression that investigations are commonly done before an execution, not after."

"This is Tibet. We are never constrained by the patterns observed elsewhere in the world."

"I don't know anything about a civil engineer named Metok."

"Professor Gangfen knew Metok. And I didn't tell you he was an engineer." He returned Pike's unblinking stare. "Metok was a friend of your daughter's?" Shan realized that although Tink had carried away the dishes, she wasn't washing them, she was at the window, watching the street. "The dead man on the train had a card for the bar where Tink works, with a clue to this address handwritten on it. He was coming here. Accompanying that crate was a convenient cover for him. Or maybe the crate being there was just a coincidence. Why did you want to speak with him? Was this the professor's apartment?"

Pike did not reply.

"Your daughter died three weeks ago," Shan observed. "I would have thought there would be arrangements needed at home. Usually takes two or three weeks to have remains shipped back across the Pacific."

"Let's just say I wanted to understand how she died. She was my only daughter."

"You mean going to her place of death would bring closure."

"Something like that."

"Then why stalk someone from the Institute? Why hide in this apartment? And why," he added in afterthought, "did the distinguished professor have an apartment among the brothels of Jamalinka?"

"It's all those millions of cameras," Pike said. "This is Tibet's Vegas Strip."

"Sorry?"

"All the bright neon. In other cities like Kashgar where Public Security worries about unrest they can spot any individual they seek in about ten minutes because the cameras are everywhere, and everyone has been required to submit to facial recognition scans. But in Lhasa there is an oasis, a black hole if you will. They watch the streets in and out of Jamalinka but inside the district the cameras are blinded by the brilliant lights. And it wasn't his apartment, just an operating base, you might say, an oasis. Tink keeps a lot of interesting friends."

Shan weighed the words. "You make it sound as if Professor Gang-fen had something to hide."

"Of course he did. His independence. What freedom-loving man wouldn't want to evade the big brothers constantly watching on their cameras? In another few years, half of China's population will be watching the other half."

"He was just an archaeologist."

"In China archaeology is such a politically hot topic that anyone true to the science has to engage in subterfuge," Pike replied. "Beijing goes into violent spasms if anyone suggests there has ever been a drop of non-Chinese blood within the boundaries of its current empire. Natalie wrote me about him and about Tink. Gangfen had two sets of records, one for his university that were well scrubbed to support the case that China had long-established roots in Tibet."

Shan knew well how Beijing aggressively suppressed any suggestion of outside influence whether in modern times or centuries earlier. "And another set, kept here, that were not so politically correct," he suggested.

Pike nodded. "He found a spirited, educated woman who lived at the edge of society, on her own terms, and who could keep her own apartment without questions being raised about how she might afford it. Tink is a courtesan, you might say, and courtesans are always given lots of latitude in their private lives." Tink turned from the window long enough to wrinkle her nose good-naturedly.

"You seem to grasp the realities of modern China very well, Mr. Pike," Shan said.

"I left the army for a higher calling with the American government. They sent me to Beijing for two years. Then later I spent a year in Shanghai, in private security, you might say."

"I don't imagine you would make a good paper pusher."

"Someone tried to make me one a long time ago. Didn't work out. Bureaucrats have to obsess over every little detail. I just spend my life on the important things," Pike added with a dangerous gleam in his eyes.

"Was your daughter engaged in something illegal, Mr. Pike? Or just something important?"

"I just met you, Shan. And I've never met a man from Beijing I could trust."

"Five years in hard labor scoured Beijing from my soul. I am from Tibet."

"But I have never met an investigator anywhere in China who was interested in truly investigating and damned few who could even accomplish what I would call a true investigation."

"I was sent to prison for truly investigating."

When Pike just fixed him with another of his intense, stabbing stares, Shan added, "Spoken like someone with experience in law enforcement."

"A dozen years with the FBI, including in Beijing. Didn't suit my temperament, but gave me perspective, you might say. I quit, became a professor."

"And here you are, hiding with a sex worker in the black hole of Lhasa."

"Careful how you speak about Tink. Only a dancer and masseuse, nothing more. And all work is great if greatly pursued. I tend to think of her more as someone of diverse skills and interests, kind of a Renaissance woman."

Shan looked at his watch. "I have to go."

"I'm not convinced I can let you."

"I'll be missed."

"Somehow I suspect that Jamalinka is the last place anyone would look for you."

Shan nodded his agreement. "If you are going to kill me, I'd prefer that you take my body somewhere else."

Pike grinned. "Nothing so dramatic. But maybe I should bind you to that chair again and let Tink tend you for a couple days. Or I have a syringe with some magic medicine that would keep you unconscious for the rest of the week. Might be easier."

Shan sighed. "Can I have a piece of paper, please?"

Tink tossed him a small notepad, and he wrote down two rows of numbers and pushed it toward Pike. "This is my fatal combination. The first is my *lao gai* number, my inmate registration, which you can verify by my tattoo. The second is my badge number. Officially a former hard labor prisoner is banned from holding a law enforcement badge. The badge was granted by the county governor, so I am protected anywhere in Lhadrung. Outside of Lhadrung I am not, but no one understands my particular circumstances. There are officers in Lhasa who would arrest me in an instant if they knew that history. Public Security knows how to find me, at the constable station in Yangkar. Take the numbers. You can destroy me with them."

Pike exchanged a long glance with Tink, then folded the paper into his pocket.

"If you knew about Metok and Sun Lunshi, then you knew about the Five Claws project," Shan ventured.

"Natalie mentioned it in a letter, although she only used that term once. She called it the Roost for some reason and said it was the most exciting place she had ever visited, professionally speaking."

"I believe your daughter was killed there when a cave was imploded, not in a car accident. I think those who did it knew she and the professor were inside. Metok knew it as well, and they didn't trust him to keep quiet. So they arranged his execution."

Pike's gaze grew more intense, then the fire in his eyes turned to melancholy. Shan stood and thanked Tink for the meal. He was almost at the door when the American spoke.

"You asked why I was here so soon after Natalie's death," he said to Shan's back. "They sent me her ashes. We had a memorial service." Shan turned. "But it was all so abrupt, so neatly wrapped up with a press report that explained the terrible car accident when Professor

Gangfen drove off the mountain road. But something nagged at me. I dug out an old letter she had written that mentioned she was serving as the professor's driver, among other enjoyable things, because like a lot of Chinese who live in cities, Gangfen didn't drive. I dug up the ashes and had a friend in the FBI test them. I had buried a sheep."

CHAPTER SIX

"It was 1720 when the horde of Dzungar Mongols descended upon Tibet, slaughtering and looting all the way to Lhasa," Shan's guide said. Shan and Cato Pike were standing in the middle of the archaeology excavation that had brought Natalie Pike to Tibet. Their escort, the junior professor who had taken over after Professor Gangfen's death, gestured to several students who were guiding a small machine on wheels over the flat terrain. "Ground radar," the balding man explained. "The most efficient way to find anomalies under the surface."

Their guide had seemed worried when Shan had shown his badge, but Shan soon realized the junior professor's awkwardness was more about being with the father of the American who had died while working on their project. "Anomalies?" Shan asked.

"Building foundations," he said with a nervous glance at Pike. "Cavities that were dug out and refilled, which could mean culverts, wells, latrine pits, defensive entrenchments. We love latrine pits. Nothing like a latrine pit to inform about daily life!"

"And graves," Shan suggested. He was watching Pike now, who lingered at a six-foot-long hole. He had not expected the American to take him up on his offer to join, but Pike had been at the waiting place by Barkhor Square when Shan had arrived at dawn, after a restless night at a cheap hotel at the edge of the city.

Pike had said very little during the long drive to the site, and Shan had realized that the American felt obliged to visit the dig, which after all was why his daughter had come to Tibet. Doing so with Shan as a companion was probably more palatable than going alone.

"Graves, of course. That's how Professor Gangfen discovered the first evidence of the importance of the site. We have found several others since."

"Evidence?" Shan asked.

"Proof, really. Of the Tibetan acceptance of Chinese authority. Skeletons wearing Tibetan amulets around their necks but in remnants of Green Standard Army uniforms. The fabric was mostly disintegrated but the professor was a wizard at using microscopes to confirm weave, material, and color. There can be no real argument anymore. The Tibetan people embraced the Chinese emperor as their protector, their savior against those barbaric Mongol hordes."

Shan swallowed hard and forced himself to say the correct thing. "No doubt the motherland will be proud of your work."

"Yes, yes! We've already had letters of commendation from Beijing. But the most exciting work lies ahead. We hope to find evidence of the amban's presence here. We have reason to believe this unit was escorting him to his high office in Lhasa."

"I'm afraid I am not entirely clear on this history," Shan confessed as Pike approached. "The Green Standard Army?"

The acting director beamed, and they listened for several minutes to a lecture on how the Dzungar Mongols, last survivors of the great Mongol khans, had invaded Tibet in 1717. The Dalai Lama had requested aid from the Qing Empire and the Kangxi Emperor had generously sent a force of regular infantry and his special Green Standard Army troops to subdue the bloodthirsty Dzungars. The Green Standard Army, a unit used to placate civil unrest and to impose order on conquered peoples, had stayed, establishing garrisons in several Tibetan towns and stabilizing the land for the Chinese ambans who had served as direct representatives of the Emperor. "The unity of

China and Tibet has been unbroken ever since," the young archaeologist exclaimed.

Shan and Pike exchanged a pointed glance. The theory of such unity ignored the violent years-long invasion by China in the mid-twentieth century. A million Tibetans had died disputing that theory, and China had been forced to maintain massive garrisons of occupying troops, who had never left. Shan knew enough history to know that the ambans were little more than ambassadors, and their office had only survived a few decades. Gangfen probably knew those same facts but if his goal had been to find a way for the government to sponsor a project so close to Lhasa, he had been astute in choosing his subject. Had Gangfen indeed been playing to the propaganda machine for some hidden motive? Archaeology was one of the most political of Chinese sciences. Excavation sites in Xinjiang Province to the north had often been shut down because they had found images on ancient murals and coffins with blue eyes, even mummies with red hair. Archaeological excavation of old monasteries had been blocked for fear they would reveal more signs of an independent Tibetan culture. The independent-minded senior professor who maintained an anonymous operating base in Jamalinka had kowtowed to Party bosses by designing a dig that would bolster Beijing's political paradigm of a long-standing, expansive Chinese motherland. The government had been so excited, and so confident of the outcome, that they had even cleared an American to join Gangfen.

Pike asked in a grim tone whether their guide knew where the accident had occurred, and the junior professor spent several minutes drawing a meticulous map and emphasizing the dangers of traveling on mountain roads. "Half an hour from here. I don't know what they were doing on those roads," he said, then added with a shrug, "the professor was always watchful for any signs of old ruins and sometimes went up on higher ground for perspective when drawing the maps which would accompany his reports. My theory is that he was trying to pinpoint the most likely route for the eighteenth-century army when

it was escorting the amban to his glorious role in Lhasa. Dedicated to
the very end."

Pike gestured toward the students. "Must be a challenge to maintain a team in such a remote place. I don't see any sleeping quarters."

"Oh, no, not here," the professor replied. "There's a crossroads ten
miles south of here with an old inn. We stay there."

"Where my daughter stayed?" the American asked.

Their guide did not look at Pike, just bobbed his head up and
down in an affirming nod.

"Did the professor have an office of some kind?" Shan inquired.

"A desk in our shared office," the acting director said, nodding
toward a small modular building near the road.

The building held only one large chamber, serving as a kitchen and
meeting area on one side, and on the other an office consisting of three
desks, one of which was separated by folding screens. Shan gestured
toward the desk behind the screens. "Gangfen's?"

Their guide hesitated. "I am quite sure there's nothing related to
the accident."

"Of course not," Shan said, and lowered his voice. "This is mostly
a courtesy call for Natalie's grieving father. Who happens to be an
important official in America," he added in a whisper. "We thought
there might be a memento, something about his daughter's work here
that Mr. Pike might take home. Perhaps a glowing evaluation of her
work here. It might bring some solace to grieving relatives back home."

The acting director gave a reluctant nod, and Shan sat at the desk
as Pike leaned over it. Papers were strewn haphazardly, all seeming to
be reports and files on Dzungar artifacts, camp structures, and the
Green Standard Army. Shan opened drawers with careful disinterest
and lifted another file from the bottom drawer.

He read the caption with a question in his voice. "Religious
Affairs?"

The balding professor sighed. "One of Gangfen's many projects.
Ever vigilant for opportunities to help the motherland. More than a
scholar. A patriot hero, really. He will be sorely missed."

Shan opened the file and read the subject matter of the report inside, not bothering to conceal his surprise. "Weather Magic Folklore?"

"What the professor called a subthread of a new Religious Affairs campaign. They are assembling proof of the many pagan practices that were poisoning the Tibetan working class before we intervened."

"The motherland benefits all it touches," Shan replied, choosing the safety of a popular Party slogan.

"Exactly. These people were practically living in the Bronze Age."

"No cars, no trains, no flushing toilets, no factories, no compulsory boarding schools, no prisons," Shan observed.

His host nodded enthusiastically. "Yes, yes, exactly, comrade!"

Shan quickly scanned the file, attempting not to seem too interested. Gangfen had notes from interviews with over a score of old Tibetans, some prominently labeled *Bonpo*, practitioners of the old Bon religion. Most of the statements reflected memories from the middle of the prior century, when itinerant weather tamers roamed the countryside and took money or barter goods to keep hail away from crops. The interview subjects seemed to agree that the tamers were all lamas who had received their calling only after years of study, but they described them with many different labels. Hail chasers seemed the most common, but cloud master, rain sorcerer, weather witch, cloud wizard, and even sky conjurer were also used. Shan recognized several of the locations of the interviewees. "Some of these places are hours away. Did he leave the site often?"

"He had been compiling that report for years. This year I believe he met a couple new sources in Lhasa, others at their homes in the countryside. Some of the old ones refuse to travel to a city. So reactionary, but Gangfen always humored them."

As he leafed through the file Shan realized he had neglected to ask an obvious question. "Whose car was he driving when they had their accident?"

"Ours, leased to us for the duration of the project. Fortunately, the government quickly provided a replacement."

Shan paused over the last two statements in the file, given months earlier. They both referred to a contemporary weather conjurer and urged the professor to meet with him upon his release from a re-education camp. Gangfen had been planning to meet with Yankay Namdol.

Shan gave Pike the choice of going to the accident site or the inn used by the archaeology students. "I knew the story about Natalie dying in a car accident was a lie even before you explained what Metok said," the American replied. "No point in wasting time there."

The original crossroads inn, an aged structure of stone and timber, looked as if it had been built for the caravans of yak, sheep, and some-times Bactrian camels that had once crisscrossed Tibet. Most of the caravan routes had been paved over into roads, and the inn had evolved into a rambling truck stop with two cinder block wings painted in gar-ish red and yellow.

As Pike pushed on the door handle Shan held up a restraining hand. "You need to see something," he said, and handed the Ameri-can the envelope sent by Amah Jiejie.

Pike read the first line and tossed it back at Shan. "As they say, fuck you. I can catch a bus."

"I debated with myself last night about what to do with this," Shan said in a level tone. "I could have just kept it secret from you. I could have given it to Public Security in Lhasa so I could be rid of you. I chose to share it."

"So, this is how it's going to be," Pike said, his anger thinly veiled. "Just when I was thinking you might be the real deal, you turn into another sniveling, backstabbing bureaucrat."

Shan unfolded the paper and read it. "From Public Security. Bei-jing Headquarters, Counterintelligence Unit." He raised his eyebrows. "You were getting attention in very high places." He turned back to the report Amah Jiejie had obtained through back channels in Beijing. "The surveillance of the embassy attaché Cato Pike is hereby transferred to the Great Wall Team," Shan read, then turned again to Pike. "An elite team. You got upgraded."

"Is there a point to this?"

Shan refolded the paper and summarized the remainder. "A case was being assembled against you for espionage so you could be deported. Then suddenly the deportation file was closed and you were transferred to a team that evaluates candidates for service as double agents. They thought you might be turned and willing to work for the People's Republic. Why?"

"Because I broke my ambassador's nose. He didn't take it well."

"You mean you were involved in some sort of accident."

"Not at all. I struck him. If I ever see the bastard again, I'll break it a second time."

Shan gazed at his companion in surprise. "Could you possibly explain why?"

"Public Security had it right. I was running a couple agents in my job in FBI counterintelligence. One of them was supplying low-level stuff, some codes and warnings on where Chinese hackers would strike next. He was arrested. The ambassador could easily have arranged a deal, exchanged him for one of the two dozen Chinese spies we were holding, but he refused. My man was executed. Damn right I hit the ambassador. Wish I had done worse."

"That was the end of your FBI career?"

"I got shipped home. Just say the FBI and I mutually parted ways."

Shan reached into the console and fished out a lighter. He lit a corner of the report, waited for the flames to catch and dropped it out the window.

Pike gave a bitter grunt. "I don't work with partners," he said.

"Good. Me neither," Shan replied. He motioned to the inn. "Shall we?"

A café occupied most of the cramped lobby, in a corner of which sat the registration desk.

Shan showed his badge to the plump Chinese woman at the desk and asked if any of the students from the university project were there.

"One of 'em took the day off, gonna catch the bus to Lhasa, he says," she reported, nodding toward a scholarly looking, bespectacled Chinese man in his twenties who sat reading at a table with a pot of tea.

"Excuse me," Shan said as he approached. "Are you with the university project?"

The man slowly nodded.

"I was hoping to speak with you about the accident."

The student obviously didn't have to be told which accident. His countenance twisted with pain, and he shook his head.

Shan was not sure how to take his reaction, so he stepped aside to fully reveal Cato Pike, standing behind him. "This is Natalie's father."

The young scholar's face went pale. He looked up at Shan with something that might have been desperation. "I wouldn't know what to say," he said. "It was so horrible. And I don't speak English," he added.

Another of Pike's sad smiles appeared on his countenance. "How about a ride to Lhasa?" he asked in his flawless Mandarin.

The student's name was Cao Li, and while they drove Shan eased his reticence by speaking of the work at the Green Standard Army camp, then of his own father's great interest in history. As they neared Lhasa, Cao opened up, reflecting on his great respect for Professor Gangfen, who had been his mentor for years, teaching him, in Cao's words, "the proper approach for archaeology in China." Cao seemed to evade questions about the accident but finally admitted that the professor and Pike's daughter had not been seen for three days before the crash.

"So the professor was out doing interviews with some of the indigenous inhabitants?"

Cao hesitated, clearly worried about Shan's prying. "The professor was deeply committed to the advancement of knowledge. He loved his work. 'Science doesn't lie,' he would tell us." Cao winced, as if again he had gone too far.

Pike and Shan exchanged a glance. *Science doesn't lie.* The professor's words could have been taken as a truism used in teaching or as a warning for those who participated in the Party's particular form of science.

Pike broke the silence with a question Shan should have asked earlier in the day. "What happened to the car after the crash? I think it probably had some of my daughter's belongings in it," he added.

"Gone. They brought a new one the next day, a better one."

"What kind was the one in the crash?" Shan asked as he checked his watch. Zhu was supposed to meet him again at the tea shop.

"One of those heavy utility vehicles with high suspension for travel on rough terrain, a white one, with a cargo rack on top. But I'm sorry, like I said, it is gone. They say the gas tank exploded." He glanced awkwardly at the American. "They said that she died instantly."

"They," Shan stated. "The same ones who brought the replacement car?"

"Sure. Public Security out of Lhasa. They had to be involved, everyone said, because a foreigner was one of the victims."

"Do you know the name of the officer? We'll want to see if he found any belongings in the vehicle," Shan said. "It would save me time if you had a name."

"The new director dealt with them. It was a lieutenant. I remember afterward one of the younger students said it would be fun to check his DNA, and the director snapped at him to stop suggesting such things."

"His DNA?"

"When the sun hit his hair at a certain angle, you could see red in it, or at least a deep auburn hue. That's from the Turkic population. His people must be from Xinjiang, probably Kashgar or Khotan. I'm surprised he hasn't dyed his hair to remove the reminder that not all

China is Chinese." Cao looked up with an awkward glance at his companions, seeming to catch himself. "But good archaeology students can't be heard saying such things, or we can find ourselves shifted to some school for computer technicians or accountants." Cao grew very sober. "I would never say such things," he assured them.

Shan studied the student. Cao may be a scholar, but he was something more. Had Gangfen nurtured a dissident? "The professor was a good man," Shan said, as if to comfort him. "An honest man. He deserves a memorial." They were approaching the Jokhang Temple complex, where Cao had said he wanted to be dropped.

"Yes, yes," Cao agreed. "I would gladly help with one."

"Good," Shan said. "The memorial I am thinking of is the truth. Not the new director's version of the story, not the report of Public Security. I think Gangfen was trying to make a difference in the world. That effort shouldn't die with him."

The words sent the student into a brooding silence. He did not speak until Shan stopped the car. He climbed out and paused as he closed the door. "They died for the truth," he blurted, then darted into the crowd.

Pike climbed out of Shan's car as Cao disappeared into the crowd. He turned to Shan, his hand still on the door. "I suppose this city has more than one crematorium. Which do you suppose the police would use?" Shan considered a moment and told him, and the American pulled the hood of his jacket over his head and set off in the direction Cao had taken.

Zhu was waiting once more at the tea shop with the red door and seemed excited to see Shan. He handed three photocopies to Shan with a victorious gleam. "Took some digging to get what you wanted but the colonel's office helped."

The first page was the list of official attendees at Metok's execution. There had been two Public Security officers in the gallery, the captain who had read the statement and the young lieutenant with reddish hints in his hair who had pulled the trigger. The young lieutenant had been Huan Yi.

The second page was a printout of a scanned document that had been sent from a Lhasa office to Tan's office. It was the official cover letter to a submission to the Party tribunal that had determined Metok's fate, with the recommendation for punishment listed as Swift Resolution, one of the knob euphemisms for a death sentence. It was signed by Lieutenant Huan Yi, and the higher-level clearance for the execution had been signed by the provincial governor with the added seal, the chop, of the head of Party discipline for all of Tibet, the aged, treacherous man feared by many even in Beijing. His name was Yang Chouzi, but he was known simply as the Commissar. The Commissar's chop had sealed Metok's fate. In other jurisdictions, in other cases, a half dozen Party signatures would have been needed for the execution of a Party member, but the seal of the Commissar preempted all others.

The third sheet was from months earlier. It was the official instruction from the Party's Disciplinary Board accepting Colonel's Tan recommendation that Lieutenant Huan Yi be transferred from Lhadrung and suspended from the promotion lists for three years.

"Huan's been busy," Zhu observed. "Another man would have kept his head down after being disciplined so severely, probably would have asked for transfer back east to put it all behind him. But Tan gave him a break."

"A break?"

Zhu pointed to the bottom of the last page. "Right there, over the colonel's signature. It says that Huan should be transferred to the Lhasa regional headquarters to give him investigative experience. Awfully forgiving of the colonel."

Shan heard the questioning tone in Zhu's voice and stared at the typewritten words. Everything but the last sentence sounded like Tan's heavy hand. But it was more likely that Tan would have recommended traffic duty in some smog-laden eastern city than a berth in Lhasa that would have given Huan more power than he would have had in the local district office.

"Funny thing about that death sentence for Metok," Zhu added. "I saw a television show where a detective said you had to check every single fact. So I checked about the location of the provincial governor on the date that death order was signed. He wasn't in Tibet, he was at a Party conference in Fujian Province, at some beach resort a couple thousand miles away."

Shan offered an approving nod for Zhu's diligence. "There's a missing piece," he said. "How did Huan go from prosecuting the weather wizard to targeting an engineer at the hydro project for corruption? Why would they have assigned him the lead on such a significant case so soon after being disciplined?"

"They wouldn't," Zhu said. "It would only be if he initiated the case, if he brought in the complaint and evidence."

"Meaning he had a connection to the Five Claws project before he prosecuted Metok."

Zhu considered his words then reached into the canvas case at his feet, used for carrying orders and maps in the field, and extracted a copy of the weather wizard's prosecution file. Shan sipped at his tea and watched the earnest young officer, wondering if he fully grasped the danger of working for Shan. "The hail chaser was a zealot," Zhu suggested. "The Tibetan Yankay Namdol was engaged in feudalistic behavior that was an affront to the motherland." The lieutenant saw Shan's confused glance. "It was what Huan wrote, his words from his report."

"Not enough," Shan said. "Perhaps he knew the managers of the Five Claws project? I mean from somewhere before, somewhere in the east," he added, meaning outside Tibet. A deep foreboding was falling like a shadow over Shan. Powerful, unseen forces were at work, the kind of forces that had once condemned Shan to the gulag, the kind of forces that had killed four people with impunity. If the Commissar was behind the conspiracy there could be no hope for justice. The Commissar was the demon deity of the Party. He didn't trouble himself with meetings or conference calls to resolve differences, he just sent thugs in dark suits to silence opposition. "Do you have family, Zhu?" Shan asked.

"Only my parents, no one else." It was a familiar story. After two generations Beijing's one-child policy had transformed a society which for millennia had been built around large families by eliminating siblings, uncles, aunts, and cousins. "They're old, had me later in life. They've moved into one of those homes for the elderly." He shrugged and for a moment Shan saw the awkward boy who still lived inside the young soldier. "I met a girl in Lhadrung. I'm thinking of asking her out."

"Good. Go back and ask her out. I'll tell the colonel about the great job you have done and tell him you are ready for a new assignment."

Zhu seemed offended. "You think I'm frightened?"

"That's the problem. I don't think you are, but you should be."

Zhu seemed about to argue, then calmed and drank his tea. "You have family too."

"A son," Shan said, though if Ko were ever released he knew he would have a daughter-in-law soon thereafter. He acknowledged Zhu's point. "I'm an old warrior scarred from many such battles. We are going into dangerous terrain."

"I'm a mountain commando, not some military clerk," Zhu reminded him. "That's what I do, fight in high-risk terrain."

Shan shook his head. "You won't see them coming until it is too late. Go back to Lhadrung. There's work you can do there. Locate that Institute crate from the train and find out what's inside."

Zhu grinned. "It never went to Lhadrung. It was picked up by an Institute worker with four knob guards and taken to the Public Security office here in Lhasa, even though it was marked for the Lhadrung depot. The fools didn't know that there were shipping papers taped to the back of the crate. The colonel told me to quietly remove them when we unloaded the military cargo. It was military cargo too."

"The Institute had military goods?"

"It was not the first time. They don't know that everything that gets loaded into the secure compartment goes through the hands of an army quartermaster back in Xining. I made a call. They had shipped military-grade explosives a few weeks ago. This time it was one of the army's battlefield surveillance drones, one with four propellers and a video camera with a two-mile range."

Shan recalled the rock fields around the top of the valley of the Five Claws. They provided perfect cover for someone worried about pursuit on the ground but anyone hiding in them would be conspicuous from above. The deputy director was raising the stakes in his fight against indigenous intruders.

"Then return to Lhadrung and check out that officer in Hong Kong who gave the statements against Metok. See if he had any connection to Huan."

Zhu gave a reluctant nod of his head, and Shan watched the lieutenant wind his way through the thinning crowd on the square then called for another pot of tea. He was exhausted and had the long drive back to Yangkar ahead of him. Being in the city only made him appreciate his simple life in the remote town even more, and he pushed down the sense that he was on a path that would drive him out of the town forever. The more he asserted Tan's authority, the more the gentle Tibetans of Yangkar would resent him. The more he resisted Tan's efforts to make him one of the colonel's key deputies, the more likely it was that Tan would recall him back to Lhadrung, which, like Lhasa, was rapidly becoming one more soulless Chinese enclave.

He noticed the little jar of toothpicks on the table and extracted one, then with his pen drew the numerals one through six in a circle on his napkin. He held the toothpick a few inches over the circle and dropped it four times, pausing each time to record on the corner of his napkin an inch-long line, a line divided in two segments, or a line divided into three segments, depending on which number it fell on. Together the four lines, stacked over each other in sequence, would combine to create a tetragram, used in *Tao te Ching* meditations.

He worked slowly, ritualistically, and created a tetragram of a solid line on top, then a second solid line, a line of two segments and a line of three segments. In the chart his uncle had made him memorize as a boy it signified Chapter Six of the *Tao te Ching*, called *Perceiving the Subtle*. He smiled as he silently mouthed the long-remembered words. *The mystery of the valley is immortal,* they said. *Its gateway is the source of heaven and earth.* To the old master of the Tao the valley meant human perception but sometimes, his uncle had taught him, you just had to take the words for what they were. He knew of a valley that brimmed with mystery, and he knew he had been avoiding the peril of its gateway for too long.

He had one more stop to make before leaving Lhasa. He bought a sweatshirt with a cartoon of a smiling yak over the words *Gem of China*, and a visored cap that he pulled low over his face as he crossed the bridge to Jamalinka. He was beginning to understand Professor Gangfen's appreciation of the island community. It was a world of many layers. If you could ignore the obvious shell of hedonism— probably difficult for many visitors—there were many other rich and varied realities. In the eyes of the dancers, the prostitutes, the pimps, the hawkers of cheap goods, and the barkeepers he often saw shades of shame and desperation but also flickers of defiant, independent spirits who had found an unexpected oasis shielded from the world outside. He had read that many cities of China and Europe had once had enclaves of sanctuary where warrants and legal process could not be served, and the hand of the law was suspended. Had places like Jamalinka become the modern equivalent of such sanctuaries?

Once again he watched the apartment on the darkened side street for several minutes before climbing the stairs. Tink answered on his first knock, as if expecting him, then quickly closed and locked the door behind him.

Cato Pike sat at the table, staring at a glass of amber liquor in his hand.

"I think we might track the car that was in the reported accident," Shan said. "I wondered if perhaps your daughter sent you a photo that would have had the car in it. There would be records from the office that administers the university projects and I could—" He stopped mid-sentence as Cao Li stepped out of the shadows of the hallway. The Chinese student froze then took a stumbling step toward the door.

"Hold on," Pike said to Cao, and swallowed what was left in his glass. Shan could smell the strong liquor from several feet away, an acrid Japanese whiskey. "Inspector Shan isn't here to arrest anyone. He wants justice for the professor just like you do," he added, then turned to Shan. "I wasn't exactly shocked when Cao led me back here," the American said, and reached into a pocket to extract a photo. It showed a blond woman wearing a broad smile as she listened to an older Chinese man who was pointing to a statue of diety on the steps of the Potala. "The professor and my daughter," Pike explained. "I had been wondering who the photographer was until I met Cao." He nodded at the Chinese student "There's still a lot he hasn't told us, but we are making progress," he said, then poured another glass and saluted Cao with it.

Tink, gazing at Pike with a worried expression, turned to Shan. "We had the same idea. Cao knew the car well," she said as she lifted a steaming kettle from the stove and filled a teapot.

Shan accepted a cup of the green tea and sat across from Pike, whose dark expression was beginning to worry him as well.

"There's a big police lot south of the city," Tink continued, "an impoundment lot where they take cars that are towed. I convinced a friend to park her car illegally. We waited a couple hours after the tow truck came and went to claim it. I waited on the street while she and Cao went in."

Cao sat at the table with his steaming cup. "I drove the professor in it many times," he said in a tight voice. "I would know it anywhere. It had a scrape on the right side where I drove too close to a boulder two months ago. In the back seat were two of our hard hats with the university emblem. The only damage was a dented fender where it had been rammed. Black paint had rubbed onto the fender."

"Black," Tink said, "like the color of knob cars. They did it, just to show it was damaged."

Cao spoke in a forlorn whisper now. "It didn't tumble down a mountain slope. It didn't explode in flames. They lied. They all lied."

Pike was looking at Shan now. He showed no effects of the alcohol. His eyes no longer burned with rage. They were more like the cold, calculating eyes of a predator beginning a hunt. Until now he had only suspicions of foul play—even the shipment of animal ashes might have been a mistake, however unlikely—but now he had proof.

"Give me some time," Shan said to the American. "These are things of my world, not yours."

"Things of your world," Pike repeated, making it sound like an accusation.

Shan turned to Tink and Cao. "You don't understand the dangers," he said.

Tink replied with a peeved grin and rose to open a closet door. "When we went today I was a redhead, my friend a brunette." The inside of the door held over a dozen hooks, on which wigs of various lengths, colors, and styles hung. "I learned a long time ago that if I dress the right way, no one looks at my face," she quipped, and pushed out her chest.

Cao looked away, embarrassed.

"Why were you coming to town today?" Shan asked the student.

Cao nodded. "To see a friend of Professor Gangfen's. He was helping us, the professor and me. And Natalie," he added with an awkward glance at Pike.

"Helping?" Shan asked.

"There's a place in the north where the professor and Natalie were when they went missing. His friend was helping us collect data we needed to stop the . . . to help preserve a vitally important archaeological site."

Shan's eyes found Pike's. The American cursed and drained his cup of whiskey.

"You mean the Five Claws project," Shan said. "And the friend was Metok Rentzig."

Cao seemed bewildered. "I had something to leave at his apartment, from the professor's records. I knew the professor would want our efforts to continue."

"Metok is dead."

Cao's countenance went rigid. His hand shook so hard tea spilled from his cup, but he seemed not to notice the burning liquid on his fingers. "How?" he asked.

"A Public Security bullet in the head. Someone wanted him dead and they accused him of corruption."

Pike leaned over and poured whiskey in Cao's tea. The student took a long swallow. "Then I'm the only one left," he murmured.

"The only one?" Shan asked.

"The only one who can make the case the professor and Natalie were trying to build with Metok's help."

"You were going to leave Metok something about the Five Claws?"

Cao nodded, and extracted an envelope from inside his shirt which he pushed across to Shan. It held a dozen square photographs taken with an instant camera. The lighting of the images was so bad Shan struggled to make sense of them. "Better to start with this," Cao said as he extracted a folded paper from his wallet. It was a photocopy of six more photographs on the same page. Two of them showed a rectangular field filled with scores of upright stones, evenly spaced in over a dozen long rows. Judging by the horses grazing at one side, the field of raised stones must have been perhaps three hundred feet long and sixty or seventy wide. None of the stones were over five feet high.

Three of the remaining photos were of marks on stone walls that might have been primitive renderings in yellow ochre of animals or supernatural beings. The last was another ochre image on a wall but this one was clearly identifiable. It was a Christian cross.

"A Tibetan herder took the professor and me to the valley two years ago," Cao explained. "The local people have many names for it. Valley of the Gods, Holy Home, Gekho's Roost, for the earth god who was said to reside there." He pointed to the photo of the rectangle of standing stones. "There have been over a dozen of these fields identified in Tibet, mostly in the western regions. They were erected more than three thousand years ago and seemed to have had a religious purpose. As far as we could tell it was the best preserved of all the stone fields, sort of Tibet's Stonehenge. The same grids of pillars are seen in Siberia and in the Scythian culture in central Asia. It would take years of study to understand it. We were going to take some days off from the Green Army dig to take more photos and begin to formulate plans for closer analysis.

"But the first thing they did, as a dramatic gesture for what they called their project launch day, was to bulldoze the field. By the end of the day it was leveled and scraped so no trace was left."

"The stone wall images are from the cavern?" Shan asked.

Cao nodded. "The local people said that on the spring equinox the shadow of the central row of pillars at sunrise pointed to the mouth of the cavern. The earliest images on the walls were carved petroglyphs made with iron tools. The others are of ochre paint, some probably dating back two thousand years and more."

"And this one, much more recent," Shan said, pointing to the cross.

"There was a Jesuit explorer, Father Ippolito Desideri, who visited Tibet in the early eighteenth century. He was intensely curious about Tibet and its origins, wrote that it was the best evidence of the complexity of the human soul he had ever found. He spoke of being taken on a tour of religious sites by some lamas, some of the sites secret and ancient. We think it is likely that the valley was one of the sites he visited. When the professor first visited the valley, he said it was one of the most important archaeological sites in Tibet, perhaps in all of central Asia. I could have spent the rest of my career studying it. Now it is all gone."

"Natalie was in the cave," Pike stated.

Cao glanced up at the American then quickly away. "Yes. She was going to help make the case to the United Nations cultural office to preserve it, to focus international attention on it. She was going to take our report back to America."

"Who knew that?" Shan asked.

Cao shrugged. "At first only me, Natalie, the professor, and Metok. Later Metok included a friend of his, another engineer named Sun Lunshi." Cao seemed not to notice the glance exchanged by Shan and Pike. He was the only one of the five still alive. "We wanted to work up a more scientific profile at the site before we introduced it to others. It was remarkable for the way it showed the evolution of religious dialogue, from the very early animists to the Bon, the Buddhist, and Christian, all existing harmoniously in the same place. I remember the professor saying it was like a convergence of different paths of the human spirit. He called it the Rosetta stone of the soul."

Shan disposed of his hat on the first block after crossing the Jama-linka bridge, his sweatshirt on the second. The news of the cavern had excited him and saddened him, and now scared him. He had warned Cao to hide all evidence of the cave, and stop all discussion of it, even offered to drive him back to his dig site, but the quiet scholar had not replied, simply gazed at him defiantly.

Shan longed for the peace of Yangkar and realized he might at least make it back in time for one of his treasured breakfasts with Marpa. The anticipation put a new energy in his pace and he had eagerly pulled out his keys as he approached his car. But as he reached for the driver's door a voice spoke over his shoulder.

"Not just yet, Comrade Constable."

He turned to face Lieutenant Huan in a well-pressed Public Security uniform, fixing him with a smug smile. Two knob soldiers appeared out of the shadows, flanking Shan. One held a pistol on Shan as another frisked him.

Shan fought to keep his voice level. "Am I under arrest?" he asked.

"Of course not," Huan said. "Nothing so formal. I am just inviting you to what they used to call a struggle session. You know, where the wayward receive an overdue socialist recalibration."

CHAPTER SEVEN

"You are adrift in a treacherous sea, Constable," Huan proclaimed as he closed the interrogation room door behind him. "You are so far over your head you might drown at any moment. You have one chance, and that is to go back to Yangkar and resume counting your piles of yak dung or whatever it is you do there."

Shan pulled the pad of paper from the center of the table and wrote down a phone number then pushed it toward the arrogant knob officer.

"What's that?" Huan asked with a sneer.

"Colonel Tan's private phone in Lhadrung. Just clear it with him and I'd be happy to go home."

Huan looked like he had bitten something sour. He ripped the paper in half. "Tan's a dinosaur. He's already extinct, just doesn't know it. His friends in Beijing are gone, already turned to fossils."

"A dinosaur who still shakes the ground he walks on. Funny, I had thought you had recently experienced the sharpness of his teeth."

Huan's eyes flashed with anger. "He had no authority over me!"

"He had you transferred out of Lhadrung," Shan pointed out. "And then there was that unpleasant suspension from the promotion lists."

"The bastard made suggestions and headquarters just went along because they were so used to Tan getting his way. Those days are over.

The old man has no idea what he was dealing with." Huan fixed Shan with a simmering gaze. "I won't let some ordinary fool get in my way again."

"No one would consider me just an ordinary sort of fool," Shan replied in a level tone. "But surely it is impossible that a lowly constable could interfere with a Public Security officer in the Lhasa headquarters."

"A constable waving a made-up badge as Tan's inspector. A constable who has the nerve to be defiant to the Public Security Bureau. Yes, you are no ordinary fool. You are a blind, self-destructive fool."

"I ever endeavor to follow the shining light of socialism," Shan stated. It was one of the scripted responses from the old struggle sessions. Many subjects had been brutally beaten before finally mouthing the prescribed words.

"You just prove you are another dinosaur by speaking slogans from decades ago."

Huan himself wasn't much older than thirty, and struggle sessions had been a favorite Party tool in the sixties and seventies. "I'm impressed, Lieutenant, that you are so well versed in the ancient lore of the motherland," Shan said.

"The history of the socialist dialectic is taught in every Red Hammer school," Huan said, referring to the special summer schools run for the children of Party elites. "I also learned of the importance of silencing reactionaries before they can inflict harm to the motherland."

"Reactionaries. I confess I never fully grasped that word. Everything in life is a reaction. You saw two soldiers die in a hailstorm. You reacted out of your own personal animus against a harmless old Tibetan. No one agreed with your charges. Your superiors reacted by sending you out of Lhadrung. You reacted by sending the Tibetan to administrative detention. He reacted by causing an earthquake at his camp, at least by your theory. Who is the reactionary, Lieutenant? I am not the one charging crimes based on ancient myths."

Huan took an abrupt step toward Shan and with a lightning-quick snap of his arm slapped him. "Why are you in Lhasa?" he shouted.

Shan shook his head to clear his eyes. "Metok Rentzig."

The name caused the knob officer to hesitate. "His case is closed."

"Colonel Tan is fastidious. He can't believe there can be conspiracy of corruption without other conspirators." For an instant Shan saw worry on Huan's face. "Corruption is never a solitary crime," he added.

"The prosecution file was handled by Public Security, the most advanced investigative service in the world. Other suspects were reviewed. There was insufficient evidence to pursue anyone else."

"Then I will have to admit to the Colonel that I am wasting my time. But I did want to ask you something. Why did you take the Ice Ball Alley road that day when you brought prisoners into Lhadrung?"

Huan frowned. "The damned Tibetan driver. It was a long, boring drive from Larung Gar. He said we could cut hours off our journey by taking the old road." The lieutenant moved back to the door and locked it, then stepped to a chair with a stack of files in front of it. "None of that explains why you were at the university dig today."

Shan weighed his words. Here was a link he had not foreseen. The dead professor's deputy and Huan were communicating with each other. "Surely the acting director at the dig told you I was escorting a grieving father who sought the comfort of experiencing his daughter's final days."

"A grieving father who had no connection to you or Lhadrung County."

"I met him in connection with the incident on the train. I speak English. He had suffered a terrible loss. It seemed to be the compassionate thing to do."

An icy grin rose on Huan's thin face. He sat and opened one of the files. "The incident on the train is being investigated by my office and the Lhasa police as a possible homicide. Your American Cato Pike is a prime suspect."

A cold lump formed in Shan's gut. "What happened on that train is under military jurisdiction."

"The victim was found in the military's compartment, yes. But he was a civilian. There is a protocol. All crimes discovered on the Lhasa train are the responsibility of the Lhasa authorities. I have witnesses who say the American visibly disturbed the victim, that he followed him, some say chased him, toward the back of the train. That was outside the military compartment. Assault with intent to commit a felony is a serious charge in itself. The medical report indicates the American struck him, another felony."

Shan had not seen the report and had very expressly ordered the train doctor to send the report only to Tan's office. Huan had intercepted it. "Like I said, call Colonel Tan. He will correct any misunderstanding."

"If you were found to be protecting, even aiding the suspect, then you too are guilty of a crime, comrade, a crime clearly in my jurisdiction."

"So this is why you sent someone to Yangkar to find me," Shan stated. "Was she going to interrogate me herself or just drag me back to Lhasa?"

Huan hesitated, not masking his confusion. "I sent no one. Do not try to distract me, comrade. I have enough to detain you. The colonel can call me, when he misses you in a day or two."

Shan gave an exaggerated sigh. "So much paperwork. Just think of it. Public Security detaining an inspector working for the military governor. Public Security interfering with an investigation into matters that may affect the security of the motherland. Public Security has its lawyers. The army has its own lawyers. We will write our reports, then the lawyers will write theirs, which will be ten times as long. Then the provincial Party authorities will get involved. They'll start citing the scriptures of Chairman Mao to let everyone know they have the ultimate authority. And eventually Beijing will step in. Generals and Party officials on special joint committees. By then they will view the whole thing as an embarrassment to the state and ask, who is the imbecile who started it? The answer will be obvious, the unreliable officer who started a prosecution based on myths and religion that the government could never officially acknowledge. Remind me. Who will be called the reactionary?"

Huan's face flushed with fury. "You won't dare start those wheels moving!" he hissed. "You are more vulnerable than me!"

"Not true. I have no ambition to higher office or higher rank. But not so with you. What was it last time? Three years' loss of seniority? It'll be four years next time, even five, and a posting to some Himalayan hill station that's covered in snow nine months of the year."

Huan quieted. He stood and went to the window, where he lit a cigarette as he stared out over Lhasa. The Potala, glowing on its well-lit hill, seemed to hover over the darkened city. "Such an imagination," the lieutenant said. "You are out of your element, comrade, in a minefield you cannot navigate. You will come to realize I am doing you a favor." He turned and exhaled smoke toward Shan. "Do you want a blanket to sleep here on the table or shall I take you down to the holding cells?"

Shan refused to be provoked. "While I'm here perhaps you can give me the contact information for Officer Daoli."

A snarl formed on Huan's lips.

"You know, the officer in Hong Kong who did that amazing fieldwork. Not only uncovering Metok's secret account but also spotting the corrupt Tibetan on the streets on the very day he set up the account. What a workhorse! And what a memory, considering Metok had not yet been identified as a criminal!"

"Details of our secret investigations are never disclosed," Huan warned.

Shan held up his hands as if to concede the point. "You would know the bureaucratic rules better than a lowly constable. Who should it be then? The banking authorities?"

Huan hesitated. "I don't follow."

"The secret fund. The corruption money. It is the property of the state now. You must never have been involved in the feuds that always arise over the allocation of such windfalls. Colonel Tan will want to make a claim, of course, since it relates to a project in his county. The old veterans from the early days in Tibet called them gate fees. You know, the way warlords used to charge a toll for passing through their territory. No bribe may be received without sharing a piece with the warlord."

Huan studied him with a treacherous gleam, then shrugged. "You have only a year or two but I doubt you'll survive that long."

"A year or two?

"The master development plan, Constable."

"You mean the work the Institute is doing for Deputy Director Jiao."

"Exactly. Yangkar is the closest town to the project. It is to become the administrative center for the dam. Hundreds of immigrants. New office blocks and dormitories. Deputy Jiao will be in charge, the mayor if you will. He will want his own constable." Huan laughed at the stunned expression on Shan's face. "Let's do the cell then. No one will be able to release you without my approval. It's such a busy time for Public Security in Lhasa. I may not be available to the jailers for two or three days." As he unlocked the door it flew open, pushing him back.

"Lieutenant Huan!" came a worried voice from the corridor. "There are some—"

"Fool!" Huan interrupted. "You were not to interrupt me, Sergeant! Do you not understand that—" Huan's own words were cut off as his sergeant stumbled into the room, shoved from behind. His nose was bleeding. The pocket of his tunic was torn.

"There you are, Inspector Shan!" Lieutenant Zhu exclaimed as he pushed past the stunned Huan. "What a difficult man you are to locate!"

Two soldiers in fatigues, holsters at their waists, stepped in behind Zhu, who himself now wore his uniform and a weapons belt. Two more mountain commandos were visible in the corridor.

"Inspector, you must have forgotten your appointment with Colonel Tan!" Zhu continued and nodded to Huan. "Gratitude for keeping him in one place for more than an hour," he added, then grabbed Shan's arm and pulled him out of the room.

Shan smiled at the furious Huan as he left. The surly knob did not understand that he had provided a new piece for Shan's puzzle.

The sun was inching over the horizon, glinting off a new strand of razor wire, when they arrived at the 404th People's Construction Brigade. Zhu had insisted Shan ride in his car so Shan could sleep in the back seat during the hours-long drive to Lhadrung as one of the soldiers followed in Shan's own car. The resourceful young lieutenant, who had been watching Shan and seen him taken by Huan, had brought friends from the city barracks. He now insisted that Shan stay quiet as they reached the prison gate. The guard waved Zhu through, then Shan's car, driven now by a sleepy army clerk they had roused from sleep in the Lhadrung barracks.

The prisoners were moving in and out of the washrooms and beginning to line up at the mess hall door for their morning meal of porridge. The clerk from Lhadrung disappeared into the administration building and minutes later the building erupted with senior guards and administrative officers who hurried toward the inner barracks compound. Colonel Tan was notorious for his unannounced audits, and this morning not even the clerk from the town garrison had known there was to be a surprise prisoner census until Zhu and Shan had awakened him. The camp officers had not argued when Zhu explained the procedure, though they seemed surprised that he knew the compound well enough to tell them that a small utility shed behind the mess hall would be used by the audit team. No one seemed to recognize Shan, who wore Zhu's army trench coat and a cap pulled low over his head. Zhu had quickly accepted that Shan could not antagonize the guards for fear of losing his upcoming family visit. The lieutenant also reminded Shan that Public Security often had its own informers among the prison staff.

The inmates were directed to step inside the front door of the unused storage shed one at a time for a corroboration of their names and registration numbers against Tan's central records, then leave through the small chamber at the rear that had its own door to the compound outside. Shan had once been locked in the chamber for several days with only water when he been discovered sneaking food to a prisoner too sick to rise out of his bed. The clerk was efficient in processing the prisoners, tolerating Zhu's impromptu questions for the inmates as Shan listened from the shadows of the back room. He struggled to keep focused on the dialogue, for he was being nagged by the nightmare that haunted his sleep in the car. Deputy Director was going to take over Yangkar. It would be the end of everything he held precious in the town.

Shan forced himself not to acknowledge old Tibetans he had been imprisoned with as they passed through, casting nervous glances at the shadowed figure leaning against crates. Finally, a tired, familiar voice called out in response to the clerk's question. "Shan Ko, Barracks Nine."

As Ko entered the back chamber, Zhu shut the door behind him. Shan stepped into the light.

It had been nearly two months since he had last seen his son, and they had only a few minutes at most now, but the weary, determined smile on Ko's face spoke volumes. His first few months in the 404th, like Shan's, had been about learning how to survive the brutal conditions of the hard labor prison, but now he was learning about more important things from the older prisoners, most of whom had been monks and lamas.

"Is life really so dull in Yangkar," Ko said as the door latch clicked shut, "that you wanted to join one of our ridiculous audits?"

"Never boring. And the audit was staged so I could speak with you."

Ko was no stranger to the intrigues that surrounded his father. He just nodded, but before Shan could continue, he spoke one word. "Yara?"

"She thrives and looks forward to our visit. But for now, I must ask about six prisoners who arrived here a little more than a year ago. They came in a special convoy, from the east, from Sichuan. Try to recall."

"Of course, I remember because the convoy brought in two dead soldiers. The windshields of every vehicle were shattered, the roofs and hoods all pockmarked. Everyone talked about it for weeks. The old ones said the fools must have come down Ice Ball Alley, a high mountain road that gets hail almost every day in the summer. They say the hail protects an old god who lives in the great mountain above."

"Who were the prisoners?"

"Six Tibetans, all from that Larung Gar place, the big Buddhist school. Most seemed to be monks, though not all of them. Word was that they had resisted the rationalization, when thousands were forced to leave, though everyone assumed they had done more than simply protest for them to be sent here instead of the Shoe Factory."

Shan considered the report. Huan had not understood the significance of revealing the name of the teaching center to him. Larung Gar, in the traditionally Tibetan region of western Sichuan Province, had been a highly popular Buddhist learning center, one of the few that had been allowed to grow in recent years. But then the population had swelled to over ten thousand monks and nuns, including scores of Chinese students. After busloads of tourists started arriving, the government had decided it had grown a little too popular and announced that half the population must leave. Without warning it had begun bulldozing homes and classrooms.

"Who were they? Why those six?"

Ko shrugged. "Because they frightened someone in the government. They're very quiet, very learned. The eldest was from old Tibet, they said, a learned lama named Tsomo. Some of the other prisoners, not just the ones from Larung Gar, were beaten for bowing to him when they saw him. I'll never forget the day he passed."

"The lama died?"

"It was a holiday, National Day. We were assembled that morning to hear a speech from the warden when suddenly the old man cried out as if in great agony. He staggered out of the ranks and raised his arms toward the north. He stumbled toward the northern fence, crying in alarm, seeming deaf to the warnings of the guards, even to the guns they shot in the air. The five others who had arrived with him cried out and ran to him until they were beaten back by the guards. They started a mantra that was quickly taken up by the other prisoners. The warden was furious. He seemed to take the old man's actions like a personal affront. 'Not again, you bastard!' the warden shouted, though there had never been a prior incident with the old lama. The warden yelled for the guards to shoot him, for he had reached the kill zone line painted on the ground. But they just stared. The old man was shouting by then, what sounded like a furious mantra, a curse maybe, then a long terrible groan came from deep in his throat. It was like nothing I've ever heard. It was as if his life was being sucked out of him. Then he dropped dead."

In the outer chamber Zhu's voice was rising, as if warning them to hurry.

"Then the warden ordered the administration buildings evacuated, though no one knew why."

"As if he expected an earthquake," Shan said. Ko nodded. "But none came. Afterward none of the guards would touch the lama's body. One of his friends was allowed to phone and the next day some people came down from the hills with a horse cart and took him away. Until then his friends kept a vigil over him. Right there by his body, not just prayers in the barracks."

"Surely the warden didn't allow prisoners to keep a vigil."

"I wouldn't have believed it if I had not been there. He was scared for some reason. One of them was allowed to stay beside him to recite the Bardo, the death rites. Two hours at a time, then a new man would come, always escorted by a guard."

"The warden," Shan said, trying to make sense of what had happened. "He's new too."

"Captain Wenlu? Been here a year or so. Arrived not long after those six prisoners came from Larung Gar. I had a sense that he had known at least some of those prisoners before."

The latch on the inner door rattled. Zhu was telling them to finish.

"See what you can find about those men from Larung Gar," Shan told his son, then gave him a quick embrace, wishing he could part from him the way other family visitors parted, with the number of months and years left before their loved one's release. But Ko's sentence had become indeterminate. He could be out in two or three years, or twenty. "Strength," he said instead. It had become his usual parting word.

Shan tried to recall what he had been told by his Tibetan friends about the destruction at Larung Gar as he drove back to Yangkar. Thousands of monks and nuns had been relocated from what essentially had become a huge Tibetan seminary, forced to sign pledges that they would never return, under threat of imprisonment. Many were also forced to swear they would remove their robes and never pursue religious activities again. They had been herded onto buses then driven hundreds of miles away and dumped into city depots, strangers in a very strange land. But he had not heard of any being imprisoned. He had also never heard of a warden allowing Tibetans to keep a vigil over a dead prisoner.

Yangkar seemed quiet as he drove in. Spotting Yara standing by the fence as students played in the schoolyard, he stopped to let her know he had seen Ko, and his son eagerly anticipated their coming visit.

As he turned to leave she spoke in an uncertain voice. "There's been complaints from the Committee of Leading Citizens," she reported. "I tried to help, to keep her here since that woman with her, her aunt or nanny, I guess, asked if the girl could experience a Tibetan country school, but she ran away and I couldn't leave to retrieve her.

She stomped on Mrs. Lu's sprouting vegetables, kicked a cabbage off the barber's front step. Choden brought her back here but she bit his hand and ran away again."

"You're speaking of the girl who ravaged the town square?" Shan asked, not sure why the girl would have returned to Yangkar.

"The same little demon." Yara shrugged. "I'm sure they'll be gone soon. Visitors don't find much to keep them in Yangkar."

When Shan arrived at the station Choden was bandaging his hand. "She saw some yaks on the slopes," his deputy reported when Shan asked about the girl, "so now that woman with her took her up one of those paths above town, praise Buddha. What a brat. Reminds me of one of those cartoon characters who spin around like a cyclone and have jets of steam coming out their ears." He gestured to a print-out of a bulletin. "You must have just missed the excitement in Lhasa. Makes you want to laugh, though I'm sure that poor bastard wasn't laughing."

Shan picked up the law enforcement bulletin as Choden continued. "Public Security is on it, but they ask that the news not be given to the public."

"The crematorium in Lhasa?" Shan asked as he read the first line.

"Yeah, someone tied the manager to one of the cremation racks and locked him in an oven. He was stuck in there all night."

Shan stared at the bulletin, stunned at Pike's audacity. The American had looked like a hungry predator when Shan had left him and had asked about the crematorium that had sent him a box of animal ashes. He looked up, realizing that Choden was still speaking to him. "You said something about Public Security?"

"I said if you slip out the back door and go up to your house in the hills maybe she'll give up. She is damned persistent, that lieutenant. She started yelling at the girl herself, almost like she knew her. And there was only one unfamiliar car on the square, as if they all came together, but that wouldn't make any sense. A knob would probably just knock a kid like that unconscious and toss her in the trunk."

"Where is this knob officer?"

"Mrs. Lu saw her in the square and ran over and invited her into her house, no doubt to give her an earful about the sorry state of law enforcement in Yangkar. The old bitch probably called an emergency meeting of her committee and is reviewing her hundredth complaint by now. Maybe it's that underwear you never recovered when it blew off her clothesline. Or perhaps it's the wild yak that wouldn't stop doing mating bellows at the edge of town last fall, waking her up every night."

At least, Shan decided, Mrs. Lu had given him time for a quick meal before retreating to his farmhouse. Marpa was cleaning up from his midday business when Shan walked in the back door. The Tibetan handed Shan a bowl of steaming soup. "I think Shiva can give you a charm against angry wolves," he said as Shan headed into the dining room.

He didn't understand the words were a warning until, having set his bowl on a back table, he stepped to the counter to pour himself a cup of tea. He froze with the thermos in his hand. A woman in her forties wearing a gray uniform was speaking with Marpa's young assistant, who had tossed a rag over his shoulder before sitting, probably to practice his Chinese. The woman glanced at Shan.

He took a step backward, upsetting his tea, and fled out the back door.

She found him sitting on a bench in the square.

"I'm sorry," he said as she sat beside him.

"My fault," the woman replied in a small, tentative voice. "I thought about giving your deputy my name but was worried it might scare you away."

Shan was ready to face imprisonment by Huan, Tan's bullying, Ko's suffering, and the murders of Metok, Gangfen and Natalie Pike, but he had not been prepared to encounter the woman who had briefly been his lover years earlier. Meng Limei had been the Public Security officer in the town of Baiyun, where Shan had been unofficially investigating several brutal killings. Their relationship had been shattered when she had killed a clandestine Public Security agent who had been about to infiltrate the exiled Tibetan government in India. The man had been responsible for the murders, but Shan had been arranging a nonviolent resolution so as not to upset the Tibetans. Afterward he had come to realize that she had been right, and her bullet had saved Shan and several Tibetans from disaster. She had killed the murdering spy, then anticipating his reaction, got in her car and drove away to a new assignment in Inner Mongolia. He had not heard from her since.

"Your town is out of one of those American Western movies," Meng said. "Horses tied up outside stores, tumbleweeds blowing down the streets."

Shan had no idea what to say. "The wind seldom stops here," he tried. "I thought of writing you last year but didn't know where you were."

"No problem," Meng replied with an awkward smile. "An awful place at the edge of the Gobi. The wind blew there too. There was always sand in the food." She gestured to a battered bust of Mao at one end of the square. It was made of fiberglass and losing its color in blotches. He seemed diseased. She jerked a thumb toward the statue by the chorten at the opposite end, the old Buddha made of stone. "That one seems to be healthier."

"The Chinese citizens were removing him every few weeks, but he always makes it back. Then the town astrologer told them they were upsetting the local spirits and they must stop harassing him or all their rice would be infested with weevils and their vegetables rot."

"Ah, Mrs. Lu and her committee. Onions, underwear, and a cabbage. She has a long list of unresolved crimes, Constable."

"A goat and the wind are prime suspects in the first two. I still have an open file on the cabbage."

A wider smile lifted the lines on Meng's face. She had always had the most compassionate countenance of any knob he had ever known, with a deep intelligence behind her dark eyes. Her face, however, had grown thinner, tinged with sadness.

Somehow he knew she was not on duty. "I doubt many officers

stationed in the Gobi Desert would choose Yangkar as a vacation destination. Although Marpa's soup is becoming famous."

"Come back inside and finish your lunch, Shan."

"My deputy thinks you are here to arrest me."

"I left my handcuffs in the car."

Shan rose with her. "I'm sorry, Meng. I don't have a lot of time.
Maybe if you had let me know in advance."

"Limei. You used to call me Limei," she said and pushed him
toward the café.

Snowflakes were drifting down from a solitary cloud over Yangkar as
Shan reached the garage, the crystals glistening in the moonlight. It
was what his old friend Lokesh called an ice blessing, when the flakes
tumbled down without a wind to gently kiss the creatures of earth,
reminding them of the power and beauty of the earth gods. He paused
to look to the northwest, where the beloved old Tibetan labored over
the task of preserving ancient texts in an illegal outpost of the *purbas*,
the resistance, and wondered if he had received the letter Shan had
dispatched in the purba's secret network

The garage was dark, except for the back room where Tserung's
teenage son lived, from which Chinese rock-and-roll music could be
heard. Shan cautiously worked his way through the labyrinth of the
junkyard, pausing halfway down the path to watch behind him.

Shan had an irrational premonition that the rowdy little girl traveling with Meng's companion might have followed him. He and Meng
had actually been enjoying a quiet lunch, speaking of small things like
the weather and her life by the Gobi, but after a quarter-hour the pair
had burst in to join Shan and Meng as they ate. He had quickly come
to view the girl as one of the monkey imps that plagued unharmoni-
ous households in old Confucian tales. She had broken a plate and a
mug by willfully flinging them at the wall, squealing with delight, then
scared away an old Tibetan couple by making faces at them, a sign of

bad luck for the town's traditional residents. Through the window he had watched them go straight to Shiva, no doubt for the astrologer to provide them with a protective charm. Not once had Meng offered an explanation of why she had brought such unlikely companions, but Shan had recalled that she had been raised in a rural area where the one-child policy would not have been strictly enforced and decided that they must be her sister and her unruly niece.

Although Shan rejoined Meng in late afternoon after spending hours at his computer searching for details of the Five Claws and La-rung Gar, there had been no more quiet time. They had spent much of the time picking up the child's detritus, including shreds of notices she had ripped from the town bulletin board and shards of another smashed mug, this one thrown against the wall of a cell. He had surrendered his quarters in the building behind the station to them, telling them he would take a room at the little inn off the town square, then gone to sleep for an hour on a jail cot.

Finally convinced he had not been followed by the female imp, Shan hurried on to the concealed door and descended into the clandestine library. He paused as he reached the bottom of the stairs, resolving not to breathe a word about Jiao's plan to take over Yangkar. Tserung and Yara were at the table in the first chamber, looking bleary-eyed as they studied old manuscripts. Tserung brewed a fresh pot of tea as Yara guided Shan through a stack of old peche marked with slips of paper.

"The journals kept in the old *gompa* go back over five hundred years," Yara reminded Shan, "and even in the earliest there is mention of the Valley of the Gods. When the foundations of the Yangkar gompa were laid, an old hermit who had meditated in the valley for fifty years came to bless it. There are frequent references to Bonpo pilgrims en route to pay homage to the fierce old god who lived there, and to an annual ceremony in which representatives from the medical school up in the mountains asked the abbot's permission to gather medicinal herbs there. The records mention that healers had been gathering sacred herbs there for centuries." The young teacher looked up. "That means before Buddhist teachers arrived."

"There was a stone field there," Shan explained, "a cemetery or perhaps a shrine that was probably thousands of years old. Was," he repeated.

A flicker of pain twisted Yara's face. "There are similar references through all the decades we've sampled, though our page-by-page review is just reaching the eighteenth century tonight."

"There are other records about Bonpo pilgrims that refer to it as both the Valley of the Gods and Gekho's Roost," Tserung added. The mechanic had taken to carrying an old silver pen case on his belt, in the traditional style of novice monks.

"Gekho was a mountain deity for the local people then?" Shan asked.

"No, not just any earth deity," Tserung corrected. "For the Bonpo he was the primary earth deity, Wolchen Gekho, the Wrathful Demon Destroyer, maker of lightning, thunder, and hail. Gekho the Blue some called him, for his skin was the color of the sky. When he got angry he would shake the ground humans walked on. Twice I found very old references to the place as Gekho's Cradle, as if the valley was where he was born, when the earth was still young."

Shan sat and went through the laborious process of opening each of the long, loose-leafed peche on the table, reading the marked passages himself, getting lost for an hour in the aged, fading ink of the one-of-a-kind books, pausing over a delightful passage about a yak cow who would only yield milk when mantras were sung to her.

He gave his eyes a rest by walking up and down the corridor, marveling as always at the vastness of the collection and the labor of the dedicated monks who had written, then carved plates and printed, the books. Pausing at the end of the corridor, Shan bent over a pile of little brown pellets in a shadowed corner, then plucked a tuft of coarse white hairs from where they had rubbed off on the stonewall above them. He contemplated his finding for several long breaths then returned to his friends, freshening their tea before taking a seat at their work table.

"I couldn't really understand why Lhakpa came to Yangkar," he started. "A snow monk usually has friends somewhere who would gladly put him up when the weather is bitter. He lived in a village only a few day's journey from here. But only Yangkar has an archive of the region, although its existence is supposed to be known by only a handful of us."

Both Yara and Tserung suddenly seemed to take great interest in their mugs of tea.

"Lhakpa was at Gekho's Roost, just days ago. I saw his goat there and she wouldn't be there without him. He fled when that team from the Institute came here and went straight there from Yangkar. He left abruptly but wanted me to go there as well, because he left me a map."

His friends remained silent.

"You've spent hard hours here, I know, but I was thinking it was nothing short of a miracle that you had already gone through hundreds of books. He had already been looking at them. He had already marked many."

"He said to say nothing to you, Shan," Tserung confessed in a worried voice. "But we would never lie to you."

"So he swore you to secrecy," Shan said, and held his weary head in his hands for a moment, then went to the shelf where Tserung kept supplies and retrieved a stick of incense, lit it, and set it in its wooden block holder in the middle of the table. It was a way of calling the gods to witness.

"Then I will tell you some of my secrets," he declared, "and you can decide if I should know yours." He explained the terrible morning when he had watched the execution of Metok, the false charges against the Tibetan engineer, and the deaths of the American woman and the professor in the ancient cavern shrine.

"The cavern was not just a shrine," Tserung said in a whisper. "For all of time the great earth deity, the grandfather of mountains, lived there." He paused and pulled a book from the pile at the end of the table, then opened it to a page marked with a tattered silk ribbon. The image on the page was of a fierce, sixteen-armed demon protector whose skin was cobalt blue and whose hands were filled with weapons and tools. Tserung pointed to each object and identified it. "A sword, a sledgehammer maul, a bow and arrow," he began then looked up when he had finished. "All used for battle or for shaping the earth. Lhakpa thought that was important. He was trying to learn all he could about this Gekho, to see if he could find a new way to reach the earth god, he said. If he had gone earlier, he would have been killed too with that Chinese professor and the American. But he was here," the monk mechanic said, and gestured to the stacked peche. "The old books saved him."

"A new way?" Shan asked. "Meaning what?"

"I don't know. It troubled me. I think now that maybe he had been without the gods earlier in his life and now he wanted to change that."

"What exactly was he looking for?"

Yara looked to Tserung, who nodded. "The words," she said. "The prayers forgotten in time, the prayers that might let Gekho know not all have forgotten him. He didn't find any, said they are probably all lost now."

"Lost to the black years, he meant," Tserung added, his voice bitter now. The black years were one of the many terms Tibetans had for the apocalyptic period of the initial Chinese invasion and the bloody Cultural Revolution that followed. He hesitated, with a nervous glance at Shan, as if just realizing what he had spoken in front of the Chinese constable, but Shan only nodded to him.

"What does it mean, Shan," Tserung asked in a mournful voice, "when all the prayers have been taken from us? Prayer is the lifeblood of a god. When no one prays to a god, my grandmother told me, the god will eventually shrivel up and die. I would pray for a Bonpo god, if only I knew what to say."

Yara broke the heavy silence. "There aren't too many Bonpo left," she said, "and almost no Bonpo monks. Many of the few who truly understood the old ways are unregistered, always moving about and hiding because they know Religious Affairs has informers everywhere."

"Are you saying Lhakpa was a Bonpo monk?"

Tserung sipped his tea. "More like an educated man who needed to urgently study the ways of a Bonpo monk."

"A very educated man with a goat niece," Shan observed.

Yara shrugged and cast a sympathetic glance at Tserung. "In this age the path to becoming a monk is not well charted."

"Lhakpa's is a complicated spirit," Tserung said. The mechanic himself was speaking more and more like a learned man. "Some days I had the impression he had been trained as a scientist, others as a historian. The goat was not make-believe, not a prop for a man pretending to be a hermit. I think she played an important role in his changing, in his taking the role of snow monk so seriously. I was in the hall one night and I came upon him sitting here, stroking her head. He didn't know I was behind him. 'Who knew this would be your journey,' he said to Tara, then added, 'Transmigration of the soul. You are the proof of the unproveable.'" Tserung shrugged, and he touched the gau that hung from his neck. "Not entirely sure what he meant, but those were his words, to his niece the philosophical goat." The mechanic looked at Shan as if for an explanation.

"One thing I have learned in the Tibet we live in," Shan offered, "is that everyone has their own unique path to enlightenment."

Shan left Yara and Tserung energetically reviewing more dusty manuscripts and ventured onto the cobbled alley behind the junkyard. Seeing a light on in the rooms inside, he knocked then opened the door, on which was painted a sun cradled in a crescent moon, surrounded by a number of small protector demons.

The astrologer was sitting at her easel, working on one of her elegant horoscopes. A broad smile lifted her wrinkled countenance as she saw him. She made a clucking sound, and with a blur of motion a furry brown creature hopped from a nearby table onto her shoulder. "Look who's here, Uncle Kapo!" she exclaimed. "Our friend the constable!"

Shan put a hand out and the gerbil leapt onto it and climbed to his own shoulder, where it began making a purring sound. He and the gerbil were well-acquainted. Kapo had once been a renowned lama.

"There's tea," Shiva said, gesturing with a paintbrush to the small brazier by the window.

Shan poured two cups and pulled a stool to Shiva's side as she painted a tortoise, the foundation of many horoscopes, on the heavy paper set in the easel. She was devoted to her work and as one of the last of the traditional astrologers was in great demand, receiving many of her commissions by mail.

"I remember the day last month when I followed the snow monk's goat through your open door," Shan said. "I thought she would wreak havoc with your charts and paints but she just came in and laid down beside Uncle Kapo's cage."

Shiva nodded. "Tara's a sweet girl, very respectful. She was too feisty before, Lhakpa says, so this goat life has been good for her."

"She was so comfortable because she was familiar with your rooms," Shan ventured. "She had been here before, more than once, I think. Because Lhakpa was here more than once."

Shiva glanced warily at Shan then went back to painting her tortoise. "A snow monk is owed charity. It is the obligation of the devout."

"I know how you work, Shiva. Special charms require much discussion with the person requesting them, so they can be tailored to the person and the place he is going to."

"Or the demon he is going to encounter when getting there," Shiva added in a professional, matter-of-fact voice.

"What charm did you give him, grandmother?"

Shiva lowered her brush and weighed his words. "In the old days astrologers were almost always monks or nuns. Words shared with a monk or nun are personal and confidential. What can be more personal than a horoscope?"

"But he wasn't looking for a horoscope," Shan suggested. "He wanted a charm. It would have been an old one, a Bonpo charm. The deity he was going to meet was Gekho the protector god." He pointed to a spatter of paint on her easel. "You would have needed that blue paint for it."

Her eyes flared for a moment, and she looked around as if worried someone might be listening. "Speak softly of such things," she said in a low voice, then slowly nodded. "The Wrathful Demon Destroyer, they called him. I hadn't heard his name spoken for years. They say he was one of the original gods, from when the mountains and humans were still being shaped. People say they are dead, but we don't believe it. They are just sleeping. But it is very difficult to wake them," she added in a troubled voice.

"We?" Shan asked. When she did not reply, he looked about the room, wondering if he had missed something. He discovered it on her little altar, a reversed swastika sign behind her little bronze Buddha, and realized he should not be surprised. Shiva herself respected the old Bonpo ways.

"You know that Gekho's valley has been overrun by machines," he said. "They are scouring everything from the surface."

"We are taught that surfaces can be misleading," the astrologer observed.

Shan was no longer sure what they were talking about. "I need to find Lhakpa, which means I need to find the path to Gekho."

"Some things are more likely to come to those who don't seek them."

"I fear he is in grave danger."

"The dangers, as the joys, of this life are fleeting. What endures is the truth."

Shan was beginning to feel like he was participating in a Bonpo teaching. He tried a different approach. "I want the same charm you gave to him," he said.

Shiva's eyes went round. "No! You mustn't ask! A charm for one man can be a curse for another. I told him so, especially for an outsider."

Shan hesitated. "How would Lhakpa be an outsider?"

"When he asked, he was so detached, I think a little ashamed in the asking. Sometimes he seemed to be more like one of those scholars who come and speak with me, like they don't really believe in what I do but still have to record it all in their books." She shrugged. "But his heart was pure, and he embraced the Buddha."

"I don't have time to argue, Shiva," Shan pressed. "I am leaving for the valley at dawn, with or without that charm."

There was pain in her eyes as the astrologer gazed at Shan. "That path could be your death, Shan."

"Death already stalks that valley. I can't stop more death unless I put myself in front of it. Am I better doing that with or without the charm?"

"You're a fool."

"You're a witch."

Shiva gave a cackling laugh that seemed to confirm his assertion. She gazed in silence, first at Shan then at the gerbil, who returned her gaze with his huge questioning eyes. "I don't want you to die, Constable. That valley is full of old demons and new demons. The worse lies ahead."

"Surely there must be room for a good demon. That's what my friend Lokesh calls me. A good demon."

"How is my favorite old rebel?"

"I wrote him to invite him to come when the passes clear of snow. Hopefully one of his young aides will join him. He is finally beginning to show signs of his age."

"It would give me joy to see him again," the astrologer said. "We always have so much to speak about." Kapo climbed back onto her shoulder and she sighed, then lifted the half-completed horoscope off her easel. "Come back at dawn."

Shan rose, then realized Shiva might be the only one in town who could answer another question that had been nagging him since his last trip to the secret archives. "The old books speak of patrols of black bulls leaving each spring for the Valley of the Gods."

"The bulls were *dob dobs*," she explained, using the nickname for the monastic police who served at the large monasteries of old Tibet.

Once Yangkar had held the largest monastery in the region. "They wore black robes, and some would always spend the warm months keeping the sacred valley protected and helping the pilgrims who came from afar."

Shan considered her words. "You make it sound like Yangkar was the protector of Gekho's valley."

Shiva solemnly nodded. "But we are down to only one dob dob. Should I find you a black robe?"

CHAPTER EIGHT

Shan went from his truck back to the door of his quarters three times, each time tearing up the note he had left and replacing it with another. Although he had buried his sentiments for years, he had genuine affection for Meng, more than he had ever felt for any woman, but their lives had no overlap. They had almost nothing to share, and now he was not even able to share time with her.

I'm very sorry, he finally wrote. *I am glad that you sought me out, but my work demands I be elsewhere. Now that you know where I am, come again, but give me some notice. Be safe.*

Shan felt ashamed to leave Meng such a cold, meager note, but he could settle on no other words and his foreboding about Gekho's Roost would not let him linger.

He sped down the highway, twice dodging antelope in the gray light of early dawn, then slowing after half an hour to find the rough dirt track that Lhakpa had marked on his map. He drove faster than he should on the rutted, uneven road, then realized he was raising a long cloud of dust that could be seen for miles and slowed. After crossing the first of the long ridges that ascended like stairs toward the high mountains, he pulled over and unfolded the charm Shiva had given him in the dark alley outside her door.

The astrologer had looked not simply exhausted but somehow drained, almost battle-weary, as if she had spent the night locked in some war to empower the ancient symbols and words on her paper. He was not surprised that he did not entirely understand the images and shapes she had rendered. Gekho the blue god was in the center. Each of his eight arms on either side extended one of the weapons or tools used in aid of the sacred earth. Along the top right border were goats on a grassy slope, then, in a clockwise sequence were three small hills with a white chorten on the center one, and one of the long woolen caps pilgrims sometimes wore. Next was a pair of what looked like stone pillars with little balls on them with one of the auspicious signs, a parasol, inked below them. In several places on the heavy sheet were *bharal*, the rare blue sheep of Tibet's high alpine slopes, and Shan surmised that meant to follow the paths of the bharal. Blue sheep lived on the blue god's mountain. At the apex, above the god's head, was a *garuda*, a sacred bird known to protect the gods, and though it had its wings extended for flight, its talons seemed rooted in the mountain, as if made of stone. To the left of the great bird was a line of yaks, each with a tiny glowing Buddha riding on its back.

"This is the same as you gave to Lhakpa?" he had asked the astrologer.

"Everyone has the same destination in the end," she had said enigmatically, then stepped inside and shut her door.

He studied his official public map, the military map marked by Lhakpa, and a satellite photo Zhu had given him before they had parted company in Lhadrung. Each told its own story. The public map delineated the road from the east, from Sichuan, in a long sloping line along the bottom that he knew was only a general approximation of the route. The photographic image, over a year old, showed only a flat compression of the landscape with peaks indicated by splays of white snow but clearly captured the Valley of the Gods, marked by its turquoise lake of glacial water and even a smudge of shadow where the standing stones stood. The military map showed the road in much greater, more accurate detail, had altitudes for several mountains, but its printed version showed no trails and none of the rough tracks like the one Shan now drove on. These had been carefully inscribed by Lhakpa, sometimes with tiny Tibetan annotations like *antelope passage* or *fresh water here*. He estimated he was ten miles southwest of the Five Claws project, and Lhakpa's dotted lines over a steep saddle of land on the high mountain slope made it clear he would have to complete the last few miles on foot.

Scanning the terrain with his binoculars, he could make out more trails that traversed the verdant slopes, made by bharal and the more common mountain goats over the course of centuries, all converging on the massive peak, as if the animals too had been making pilgrimages. The peak itself was unmistakable, the jagged tower pointing toward the heavens, its western side split by the narrow pass where the Five Claws dam was being built. Something moved on the heights and he braced the lenses against a ledge rock to focus on a line of figures. They were so distant and the slope they traversed so mottled in shadow that it took several breaths for him to make them out, then he paused in surprise and looked at them with his naked eye. He was seeing something very rare for that sparsely populated quarter of Lhadrung County, something so improbable that he bent to study the figures again with his lenses. He was looking at a yak train, a convoy of eight or ten yaks loaded with packs, heading toward the deep mountains of Kham, the most rugged and inaccessible of Tibet's regions.

It was an image from old Tibet, when yak convoys had been the predominant link between distant communities, when commerce depended on such convoys, and the role of caravaner was a romantic and honored profession. But this is not old Tibet, he reminded himself, then reconsidered as he recalled that Shiva had drawn a train of yaks carrying Buddhas, and realized the yaks were coming from the direction of the Five Claws project. Old Tibet was there in the valley, at least dying vestiges of it, as well as the forces of modern China. The conundrums he faced were rooted in both worlds, and he was the inadequate black bull dob dob sent to resolve them.

He laid out his maps on the flat rock, then set Shiva's chart beside them, for he had realized it too was a map of sorts. He had passed herds of sheep on grassy hills, then a trio of steep hills with a decrepit chorten on the center one. The signs and symbols the astrologer had painted were a guide. Each of the maps embodied the perception of the world from a different view, that of soldier, scientist, snow monk, and Shiva. Most called her an astrologer but some whispered a different name: sorceress. How could the old woman, who almost never left Yangkar, know this terrain? And what were the secrets she was trying to lead him to? He put away the map and the satellite photo, keeping only the guidance of the snow monk and the sorceress.

Every few hundred yards along his road were lhatse, rock cairns, most so overtaken by lichen they almost seemed like misshapen ancient statues. The track he drove down had clearly been a pilgrims' path, which aligned with the path Lhakpa had shown. There was another line on Lhakpa's map that intersected his own track a few miles ahead. He saw now that the snow hermit had inscribed one of his tiny legends under it. *Ice Ball Alley.*

His utility vehicle groaned more loudly with each slope. The cairns became more frequent as he climbed higher, and several showed recent additions of mani stones, carved, or simply scratched, with the mani mantra on their face, invoking the Compassionate Buddha. Here and there the spars of old withered pines extended out of the heather. All those near the track held wind-battered prayer flags. He had an odd sense that as he ascended he was going backward in time, into Old Tibet.

He halted at the intersection with the Ice Ball Alley—a wider, firmer gravel track—and got out to walk eastward, in the direction the prisoner convoy from Sichuan would have taken over a year earlier. Something yellow fluttered in the wind two hundred feet in front of him and he hastened his pace. It was a tattered length of plastic tape, anchored under a rock and printed with the bold words *Public Security Crime Scene.* The knobs had their own sacred flags.

This then was where the hail chaser had called to the skies and done his dance, where two soldiers had died, where Huan had arrested the old Tibetan for murder. Shan sat on a boulder and studied the scene. It was at the crest of the highest ridge that reached out from the massive snowcapped peak above, which itself was the highest summit for scores of miles to the south, probably the highest until the mighty Himalayas, which were visible as a gray smudge on the horizon. It would be a cloud catcher, where moisture-laden clouds that had made it over the barrier of the Himalayas would pile on, colliding with the frigid air of the peak. It didn't require sorcery to know that if hail was going to fall anywhere in the surrounding countryside, it was likely to be on this slope.

As he approached his truck he saw two stone pillars matching those of Shiva's drawing. They led to a little flat overlooking the vast landscape, beside a spring that bubbled up out of the ground, surrounded by more of the overgrown cairns and a jutting ledge that made a roof under which three or four people could have slept. It would have been a stopping place on the pilgrims' path. It also had to be where the hail chaser would have sheltered when the hail had pelted down on the nearby convoy. Not just pilgrims had stopped there, for Shan found the faint traces of hoof prints. He turned and studied the landscape to the south, then lifted his binoculars, locating more gray blots on the land below. The distance was too great to make out specific structures, but he knew the pattern of the blots, and he realized he had looked at these same snowcapped peaks many times during his years behind razor wire. The gray blots were Tan's prison camps. On the day of Yankay Namdol's release the hail chaser had come in this direction, on horseback, with the young woman who released prayer flag kites over the dam construction site.

Shan folded his legs into the meditation position and sat in the pilgrims' flat, facing the high mountains, reciting first the mani mantra then the mantra Shiva had written at the bottom of his chart, a mantra that invoked the mountain deities. Eventually he rose, parked his truck off the road, and pulled his pack from the back seat. He emptied his water bottle from Yangkar and refilled it in the pilgrims' spring, then proceeded up the trail. He might have driven another two or three miles, but this was the respectful approach, as a pilgrim trying to meet the mountain god on his own terms.

He walked for nearly four hours, alternately contemplating the pilgrims who had trod the path for centuries before him or trying to fit together the pieces of the puzzle that somehow included the hail chaser, the snow hermit, Larung Gar, and the American archaeologist. At each cairn he encountered he followed the tradition of reciting the mani mantra and adding a stone. He often sensed having his old friend Lokesh at his side and recalled with a pang how when released from prison, they had naively vowed to spend a year walking pilgrims' paths together. He and the old Tibetan had still been able to spend days off from time to time exploring and rehabilitating ancient pilgrim trails. Once, for a moment, he was sure he heard the old man's joyful laugh, then realized it was just the chuckling call of a snow partridge sunning itself near the trail.

The air had grown thin, and much cooler, when he crested a small ridge and looked down into a north-facing flat at the base of a huge rock formation from which four long spines protruded. He extracted Shiva's chart and saw that the spines matched the talons of her garuda bird, the last in her sequence of landmarks. With a bit of imagination, he could see that the curving expanse of stone above the talons might be seen as the wings of a giant bird. The flat was shielded from the wind and opened onto a grove of thick junipers beyond which lay a long field of ragged rock outcroppings. A dozen paces past the talons the flat disappeared into the sky, its thin lip of shale hanging over a cliff that had to be hundreds of feet high. Two horses were tethered by a small spring that ran along the edge of the trees. Folded blankets were stacked by a smoldering fire pit, and at the back, just beyond the farthest talon, a length of heavy black felt had been draped across a rope strung between two trees to make a makeshift shelter, in which he could see a few pots and kettles. He studied Lhakpa's map, realizing that he was at the opposite side of the rock field where he had chased the kite flyer.

No one called out in challenge as he reached the fire pit. He circled the campfire then knelt at the little spring to rub water onto his face. Suddenly he heard a grunt, a rush of small feet, then something slammed into his hindquarters, sending him sprawling into the spring.

"It requires real effort to accidentally find this camp," came a simmering voice above him. He righted himself slowly, rising to his knees to find a young Tibetan woman with a wool cap pulled low over her head and a heavy shepherd's staff raised in her hands. But it hadn't been the staff that struck him. With a now joyful bleat Tara the goat charged him again, but this time to push her face against him, mouthing his jacket in her usual greeting.

The woman relaxed her hold on the staff. "She acts like she knows you," she said, question in her voice.

"Animals like me," Shan said, and slowly rose to his feet. "I was on the pilgrims' path," he offered. "Does it continue into the stone field?" He took a step toward the outcroppings.

Tara, however, would not let him avoid her. She leapt up on her two back feet, nuzzling his belly.

"No, she does know you," the woman insisted, raising the staff again.

Shan sighed and sat on a flat boulder, putting his hat beside him as he rubbed Tara's head. "Can we perhaps start over?" he asked. "Yes. Last month Tara ate a pair of my shoes, then a shirt she pulled off my clothesline. And she seems to enjoy visiting the cells in my jail."

The woman stiffened, raising the club higher as she retreated toward the shadows, calling Tara. The goat looked at her with a curious expression but did not leave Shan. The Tibetan hesitated. "She trusts you," she said in surprise.

"I was there when you took Yankay away from his detention camp. I never liked those reeducation camps. Not really a prison, not really a school. Just one of those limbo hells where souls bide their time for life to begin again."

"We've done nothing wrong!" the woman snapped.

"I am not your enemy," Shan said.

"You are Chinese! You admit you are a government officer!"

"Officer seems too big a word for what I do. Just a lowly constable. And I am outside my jurisdiction."

"No," came an amused voice from the shadows. "Shan is more like the Abbot of Yangkar. And the gods' valley was always in the jurisdiction of Yangkar gompa." Lhakpa emerged into the daylight.

"He is a policeman, Uncle!" the woman pressed, alarm in her voice. "And there is no more gompa at Yangkar."

"No. The gompa remains, just harder to see than it once was. Shan is a policeman who opens his jail beds to half-frozen monks and helps paint the chorten in the town square, always ignoring the Mao at the other end."

"He was trying to deceive me when he arrived," his niece pressed.

"In Tibet a wise man learns to test new ground before revealing himself." Lhakpa turned to Shan. "This is Jaya, my other niece."

"I can barely tell them apart."

Lhakpa laughed. "She is the human one, though I warn her often that she gets dangerously close to transmigration these days."

"As when she flies kites over bulldozers."

Jaya cocked her head at him. "It was you who followed me on the ridge that day."

"I thought it silly when she first suggested it," Lhakpa said. "But it makes them hesitate when they find prayers mysteriously draped over equipment. I especially like the night flights. The director came out of his quarters one morning and prayer flags were all over the trees by his door. He was furious, cursed his security team for allowing it, but they said they were certain no one came close in the night. So they installed security cameras. They were even more disturbed when it happened again, and the cameras proved no one had set foot in his compound. Tibetan ghosts!"

Shan chewed on Lhakpa's words. Was the snow monk revealing that they had helpers secretly working in the valley below? "They have a drone now," Shan warned. "One of those used by the army for battlefield reconnaissance. You won't be able to hide in the outcroppings when they watch from above."

Lhakpa cast a worried glance toward the sky, no doubt realizing that their camp would be conspicuous from the sky.

"Maybe the gods would send an eagle," Jaya suggested. "Eagles don't like drones."

"You have a relative who's an eagle perhaps?" Shan asked. "I've always wondered, is that a lower- or a higher-level reincarnation?"

Jaya gave him a dangerous smile, then began moving the blankets under the lean-to of black cloth, which would look like just another shadow from above.

"You're not really a snow monk," Shan said to Lhakpa.

Lhakpa shrugged. "I think I have the heart of a snow monk, and I was looking forward to a few months wandering the remote peaks. But I was needed for the valley."

"For the valley or for its cavern?" Shan asked. "I saw heavily loaded yaks coming out of the mountains when I was climbing up."

As Lhakpa motioned Shan toward the lean-to, Jaya uttered an angry protest and stubbornly planted herself, arms akimbo, in front of it. "Uncle, no! We don't know him well enough."

Lhakpa raised a palm to quiet her. "If he meant to do us harm, he would not have come as a pilgrim. He stopped to pray at each of the cairns. He had no idea anyone was watching, niece."

As Jaya reluctantly stepped aside, Lhakpa opened a flap in the back wall of the shelter and Shan discovered it was an entry into a wide, dry cavity created by a huge overhanging ledge that was obscured by the juniper trees. Crude shelves had been constructed of long flat slabs of slate set on smaller, squarish rocks. The entire hundred-foot stone wall at the back of the chamber was lined with the shelves and two-thirds of the shelves were full of artifacts.

"The local herders say that Gekho's cavern was used since the first man met the gods," Lhakpa explained as he guided an awestruck Shan along the shelves. "There were many small chapels off the main tunnel of the cavern, and each chapel's contents were kept together here, as the professor recovered them, with the more modern images, probably one or two hundred years old, at the shelf to the right, progressing to the oldest at the other end." Among those more recent images Shan recognized exquisitely carved and cast representations of the Buddhas of the Three Times, the five peaceful meditational Buddhas sitting astride golden lotus flowers, then many of the twenty-one aspects of Mother Tara. He lingered for a moment at a particularly fierce-looking Red Tara, painfully recalling how Metok had invoked the protectress with his last breath. As they progressed along the shelves the images grew less familiar, many of them appearing to be angry demons and protector gods. The last images left on the shelves were a group of primitive figures that looked more like tigers than gods, frightening in aspect. Lhakpa pulled away a large piece of dark cloth. Under it were two intricately crafted figures, one of the blue mountain god and one of Yamantaka, the Lord of Death. Propped between the small statues were photographs of Professor Gangfen and a blond Western woman who had to be Natalie Pike.

The grainy photos were from an instant camera, close-ups taking in only their subjects' upper bodies, but Shan saw the joy in both their eyes as they held the same two figurines. There was sadness there too, for the only reason they had been collecting the treasures was because they knew the sacred cavern would be sacrificed in the building of Beijing's dam.

The woman who gazed out of the photo had Cato Pike's intelligent-but-defiant blue eyes. She was in her mid-twenties, and her high cheekbones would have given most women an elegant beauty, but he could see from her smudged face, tangled hair, and dirt-stained clothing that she was not one much concerned about outward appearances.

Professor Gangfen reminded Shan so much of his own father that he felt a pang as he studied the archaeologist's image. Even without his wire-rimmed spectacles he would have looked the scholar. Shan imagined that the many pockets of the photographer's vest he wore were filled with little brushes, dental picks, glassine envelopes, and other tools of his beloved trade. A pencil was lodged behind an ear, sticking out of shaggy salt-and-pepper hair. Like Natalie Pike, he had died an unsung hero, perhaps even more so than the American woman, for he had known that his government would severely punish him if they had discovered what he was doing. He had not only defied his government, he had given his life to save a vital history, to preserve the truth.

"Shan," Lhakpa urged, standing at the flap in the felt wall. Shan realized the Tibetan had been calling his name. Shan bowed his head respectfully to the images of the two dead archaeologists and rejoined the snow monk.

"They must have gotten most of the artifacts out," Shan observed as Lhakpa led him back to the campsite.

"Three yak trains have already left. But even so, and including those still here, it is only part of the total. It wasn't just one cavern shrine, there were tunnels and chambers deep in the mountain, an unexplored labyrinth of shrines. Just imagine all those people for all those centuries, carrying dim butter lamps for half a mile or more into the darkened corridors to reach the gods."

Lhakpa stepped across the camp into the shadows of the field of outcroppings with a summoning gesture to Shan, who retrieved his pack and followed. He heard footsteps behind him and turned to see Jaya behind him.

"I don't understand how they could have taken so much out of the cavern without being spotted," he said to the Tibetan woman as they caught up with Lhakpa.

"There are friends below. There's a Tibetan named Metok, a senior engineer, who helps sometimes. He had trucks and other equipment parked across the mouth of the cave at the end of the workdays before . . ." her voice trailed off.

"Before the explosion," Lhakpa finished. "He gave us cover that way, so we could move in and out of the cave at night without being seen. Metok took a great risk. He's a good friend."

"Metok loved going inside," Jaya explained. "He came back again, and again, each time more worried. He wanted us to give him our photos and inventory lists, so he could persuade the authorities to stop the project." Jaya winced. "I asked him if he had somehow missed the fact that six thousand temples and monasteries had already been destroyed. Where was the big monastery at Yangkar, I asked him, or the one at Lhadrung? Where were the millions of artifacts already taken by the government? When Natalie told him that some of the artifacts here were truly ancient and showed that riders had likely come here from Scythia and Central Asia, that the standing stones were from those cultures, he said yes, that was his point, that the stones proved that this was a unique site, that it was so important it could be one of those heritage sites protected by the United Nations. But then just days later the standing stones were bulldozed, all signs of them destroyed. He never argued with us again, just asked how he could help. So I said move the trucks in front of the cave. He has a good soul, that Metok. The gods are in his heart. He thinks he might convince the government that the site is too unstable to continue the work, says he knows of maps in Golmud that show a fault line here that was left off the maps used by the Five Claws engineers. He was called away unexpectedly but before he left, he said he sent a friend named Sun to bring them back."

Shan looked away. Sun had abruptly gone to Golmud to retrieve maps, but there had been no maps with his baggage. He spoke no more until they emerged onto a field thick with grass and wildflowers. They were at one of the highest points overlooking the valley, a few hundred yards from the narrow pass where the dam was to be constructed, looking down at the frenzied construction activity at the bottom of the valley.

It was Shan who broke the silence. "I pray you will not hate me for the news I must give you." He sat on a ledge and motioned them to join him.

"I was forced to witness an execution in Lhadrung town," he said, his heart feeling like a cold stone. "I didn't know about all this," he said, gesturing to the huge work site below. "I just saw a man convicted of corruption, who had defiance in his eyes and a prayer in his heart." He looked each of his companions in the eyes. "It was Metok Rentzig."

The color drained from Jaya's face. "No! No, no, no!" she cried. "Impossible!"

Lhakpa sank his face into his hands.

"Impossible but true," Shan said.

"He was not corrupt!" Jaya said with a sob.

"I know that now. He smuggled a note out. He said he was being held because he had seen the professor and Natalie Pike murdered. I know now that he meant that he was there when the cave was collapsed, and that whoever directed it knew he was killing those inside."

Jaya wiped at her tears. "They killed Metok. The government murdered him."

"And his friend Sun died on the sky train. But it wasn't the government, only certain people in the government," Shan said, and gazed despairingly down at the construction. "We can't stop this, but we can expose the truth," he said.

"For whom?" Jaya snapped. "No one in the government will care!"

"For us. For Metok and his friend Sun. For Professor Gangfen and Natalie Pike. For Gekho."

Lhakpa shook his head as if disagreeing. "We have more chance of stopping the dam than finding the truth. Buddha's blood, Shan, you're talking about Public Security and a project led by Party officials from Beijing. The deputy director, that man Jiao, has a satellite phone. He talks with Beijing almost every day."

Shan decided not to ask how Lhakpa could possibly know that. "If you keep resisting, they'll call out armed patrols."

"If they call out patrols," Lhakpa said, heat entering his voice, "we keep resisting." Jaya murmured her agreement, then whispered a mantra to the Mother Protector.

"I'm going down," Shan announced.

"Bad timing. They've had a high-level visitor," Lhakpa said, and pointed to the Five Claws office building. Shan made out the shape of a white utility vehicle parked between the flagpole and the director's office.

"Good. I'm not going down to see the director. I am happy for him to be distracted."

"Then wait," Jaya said, and reached into her pack, extracting one of the lanyards with a security badge Shan had seen the workers wearing. She reminded Shan that there were usually spare hard hats in the bin by the mess hall, then had one question before he turned away. "What can you tell us about that drone?"

It was midafternoon by the time Shan reached the administrative compound at the bottom of the valley. He found a hat in the bin described by Jaya and a worker's tunic hanging on a row of pegs inside the now-empty hall. He went as close to the headquarters office as he dared, wary of the guard now posted there, but near enough to see the nondescript white utility vehicle parked by the front door and the young Chinese driver slumped behind the wheel, asleep.

Beyond the compound of modular units that comprised the administrative center of the huge project was the equipment yard. The fence had been completed around the equipment and in one corner, two more walls of wire had been added to create a square perhaps two hundred feet on each side. Inside the wired-off corner, canvas tarps had been spread overhead and cots placed underneath, creating what looked like temporary living quarters for a few dozen men, some of whom were lying on the cots while others played cards or walked along the perimeter of the wire. They were all Tibetans.

"New rules," came a voice over his shoulder. "Gotta' sign in at the office if you need any laborers and register each name and identity card number." A sturdy, square-shouldered Chinese man was at his side, casting an appraising eye over the Tibetans. He wore a red safety helmet, which Shan took to be the sign of a foreman. "Took me almost an hour just to get six ditch diggers this morning," the man groused. "Deputy Director Jiao tells us in all his speeches that we're on the urgent business of the Chairman, then he puts more damned obstacles in the way."

"Only the Tibetans?" Shan asked.

"Right. Suddenly Jiao doesn't trust them. Too much talk about the blue god and such. He says all the troubles we're having can't be coincidence. But the Tibetans are the hardest workers we got and trying to bring in others from the east could take weeks."

"More troubles?" Shan asked. "I just got back," he added, trying to cover his curiosity.

"Yesterday the brakes on a truck failed and it drove right into the lake at the end of the valley. Into Gekho's belly, one of the Tibetans said. Today a bulldozer broke down with dirt inside the engine. Could be a bad gasket, could be someone put dirt in the fuel tank. Either way, it'll take days to strip the engine and get it running again. And more of those Tibetan prayers materializing out of the sky. They just drift down out of the clouds. That spooks people the most. Anyway, Deputy Director Jiao ordered the fence erected and ordered most of the Tibetan laborers to stay inside it when not assigned to work crews. For their own good, he told them. They'll take meals in the mess hall with the rest of us but are kept under watch by one of us foremen until the real guards arrive. He called Public Security in Lhasa."

Shan tried to push the worry from his voice. "He can't just arrest people," he said.

A guttural sound that might have been a laugh came from the foreman's throat. "I guess you haven't crossed Jiao yet. He's the one with the real power. One step out of line and he becomes like a scolding schoolmaster. 'Would you defy the Chairman?' he'll demand.

That's his response to anyone who even hints at not agreeing with him. 'Why would you add another reinforcing rod to that new wall, would you defy the Chairman? Why are you digging that foundation so deep, would you defy the Chairman?'" The foreman lit a cigarette. "Never knew the Chairman had an engineering degree," he muttered, then walked toward the gate that led into the pen of Tibetan workers.

Shan was about to follow, to talk with the Tibetans, when he saw someone darting toward the white utility vehicle. It was the driver, coming from a side door in the administration building, who now climbed back behind the wheel as several men emerged from the main entrance. Snippets of loud conversation came from the group. The director was using his public voice, boasting proudly of his project to a Westerner in a business suit, who was replying in perfect Mandarin. Shan froze as the man turned toward him. It was Cato Pike.

He watched from the shadow of a truck as the director helped Pike into his own car, driven by Deputy Director Jiao, and they pulled away, apparently on the same tour Shan had received the week before. The white utility vehicle followed. The driver was Natalie Pike's friend Cao.

As they disappeared down the valley, Shan moved toward the administrative complex, casting nervous glances toward the twisting road on the slope above that connected the project to the outside world. Public Security was coming, and soon there would be jackbooted guards stationed in the complex. He paced along the long message board outside the mess hall, reading notices about work shift schedules, meal hours, meetings of a Patriotic Workers Alliance, and sun-bleached photos of the ceremony that had launched construction months earlier. On October 1, the first caption read, the provincial Party chairman had come with a small brass band to celebrate the glorious event. The photos showed the first few modular units of the administrative compound, the first busload of joyful workers who would work on site preparation during the winter, and included a staged image of the provincial chairman at the controls of a bulldozer. *The first step in the historic event happily coincided with the destruction of the feudal remnants that blighted the valley*, boasted the caption. The bulldozer was plowing down the ancient standing stones. Shan paused, trying to understand several tiny tear-shaped blue objects in the photo, then realized that someone had deposited a line of blue paint along the top that had dripped below. Blue was the color of Gekho's blood.

On top of an announcement about evening entertainments someone had pinned a photocopy of an aerial photo of the project. Shan took it down, puzzling over the annotations that had been made on it. Buddhist symbols were drawn along the top in a crude hand, then lines had been drawn along the edges of the valley and what looked like eyes drawn in the lake above the waterfall that dropped into the valley. More drops of blue paint had been added to the bottom. Seeing that two more identical images had been pinned elsewhere on the board, he folded the paper into his pocket.

Shan returned the tunic he had borrowed to the peg he had taken it from, tossed his hard hat into the bin, and marched into the administrative offices. The director's secretary fortunately recognized him and expressed chagrin that he had not arrived in time to join the director and their distinguished foreign visitor.

He feigned surprise. "A foreigner?"

"Our first of many to come, the director told us," she exclaimed. "We didn't really expect him, although a woman from the United Nations office in Lhasa did call this morning to leave a message for him to call some ambassador, so we had a couple hours' notice. At least he brought a copy of the letter he had sent, which we haven't even received yet. We apologized and said in the future email would be sufficient." She lifted the letter with a proud, excited expression. "The United Nations!" she exclaimed.

"May I?" Shan asked and accepted the letter with a respectful nod. It explained that the global director of Hydrogeology Development,

Mr. Constantine Speare, was in Lhasa on official business and would be visiting the project to witness its remarkable construction and see if the director would be interested in speaking at a global sustainability conference in Kuala Lumpur. "The director must be very proud," Shan said as he handed the letter back. Pike had known how to get his foot in the director's door

The woman gave a vigorous nod. "Director Ren was disappointed in his offer to host a banquet tonight in honor of Mr. Speare, but the gentleman has to return to Lhasa today." She gave a sigh of relief. "As if such an important personage would care to eat in our simple executive's hall," she added in a whisper, then she brightened. "But maybe we can get a photo of him for our wall," she said, pointing to the wall of framed photos between the empty offices of the director and deputy director.

Shan paced along the wall, offering polite exclamations over the distinguished visitors in the images. At Jiao's door he pushed aside a windbreaker with Jiao's name, ostensibly to view another photo, making sure it dropped to the floor. He was out of sight of the woman as he bent to retrieve it, and quickly searched the pockets. He found them empty, but he paused over the embroidered badge over the breast pocket. It showed a red hammer over a white chorten, encircled by the words *Safety in Serenity*. The secretary noticed his interest in it as he hung the jacket back on its peg.

"From an old job," she explained.

Back outside, Shan walked along the perimeter of the compound and found himself facing the caged Tibetans. None of them would make eye contact with him. He took out his gau and murmured the mani mantra several times. Heads snapped up. Three men darted to the wire in front of him.

"We didn't do anything!" the nearest said in a plaintive tone. "We just want work! I need to feed my family!" Another man produced a little red book as if to prove his loyalty. He was, no doubt, a graduate of a reeducation camp.

"Don't argue with them," Shan said. "The director will soon realize he can't treat his best workers this way."

"The director?" asked the third, older Tibetan. "It wasn't the director, it was that damned deputy of his. At least the director overrruled him when he said we would have to take all our meals in here."

"Tell me," Shan said, with a worried glance toward the high road again, "were any of you here on that first day, when they leveled the standing stones?"

The man with the book turned and called out, summoning a compact middle-aged man in a herder's coat. "Where are the old stones they pushed down last October?" Shan asked him.

"Gone. Back to the gods, sir," the man explained.

"To the gods?"

"There was a great long crack in the ground that led toward the cave shrine from the standing stones, a half-mile long and who knows how deep. My grandmother said such things were openings to the *bayal*, to the land of bliss where the gods waited for the human world to improve. But the director said that was to be our first task, to fill it in and cover all traces since it would be a distraction to the engineers. So he had all those stones pushed into it, even the ones that had old writing and images cut into them. Then he ordered more big boulders to be pushed in and block the crack and used all the gravel that had been brought in for the roads, so the bulldozers could drive right across. All gone now."

"The cave is gone too," Shan observed.

The Tibetan replied in a forlorn whisper, "If the cave is truly gone, the gods are trapped."

Shan found himself unable to answer. He reached into his tunic pocket and searched for the cones of incense he often kept there, then handed the man all he had, six cones, and his box of matches. "You are not forgotten," he said, feeling painfully inadequate.

"Maybe we should be," the worker said. "Maybe we shouldn't light incense to call in protecting spirits. I'm not sure we deserve it."

Shan cocked his head in question.

"Because of what we're doing," another man explained. Half a dozen Tibetans had now gathered near Shan. "We're destroying the gods' home."

"The gods' home isn't a few feet of soil on the valley floor," Shan said, and gestured toward the surrounding mountains. "You haven't destroyed their home. You haven't trapped them, at least not for long. You've just confused them. Let them know you are here."

The man who had taken the incense considered Shan's words and began to nod, joined by others. Someone brought a flat rock and put a cone on it as another struck a match.

"Is there anything I can do for you?" Shan asked.

"Yeshe," a man said, and reached inside his shirt to produce a small copper gau on a strand of braided leather. "He was attacked. We worry about him." The Tibetan nodded toward a small building behind the mess hall, fifty yards away, that Shan had not noticed. A sign on the path leading to it said *Infirmary*. Shan accepted the gau and the man backed away with a grateful nod.

The well-fed Chinese woman at the desk inside the infirmary door was watching a movie on a laptop and gave only a disinterested glance as Shan walked past her. Behind the screen that separated her desk was the ward, with six beds. Only two were occupied, one by a sleeping Chinese man with his ankle in a fresh plaster cast. The second patient was a Tibetan in his thirties who shuddered as Shan drew near. He closed his eyes as if pretending to sleep.

"My name is Shan," Shan said in Tibetan. "I come from Yangkar. The monastery town." It was the first time he had given voice to the description, but it was how he was beginning to think of the town. "Hold the dagger in your heart," he added after a moment.

The man's eyes snapped open. Shan had spoken one of the secret signs of the purba, the resistance. The purba was a ritual dagger meant to pierce the demons of fear and confusion. Shan extended the gau, which the man instantly snatched away, pressing it in both hands over his heart. As he did so, Shan saw the healing bruises and scrapes on the back of his hands and forearms and saw fading bruises on his face. The young Tibetan seemed about to speak but as he opened his mouth he grimaced in pain. He had cracked or broken ribs.

He tried again. "I fell off some rocks," he said with a wince.

Shan was familiar with the pattern of the man's injuries. "No, Yeshe. Someone beat you."

Yeshe looked down at his gau and slowly nodded, then held up four fingers.

"Four people beat you."

He nodded again and gestured Shan closer. "The cleanup crew they call them. Special janitors, though you never see them actually cleaning anything."

Shan was not sure he heard right. "Janitors?"

Whispering apparently did not cause Yeshe as much pain, and Shan bent to listen. "That's what they call themselves, because they wear the gray coveralls and gray windbreakers that the custodians wear. They drive a pickup with a mop stained with red paint like blood hanging off the tailgate. It's like their banner. The cleanup crew they may be called, but my bet is that they are soldiers."

Shan studied the Tibetan. "What do you mean?"

"I just left the army five months ago. They're all in good shape, all follow a strict discipline. And I heard them call their leader sergeant. They sing an old battle song sometimes, about holding the flag high as the bullets fly."

The news struck a nerve. Shan had heard the song often, sung by guards in his former prison. "But why attack you?"

"Fireworks."

"I'm sorry?"

"I worked in demolition in the army. Ten years, then I came home."

"You mean you worked with explosives."

"Right. When the construction company heard that, they hired me right away. Good pay. Blast a ledge here, a stubborn boulder there. Shatter a rock face so it can be straightened."

Shan cast a glance toward the entrance. He could see the back of the nurse, still watching her laptop. "Why assault you for blasting rocks?" he asked

"More like for not blasting," Yeshe said. "The deputy director told me to destroy that old cave and I said I couldn't, that I would have to ask a monk before doing so, because it was a holy place. That night the cleanup crew pulled me from my bunk."

Shan saw the torment in the Tibetan's eyes. "But the real reason you wouldn't help was that you knew there were probably people inside."

Yeshe looked away, staring at the wall. "So the deputy director did it himself," he said toward the wall. "He could have sent men to clear it, to check it to be certain there was no one inside. The deputy engineer argued with him, said people might die. Jiao struck him, then had him escorted to his room. Then Jiao managed the detonations himself. The next day the deputy engineer was gone, summoned away on urgent business, Jiao said."

The Tibetan stared forlornly at his prayer amulet. "Later, some of the hill people came down and told us a man and a woman had been inside. Such a terrible way to die. I have nightmares every night now, like I was one of those trapped inside. I am lingering for hours, slowly suffocating, dying with the agony of broken bones and pierced organs, alone in the total darkness with the trapped gods screaming all around me."

CHAPTER NINE

The valley was washed in shadow as Shan planted himself in the road between two boulders, just beyond where the road leveled off at the top of the ridge. He had watched the white utility vehicle slowly mount the long switchbacks that led out of the valley, and now stood in its path with folded arms. As the car approached he took off his hat. He could see Cato Pike in the passenger seat, muttering to Cao as they skidded to a stop.

"Constantine Speare," Shan said when Pike approached him. "Another Roman name and another pointed weapon."

"Glad someone here appreciates my subtle wit," Pike replied with a peeved grin. The American glanced in the direction of the valley, out of sight below. "I'd rather not linger."

"Afraid someone will discover there is no UN office of Hydrogeology Development? Or that you don't even work for the UN? Back in America that might just be considered a prank. Here it is suicidal."

"Think of it more as vengeful curiosity," the American said. The glint in his eye made Shan uneasy. Once again he became aware of the beast that seemed to hover behind Pike's gaze. "And you're the one who told me about this valley. Did you honestly think I would stay away?"

"I thought I would eventually find a way to bring you here, to pay respects to where . . ." Shan searched for words. "Where the deaths actually occurred." He nodded to Cao as the Chinese student climbed out, standing behind the car to watch the road below. "You probably think you know China, Pike, that you probably would just be deported if they found you out. But not here, not in Tibet, not if you interfere with this project. They will shoot you and drop your body where no one will ever find it but the vultures."

"They? Give me their names and you and I don't have to cross paths again."

Shan gestured to Cao. "Think about him. If they didn't kill him outright, they would ruin his life if he were caught aiding a foreigner in some illegal activity. Assuming false credentials sounds like espionage. Beijing is ravenous for American spies."

"Actually, today was mostly Cao's idea. I was just the decoy, although I did want to see the place and meet the men responsible for it. I made an interesting discovery. Director Ren is a figurehead. It is Jiao who runs this place."

"Very astute. Took me two visits to figure that out," Shan said, then gestured to a flat boulder where they could sit and told the American what he had learned.

"Need a ride?" Pike asked when he had finished.

Shan gestured up the darkening slope. "My truck is up in the mountains," he said with a sinking feeling, knowing he would never find it in the night. As Pike opened the door to climb inside, he realized the American had not reciprocated. "You said you were a decoy. To distract them from what?"

Pike grinned. "You have your ways and I have mine. China breeds the best talent in the world for surveillance of electronic communication. I used to pay a lot of Uncle Sam's money to buy black-market surveillance software in Beijing. I kept my own copies, but Cao had even better ones. Kind of a hobby of his it turns out."

Shan remembered seeing Cao dash from the administration building. He hadn't been sleeping, he had been waiting for someone to come out the side door, for a chance to sneak inside while the senior managers were distracted with Pike.

Cao returned Shan's inquiring gaze. "You're just an archaeology student," Shan said.

"I'm just an archaeology student," Cao repeated. A student, Shan reminded himself, who helped his professor keep records of work that would have been banned by the government if it had known.

Pike held up a memory stick. "And now because of him we have a copy of all the office emails for the past six months." He pulled his door shut and rolled down the window. "Oh, and right about now their communication link with Beijing is crashing. Probably take a day or two to recover."

Shan paused to catch his breath on the steep climb up to the outcropping field. He could see the work site far below, where some equipment was still being operated with headlights on. In the distance a huge pile of toppled trees burned. Something still nagged at the back of his mind, a lurking question about his visit that he couldn't quite articulate. Something else still tore at his heart, the destruction and burial of the ancient standing stones. He had begun to grasp the excitement the professor and the American woman had felt about the valley. They hadn't been doing archaeology of long-ago tribes, they had been engaged in archaeology of the human spirit, at the place that anchored all the bones of the earth.

He had to climb the final heights in short stages, pausing when his lungs strained in the thin air. At the next stop, as he looked down at the shadowed place where the standing stones had once stood, the engima of his afternoon found his tongue.

"October 1!" he said out loud. October 1 was the day the stones had been destroyed. October 1 was National Day. National Day was when Tsomo, the old lama at Ko's prison, had suddenly gasped, thrust his arms toward the north, and died.

. . .

Two hours later Shan sat at the campfire in the little sheltered flat below the stone talons and told Lhakpa and Jaya of his afternoon at the work site, ending with his realization that the standing stones and the old prisoner from the Larung Gar monastery had essentially died the same day.

"The same hour," Jaya said. "2:00 p.m. on October 1." She knew. She knew more than Shan. "The mysteries of spiritual transmigration in Tibet," she added, then saw the confusion on Shan's face. "Yankay calls in hail and two soldiers die. They destroy the ancient stones and an aged lama dies. Maybe it's true what the old Bonpo say. We are all puppets. The gods decree it all."

Lhakpa murmured something in a voice that had grown desolate, and Jaya kicked him. He gave his niece a stern shake of his head, as if chastising her. Shan did not react, acting as though he had not heard. But he had heard. Lhakpa had said *I should have been the one.*

"On the road you stopped that white car, Constable," Jaya said.

Shan hesitated. The Tibetan woman seemed to spend much of her time watching the valley. "I discovered that I knew the visitor, someone from Lhasa," he replied.

Lhakpa stirred the embers of their dung-fed fire. "Tell me, Constable, are you investigating the death of Metok or the death of the gods?"

Shan leaned closer to the fire. "I only have jurisdiction over the former."

"That is just the jurisdiction that other men give you," Lhakpa replied, seeming to disagree.

Shan, suddenly feeling very small and very cold, pulled his borrowed blanket around his shoulders.

"There are many old statues of deities up in the hills above Yangkar," Lhakpa continued, "toppled by the government. Marpa told me how on days off you go up by yourself with a shovel and bar to stand them tall again."

"Sometimes herders come and help me."

"And if Religious Affairs knew of this, or what you do below the streets of Yangkar, they would call Public Security on you. You talk of jurisdiction but you act based on higher duties."

Shan looked up at the Tibetan. Talking with the snow hermit was like talking with Lokesh. Nothing could be hidden.

"So again, who was in the white truck?" Lhakpa pressed. "Jaya said it might be Public Security. I said no, because I trust you." The two Tibetans stared at him with expectant, impatient expressions.

"It was a student from Professor Gangfen's dig. He was driving Natalie Pike's father."

"Uncle!" Jaya cried out and threw a hand out to grasp Lhakpa's shoulder. Shan's announcement seemed to stun both Lhakpa and his niece.

"He came from America?" Lhakpa asked at last. "What does he hope to do?"

Shan thought about describing Pike but he was not sure how to do so. "He received notice that she died in a terrible accident. The government sent her ashes and they had a funeral for her. But he has been in law enforcement and possesses a great curiosity. And he lived in Beijing, knew the ways of Beijing and its police. He tested some of the ashes. They had sent him the remains of a sheep."

Lhakpa stared into the fire with a solemn expression. "A cruel thing to do to a father."

"He asked me where the crematorium was that had done it," Shan continued. "Two nights ago he went there and locked the manager into one of the ovens for the night."

Lhakpa gave a surprised laugh and patted Jaya on the back, as if she needed comforting. Shan realized she must have been a friend of Natalie Pike. "I like this man Pike," the snow hermit said. "He does what an old teacher told me the best lamas always did. He puts teeth in his virtue."

One of the horses tethered in the trees wickered and Jaya rose to investigate. Whispers came out of the darkness, and she returned with three Tibetans who eagerly accepted servings of the stew she had made. The two men, judging by their sheepskin vests and caps, were herders.

The third, a sturdy woman of perhaps forty years, nodded at Shan as she accepted her bowl from Jaya. He had a vague sense that he knew her but could not put a name to her face. Only when one of the herders added sticks from the bundle of fuel he had carried into the camp did Shan make the connection, for the flames illuminated the big leather bag she kept at her side, clearly showing the painted image of Menla, the Medicine Buddha. The woman was the nurse who usually roamed the Yangkar hills.

The matronly Tibetan woman remained silent as Jaya filled a small pot with stew and kept her head bent down in a melancholy expression. She did not eat, only murmured her gratitude to Jaya, picked up the pot and a bundle of incense that had been left near the fire, and stepped back into the shadows behind the wall of black felt.

Ten minutes later a Tibetan man in the denim clothing of the construction workers appeared at the edge of the trees and Jaya and Lhakpa quickly stepped to his side, speaking with him in urgent, worried tones. Shan slipped behind the felt wall. At the end of the rows of artifacts, past a bend in the mountain, he discovered a smaller campfire. The nurse and two other Tibetans sat there, one an older man with long, ragged, graying hair that hung about his shoulders, the other a squarely built woman who was working a strand of prayer beads. The man looked up and cocked his head as if hearing Shan's approach.

The two women gasped as he stepped out of the darkness. The man's leathery face lifted in a small, uncertain smile, though he did put one hand on the carved staff that leaned on a tree beside him.

"He was talking with Lhakpa," the nurse explained to her companions.

"I was hoping to get better acquainted with the hail chaser," Shan said, nodding to the old man.

"The constable of Yangkar," the nurse added in warning. The other woman grabbed the pot of stew and fled into the night.

The hail chaser spoke in the quiet voice of a lama. "Come share our fire, Constable." As Shan moved to sit on one of the flat stones by the flames, the nurse rose, lifted her medicine bag and a smaller, bulging leather bag of the kind used for collecting yak dung for fires, and disappeared in the direction of the other woman.

"Such an effect you have on women," the old Tibetan said with a low chuckle.

Shan looked down the path the nurse had taken. She had always been standoffish with him. He did not even know her name, only that she was called the walking healer. The herders she served always praised her abilities.

"I wouldn't have thought the sick would stay so close to the Five Claws," Shan observed as he extended his hands over the warmth of the flames. He glanced back toward the trail. There was plenty of firewood but the nurse had taken dung for fuel, which he did not understand.

"There are many forms of healing needed on this mountain," the hail chaser said. Shan saw that beside him were half a dozen bunches of juniper twigs, bound with vines.

"I am honored to meet you, Yankay Namdol. I am called Shan. I regretted not being able to speak with you when I saw you released at the Shoe Factory." Shan recalled the strange movements the hail chaser had made that morning. Now he realized part of the strangeness had been because the old man seemed subtly deformed. A hand was bent at a slightly unnatural angle. One shoulder seemed higher than the other. His left forearm was twisted, and his jaw seemed a bit off-center, giving his grizzled face a crooked appearance.

The old man tightened his grip on his staff, which Shan now saw was intricately carved with Buddhist and Bonpo symbols.

"I had never seen a man summon an earthquake."

Yankay's smile showed a row of uneven yellowed teeth. "You're mistaken. I don't summon earthquakes. Earthquakes summon me."

"At precisely the moment of your release. I was deeply impressed. It was magical. I think the warden might have fled if the colonel hadn't been there. And I expect the prisoners were treated with a bit more respect for a few days."

"You aren't prepared to understand how the earth works here," Yankay said, in the tone of a patient old teacher.

Shan stared into the fire, weighing the man's choice of words. "No," he admitted, "I always thought as I grew older I would grow wiser. But I only learned how ignorant I am."

Yankay let go of his staff and extended his hands over the flames. "Good. The first step to wisdom."

"And the next?" Shan asked and realized he sounded like a nervous student.

"Surrender to the wonder of it all."

"The wonder of men who would kill gods?"

Yankay sighed and did not reply right away. "There is an ice cave near the top of the mountain," he said eventually. "If you sit there long enough you can hear the vibration coming from the heart of the mountain. Like a heartbeat."

"Sounds cold."

The hail chaser seemed disappointed. "So you are one of those who has to be beaten into surrender."

"I tend to think that I am simply a survivor, hardened by long experience." He looked up into the open, inquiring countenance of the disheveled man. "How does one become a hail chaser?" he asked.

"You could never do it, Constable, if you couldn't sit to listen to the mountain."

"You mean it is a gift. A heavy burden of a gift, I suspect. Men die in hailstorms."

Yankay grimaced. "There used to be shrines dedicated to those who died in hailstorms. The lamas always had a hard time knowing how to treat them. Those who died violently usually can't attain a higher level of existence, but many people felt a man killed by hail had been called by the gods." He stood and dropped more wood on the fire. "I never wanted those soldiers to die. Sometimes I think that Lieutenant Huan was right, maybe I had committed murder that day. If I hadn't stopped the convoy, they would have lived."

"If they had worn their helmets, they would have lived," Shan said.

"If the trucks had broken down climbing the mountain, they would have lived. If Huan had not been in such a hurry and taken the short-cut, they would have lived. If they had left that morning ten minutes later, they would have lived." He shrugged. "Murder is a construct of human law," he observed. "I'm not sure those laws apply on this mountain."

"They don't," Yankay agreed.

"Then one year in the Shoe Factory seems penance enough."

Yankay lifted a foot, showing a heavy boot. "Every graduate gets a pair of the army boots made there, did you know that? Best boots I've ever owned. Cost one year of my life. Sometimes I think I should put them on a shrine." The old man sighed loudly. "But the stones of the trails are sharp, and my bones get weary."

Shan had so many questions, about how Yankay had become a hail chaser, about how he had sensed the earthquake, about how he had evaded capture by the authorities all these years, and what he knew about the sacred valley before the heavy equipment had arrived, but he said nothing. He felt like a nervous young novice in the presence of a renowned lama. Even after so many years of living in Tibet there were so many things about the land, about such Tibetans of the old world, that he didn't understand. He knew Lokesh would say his compulsion to understand everything was Shan's particular weakness, that he had to stop questioning and, as Yankay suggested, immerse himself in the wonder. But wonder was proving elusive in the Valley of the Gods.

They sat in silence. A night bird called from the trees. The shadows shortened as the moon rose higher.

"The ancient ways are always just beyond," Yankay suddenly said. He seemed to be speaking to the fire, for he then nodded as if the flames had replied with something profound.

"Once it was a noble profession," he declared, lifting his eyes toward Shan. "Only very learned men would chase the hail. It took as many years of study as that for a lama abbot, with hundreds of long prayers to memorize. But all those teachers fell off the earth in the last century."

He raised a hand and pointed to the northwestern sky. A moment later a meteor shot across the heavens, exactly where he pointed. It had to be a coincidence, Shan told himself. There could be no explanation for it, just as there could be none for Yankay's knowing of the earthquake at the Shoe Factory. He heard Lokesh's whisper in his ear. *Just accept the wonder.*

"There are many evil demons roaming the earth in our time. That was the true job of the hail chaser, to use lightning, hail, and earthquake to subdue the demons that sought to harm humans." He poked the fire with a long stick. "The charm against the inner-earth demon is soil that has been fused by lightning. The charm against the lesser female water demons is hellebore. The charm against the more powerful ones is powdered copper and black sulphur mixed with soil from a crossroads. The list is long, and some charms are lost forever. I didn't have the right training. The gods speak to me, they tell me about hail, and lightning, and earthquakes, even meteors, but I don't really know how to speak back to them. I am a mute wandering alone in the house of the gods," he said, with a tinge of anguish in his dry voice.

The hail chaser shrugged. "I can always dance and have people think it is magic but it's not magic. It's the gods whispering in my ear. That day at the Shoe Factory, did you not hear all the dogs barking and see the mules bolting? There's a special bark dogs have when an earthquake is minutes away. My early teacher taught me that much. All the birds had gone from the camp, though no one else seemed to notice. There's a vibration in the air just before the ground shakes, though most humans have forgotten how to feel that as well. Maybe I just have obsolete senses that have died out in other humans." He sighed. "I hear that down in the lower lands there are actually rivers a man can't drink from and air that makes a man sick to breathe. If that's true, it's because no one knows how to speak with the earth gods anymore. I'm just a miserable fool who can only hear them. Which makes it a curse, really."

The words pressed against Shan's heart. Not for the first time he felt a deep loathing for what the world had done to such men. Why, he wondered, was Yankay confessing such things to him? And why was his old body so misshapen? He gazed into the shallow cave where Yankay stored his belongings and saw a dented helmet. "Tell me, Rinpoche," he said, using the form of address reserved for learned lamas, "how many times have your bones been broken by hail?"

A sad smile rose on the old man's face. "You do me too great an honor, Constable. Maybe in the former world I would have become such but never in this one." He shrugged, then began touching parts of his body and counting. His left collarbone, his right collarbone, his left radius bone, his right ulna bone, the back of one hand, the wrist of the other. He stopped counting at ten. "I tend to think of these as blessings, for each time the gods decided not to kill me. 'Here we are!' they are saying. 'We have decided to let you live a while longer, you old fool!'" He touched his crooked jaw. "This one was just my stupidity. Never look up into a hailstorm."

The hail chaser quieted and added more wood to the fire. "How well do you know the dead?" he suddenly asked Shan.

A chill ran down Shan's spine. "I'm sorry?"

Yankay motioned in the direction the nurse had taken. "Our walking healer says you are the constable of Yangkar. Surely the constable of the old gompa town must know the dead. They say the dogs there are always barking because more ghosts than humans live there."

"I have experienced the dead far too often," Shan admitted.

The ragged old man gave a sympathetic nod, then pushed the end of one of his bundles of juniper into the embers. "We all know the Bardo, the words for the truly dead. But how do you deal with the half-dead? How do you raise them from in-between?"

"I don't understand," Shan confessed.

"When the body and soul change their mind. I keep thinking if I let the gods take me, I might see enough to—"

"There you are, Constable!" a female voice interrupted. Jaya appeared out of the shadows. "The worker who came to visit wants to thank you in person for helping Yeshe in the infirmary. He wrote a prayer he wants you to keep in your pocket." She pulled Shan to his feet with an insistent gleam in her eyes. As they left the little clearing Shan looked back at the old man, then paused until Jaya yanked his arm. Yankay was shaking his staff with one hand and waving the bundle of smoldering juniper with the other as he murmured beseechingly to the heavens. He was trying to raise the half-dead.

The next morning Jaya insisted Shan ride a horse back to his truck and she accompanied him so she could lead the mount back to their mountain camp. They left under the harsh gaze of four rough-looking Tibetan men, who had arrived in the night, all of whom wore red yarn in their long shaggy hair, marking them as *khampa*, the fierce, defiant people of the Kham highlands who would probably still be fighting the Chinese if the Dalai Lama hadn't implored them to stop years earlier. The khampa were filling the packs of half a dozen yaks with artifacts from the hidden cache, assisted by Lhakpa, who packed the more fragile pieces in layers of dried grass. The khampa did not acknowledge either Jaya or Shan as they rode past, other than to pull scarves up to cover half their faces, which suited Shan. He did not want to know who they were or where they were going with the treasures. As he watched them he recalled how Shiva had painted a line of yaks with Buddhas on their backs. How could she have known about the convoys carrying Buddhist treasures?

As they rode, Jaya frequently looked up at the sky. A storm had passed through in the night, but the sky had cleared. He knew she was skittish about the aerial drone, which could reveal their secrets to Public Security. Her worries faded as they began to descend the southern slope of the huge mountain and she spoke to her horse in admiring tones, sometimes even singing old songs from Tibetan horse festivals. She even asked Shan wary questions about Lhasa and asked him to explain what the Olympics were. She reminded him a lot of Yara, another bright, inquisitive woman who had been denied a broader engagement with the world.

"I was honored to meet Yankay last night," Shan said.

"He seemed . . ." Jaya tried to find a word, "comfortable with you."

"I sensed he was somehow sad about being a hail chaser."

Jaya nodded. "He says his soul is always itching, and he does not know how to scratch it. Sometimes Uncle Yankay says he is just the edge of a sword that can never be sharpened."

Shan looked at her in surprise. "Your uncle? Yankay and Lhakpa are brothers?" He had not understood the connection between the two men, just as he had not understood Lhakpa's bitter statement uttered when Shan had described the death of the old lama at the 404th. *It should have been me*, he had said, as if Lhakpa had wanted to die.

"Yes. Yankay is many years older and as the first son had gone to a monastery. He was still a novice when the Chinese army came. He had always felt he would be a hail chaser, for even as a boy something inside him stirred at the coming of storms and earthquakes. His gompa had two of the most celebrated hail chasers in all of Tibet, who had begun to teach him. But they died when the Chinese came, and he fled into a cave with some of their books. Once when I was seven or eight I saw a demon dancing above our barley field, dressed in twigs and grass, with a long white horse tail fixed to a staff. My mother said, 'That's no demon, that's your uncle Yankay.' He would come like that every few months, and my mother would have me take a sack of barley and leave it at the edge of the field for him.

"Then after my parents died, I lived with neighbors and he would still come, though my new family had little to spare. I would save half the barley I was supposed to eat and give it to him. Once there was a letter on the rock where I left his food. It simply said, *Jaya, I will try to be near, but I cannot be at your side, for your own safety.* After that, he would leave letters each time he came, and when I was twelve he wrote that I must go to school and bloom into the flower I was meant to be." She grew melancholy for a moment, then brightened. "He didn't know I was going to be a prickly rose," she said and urged her horse down the trail.

When they reached his truck, he expected her to quickly ride back up the mountain, but instead she dismounted and tied the horses to a gnarled pine. At first, she walked cautiously toward the truck, watching the surrounding outcroppings, but then she abruptly gasped and ran past him.

Shan stared in some chagrin as she excitedly pointed to half a dozen pockmarks on the hood and roof of his truck. The storm from the night had brought hail to Ice Ball Alley.

"Look!" Jaya exclaimed, pointing in turn to each of the dents, which looked like they had been made by hail the size of ping-pong balls.

"I should have parked lower on the slope," Shan said.

"No, no! You don't understand! The water from the melted hail is in each of the dents! The old ones claim such water is very powerful, straight from the hands of the earth gods. They soak charms in it. We must save it!"

In an energetic search of Shan's truck, the Tibetan woman found an old drinking straw and an empty soda bottle left by the soldier who had followed Zhu in Shan's vehicle the night they had driven to Lhadrung from Lhasa. Jaya cleansed both in the spring at the nearby pilgrims' rest, then, clamping a thumb over one end of the straw, used it to suction up the water. She collected less than two inches in the bottle but pressed the sacred water to her breast for a quick prayer, then made Shan hold it while she carved a plug from a piece of the old pine. She carefully secured the bottle in the bag behind her saddle but hesitated before mounting. "Do you need that old newspaper on the seat?" she asked, then quickly snatched it up when Shan gestured to it with a nod. "Do you have any tape? String?"

Despite his confusion, Shan let her search the truck more thoroughly, and soon she added to her saddlebag a roll of adhesive tape from his small medical kit and a length of thin wire from his glove box. She looked longingly at Shan's high boots, and with a grin he gave up his laces. Then she put her hand on the canvas medical kit, emitting a joyful cry when he nodded again. To his surprise she gave him a quick embrace before darting to the horses. He watched, amused and still confused, as she trotted up the slope, then he filled his water bottle at the pilgrim spring and climbed back into his truck.

He had driven almost an hour before he noticed that in searching the glove box Jaya had left his new satellite phone on the seat, under his maps. He switched it on. Five minutes later it rang.

Amah Jiejie spoke in a peeved tone. "The colonel gave you the phone for communication, not as a paperweight. He's been trying to reach you since yesterday afternoon."

"I've been in the mountains," Shan said, before he realized it was no excuse for a satellite phone.

He could hear her sigh. "I'll tell him you had battery problems. Hold on."

Tan was never one for the niceties of conversation. "My janitor was attacked," the colonel declared. "He's in the hospital."

"I'm sorry?"

"Jampa, the one who smuggled out the message from Metok. Thieves assaulted him. How soon can you get to the hospital?"

Lhadrung's small infirmary had grown as the army had expanded its presence in the town, so that it now sat not at the edge of town but at the edge of the sprawling military compound that adjoined the town, with a new wing that provided a door for civilians at the front and one for military patients at the rear. The hospital's handful of doctors were all army officers.

Major Xun was waiting at the front steps and escorted Shan around the building to the military entrance. Tan was pacing, very impatiently, outside a patient room on the first floor, next to the small emergency center. Jampa, the old Tibetan Shan had met at Tan's office, lay in the solitary bed inside, his face and hands swollen and bandaged. His eyes were fixed so blankly on the ceiling that Shan thought he was dead. Tan motioned Shan inside and shut the door, leaving Xun in the corridor.

"I don't care about Metok or Huan right now," the colonel snapped. "I want the bastards who did this!"

"What happened?"

"He was set upon in an alley last night. In my town! Took what little money he had and fled, the cowards! I want you to find whoever did this and I will personally inflict blows to match what they did to him!"

Shan lifted the chart from the bedstand then looked again at the man's arms, one of which was broken, held up in a sling, exposing its tattooed number. Jampa had been a prisoner, one of the many who found menial jobs in Lhadrung after release because travel papers were denied them. He gazed for a moment at the man, wondering what he had been before imprisonment.

Tan followed his gaze. "Yes, a convict. But he was a good man. He had been a scribe in the old days, you know, making those manuscripts the Tibetans use." The colonel caught himself. "He was tainted by his reactionary ways but was cured of them. We never talked about all that. He paid his price and learned very passable Chinese during his time. Reformed his ways," Tan added uneasily.

Years earlier it would have been unheard of for the tyrant of Lhadrung to engage in conversation with a former prisoner, let alone befriend and defend one. Was the colonel just finding compromise, or growing weak? Probably, Shan decided, Tan would consider them the same thing.

He read the rest of the chart, then studied the old Tibetan more closely. Broken arm, broken ankle, and a skull fracture. His assailants had used a metal bar on him, probably a reinforcing rod from one of the construction sites, judging by the ridges Shan saw along the fracture of his skull. But none of these would kill him. What was killing him was his ruptured kidney.

"Jampa!" Tan said, barking the name like an order. The old man stirred slowly, painfully turning his head toward Tan to smile. His chest rattled as he breathed. His body seemed to shake and he nodded. Then he looked at Shan with pleading eyes and the rattling stopped.

"Jampa!" Tan shook the man's shoulder.

Shan lifted the Tibetan's wrist, searching for a pulse. "He's gone, Colonel."

Tan seemed not to hear. "Jampa!" he repeated, then turned to Shan. "Get a doctor!"

"He's dead."

Tan collapsed onto the bedside chair. "He wasn't so old really, only seventy-four, he told me last week. He said he knew a place where we could go fishing, up in the hills." He looked up with despair. "Find those damned thieves!"

"It wasn't thieves," Shan said, still feeling the shock of those beseeching eyes. "Somehow the killers found out that he had delivered the message from Metok. They had to silence him. What else did he know?"

"He never said anything more to me. I only saw him once since the day he delivered Metok's message. He was terrified. He said he had stopped sleeping so he could spend his free time praying."

"Lieutenant Huan," Shan said. "You need to find out if he was in Lhadrung last night."

Tan cursed, then nodded. He lifted the dead man's gnarled, withered hand and clasped it between his own hands. After several breaths he turned away to summon an army doctor, who bent over Jampa for a moment, glanced at his watch, and made a note on the dead man's chart. "Dr. Anwei," Tan muttered in introduction to Shan, then threw an unwelcoming glance at Xun, who had followed the doctor into the room.

"The other one has to go now," Anwei declared.

"Other one?" Shan asked.

The doctor gestured with his pen toward the door adjoining the room. "The old man in the bathroom. He said he could make any place an altar." The doctor suddenly saw Colonel Tan's withering glance. "They were friends. It seemed to calm the patient," he added.

The scent of incense wafted from the darkened bathroom as Shan opened the door. He could hear a whispered mantra and the rattle of rosary beads. Major Xun pushed past Shan and switched on the light. Suddenly the painful visit to the hospital became a nightmare.

Sitting on the floor before a smoky cone of incense was Shan's old friend Lokesh. The aged Tibetan looked up, blinking from the harsh, sudden light. "You can join me!" he said as he recognized Shan. Lokesh, who had once worked in the Dalai Lama's government, had spent most of his life behind the wire of prison camps. Shan had been nearly dead, in body and soul, when he had first collapsed onto a bunk in the 404th People's Construction Brigade. More than anyone else, Lokesh had been responsible for reviving him, first nursing him to health and then nurturing his spirit. The gentle old Tibetan, long suffering from guilt over being a citizen of the government that had destroyed Tibet, had absolved it by destroying his identity card and now lived in a secret outpost helping the resistance preserve old manuscripts.

"Whatever are you doing here?" Shan demanded. Tan's anger was visibly rising. Xun pushed forward to see Lokesh.

"Helping Jampa recover!" Lokesh explained in Tibetan. "He had written to me, said terrible things were happening in Lhadrung, and that he and I should take some days together to build a mandala in the old style, so the gods would pay better attention to events here." He was referring to the sand paintings of intricate symbols and patterns that once had been one of the most sacred elements of Buddhist ritual.

Shan helped the old man to his feet. Xun had fixed Tan with an expectant look, waiting for the signal to detain Lokesh. If arrested, he would spend the rest of his life in prison, assuming he would survive his interrogation. "It's too late," Shan said as Lokesh rose. With a wrenching groan Lokesh stumbled to the dead man's bed. Low sounds of despair escaped his throat, and he bent over Jampa, urgently whispering the first words of the Bardo, the death ceremony that was needed to ease the old man's passage into the next life.

Surprisingly no one uttered a word, and no one tried to stop Lokesh. After two or three minutes he straightened and spoke to Shan, but switched to Mandarin as if to taunt Tan and Xun. "In the letter Jampa sent me he said a man named Metok was being falsely condemned to death, that Metok was being executed because he knew certain things about that new project on the sacred mountain."

A tight knot formed in Shan's belly. "You need to go," he said, pulling on Lokesh's arm. "My truck is outside."

"No, not possible. I will have to stay here, to help Jampa. Someone has to say the death rites."

Xun laughed. Tan glared at Shan, who desperately looked about the chamber as if it might reveal a solution. He spied a bag of clothing on a chair in the corner.

"You don't have to be beside his body," Shan reminded Lokesh. "You just have to be in touch with his spirit."

"It's better to be with the body for the first day or two of the rites," Lokesh replied.

"Not possible," Shan pushed back as he retrieved the bag of clothing. "This is an army base."

"He was one of my closest friends in prison during my first twenty years. I knew him as a boy even, Shan, before I was . . ." Lokesh had the sense not to announce his old role in the Dalai Lama's government. "I knew him before."

Shan lifted the bag. "We will take his mala and his gau. We will take his belongings. His spirit will follow. We will arrange them somewhere in Yangkar, and you can sit with them and continue the Bardo."

"But I need to confront the evil men here with the truth," Lokesh protested, still speaking in Mandarin. "I promised Jampa. They need cleansing, or more evil will follow."

Tan looked like he was close to erupting. Xun watched with a ravenous expression.

"Look to Jampa's spirit first," Shan said. Lokesh contemplated Shan's words then slowly nodded his agreement and removed Jampa's gau and mala. The old man shook them over Jampa's head, as if to get the dead man's attention, then slowly backed out of the room, the rosary and prayer amulet raised in the air as he continued the words of the death ritual.

Shan had loaded Lokesh into his vehicle under the watchful eye of Major Xun when he realized he had forgotten Jampa's shoes, which Lokesh would want for his ritual. As he lifted them from under the dead man's bed he heard a quiet sob and looked up to see Amah Jiejie sitting on a chair in the shadowed corner.

"He never hurt anyone," she said with a sob as Shan approached. "He never deserved this." The matronly Chinese woman dabbed at her cheek, then fixed her eyes on Jampa. "He was softening the colonel, helping us understand things."

"Us?" Shan asked.

She nodded. "I was frightened for my life and Jampa took away my fear."

Shan pulled up a chair beside her. "Please, I want to hear about it."

The gray-haired woman spoke in a whisper, watching the door. "Last month something terrible happened. Jampa helped me. It was a piece of paper rolled up and inserted into the eye sockets of a little animal skull, left in my lunch bag. The paper had words in Tibetan and terrible drawings. A big scorpion. A fox or a wolf, rows of human skulls, and above them a sketch of a larger skull, with three eye holes. It was a death threat, what else could it be? Jampa found me staring at it, pale as a ghost. But Jampa took it and said not to worry. He threw the skull out the window and said the paper was more like someone's bad joke."

"Why would he call it a joke?" Shan asked.

Amah Jiejie reached down and extracted a wad of paper from the bottom of the big bag she used as a purse. "I wasn't sure how to destroy it. I was going to ask Jampa."

Shan took the paper and straightened it, pressing out the many creases against the wall. It was a Tibetan death curse, or rather some-one's idea of a Tibetan curse.

"Jampa said the words weren't right and that the three-eyed skull wasn't a Buddhist thing at all, so it had no effect, it represented no danger."

Shan saw that the old Tibetan had been right. He had seen death threats, and this was just a poor imitation of one.

"It still scares me, Shan. Maybe it wasn't really a death curse but surely it was meant as one."

"No, just meant to scare you, to have you think Tibetans were stalking you," Shan told her. It meant, he knew, that whoever had done this had not been Tibetan.

She nodded. "I suppose."

Shan folded the paper. "May I keep this?"

"Yes, yes, please do," Amah Jiejie said. "But just don't . . ." her voice trailed off

"Don't what?"

"Please don't tell the colonel, Shan. He would worry."

Shan passed a desperate night at a pilgrims' rest near the road to the prison camp, keeping nervous watch as Lokesh, Jampa's belongings arranged before him on a rock, continued reciting the death rites, which would take days to complete. He relented only for quick swallows from Shan's water bottle and bites of the rice cakes Shan had in his pack, then later, long after midnight, for quick responses to Shan's questions about his trip to Lhadrung. Lokesh had hitched a ride on a truck with a Tibetan driver after riding a horse to the nearest road. The joyful old man, who was like a close uncle to Shan, was showing conspicuous signs of his age. His firm, steady stride which had taken them over hundreds of miles of pilgrims' trails, had slowed and some-times was only a tenuous shuffle. His bright eyes were watery, and at times Shan saw a tremor in one hand.

They were outside the gate when the boxy old sedan, dented and badly in need of new paint, pulled up at the 404th People's Construction Brigade. They had not been the first in line despite arriving before dawn, and Shan recalled from his years as an inmate that relatives often arrived the day before for the infrequent family visitation days, spending the night in sleeping bags or wrapped in blankets, sometimes after traveling for days.

"I'm sorry, Tserung," he said as the mechanic wearily climbed from behind the wheel. Shan had called to ask him to bring Yara for the long-awaited visit when he had realized he would never make it to Yangkar and back in time. "But at least you have a companion for the ride home. Find a safe place for him until I get back," Shan said and opened the back door of his car.

"Lokesh!" Yara exclaimed. Her cry awakened the old man, who groggily returned her embrace and let himself be pulled to Tserung's car.

Ko was no longer counted among the high-risk prisoners, so he was not chained to a chair for the visit but rather allowed into a side yard, enclosed with razor wire, with other prisoners and their families. Mothers and wives wept. Fathers and sons clenched their jaws and tried not to glare at the armed guards as the thin, ragged prisoners filed in, some supported by other inmates. Half a dozen prisoners, the oldest, never had visitors but were allowed to sit at the perimeter and contentedly watch the brief, tearful reunions. The families of hard labor prisoners never knew whether a loved one would survive to the next visit. More than once Shan had seen family members collapse, sobbing, as they were greeted not by the prisoner they had come to see but by a certificate attesting to his death.

Shan hung back as Ko appeared, letting Yara run forward and wrap her arms around him. They held each other tightly, without a word, until a couple of prisoners nearby noticed and laughed. When Ko finally released the Tibetan woman, there was a new, deep strength behind his eyes. Yara recalled the bags Shan had carried from Tserung's car. Prisoners were not permitted to take food back into their barracks but could eat in the yard, and she unpacked a bag of Mar-pa's momo dumplings. Then, in a custom she had established the year before, she walked with a second bag to the sergeant of the guards and placed it at his feet, with a murmured blessing. The sergeant responded with a stern, tight nod.

Shan gave his son and Yara time to speak alone by going to the circle of old men. He knew most of the aged lamas and pushed down his emotion as he struggled to keep their conversation cheerful, try-ing to ignore how frail some had become. He had his own bag of momos which he distributed among them, and the rail-thin prisoners accepted them with an eager gratitude that made him feel shamed for being so well-fed himself.

There were thirty minutes left in the visitation period when he re-turned to Ko. Yara stood at his side, holding his calloused hand, as Shan asked about the prisoners from Larung Gar.

"Good men, every one of them," his son reported. "They're not in my barracks but sometimes I work with them. They hold teachings in the night. Some from other barracks sneak out after curfew to go listen."

"You mustn't!" Yara interrupted. Being caught outside one's bar-racks after curfew brought at least a month's solitary confinement.

"I only went the one time," Ko said. "They had an altar made out of an old carton and they had made clever cardboard cutouts that by themselves looked like nothing more than the remnants of cardboard men stuff in their clothing for insulation. But when fitted together they made the images of gods and deity protectors. They spoke of the timelessness of who we are. At first I didn't understand, but by the end I grasped that they were saying that the difficulties of our existence don't really matter, that what mattered was the chain of compassion and truth that had connected humans for thousands of years, and that was more important than any physical chains that may encum-ber us."

Ko hesitated, seeing the surprised looks of both Shan and Yara.

They were not used to him waxing philosophically. He flushed. "Any of those momos left?"

As he ate the last dumpling, Ko recalled an odd story he had heard from two different prisoners in the barracks of the Larung Gar men. "There was one who didn't seem to belong with them at first. It was almost like they didn't know him, and one of my friends said at night they gave him extra blessings and thanked him for his sacrifice, like he was enduring a greater hardship than the others. And during those early days there were times when he seemed not to respond to his name, though most dismissed that because everyone knows how the shock of arriving here plays games with your mind."

"What was his name?" Shan asked.

"Lin. Lin Fochow."

Shan weighed the news a moment. "Tell me, son, the day those prisoners arrived, when their convoy came with the two dead soldiers, were the prisoners all wearing robes?"

Ko thought a moment then nodded. "Seven men, all but one in robes, yes. All wearing wool caps pulled low over their heads. No one would have seen except like I said they came in as we were unloading from the work crew trucks."

"Seven? I thought there were six prisoners."

"Six in robes for the 404th. Another Tibetan man who was pounded by a Public Security officer with his baton and immediately shoved into one of the knob cars after being pulled from a truck. The officer drove away with him."

Shan realized that Ko had seen Lieutenant Huan take Yankay the hail chaser away to face murder charges. He glanced at his watch. Their time was almost over, and he did not want to spend what was left speaking of his investigation. "Marpa says he wants to plan a big feast for next time you come to visit," Shan said, forcing a smile. While Ko had been given a brief parole months earlier, no others had followed, and there was no way to predict when Tan would allow another. It could be in two months or two years. Ko had been convicted of several crimes, some of which carried indefinite sentences, subject to the review of his file every two years.

"A lammergeier!" Yara called and pointed nearly straight up toward a huge bird soaring overhead. "A good sign, Ko!"

Ko lifted his head to follow her pointing arm, and Shan saw a long bruise on his neck that disappeared under his shirt. "What happened?" he asked with a gesture to the injury.

Ko snapped his head down. "It's nothing. From work. I fell down when pushing a wheelbarrow and the handle slammed into me," he said, then pointed toward a nearby family, where three children had formed a circle around a prisoner and were singing to him. Shan smiled and accepted his son's obvious change of subject, knowing he had made up the story of how the injury had happened. Sometimes there were fights among prisoners, often Chinese versus Tibetans, but Ko was smarter than to be drawn into such feuds. More painful to contemplate was the alternative. Most of the guards knew Ko was his son. Ko was his weak spot. If he hadn't been in brawls with other prisoners, then his injuries could only mean he was being beaten by the guards.

CHAPTER TEN

Tserung the mechanic laughed when Shan asked about Lokesh, saying that the old man had indeed immediately gone into the archives when they had arrived in Yangkar, as Shan expected, but had not stayed. Lokesh had recalled that Tserung had mentioned during their drive to town that Yara's grandparents were visiting for the coming livestock market and had gone to find them. Yara reacted to the news with a nervous laugh and motioned Shan back into the truck.

The compound beyond the edge of town that she directed him to had once belonged to one of the most important of the farming families in the region and had sat abandoned for decades, except for the sheep and goats who found their way into the old stables during winter storms. Most of the local residents avoided the buildings because they were said to be haunted.

"The family was executed by the Red Guard," Yara explained in a matter-of-fact voice as Shan parked the truck at the end of the rutted track that led to the farmhouse. "But my grandparents had been close friends and prayed for their spirits for many years after." They began to walk up the overgrown track, which showed no sign of use in recent years. "They're getting too old for the harsh winters. When I took them here my grandmother was frightened at first but bravely ventured inside, telling us not to follow, and prayed for nearly an hour. When she came out she was excited and said the old ones weren't angry or vengeful, that they were just lonely and would welcome the sound of laughter inside the walls again. The first thing she did was make a little altar for us to revive the prayers the house had once known."

As they reached the tall double-doored gate in the compound wall, each of its panels hanging on one hinge, Shan saw that the compound had clearly once been the center of a large and prosperous farm. A two-story stone house, wind-battered but still solid, formed the anchor of the weed-infested courtyard, with a second one-story house forming an adjacent side, probably where extended family or farm workers had lived. An open-fronted shed that included an old forge lined the side opposite the smaller house, and a sizable barn took up the entire side opposite the main house, completing the square.

"This place is big enough for a whole clan," Shan observed as Yara led him toward the smaller house, the entrance of which evidenced a fresh coat of maroon paint and several carefully inscribed auspicious signs that looked like the work of Shiva. Inside, the air was tinged with a combination of incense and smoke from the cigars that were the primary vice of Yara's grandmother Lhamo. A small dog yapped and bounded through an inner doorway to greet Yara, followed by Yara's son, Ati. The adolescent boy excitedly introduced Shan to the dog, then sobered as a droning voice carried from the shadowed door-way at the far side of the chamber. Shan stepped through the passage and discovered Lokesh at a long, low table upon which the tattered clothing, shoes, and other belongings of Jampa had been laid out in the shape of the dead man. Lokesh was continuing the death rites.

"He helped us cut fresh juniper for the room where our sleeping pallets are," came a familiar voice at Shan's shoulder, and he turned with a smile to greet Lhamo. "He recited some prayers at our altar, even sang one of the old kitchen god songs he remembered from his childhood over our cooking brazier, then said he had a sacred duty to perform."

"An old friend died," was the only explanation Shan offered, and Lhamo gave a meaningful nod. "He'll stay in there for days probably, and just take *tsampa* and water for nourishment."

Lhamo nodded again. She had probably lost count of the number of death rites she and her husband had conducted through the years. "Except he wants to go to Shiva in the morning, he says," the old woman explained, "to get a death chart started."

Shan went to a window, several panes of which were broken, and gazed out at the compound. Despite the weeds that had overtaken the courtyard, the decrepit condition of the barn roof, and the faded paint on the walls, it still had the air of a sturdy, welcoming outpost. Undoubtedly the farm's expansive fields had provided food for the monastery for decades, if not centuries, and pilgrims had probably slept in the courtyard, singing their songs of devotion into the night. The compound commanded a view of the rolling hills in each direction for nearly a mile and was obscured from the town by a low ridge that was ablaze with spring flowers. Yara's grandparents, like Lokesh, were ferals, Tibetans without identity cards, and for most of their lives they had avoided towns. The compound was probably the safest place for them, at least for now.

"I will bring food later," he said, then excused himself. Choden would be getting off duty soon.

Only two reports awaited Shan on his desk. Mrs. Lu had caught the incorrigible young girl with Meng's companion throwing stones at the bust of Chairman Mao and the Committee of Leading Citizens had demanded that Choden arrest her.

"They're still here? You arrested her?" Shan asked his deputy, who looked up with a sheepish expression.

"If I hadn't, Mrs. Lu was going to thrash her with a belt."

Shan opened the door to the back room. The cells were empty.

Choden shrugged. "She slipped out between the bars. She's very thin. But I can truthfully report to Mrs. Lu that I did put her in jail."

"And?"

"That woman with Lieutenant Meng was waiting at the back step. She seemed to expect it, as if it were not the first time the girl had broken out of jail. Buddha's Breath! She can't be more than five!"

"Meng wouldn't stop the girl?" Shan was reluctantly reaching the point at which he was going to demand they leave town. Surely Meng understood the girl could not stay.

"She was feeling poorly, took to bed."

Shan shook his head in frustration and read the second report, then looked up. "You can't file this. An 'obstruction of an emergency vehicle'? What does that mean? What ambulance? I've never seen one anywhere close to here."

"I didn't know how else to explain it. It was that old rescue truck they keep at the highway equipment station on the road to Lhadrung town for bad highway accidents. Someone called them and said a Tibetan herder had been hit on the highway and seemed to be close to death. When the rescue truck got there a herd of sheep surrounded it, so the driver and attendant got out and pushed through to the man who had been struck. But he had regained consciousness, said he was fine, and couldn't leave his herd. So they treated a few scratches, gave him some medicine and left. Except later they called to say the medical pack was gone from the back of the truck."

"Medical pack?"

"Like a big metal suitcase, they said, full of medical equipment and medicines. Except then the driver said the attendant was a damned fool and may have forgotten to put it in the truck. They have several and couldn't find any inventory list to confirm one was missing."

Shan read the report again then ripped it in half and dropped it in the trash can. A phone message had been underneath it, from Amah Jiejie. Lieutenant Huan, she reported, had been in Lhasa the night of the attack on Jampa. Shan wearily braced his head in his hands, elbows on his desk, feeling his exhaustion. He watched Choden, willing him to sign out and go home so he might nap in a cell. But suddenly his deputy was at the window, studying two figures in hooded sweatshirts who were now sitting on a bench in the square, watching a half dozen sheep who were eating one of the new flowering shrubs Mrs. Lu had planted. Shan was about to tell Choden to go disperse the sheep when his deputy pointed to a white utility vehicle parked on the square. "Lhasa plates. Everyone gets lost in Yangkar these days."

Shan studied the two figures a moment. "Go home," he ordered, then waited while his deputy disappeared down the street before venturing out on the square.

"I love this town!" Cato Pike exclaimed as Shan sat beside him. "I am a connoisseur of forgotten places, and this one looks like it has been forgotten in so many centuries it practically doesn't exist!"

"Sometimes the only way to be free is to be forgotten," Shan replied.

"In other words, Yangkar is a Chinese paradise. Hell, it's not even on the road map. We had to stop and ask a herder."

"The mapmakers are all from Beijing. They decided to call it Buzhou. There used to be a sign saying that, but a yak knocked it down."

"And the constable chose not to put it up again. I imagine your Chinese residents didn't much like that."

"Staying forgotten requires sacrifices," Shan said, choosing not to mention that the Committee of Leading Citizens had erected their own sign and Shan had knocked it down with his truck and blamed a yak.

Pike gave a quiet laugh. "My life story in four words," he said.

Shan paused, studying the American, but decided not to press for an explanation. Pike was a strong bull of a man, and his eyes burned with a penetrating intelligence, but Shan had begun to also see a deep sadness etched on his countenance. He was a man who had experienced a great deal of the world and seemed to have given up on much of it. He was a loner who seemed to have left behind the anchors that kept most lives on track, and now had lost his daughter in a forgotten land.

A melancholy grin flickered on Pike's face as he watched Cao climb up the steps of the tower at the end of the square, and Shan realized the student's energetic curiosity probably reminded Pike of his daughter. He made a sweeping gesture that took in the square and the buildings around it. "There are layers of time here," the American declared. "The scale is all wrong. Once something much bigger occupied this space."

Shan nodded. "A gompa, a monastery. The tower was part of the gatehouse."

Pike weighed Shan's words. "A major gompa. One of the big regional ones," he suggested.

Shan nodded again. "Hundreds of monks, and a medical college in the hills above town. The army left only the tower, because it was a convenient watch post."

"More of the forgotten landscape."

"The Tibetans haven't forgotten it. Sometimes I think they believe the old gompa is still here, invisible to all but the devout. On still nights when the wind isn't blowing people say they can hear the old horns that called monks to prayer. Some of the old ones walk around the square in a crooked path because they say they are avoiding the sacred chortens that stood there for centuries, as if they could still see them. More and more of the devout are coming back because of those stories. Sometimes I see them sitting and praying in front of the empty spaces. On Buddha's birthday last year flowers and boughs of juniper appeared in the night, laid out in squares where the old chortens were."

Pike gazed at the empty space with a strange longing. "My daughter Natalie found something special in Tibet, Shan," he confided. "She wrote me about it. She said she now understood that her job was to bring old ghosts to life. She said that what people didn't understand was that the ghosts are us."

The words sent a chill down Shan's back. It sounded like something Lokesh would say. He wished he had been able to meet such a wise woman.

They sat in silence, watching a ball of dried weeds blow down the square.

"You didn't come all the way from Lhasa to philosophize about Tibet," Shan said.

"I came because I know not to trust email or cell phones in this country," the American stated, and produced a thick envelope from inside his sweatshirt and handed it to Shan. It contained copies of emails from the Five Claws.

Pike provided a commentary as Shan leafed through them. "The deputy director demands that the director put a halt to a visit by the Bureau of Religious Affairs, stating that they have no jurisdiction in the valley. Next the director is urgently requesting the public works office in Sichuan Province to send more Chinese workers but is told none would be available for several months." Pike pointed to another message Shan was scanning. "The director asks Jiao where he is and Jiao says he had important meetings of his working group in Lhasa. The director asks what working group and Jiao just replies the one engaged in vital work for the motherland, that's all you need to know. Then comes a series of messages about shifting funds from bridge and highway sites all over Tibet to the Five Claws project, which were odd enough to make me pause but probably just typical bureaucratic exchanges in China."

Finally came a long exchange that Shan had to read in detail to fully grasp. Jiao was asking Huan to check on known associates of a troublemaking professor from Larung Gar, suggesting that Public Security review his colleagues at the university in Tientsen where he had once taught. Jiao reminded Huan that the professor had demanded a halt to the construction at the Five Claws pending further study, claiming the site might be too unstable geologically to support the dam. Jiao was worried that the professor may have sewn dissident seeds at his old university and that other associates might try to oppose the Five Claws.

Shan asked if Pike could search the name he had heard from Ko.

Pike laughed when he heard the name. "That's the very man, Shan, the professor Jiao was complaining about! Professor Lin Fochow. Jiao told Huan to remind his colleagues in Tientsen that the professor had been such a problem at Larung Gar that he and five other hotheads had been sent directly to the 404th hard labor prison, on the grounds that they were a threat to national security."

Shan stared at the last email, trying to understand. The dissident professor had become the prisoner who couldn't remember his own name, the professor who had arrived at prison wearing a monk's robe. Had he been beaten so badly he had suffered brain damage? Shan's foreboding began to descend on him again. Every time he thought he had found one answer, two more questions seemed to rise. He wasn't confronting a murder, he was tumbling into a black hole of violent intrigue and politics.

"You should go home, Pike," Shan said. "If you stay, you'll become another ghost."

Pike seemed not to hear. "She was just getting a foothold on life," he said in a distant voice. "She stumbled early on, raised by her mother. I was never there for her. Mostly sent to boarding schools. Then when her mother remarried, she suddenly had stepsisters who seemed determined to drive her out of their family. We only grew close later, when she moved to a college near my home. I started declining trips so I could spend more time with her. Then I introduced her to the son of an old army buddy, an officer in the Army Rangers, and months later they were engaged. When he was deployed to Afghanistan, he made her promise to finish her college work while he was away, and she made him promise they would get married as soon as he returned. But he didn't return. Killed by an explosive device when driving some Afghan girls to a school on his day off. It took her over a year to recover. This trip to Tibet was her way of starting over, making a clean break. She was enrolled in graduate school, ready to start when she returned." Pike clenched his jaw, as if choking down emotion.

"Before she left I told her she was the miracle of my life, my anchor that let me withstand all the storms that raged around me. She smiled and said then we had given each other a miracle and promised to write me every week. She did for the first month and wrote that she had discovered the importance of committing to something bigger than yourself."

"You should go home," Shan said again. "It's what she would want. Stay alive."

The American looked down into his hands with a weary expression then extracted a tattered envelope from inside his sweatshirt. "Her last letter. I must have read it a hundred times." He handed it to Shan.

Dear Papa, Shan read. *Professor Gangfen says I am learning to adeptly straddle the centuries as we dig, which I think he means as a compliment. This week I unearthed a nearly intact bridle with a bronze bit all on my own!* The letter went on to describe how she had made new friends and spent the weekend in Lhasa, where she had gone to the magnificent Potala and the ancient temple complex.

"The last paragraph," Pike said. "She added it later."

Shan skipped to the bottom of the second page. *I have seen something terrible, which I may not write about. It felt like a dagger in my heart at first, but I am learning Tibetan ways to resolve things. There's no better place to learn that you can fight monsters without becoming one yourself. If you want to have a soul here, every man must be a monk and every woman a nun, and all must be outlaws.* Lha gyal lo, *Nat.*

"*Lha gyal lo,*" Pike said. "I hear Tibetans say it."

"It means victory to the gods," Shan said as he handed the letter back.

"Is that a prayer or a war cry?" the American asked.

The letter had only increased Shan's foreboding. "You need to go home," he tried for a third time.

Pike gave a bitter grin. "You don't understand, Shan. Natalie was one of the only people I ever cared about in all this big world, in recent years. She's been the only thing in my life that has meant anything to me. And she died in an ancient cave trying to save gods. The bastards killed her. They murdered her. Did you really think I was just going to take some photos and fly home?"

"You can't do anything by yourself," Shan said.

"You can't do anything by yourself," Pike shot back.

The words hurt, not so much because they were from a foreigner, but because they were true.

"You and I aren't much different, Shan," the American said. "We hate what our worlds have become and the only way we can stay true to ourselves is to push back against those worlds. The only difference is that I push back more physically than you do."

"What you did to that man in the crematorium was cruel," Shan said.

Pike shrugged. "I didn't light the oven."

They silently watched a donkey cart filled with cabbages traverse the square. "A witness was killed in Lhadrung yesterday," Shan said at last, and began explaining what had happened to the unlucky janitor.

"You don't know for certain who did it," Pike said. It sounded almost like an accusation.

"No," Shan admitted. "It was not Lieutenant Huan. It was someone close to the colonel who is allied with Huan in Lhasa. Someone who knew about Jampa delivering Metok's message, even though we thought only the colonel, Amah Jiejie and myself knew about it. They knew that Jampa could be a witness against them."

"If you want to catch a fox, you have to set a trap," Pike suggested. "But first you have to find the bait that will attract it."

"I'm sorry?" Shan replied, with an eye on Cao, who had returned to the square. To Shan's great surprise he was walking in the same patterns as the old Tibetans, as if the Chinese scholar also saw the phantom shrines. He knelt at one of the invisible stopping places, unfolded a pocketknife, and used its blade to dig. After a few moments he nodded, as if confirming a discovery.

Cao gave a self-conscious grin as Shan and Pike approached him at the third such stop. "An earth-taming temple," the Chinese student declared, and gestured at a stone foundation he had uncovered six inches below the surface. "The gompa here must have been an earth-taming temple," he said, referring to the ancient sites that had been constructed to subdue the demons under the earth.

"I don't know," Shan admitted.

"No, no, I am telling you. This was an earth-taming temple site, a very important one." He pointed to smudges on the wall of the tower, then took out a small notepad and drew a series of symbols stacked one on top of the other. "A sun, a moon, an empty lotus throne to welcome the god, hovering over mountains. And a garuda bird, I think, though it is mostly a smudge. Earth-taming signs," he explained.

Shan stared in disbelief. He had taken the patches of discoloration on the crumbling stucco of the wall to be nothing more than water stains, but now as Cao held up his drawing so he could compare it to the stains, he could see that indeed the faded patterns corresponded with the symbols in shape and placement.

Cao bent and scooped away more of the dirt, revealing cobblestones around the foundation. "There was a great paved courtyard, and the small foundations mark the pattern used for the old dances, the ritual *cham* dances done to honor the good earth spirits and discourage the evil ones. This was the courtyard of a great temple," he said, pointing to the exposed cobbles. "The professor and I have seen this before. Religious Affairs and the army were in a great hurry to obliterate everything fifty years ago, so they just dumped a few inches of soil on top and called it a park."

Shan recalled complaints from those who tried to plant in the square about the many stones they encountered. He extracted the paper he had taken from the mess hall bulletin board at the Five Claws project, the satellite photo embellished with new lines. It had some of the same signs drawn across the top.

"Exactly," Cao said.

Shan stared at him, not comprehending. "It's an aerial photo of the dam site with some lines drawn to suggest some kind of body."

"No," Cao said. "It's more like the sketch of a *thangka,* a devotional painting. The ancient ones saw it as clearly as if they were flying overhead on garudas. It's probably why the valley is so sacred, why your town had an earth-taming temple." Cao saw Shan's lingering confusion, so took out a pencil, laid the paper on a bench, and with a few quick strokes, embellished and extended the lines drawn on the photo, making the upper lake look more like a head, the cupping ridges at the top like arms, and the bottom ridges like legs. "Don't you see?" he soberly said as he held it up. A chill went down Shan's spine as he recognized the image from the drawings he had seen in the archives. "It's the most terrible of the earth demons," the Chinese scholar continued. "The grandfather warrior, they call him, those who are awakening him now to protect the earth. It's Gekho the Wrathful Destroyer."

While Cao continued his exploration of the square, Shan and Pike sat in the station, eating a meal Marpa had delivered as Shan explained what happened in Lhadrung.

"You say this started with an execution that was a murder," Pike said. The slow fire of anger that always seemed to burn in his eyes had crept into his voice. "But it really started with the murder of my daughter and the professor." Shan nodded his agreement. "And now we have the murder of a witness in Lhadrung and a suggestion that all this may really have started at this school, this Larung Gar place. You have an annoying habit, Shan, of identifying more crimes but never the faces of the criminals. It's the story of modern China," the American observed. "Feed the outrage but never aim at the cause unless the Party bosses so direct."

"I know Huan's face, and that of Jiao, at least. And if I were in the habit of kowtowing to Party bosses, I never would have gone to prison."

"Still, you haven't a shred of evidence against Huan or Jiao, against anyone."

"I am open to suggestion."

"Already told you. When you find the right bait, you can always trap a fox. We're going to create an urgent problem that Huan's con-

tact in Lhadrung has to respond to. We'll smoke him out. If it's someone close to Colonel Tan it shouldn't be so difficult," the American
suggested, and his eyes lit with a new excitement.

As usual, Amah Jiejie responded with cunning efficiency once Shan
explained their plan. The memo he had just transmitted to Colonel
Tan on the old fax machine, which he knew was safer than email, was
only two short paragraphs, although he and Pike had taken an hour
to compose it. The first paragraph reported that Shan had discovered
a secret report prepared by Metok sewn inside the old janitor's shirt.
The engineer had reported that he was in touch with the Bureau of
Religious Affairs in Lhasa about the astounding artifacts in the Valley
of the Gods, and he believed the agency would soon declare the valley a major heritage site. Metok, Shan explained, knew that while Religious Affairs for the most part just collected and destroyed artifacts
on the grounds that they belonged to the state and were counter to
socialist imperatives, the agency was practical enough to understand
the enormous economic benefit from the tourists who flocked to significant sites. Just as the Dalai Lama's restored Potala Palace in Lhasa
brought in millions in revenue, so too could the sacred valley. Metok
had therefore taken several cartons of the valley's best artifacts to the
Religious Affairs processing center on Kunming Road on the outskirts
of Lhasa, along with a file he had compiled with the help of a renowned archaeologist.

In the second paragraph Shan simply asked permission to go to the
Kunming Road facility to interview Religious Affairs about their contact with Metok, which might reveal that the engineer had not been
driven by corruption but simply by an inconvenient belief that the
dam was being placed in the wrong valley. While doing so, Shan wrote,
he would examine and memorialize the unique artifacts that might
provide the basis for stopping the dam project. If he could verify
Metok's assertions, then Colonel Tan could contact the Commissar to

address what was rapidly developing into a conflict between different arms of the government.

Shan had to admit that Pike's plan was a clever ploy. Tan's entire staff knew that in some more remote regions of Tibet, Religious Affairs had become the dominant government agency, with direct lines to Beijing. Adding a reference to the Commissar had been Shan's idea. No one in Tibet needed an explanation, or a name added to the title, and nearly everyone shuddered at the mention of his name. Commissar Yang Chouzi had been in Tibet since the original occupation, and though he had had many titles, the one that had stuck was the one used for the Party counselors who shadowed high officials and often were the real decision makers. After decades of ruthless manipulation, the aged, retired Yang lived in a compound outside Lhasa and was still the unofficial Party boss of central Tibet.

Shan had asked Amah Jiejie to place a copy of the memo on the colonel's desk.

"No, no," Tan's assistant said. "On the corner of my desk. His aides are always lingering at my desk with an eye for the colonel's mail."

Shan had listed the aides for Pike before dispatching their bait to Amah Jiejie. The quartermaster, the wardens, the administrative officer, Major Xun, and Lieutenant Zhu all reported to Colonel Tan. The quartermaster, Shan had explained, would have authority to order the drone that was delivered to the Five Claws. The administrative officer could have changed Tan's recommendation on Huan's discipline to assure the lieutenant went to a powerful position in Lhasa. And Xun as chief of staff touched every aspect of Tan's operations.

"Which of them are in Lhadrung now?" Shan asked Amah Jiejie, wondering how they might narrow their list of suspected conspirators.

"Only Major Xun, Captain Chi the quartermaster, and Captain Bing of the administrative office. The colonel sent Zhu to Hong Kong and the others are at a conference in Chengdu. But I can guarantee you that if I leave it in plain sight, it will be seen before the end of the day."

As they finished their plotting with Amah Jiejie, she volunteered that Metok's poor widow, Lekshay, had called to ask if the government had any personal effects of her late husband. "She seemed so melancholy. I told her I had a brother who died in prison and I knew it would do her good if we could just get together and talk. She said it still felt too soon for her to put her pain into words but maybe in a few days. Poor girl, she suffers so, even though she did no wrong."

Pike grinned as Shan put the phone down. If one of Tan's top deputies was indeed Huan's invisible ally in Lhadrung, then Huan would hear the news by the end of the day. Shan glanced at his watch. "If you are going to set up a camera to secretly watch that building on Kunming Road you'd better be underway."

Shan watched the white car leave for Lhasa then turned reluctantly to the pile of paperwork at his desk. If he did not keep up with it, terse reminders would arrive from the judicial administration center and then auditors might arrive. He poured a cup of tea and settled into his desk. An hour later he was about to refresh his tea when a sudden groan then a crashing sound came from the cells. He pushed open the door, which had been left ajar, and turned on the light in the rear chamber to reveal Meng lying on the floor beside an overturned chair. When he rushed and knelt over her, she reached up and for a moment clung to Shan like a frightened child. Then she collected herself and let him help her up.

"Sorry," she said. Her voice trembled for a moment, then she pulled away and straightened her clothes. "I came in the back door but heard you speaking with someone so I just lay down in a cell. I fell asleep and was still groggy. Sorry," she repeated.

He hesitated, thinking of the pile of paperwork that waited for him at his desk. "I was going to eat," he lied. "Come with me."

Meng bit her lip and gave a small, shy smile that for a moment made her seem more like a young self-conscious woman than a stern Public Security officer. He realized that she had changed into blue jeans and a silk blouse and sweater and asked her to wait a moment as he went into the washroom, taking off his tunic and uniform shirt and replacing it with a simple white one.

She gave him another shy smile as he appeared. They were just another couple going out for dinner. Mrs. Lu, walking her terrier, stared in mute surprise as they stepped outside.

Marpa took one look at them at the kitchen door and held up a restraining hand. "No, no. Front door."

By the time they had gone around the building he was spreading a cloth on the table at the center window then excused himself after seating them, darting into the kitchen then returning with the stub of a candle which he forced into a soda bottle and lit before disappearing once more. This time he returned with a dusty bottle of cheap rice wine. Shan had never before seen any kind of alcohol in Marpa's establishment and knew that Marpa himself never drank any. The café owner filled two small tumblers halfway with the wine. "I had some wineglasses," he apologized, "but I forget where they are."

"It's not like—" Shan began, meaning to say it was not the romantic event Marpa had inferred, but then he saw the anticipation in Meng's eyes. "Not like we are connoisseurs," he said instead.

They spoke of little things, of the occasional shifting of the wind that washed the town with the scent of wildflowers, of the vast high meadows above them where deer and wild goats grazed, of Meng's journey from the Gobi, during which they had stopped at a camel market, and of the horse festival the local herders were planning for late summer. Shan let Marpa decide their menu, and the Tibetan brought out small spiced dumplings, then a rich fragrant stew. Meng seemed not to have much appetite and when she stopped eating altogether, Shan followed her gaze toward the square.

Meng's traveling companion was shouting up a tree, dodging twigs being thrown down by the young girl, who had climbed to a remarkable height.

"I should go help," Shan said. "Your niece could fall."

Meng hesitated, glancing at Shan, then she nodded and turned back toward the window. "No need. She climbs like a monkey," Meng said, sipping at her wine.

As they watched, the girl climbed down a drooping limb then

slipped around it on her hands and dropped directly onto the bust of Mao, straddling it. She began beating the head of the Great Helmsman like a drum.

Meng shook her head in dismay.

"Negligent parents," Shan suggested.

"I am certain of it," Meng replied with a hint of a smile. "We had to wash paint off her face today."

"Why paint?"

The old woman who makes those charts and horoscopes seems to enjoy the girl. She has a gerbil as a pet. The only time Kami was quiet all day was then, just like on our prior visits."

"Kami?" Shan had not heard the girl's name before.

"Kanmei, but Kami suits her. It's funny, but when the gerbil looks at her, she gets very quiet. I watched them today. The gerbil and Kami just stared silently at each other, the gerbil with his head cocked at her as if he recognized her. Those big eyes of his must hypnotize her."

Shan smiled. "The Tibetans would say they knew each other in a prior life. The gerbil is the reincarnation of a famous lama."

"I thought famous lamas went on to some higher level of existence."

"Some do. But most in this region had disturbances in their devotion at the end of their lives. They couldn't prepare for death the way they should have, or even broke their monastic vows in their final days." He saw the question in her eyes. "Some monks and nuns were forced to marry and then forced at gunpoint to consummate the marriage in front of soldiers. Some were forced to disavow the Dalai Lama. Some picked up a gun to resist."

Meng sipped more wine and offered one of her melancholy grins. "What will we come back as, Shan?"

"I tend to think I'll be a surly yak. And I recall someone in prison telling me that every knob would be coming back as a beetle," he said, and immediately wished he had not spoken the words, for she winced, not seeming to take them as a jest.

Meng touched her glass to his and spoke in a whisper. "Then try not to step on me, Constable," she said.

A warm meadow-scented breeze was wafting over the town as
Shan guided Meng down the dusk-lit street to see the carpet factory,
where the night crew was hanging brilliantly colored bundles of yarn,
still damp from dye, on scaffolds. He introduced Meng as a friend to
the old women who worked the looms, and one laughed and pounded
Shan on the back with a mischievous wink. He realized he was enjoying the rare time away from his troubles and, as the sky turned deep
shades of purple, asked if Meng would go for a ride. Without really
knowing why he found himself parking at the end of the rutted track to
the old farm compound. As they approached the buildings he cursed
himself for thinking he could take a Public Security officer into a nest of
ferals but as they reached the gate Meng gave a cry of delight and ran
forward. Lokesh had found an old horn and was standing by a flaming
brazier in the center of the yard, playing an old herder's song.

As he passed through the gate, Shan was struck by how much
work had been done. The weeds had all been plucked and the courtyard swept, revealing a surprisingly intact cobblestone surface. The
front wall of the stable had a fresh coat of maroon paint, and two of
its support posts had been replaced.

Yara was there, washing dinner dishes in a basin, and warmly introduced her grandparents. Her grandfather Trinle offered Meng
some dried apricots. Her grandmother Lhamo offered a cigar, which
Meng politely declined.

"You have a wonderful home," Meng said to them, causing them
to glance anxiously at Shan.

"We're just settling in," Yara interjected. "With Shan's help, it may
become a home."

Shan hesitated over her words, for he had thought of the compound as just one more temporary refuge for the ferals. Then Yara
pushed him away, toward Trinle, who led them inside to see the new
altar, new kitchen alcove, and fresh pallets in the sleeping quarters,
well-scented with fresh juniper.

When they returned to the courtyard, Yara had produced benches and they sat around the brazier drinking tea as night crept over the hills. Meng asked if she might borrow the horn, which reminded her of the recorder she had once played in a student band, and to Shan's surprise she began an excellent rendition of "Beautiful Dreamer." Stephen Foster was a favorite not only of Chinese schoolteachers but also of public-address systems in buses and trains.

Shan felt an unfamiliar tranquility, letting himself be immersed in the domestic warmth, and for a moment found himself thinking of the impossible, but beautiful, dream of Yara and Ko raising a family in such a home.

Meng leaned her head on his shoulder as they walked back to the car, and he prolonged the sense of leaving the world behind by slowing to point out Tibetan constellations to her. "*Lak Sur*," he said, indicating Scorpio, then "*Mindruk*," which was the Pleiades. "And there, a most important one," he said, pointing to the Little Dipper. "*Karma Pur Dhun*, or the Seven Siblings. The seven stars are children racing but the little boy fell down." He indicated the star at the end of the handle. "And fortunately, he could not get up, so he is stuck in the same place for all of time."

Meng gave a girlish laugh and held onto his arm. "Polaris. I never thought it was just a clumsy Tibetan boy." She abruptly clutched him tighter, then doubled over, clutching her belly.

"Meng?" Shan asked, helping her to a flat boulder.

"It's nothing," she said in a strained voice. "I just ate those dumplings too fast," she explained, then reached into a pocket and produced a small jar of pills. Shan recalled that she had barely touched her dumplings. "I'll be fine," she said as she swallowed a pill. "Tell me more about Tibetan stars."

When he finally parked behind the station and began walking her to her quarters, they could hear Kami singing loudly on the other side of the door.

Meng pulled him away, her grip suddenly tight on his hand. "Isn't there somewhere we can go?"

"Not really," Shan said.

"Yes, there is," Meng replied and led him into the jail.

It was nearly dawn when the satellite phone on his desk rang. Shan slipped out of Meng's arms and rose from the jail cot, wrapping a blanket around his body before going into his office.

Pike did not wait for greetings. "Our man is one of those Amah Jiejie mentioned. Huan got word from Lhadrung and arrived at the Religious Affairs building on Kunming Road just after midnight. The whole beautiful scene is on video," the American reported. "Huan's got balls, I'll say that for him. He didn't bother to search the building. He just burned it down."

CHAPTER ELEVEN

Marpa broke into a wide smile when Shan and Meng arrived at his
back door for breakfast. The owner of the noodle shop protested when
Shan took a step toward the little table at the back of the kitchen, insisting that they return to their table in the now dim dining room,
where he quickly brought them tea. Meng asked him not to switch on
the lights, so they could better watch the dawn light up the mountains.
In the dark, with the town beginning to blush with tones of pink and
gold, they whispered. Shan spoke of the joy of being up among the
wildflower meadows in such a dawn, Meng of the stark beauty of sun-
rises she had seen in the Gobi.

"I have to go to Lhasa today," she said in a louder voice as Marpa
brought a plate of thin cardamom pancakes, Shan's favorite.

"Have to? I thought you were on leave."

"And I thought you wanted me gone."

Shan winced. He was adrift in such conversations, having built a
hard shell around his heart for so many years. "Maybe it's safer for
you. Last night was like a dream. In my waking world, people are getting killed."

"In Yangkar?"

"In Lhadrung County." Shan pulled out his badge from Tan and
dropped it on the table.

Meng stared at it longer than he expected. "Is that good news then?" she asked, forcing a small smile.

"I wasn't given a choice. And if I don't find an answer the trouble could come here."

"An answer? You mean arrests and justice."

"It started with an execution that turned out to be a murder by the government. By certain members of the government. I know some of the guilty but not all."

"And if you don't discover all of them, you will be the one who's punished," Meng suggested, nibbling at her pancake. "Do you ever have cases that actually go to trial, Constable? I think it's your specialty. Only take the cases in which the government would rather kill you than the criminal."

"It's less paperwork," he ventured. When she didn't smile, he shrugged. "I'm still alive," he said, then looked out over the brightening square, trying to push down the new foreboding that had been gnawing at him since Pike's phone call.

"Maybe you should spend more time on tracking missing cabbages and less on corrupt soldiers and knobs."

Shan paused. "You heard us yesterday, when we were talking in the station."

"A bit. Enough for me to smell the same kind of disaster as when we first met."

"Not your problem this time."

Meng seemed strangely hurt by his words. She sighed. "Not my problem," she agreed. "I'm on vacation. I can practice my recorder songs."

Shan smiled at the memory of the prior evening, then suddenly a fist seemed to seize his heart as his foreboding found its voice. "Lokesh!" he cried and sprang to his feet. "They killed the janitor, then burnt that building. The only other connection is Lokesh. Burning the building proves Huan is working with one of Tan's senior aides. If it is Xun, then Lokesh is in danger. Xun was there in the hospital! He heard Lokesh say he had a letter about Metok."

"I have no idea what you mean," Meng said. "But go. Marpa can finish the breakfast with me."

Ten minutes later his car skidded to a halt at the rutted track to the farmhouse. He ran, too hard, and he was gasping for air when he reached the gate. Yara was just leaving for her school. "You have to get him out!" he cried. "Hide him! Your grandparents can take him up to one of the caves!" Shan turned toward the smaller of the two houses. "Lokesh!" he shouted.

Lhamo appeared in the doorway, rubbing her eyes.

Shan shouted the old man's name again and ran to the doorway. Lhamo did not move when he reached her, and Yara caught up with him, pulling on his shoulder. "He's not here, Shan. I told you. He had to go see Shiva about a death chart for Jampa."

As she spoke, old Trinle came stumbling through the gate, a panicked expression on his face. He was frantically reciting the mantra of the Mother Protectress. Shan ran to the gate and followed the Tibetan's frightened gaze. The road into Yangkar from the highway was nearly a mile away but the black vehicles were plainly visible. Four Public Security cars were speeding toward Yangkar, lights flashing. He was seeing proof that Major Xun was both betraying Tan and using Huan to further his conspiracy.

Shan parked on the edge of town and ran to the square. Lieutenant Huan had taken charge, directing several knob soldiers, who were forcing people out of their houses and lining up all the men with white or gray hair in the square. Huan was searching through the older men in Shan's town, pushing and shoving them to assemble in the square. One old man fell and received the slap of a baton for his clumsiness. Huan did not know exactly what Lokesh looked like but Xun had given him a description.

Shan prayed the knobs would miss Shiva's alleyway. He might be able to reach the other side of her house and extract Lokesh through the window. But then another of the knobs appeared, leading Lokesh out onto the street, roughly pushing him toward the line of suspects.

"Constable Shan!" Huan had spotted him and was marching to

his side. "How helpful to have you here!" the knob lieutenant said with an icy grin. "We wish to speak with the old man who was with you in the Lhadrung hospital."

"Not here," Shan lied, struggling to keep his voice level.

"A friend of yours apparently. You called him Lokesh. The report on the death of a man named Jampa is incomplete. This man Lokesh apparently has some information." Shan fixed Huan with an expressionless stare. They both knew Huan had no authority over the death of Jampa.

"Just a sad, old former convict. You know the type. He was at the prison where I served," Shan said, making it sound like he had been on the prison staff.

The government had once discouraged older, traditional Tibetans from settling in the "pioneer" town of Yangkar after the annihilation of its old monastery but as Shan's town developed a reputation as something of a sanctuary, more had moved in. He knew each of the old men, had helped many get settled, and now he watched in agony, blaming himself, as they were roughly herded into a line in front of Mao's bust. Most appeared terrified. Most knew this was how Tibetans were rounded up for reeducation camps.

"Then you won't mind if I confirm that by examining these gentlemen," Huan shot back. The knobs began checking papers, questioning each man. Lokesh was in the middle of the line, no more than a few minutes from his own interrogation, and Shan recalled with horror how his oldest friend had vowed that if he were ever stopped by a policeman, he would explain that he had no Chinese papers because he worked for the true government, that of the Dalai Lama. News of the arrest of a confessed agent of the exiled government would go straight to Beijing. Not even Colonel Tan would be able to save him.

Shan studied the men in the square. All of the knobs had pistols, and two carried submachine guns. He was helpless against such odds. Even if he did try to help his friend, the action would only identify

Lokesh for Huan. He tried to speak, but no words came. His despair was paralyzing.

"Tashi, Tashi, Tashi!" came an impatient voice from behind him. A female Public Security lieutenant pushed past him, holding a cap and blue jacket. She went straight to Lokesh and pulled him out of the line. "Let's go, you old fool. Too many beers again last night, I see," she chided as she pulled the cap down over his white hair.

"Lieutenant?" Huan asked the woman in an uncertain voice. "We have an operation underway."

"Whatever it is, my silly know-nothing driver will be of no use to you. Serves me right for giving the simpleton free time last night. Where does the motor pool find these people?"

Shan stared in disbelief. It was Meng, in her uniform now, with her hair pinned up under her cap. The hat she had put on Lokesh's head was an old constable cap hanging in the cell room, from which she had torn away the emblem.

Huan stared at her in confusion.

Meng gave him a smart, but amused, salute. "Lieutenant Meng, down from the north. On the biannual law enforcement audit, at least when my good-for-nothing driver decides to work. Do you happen to have a driver, Lieutenant?" she asked Huan. "Can we switch? My report goes straight to Beijing," she added in a self-important tone. Without waiting for a reply, she turned to Lokesh. "Look at you!" she barked. "Who knows how you ever landed a government job!" She draped the jacket, an old uniform coat of Shan's, over his shoulders, then turned to Huan. "Carry on, Lieutenant."

Huan hesitated, as if trying to decide to challenge Meng, then she turned toward Shan. "What a disgrace this town is, Constable!" she shouted. "You should be ashamed! You'll be hearing from Beijing!"

Another lightless smile crossed Huan's lips, and he turned back to his men. "Carry on," he repeated.

The knobs were still questioning the detained men when Meng's car emerged from behind the station and drove out of town. Meng had to go to Lhasa, she had said, but he knew first she would deliver Lokesh back to the farmhouse. He watched the car disappear, wondering again why Meng was so abruptly trying to be engaged in his life, but immensely grateful that she had chosen to do so that morning. He went around the station, into the quarters at the rear, half expecting to see the young girl Kami and Meng's companion, but they too had gone, and he realized Meng may have taken them. He absently picked up the child's clothing, strewn on the floor, and laid it on the bed. He paused, looking at the strange, tiny clothes. Children were not of his world, had never been of his world—not even his son, Ko, who had been raised by Shan's long-divorced wife.

On the bedstand there was a book with several markers in it, titled *Comrades of Tibet*. It was an overview of the customs and historical culture of Tibetans, published more than twenty years before during one of Beijing's short-lived liberalizing periods, when discussion of separate indigenous cultures had been more palatable. Inside the front and back covers, Meng had made notes about Tibetan food, weather, traditional clothing, and festivals. The marked pages described features of Tibetan temples, dakini goddesses, the Bardo death ritual, and traditional sky burial, when mortal remains were surrendered to vultures to be returned to the cycle of life.

Shan was deep in thought as he climbed the back step of the station, deeply worried about what to do with Lokesh, whose advancing frailty might make it impossible for him to return to his outpost deep in the mountains. He walked past the cells and opened the door, then paused for a moment as he saw Choden, transfixed with fear.

Lieutenant Huan sat at Shan's desk, his boots on the paperwork. "Constable!" he greeted Shan. "At last I get to see you in your lair!" Huan gave an exaggerated wince. "Truly a dismal nest for such an overreaching bird, though I see now why you grope for greater heights." He paused, studying with obvious disapproval the faded posters on the walls, the cracked tea mugs and peeling paint on the ceiling, then continued in his sneering tone. "Wasn't there a fable about a crow who flew too close to the sun and burst into flame?"

Shan gestured Choden toward the door. "Time for a patrol, Deputy." Choden backed away, groping for the doorknob behind his back, then quickly turned and darted out onto the street.

Huan laughed as he watched Choden nervously pass the knobs who stood in front of the station and run across to the square, where some of the released men sat on benches, being comforted by family members. Two of the knob cars were gone. The remaining knobs had gathered in front of the station, obviously awaiting orders.

"What a pathetic place this Buzhou is," Huan said.

"Yangkar. The county government allows us to call it by the old name."

Huan's eyes widened. "Sounds reactionary," he said in a mocking tone.

"What do you want, Lieutenant?"

"Just to show you something, comrade. My new photo collection." Huan began laying out grainy photographs taken with one of the instant cameras all knob squads carried for recording arrests. The images were all of individual Tibetans, men and women of various ages in the clothing of farmers and herders. "Seventeen in my gallery so far. Maybe I'll make a poster. 'The Faces of Antisocialism.'" He fixed Shan with a pointed expression, then swirled his hand in the air, mimicking the act of signature, then made a backward motion like swatting a fly. A cold lump grew in Shan's chest as he realized what Huan meant.

The knob officer lifted a photo of a middle-aged Tibetan in a sheepskin vest. "This fool said, 'What about my wife?' when we snatched him. I said we will arrest her too. Then he said, 'There'll be no one to care for my mule.' 'No problem,' I said and shot the mule in the head," Huan reported with an oily laugh. "A good officer addresses the little details like that. Did you a favor. Can't have an unclaimed mule wandering through your township."

Shan, suddenly feeling unsteady, lowered himself into the chair in front of the desk. "You detained them all."

"I launched them all into a more productive life. Next year they can graduate and join the proletariat. Meanwhile they have free meals for a year."

"Where?"

"Camp New Awakening."

"Where from?"

"We drove five miles along Ice Ball Alley and picked up anyone we saw."

"Why?"

"Because you need to back off. Because you have no idea of the depths you swim in. Seventeen this time. Double that next time. Hell, keep it up and I'll detain your whole damned township. And next time my men will have orders to shoot the animals of every detainee."

"You have no authority in Lhadrung."

"From Colonel Tan? I don't need to consult that old dinosaur. His signature is obsolete. Your authority is obsolete. Five Claws is under national jurisdiction. If Tan tries to interfere, he will get a very unpleasant call from Beijing. He'll end his days in one of those pathetic homes for cast-off soldiers."

"Those people were miles from the dam site."

"Indigenous people have been seen secretly observing the construction. There have been disturbing incidents that might be interpreted as disloyal, even sabotage. Religious Affairs has long suspected illegal anti-cultural activity in the area."

"Anti-cultural?"

"From a new policy directive: 'conduct of unauthorized indigenous cultural activity.'"

"They call it praying."

"Praying! Exactly! The term reeks of reactionary conspiracy. Just a bunch of annoying whispers, as far as I can tell." Huan raised a chastising finger and wagged it at Shan. "You let them leave one of those statues of their bald-headed god on your square. Have you heard of the marvelous discovery made by Religious Affairs recently? The bald-headed god is really a symbol of the Dalai Lama!"

"More like the other way around," Shan said, looking down at the photos. Huan seemed not to hear him.

"So a statue of that old god is really a statue of the Dalai Lama. Such is the insidious personality cult that inflicts grave damage on our effort to transform the Tibetan people." Shan cocked his head at Huan. The knob officer shrugged. "I attended a Religious Affairs seminar last month. Personality cults are like poison injected into the heart of our socialist paradigm. It was written right on the chalkboard. You are empowering the Tibetans' personality cult."

"We have a bust of the Great Helmsman at the other end of the square," Shan observed. "And how surprising for you to invoke Religious Affairs. They probably need you in Lhasa. I hear they suffered a terrible arson fire last night."

The words caused Huan to falter, but only for a moment. A cool gleam soon returned to his eyes. "Steady, Constable. I'm not sure there is a lower posting in law enforcement to which you could be demoted to, but Lhadrung is probably always in need of more garbage haulers."

"And janitors," Shan added.

Huan grinned again, then stood. "Stay away from Five Claws, Constable. Stay away from anyone working on the dam. Stay away from janitors and old men carrying secret messages. You're a bug that someone might step on. Go find a distant corner and curl up in your shell."

Shan returned his steady gaze. "I have one question, Lieutenant Huan. Do you know where Fujian Province is? Thousands of miles from here. Yet somehow you got the provincial governor's signature on Metok's death warrant during a week when he was at a Party conference in Fujian Province. Not to mention the seal of the Commissar."

Huan smiled, seeming to welcome Shan's defiance, then slowly, silently, gathered up the photos, one by one. "One thing about this empty countryside, miles and miles of open road with no witnesses. Little bugs must get squashed all the time."

The knob picked up the blue windbreaker he had dropped on Choden's desk and donned it before stepping outside. "Set your goals to match your abilities, Constable," he said as he opened the door. "Like picking up the litter in your town square."

As Huan bent to enter his car an unshelled walnut slammed into the fender beside him, accompanied by a peal of high-pitched laughter. Shan spun about to discover Kami, standing in the alley by the station with another walnut in her hand. Huan instantly straightened, hand on his gun, then laughed as he saw who had thrown the projectile. With a desperate cry, the girl's caretaker darted out of the shadows and dragged her down the alley. Huan made the shape of a gun with his hand and fired imaginary shots in Kami's direction before climbing into his car.

Shan watched as Huan and his men drove away, realizing he had asked Huan the wrong question. On the windbreaker had been the same embroidered emblem he had seen on the one the deputy director had been wearing, a red hammer over the white chorten, encircled by the words *Safety in Serenity*. "There's a school for children with behavioral problems in Lhasa," came Choden's voice. His deputy was approaching from the square. "For those too young for incarceration. I checked, Constable. The civil authorities have the power to send a child there."

A shriek of laughter caused them both to turn toward the square. Somehow the girl had already circled back around them and was now trying to mount one of the sheep a herdsman was guiding through town.

Choden glanced at Shan with a hopeful expression. "I left the form on your desk, Constable. Please," he implored, then darted off to catch the girl.

Shan wandered back toward the cells, lost in thought, then saw the disheveled cot in the cell where he had spent the night. As he stripped away the bedding the sweater Meng had been wearing fell out. He lifted it and sat on the bed, staring at the sweater. She had pried open a part of his heart that he had thought forever closed. He was more confused than ever about her. He had felt an instant of revulsion when she had appeared in her Public Security uniform, but he knew she had saved Lokesh's life. In the middle of the night she had clung to Shan as if she had glimpsed something that terrified her, then had paraded onto the square like one more arrogant knob.

He stared out at the square, empty except for half a dozen Tibetans praying at the chorten, thinking of the disaster that had been narrowly avoided and the disasters likely to come. Maybe Meng was still at the farmhouse, he realized, and grabbed his keys.

Her car was gone when he reached the farm, but he tossed his uniform tunic onto the seat and walked up the ragged lane. Lokesh was in the back room again, chanting the death rite. Lhamo was standing in the doorway, holding a bowl of barley porridge.

"He won't eat," the old woman groused.

Shan took the bowl from her and stepped inside. He sat beside Lokesh, the bowl between them, and joined in the rite. When Lokesh paused after a few minutes to sip from the crock of water in front of him Shan lifted the bowl. "You'll like Lhamo's porridge. She adds heather honey to it."

Lokesh hesitated, then Shan pushed the bowl into his hands. Shan began speaking of Jampa, in the tone of a eulogy, and after a moment Lokesh nodded and began eating. Shan described how brave Jampa had been in coming to the colonel with a message from the jail. "Jampa brought you to Lhadrung," Shan said. He motioned to the clothing on the low table, arranged in the shape of the dead man. "He would be devastated if you were lost, too. It was a close call this morning."

Lokesh swallowed another spoonful before replying. "I am ready, Shan. Do not worry about me."

"Ready?"

"If the choice is to die for being a failed Chinese citizen or as a true Tibetan, there is no choice at all."

The words sent a chill down Shan's spine. "Please, old friend. You know you can't go back to your mountain home. I can get you to a cave in the nearby mountains. I promise to visit you two or three times a week."

"I was ready today. I have a small card with the Dalai Lama's photograph. On the back I wrote my name, and my job in his government. If they ask for my identity card, that is what they will get." The old man, sensing Shan's frustration, stared at the dead man's effects. "*Lha gyal lo,*" he whispered.

"You will never know freedom again if you do." Most of the old man's life had already been spent in prison.

"The gods have always looked after me, whether inside or outside the razor wire."

"I need you, old friend," Shan said.

"You need me to be true," Lokesh replied and took up the chant again.

Shan felt numb as he drove back to the station. He could not bear to lose the old Tibetan but he could not stay with him to protect him. He had just sat down at his desk when a dog began barking. Someone shouted in alarm. As he stood, something thunderous rushed in from the south, swooped over the station and receded toward the edge of the town.

The helicopter's passengers were still climbing out when Shan pulled up to meet them. He was not surprised to see Colonel Tan, but had not expected Amah Jiejie, who laughed as she stumbled on the thin rail-like step and fell against Tan. The colonel patted her affectionately on the back, then straightened as he saw Shan and marched toward his truck.

Minutes later they were at the station, where Tan conducted a brief search as if for eavesdroppers, then pulled the cell room door tightly shut and gestured Amah Jiejie forward. The cell phone she produced was of surprisingly recent vintage. "Lieutenant Zhu has only my number for calling from Hong Kong," she explained. "Seemed safer that way."

Zhu. Shan had almost forgotten that Zhu had gone to Hong Kong.

The text message under the video said simply: For Shan and the

Colonel only. The image was of a Public Security officer with a bloody lip. "So the Hong Kong knob admitted lying?" Shan asked.

"Something like that," she said and tapped a button.

Zhu, the careful professional, had orchestrated what sounded like a video witness statement. The frightened officer confirmed that he had signed two statements related to the Metok Rentzig case. The first was a confirmation of a bank account and the second an eyewitness confirmation that he had seen Metok.

"Officer Daoli, did you in fact see the account records and the subject Metok?" Zhu asked off camera. The Public Security officer was standing in front of a brick wall. Car horns and truck engines could be heard in the background. They seemed to be in an alley.

"I complied with orders," the forlorn officer said, his gaze dropping toward his feet. Zhu snapped his fingers and his head shot up.

"Orders?" Zhu asked.

"She showed them to me."

"She?" Zhu was clearly surprised.

Daoli glanced up with an oddly sheepish expression then looked away toward what sounded like a busy street. "The Public Security officer who came to interview me. The orders were from a famous soldier, a legendary officer in Tibet. Colonel Tan of Lhadrung County, who runs all those prisons. I hear that in the army they call him the Tibetan Mastiff, after the dogs that rip people apart."

"You saw the orders from Tan?" Zhu asked.

"Affirmative. Issued by Tan and signed by his adjutant Major Xun."

Although Tan had obviously seen the video already, Amah Jiejie nervously kept her hands pressed tightly around the phone, as if she expected that Tan might smash it.

The layers of deception ran deeper than Shan had expected.

"I'll rip Xun apart with my bare hands," the colonel hissed.

"You can't," Shan said. "Inserting your name was an insurance policy. If someone ever dug into Metok's case, they would discover evidence that you were implicated. And if one of them went missing, the others would say it was your conspiracy, which would ring true because you rank higher than them. This knob's testimony would prove it. He wasn't lying, he was just obediently following orders from a renowned army officer."

"Surely you don't suggest we sit back and do nothing?" Tan snarled.

"I'm not saying that," Shan replied. Amah Jiejie looked at him with a frightened expression. She understood. "What I'm saying is that they all have to be taken down for something other than what they did to Metok."

"Huan and Xun, you mean."

"Plus Deputy Director Jiao. And I suspect there's someone else in Lhadrung involved, someone who has authority to order military supplies. You really don't understand, do you?" Shan asked.

"I understand lying, overambitious pricks committing murder."

"Metok and Jampa were just nuisances for them, minor obstructions they had to swat away. They have a much larger goal."

"Speak plainly!" Tan snapped.

"Xun now has control over all government buildings and personnel in the county. Huan is getting authority in the county through his deployment on the Five Claws. Jiao is already acting like he is the supreme government in the Five Claws region. They didn't kill Metok because he was slowing down the dam, they killed him because he was interfering with their bigger plan. Killing the professor and his American student was little more than an afterthought. Metok was criticizing their project, and trying to bring in Religious Affairs, which they don't control. They destroyed him, then they thought they were destroying every connection Religious Affairs had to Lhadrung and the project by burning down that building. Religious Affairs isn't a sister agency to them, it is a competitor."

"Meaning?"

"You're the only military governor left in Tibet. It's very old-school, less and less palatable to the Party. Given an excuse, the Party won't get in the way."

"Shan!!" Tan barked.

"It's a silent, clandestine coup, Colonel. They're trying to take over your county."

Tan lit a cigarette then gazed out at Amah Jiejie, who was speaking with Choden in front of the station. A lightless grin formed on his face as he opened the door and summoned his assistant. "Call that Director Ren," he instructed her. "It's time I observe protocol. Tell him I will be at the Five Claws this afternoon."

As she extracted her phone, Amah Jiejie turned then froze in alarm. Shan twisted in time to see Kami, mounted on a sheep, an instant before the frightened animal collided with Amah Jiejie. A terrified cry left the woman's lips as she fell into a tangle of human and wool-covered limbs.

Tan and Shan leapt into the melee. As Shan helped Amah Jiejie to her feet, Tan grabbed the girl's shirt, suspending her as she flailed the air with arms and legs. The sheep fled with desperate bleats.

The colonel extended the girl with one arm then comforted the shaken Amah Jiejie with the other, patting her on the back. As he did so, Kami landed a sharp kick on his knee. Tan dropped her, and Kami was hauled away by another figure who had appeared from the alley. Meng, a jacket over her uniform now, did not react when the girl tightly wrapped her arms around one of her legs.

"It's the end of it!" Shan shouted at the girl. "Choden!" His deputy ran forward, obviously shaken. He had never heard Shan lose his temper before. "Get me that form!" Shan ordered him.

"Form?" Choden asked as the girl's caretaker appeared, then he brightened and ran into the office.

"I'm sorry," Shan said to the woman. "Either you immediately take this little demon out of Yangkar for good, or my deputy will drive her to the reform school in Lhasa."

Strangely, the woman looked at Meng.

"No," Meng said. Kami was still wrapped around her leg.

Shan hesitated. "I wasn't speaking to you," he said, realizing he had not seen the girl hug Meng in such a fashion before, nor had he seen the affectionate way Meng now patted the girl's head.

"No, Shan," Meng said again.

"I don't understand," he confessed, glancing at Tan and Amah Jiejie, who listened with great curiosity. "I swear I will send her there. I have the authority. She is a vandal, an undisciplined disturber of the peace who has no place in this town." Choden reappeared, waving his form with a victorious expression.

"No," Meng said once more. He did not understand the smile that was growing on her face.

"No, what?" Shan could not hide his impatience.

"No, you will not send Kami to the reform school."

"And why would you think that, Lieutenant?"

"Because, Shan, the little demon is your daughter."

CHAPTER TWELVE

Ten minutes into their flight, Shan removed the headphones that let him hear what the others on the helicopter were saying and numbly stared out the window. Tan, sitting beside him, would not stop laughing and repeatedly patted Shan on the knee, though whether it was in consolation or congratulations, Shan could not tell.

Tan had sent the helicopter back for four of his commandos, which they would call his security escort, and the colonel's laughter had infected them as well. "An instant daughter!" Tan exclaimed in his microphone as he twisted to see his soldiers. "She just materializes on a galloping sheep! Like some old fairy tale!"

Shan was not sure what tale he was caught in, but it did not feel like a fairy tale. His immediate reaction had been anger that Meng would mock him with such an impossible suggestion but he had quickly seen the unexpected pleading in her eyes and he had made the inevitable calculation. They had been lovers for less than a month, but that month had been five years earlier.

With her usual wisdom Amah Jiejie had eased the effect of his paralysis by rising and hurrying to Kami. "What a wonderful sheep rider you are!" she had exclaimed, then added, "I hope I didn't hurt you in the fall," as she bent over the girl with a piece of the candy she always carried. Kami relaxed her grip on Meng and took a cautious step away, gazing in confusion at Meng and Shan, then let Amah Jiejie lead her toward the square, motioning the deeply amused Tan to join her.

Shan took an unsteady step toward Meng, who now looked frightened. "I had rehearsed so many ways to tell you," she said in a tight voice. "I wrote letters every few weeks but tore each one up. I was thinking maybe we could have gone on a picnic in the hills for you to get to know her better and when she ran off to pick wildflowers I would ease into the announcement. It wasn't supposed to be like this."

Shan could not find his voice.

"She's very bright, and so affectionate, Shan." Meng was speaking quickly, nervously, now, and Shan saw moisture in her eyes. "I know she will do well with you. She's very funny, and sometimes seems wise like—" Shan had touched his fingers to her mouth to silence her and embraced her.

A bolt of lightning or a careening car can change a life in an instant. Shan's life had taken a sharp pivot with six short words spoken on the street in Yangkar. *The little demon is your daughter.* He had remained mute as emotion stormed within him. He should say something to the girl, who now seemed frightened of him. He had to comfort Meng, who was still crying as he stared at her. He had to run into the hills and find somewhere to contemplate the impossible news. He looked across the street to see Kami skipping in circles around Amah Jiejie.

"She seems healthy," he said instead.

Meng laughed through her tears.

"She has your eyes," Shan suggested.

"She has your stubbornness," Meng said, scrubbing at a cheek. She grabbed Shan's hand and led him toward the square.

Thankfully she had not pushed the girl on him, and Shan just watched with a dazed smile as Kami played, first with Amah Jiejie then with some Tibetan children who appeared with a puppy.

Choden and Amah Jiejie had brought food and they had made an impromptu picnic while waiting for the helicopter to return with the soldiers. As they ate, Tan's assistant recounted a very satisfying meeting with Metok's widow, who had come to Lhadrung to confirm that the colonel's office had none of her husband's belongings and to see the jail where he had spent his last days. She had broken down into tears when seeing the cell, but eventually recovered enough to ask if Amah Jiejie might possibly accompany her sometime to her husband's favorite shrine, a small remote chorten up in the mountains. Mrs. Lu had approached with a scowl then backed away in alarm after Choden leaned into her ear, no doubt telling her that Shan was sitting with the notorious, famous governor of the county.

"I should stay," Shan had said to Meng when the helicopter had made its return known by buzzing the square.

"The one thing you must not do is stay," Meng had replied. "Go with the colonel. He needs you. Kami and I will be here when you return tomorrow."

"As will I," Amah Jiejie had interjected, and explained that she would rejoin the colonel when the helicopter dropped Shan after their visit to the Five Claws. Choden, eavesdropping, protested that he had no accommodation for her, and was visibly shaken when she said she would sleep in the jail.

They circled high over the valley, giving Tan a full view of the hydro project before landing on the helipad at the back of the equipment yard. Director Ren nervously awaited Colonel Tan's party, wearing a suit and tie. Shan and the colonel had listened on the station's speakerphone when Amah Jiejie had called Ren. She had been most adamant about the colonel's visit, saying it was overdue and that twenty-four hours had just unexpectedly opened on his schedule.

"Twenty-four hours?" the director had gasped.

"Of course. Unless you think the military governor needs longer to become acquainted with the largest project ever undertaken in his county. Do you have vodka?" Amah Jiejie had asked. "He likes Russian vodka for the toasts at his banquet."

Ren had gone silent. "Vodka," he had repeated in a defeated whisper. "For the banquet." Before he hung up they could hear his frantic calls to his staff.

Tan's soldiers leapt out before the helicopter's rotor stopped, as if making a combat landing. They formed a corridor for Tan to walk down as he approached the director, who had an assistant snapping photographs of the esteemed occasion. Shan, in his dress uniform, climbed out behind Tan but the colonel pulled him forward so that they walked side by side toward Ren. Before they had climbed into the helicopter, Amah Jiejie had rummaged in her purse and produced several ornate medals, military decorations awarded to the colonel but which he generally declined to display. Tan had watched with amusement as she had pinned three on the colonel's breast pocket and two on Shan's.

Now the director nodded with new respect at Shan before motioning them toward his office. The loudspeaker system began playing *The East Is Red*, the favorite anthem for military parades. Halfway to the office building, Tan halted.

"What's this?" he asked as he pointed to the Tibetan workers in the fenced-off quadrant of the equipment yard.

The director seemed confused. "Just some Tibetans. We've had incidents. More efficient to keep them under some discipline. A reasonable precaution," he added.

"You're going to make my prisons look bad," Tan said.

The director gave a nervous laugh.

"Do you have any idea of the paperwork required for even a single detention?" Tan asked. "My prison auditors will need to know you are running an auxiliary jail."

Ren gazed into the colonel's face, trying to detect any sign that he might be joking, then trotted to a man wearing a foreman's red hat. The gate into the enclosure was opened, and the Tibetans started drifting uncertainly toward it. "Just some discipline," the director said, "no real detention. It was Deputy Director Jiao's idea. They didn't seem to mind."

Shan stayed with Tan as they were given the slideshow about the ambitious project then they left the building for the same driving tour Shan had been given on his first visit. Tan insisted that a utility truck be provided for his army escort and as they waited for the vehicle, Ren directed them to the billboard-sized painting of the completed dam erected by the parking lot. "We're doing a calendar with glossy photos," Ren boasted as an assistant snapped a photo of Tan and himself by the painting. "This will be perfect for it."

As they began to pull out, the door beside Shan opened and Jiao climbed in. Ren seemed a bit deflated as he introduced his deputy. "If you have any technical questions, Jiao's your man," Ren said in a stiff voice.

"Excellent!" Tan replied. "I have dozens! Like where are you hiding your army of clerks? The permits alone must number in the hundreds. The equipment licenses, explosives permits, sanitation approvals for worker facilities, not to mention all the environmental and Religious Affairs permits. And not a single one ever crossing my desk. What magicians you are!"

The director again seemed to search for signs of humor on Tan's face, then shrugged. "Everything was handled out of Beijing. Normal clearances were waived in the interest of the project's strategic importance."

"Do not concern yourself with such trifles, Colonel," Jiao smugly declared. "Five Claws is on the national priority list. It will provide power for millions back east. Our coal stations have been struggling to keep up with the Glorious Progress," he said, using one of the Party's newest terms for the country's economic advancement. "There's a green revolution, Colonel, and hydro is all green."

"The UN has shown an interest," Ren inserted. "We just had one of their officials here, who said we are on the front line in the fight for ozone," he added uncertainly.

At the turquoise lake at the north end of the valley a special operation was underway. A bulldozer was pulling a dump truck out of the water. Shan recalled his conversation about accidents with the men in the mess hall. This would have been at least the second time a truck had gone into the lake.

"A minor accident," the director explained. "Routine really," he nervously added, then had begun to point out the high-water mark on the cliff wall above them when a small choking sound escaped his throat. Tan was holding up the aerial photo marked to depict the god Gekho that Shan had given him while they had been waiting in Yangkar.

Jiao made an angry hissing sound and reached from the back seat to grab it, but Tan deftly pushed it out of his reach.

"The god was hungry," Tan said. "If I read this right, the lake is his belly."

"It's—it's just a cartoon really," the director sputtered. "Sort of thing that makes the Tibetans laugh." He took a hand off the wheel and gripped the side of the paper to pull it away, then flushed as Tan resisted.

"Carry on, Director Ren," Tan said, folding the paper back into his pocket before he lit a cigarette.

"The Tibetans," Jiao declared in a patronizing tone, "are still assimilating the strategic benefits of the project."

"Is that what your job is, Deputy Director?" Tan asked. "Calibrating assimilation?"

The colonel could not see the way Jiao's lips curled around his teeth, reminding Shan of an angry predator. "The Five Claws will put this county on the world stage," the deputy director stated.

"Funny," Tan replied. "They asked me to build all those prisons precisely because we were so far removed from the world stage." He turned and blew smoke toward Jiao. "Should I send some photos of my labor brigades for your glossy calendar?"

The silence was brittle as they approached the crew clearing the last of the juniper groves. Tan held up his hand for Ren to slow the car. "You seem to expect trouble," the colonel observed, gesturing toward a gray-uniformed man who stood at the edge of the grove, a semi-automatic gun slung on his shoulder. The knobs had arrived.

"There's an old motto for engineers," Ren replied. "Hope for the best, plan for the worst."

"If you are preparing for battle, Director," Tan observed in a scolding tone, "you really must consult the army."

"No, no! I mean, of course, Colonel, that this is just—" Ren frantically tried to collect his thoughts, "just pacification."

"Pacification of what? Do you have wolves?"

"This is Tibet," Ren said uneasily, then cast a nod over his shoulder. "My deputy is in charge of security. He is very clever in dealing with Tibetans. The guns probably aren't even loaded."

Jiao's thin smile revealed his amusement at seeing his director squirm. "Normal precautions, Colonel. A remote site of great value has to address all contingencies, here and above."

Tan was enjoying himself. He looked toward the sky. "Above? Are you worried about the gods then?" A moment later, as Ren braked the car to allow a log truck to pass, Tan abruptly hopped out. He paced along the edge of the grove, speaking with a group of drivers on a cigarette break. He was a man who was seldom at ease with his officers but beloved by his sergeants and privates. Ren watched in nervous confusion, and groaned as Tan wandered to an idle bulldozer, leapt up and started the engine. Jiao extracted a small walkie-talkie and ordered someone to proceed with their mission.

Ren's eyes went round as he watched the colonel. "Can he do that?" he asked Shan.

Shan assumed a somber expression. "One of his officers once told me that the most powerful people in Lhadrung were Chairman Mao and Colonel Tan, and the Chairman is dead. He misses driving his tanks," he added.

Ren groaned as Tan lifted the bulldozer blade and actually engaged the gears, driving the huge vehicle a few feet before climbing down with a satisfied smile. He approached the Public Security guard and spoke with the man then tossed his cigarette aside and extended his hand. The guard hesitantly unslung his gun and handed it to him. Tan examined the weapon as if on a troop inspection, then abruptly shouldered it, aimed at an empty truck, and fired. The truck's windshield exploded into shards of glass. The workers laughed, the soldier saluted, and the director looked as if he was going to be sick.

"The old fool," Jiao muttered as he watched Tan. "He's an embarrassment to his office."

Tan wagged a finger at Ren as he climbed back in. "The gun was loaded after all," he chided with an amused grin.

As they drove along the towering V-shaped pass where huge squared pits were being dug for the dam's foundation, Jiao's radio crackled and they heard a single word: "Launching." Ren brightened, then accelerated the truck onto a small flat knoll and motioned them out. "Colonel, you will enjoy this!" he exclaimed.

There was a high-pitched whine and then a large white disc soared overhead. Shan watched with a sinking feeling as he recognized it and exchanged a knowing glance with Tan. The colonel had been furious when Shan had told him that the mysterious package bound for the Five Claws had been an army drone.

Shan scanned the valley floor and spotted a black utility vehicle with a small field table set up beside it. A knob sat at the table, leaning over a laptop computer while Lieutenant Huan stood at his shoulder, watching the screen. The drone was being calibrated, he realized as it flew in circles then made several short dives. Soon it began ascending toward the slopes below the high pass, then hovered over the mouth of the imploded cavern halfway up the slope.

"The maiden flight," Shan suggested, wondering if the Tibetans above had understood the risk he had tried to describe to them. Their campsite and any yak train leaving it would be instantly spotted if the drone ventured above the field of outcroppings.

"The first operational flight," Jiao confirmed. "We have been testing, learning it is best to fly in midafternoon. Too many shadows in the morning." It meant, Shan hoped, that not only would the risk have become obvious to those above, but that the drone flights were predictable.

"Today the real work begins," the deputy director boasted. "The agitators are no match for our twenty-first-century technology."

The drone soared still higher, tracking the slope then buzzing the team of workers who were preparing the foundation for the new control house high up the slope near the road. Some of the men put down their tools and waved for the camera. Others pulled down their hats and lowered their faces. Public Security was also working on what they called personal trackers, small drones that would be programmed with facial recognition to locate and follow individuals suspected of antisocial behavior.

The drone climbed steadily toward the outcroppings, and as Shan glanced back at the flight controller, he saw a second vehicle pull up with four more knobs. They climbed out and began checking weapons. He watched in helpless agony, knowing they were waiting for the orders that would come from Huan as soon as the drone discovered the location of the Tibetans hiding above. If Lhakpa and Jaya were discovered, they would be sent to a reeducation camp, or worse.

"Watch the bird!" the director suddenly shouted, and Shan turned to see him reaching for Jiao's radio. "The bird! The bird!" he cried.

Shan saw that indeed a large bird of prey had appeared over the outcroppings and seemed interested in the drone. He had heard more than one story about eagles and lammergeiers attacking drones.

"Do you see a woman up there?" came Huan's voice over the radio. "I thought I saw her in the camera, but she faded into the shadows."

Ren darted to his car and returned with binoculars but seemed to have trouble finding the drone in the lenses. Tan grabbed them from him and watched with a widening smile.

The bird never bent its wings as it soared up and down, in an undulating pattern, getting ever closer to the machine.

"Scare it away!" the deputy director shouted into the radio, and the drone abruptly changed course for the bird. As it did so, the long-winged bird jerked upward, then dove.

"No!" came Huan's furious voice as the bird hit the drone. "No, no no!" he squawked. "Someone shoot that damned bird!"

The bird jerked upward, then seemed to hover a moment before diving again, seemingly mindless of its own safety. Tan handed Shan the binoculars and he watched as it crashed into the propellers on the left side. The drone seemed to stagger then, to Jiao's furious expletives, flipped sideways, careening toward the vertical rock wall of the pass. It slammed into the cliff, showering down bits of white plastic.

Tan said nothing, just unfolded the photo that had been overlaid with Gekho's body and made a show of positioning it according to the axis of the valley before holding it up for the director to see. He pointed to the bottom of the image, where the drone had gone down. "Public Security," the colonel solemnly declared, "just got squeezed in the god's ass."

CHAPTER THIRTEEN

As they drove away, Shan tried not to be conspicuous in scanning the outcropping. He was certain he had seen someone there. The distance had been too great for Ren and his colleagues to understand what had happened, but he recalled how Jaya had collected newspapers, tape, string, and dried sticks. She had brought the drone down with one of her kites.

Tan seemed to be having difficulty in suppressing his amusement. He had briefly watched through the binoculars and was canny enough to understand that even eagles and lammergeiers have to flap their wings from time to time. The colonel disliked Public Security nearly as much as Shan, but neither of them had many opportunities to see the knobs embarrassed.

Director Ren was visibly upset. Clearly, he was not an engineer in any technical sense. He was an overseer, a Party diplomat, and his job was mostly to polish the image of his project to a high sheen. He was miserably failing with the most important man in Lhadrung. Tan herded the director back to the car and made sure they drove away without Jiao before he pressed Ren harder.

"A report will have to be submitted, Director," the colonel pointed out. "That was a very expensive piece of military equipment. If you like, I can certify it was an accident. If only I had been consulted when someone decided to use my railcar, I might have been able to call it a loss on one of my training exercises. But I can still try. Whom should I speak with?"

Ren was still recovering from his shame. "Speak with?"

"The one who approved the use of the army's equipment for a civilian project. Corners were cut. Maybe we can take advantage of that. It must be someone else's fault. I would hate to see your record stained."

Ren brightened. "My deputy did all that. Someone in the Lhadrung military depot arranged it, and Major Xun said we should take advantage of a military shipment to keep things quiet. Jiao was hoping to surprise"—the director glanced uncertainly at Shan—"to surprise them," he said with a gesture toward the top of the mountain.

Tan weighed the response for a moment. "Does Major Xun visit you often?"

Ren stiffened. "Our first official visit from the Lhadrung government was that of Inspector Shan."

"So he visits, just unofficially."

"They are friends, Jiao and Xun. Served together somewhere before this. They have meetings."

"Meetings?" Shan asked.

"Like a working group. That Public Security lieutenant from Lhasa, he's in the group too. It's all kept very quiet, since Jiao says they are working on special Beijing assignments, very confidential stuff."

"Surely you know everything your own deputy does," Tan chided.

"Everything the Party wants me to know."

"Spoken like a true patriot, comrade," Tan said, patting Ren on the shoulder.

Ren nodded gratefully. "Even in the army there are secret missions outside the usual command structure."

"Damned right," Tan rejoined. Ren did not see the way the colonel's jaw clenched. It wasn't amusement he was suppressing now. It was anger.

"They even have a name for their group, derived from those old officials who used to enforce the emperor's word out of Lhasa. They call it the Amban Council."

"A clever name," Shan said after a moment's reflection. "Tell me something, Comrade Director. Who came up with the name for this project?"

"Believe it or not, it was Deputy Director Jiao. People in Beijing loved it. He wrote a note for our website that says Tibetans believed a mythological bird lived here, a garuda it was called. There is some rock formation on the mountain that the Tibetans call the claws."

"The Talons," Shan corrected.

"Yes, yes, the Talons. Jiao says the name pays homage to the Tibetan people."

"A garuda has only four claws," Tan observed, to Shan's great surprise.

Ren shrugged. "Beijing loved it."

The colonel exchanged a pointed glance with Shan. The name had nothing to do with Tibetans. The sign of the Five Claws was a symbol of the ambans, and of the imperial power in Beijing. In old China mortal punishment was imposed on anyone outside the government who used the sign, because, for centuries, five claws had been the symbol of the imperial five-clawed dragon.

The banquet the director threw for the colonel was surprisingly elegant. The modular buildings, arranged in rows behind the office and mess hall, looked identical from the outside, but the one closest to the mess hall had been transformed by Deputy Director Jiao into what he called his executive club, for his senior managers and visiting dignitaries. It had been divided into a lounge, furnished with thick Tibetan carpets and overstuffed chairs, and a dining room, with a small kitchen and bar in the rear. The lounge walls were hung with framed photographs of the director and deputy director with various officials. Next to the photographs hung another artist rendering of the

completed dam and the lake behind it. Along the bottom of the painting were images of joyful Chinese children turning on light switches,
electric railways, and spotlights sweeping across skyscrapers of eastern cities. The dining room was hung with portraits of Party chairmen
and several framed vintage political posters.

Pinned to the bulletin board by the bar were three pages captioned
Master Development Plan Summary. With a chill Shan read a paragraph on the second page explaining how his beloved Yangkar would
become the administrative center for the project. The first office building would be constructed on what was a vacant lot currently used as
the town square. Shan closed his eyes for a moment, fighting the ago-
nizing vision of Yangkar as a modern Chinese town, then turned toward
the dining room. His years in Tibet had taught him to fight one disaster
at a time.

The food was simple but the wines and liquor expensive, and Tan,
who could hold his alcohol better than any man Shan had ever met,
made sure the director matched his own consumption of vodka. Tan
had insisted that the Public Security officers join them, ostensibly to
show his appreciation for their service in such a hardship post, but in
fact to allow his four commandos more freedom in following Shan's
instructions for reconnaissance. A sullen Lieutenant Huan sat beside
Jiao at the other end of the table. Twice Shan caught Huan staring
balefully at the colonel and each time Jiao nudged him then refilled
his glass and offered a toast.

Shan tried not to show his impatience as he sat through the meal,
declining all liquor, and listened to a short, slurred speech by Director
Ren that ended with the announcement that in the morning the colonel would be given the honor of pressing the detonator to collapsee
the steep slope above the imploded cavern. The cave mouth, Ren explained, was still visible and presenting a great distraction to the Tibetan workers, who still went there to pray and leave offerings. With
his usual efficiency, Ren stated, the deputy director had devised a plan
to eliminate the distraction.

Shan nodded to Tan as the dinner guests finally rose, and the colonel made a show of good-naturedly helping the tipsy director out of the building, surrendering him to one of his junior managers.

Tan's commandos, all from Lieutenant Zhu's team, met Shan behind the mess hall and were about to report what they had found when a shadowy figure appeared around the corner. The soldiers crouched into the darker shadows, pulling Shan with them as the man stopped and pulled out a cigarette. As his match flared they made out Colonel Tan, in battle fatigues now. "Did you really think I would miss the fun?" Tan asked, then motioned for them to carry on.

The soldiers reported that the cleanup crew, all looking like military men, were closely guarding the equipment yards, and that several of the Tibetan workers had voluntarily gone back into the wire-enclosed compound for the night. Only one man, a young Tibetan, was in the infirmary, where the nurse was drowsily watching another movie on her computer. The cement factory was working through the night, and a reduced crew at the southern end of the valley was continuing work on the huge forms that would eventually be filled with thousands of tons of concrete. A small toolshed behind the equipment yard had armed guards outside it.

"I need a truck, and not the one assigned to us," Shan said.

The sergeant in charge gestured to the row of pickups parked behind the mess hall. "Take your pick," he replied. "We just returned from urban warfare training. Very first thing they teach is how to hot-wire any vehicle."

Tan insisted on coming and sat beside the sergeant with the air of a battle commander as he drove them out of the compound, switching off the headlights as they reached a dirt track Shan had marked that day. The going was slow, with only a gibbous moon to light their way, and it took nearly a quarter-hour to reach the flat in front of the cave mouth. Shan found a flashlight in the glove box and the sergeant handed Tan the powerful light he carried on his equipment belt.

The collapse of the cavern had started twenty feet inside the entrance, and the base of the sloping pile of shattered rock it had created began several paces inside, leaving the outermost portion of the entry walls still intact and visible to their lights. Even that small section revealed the working of multiple cultures. On each side intricate images of Bon deities had been painted above a row of elongated stick-figure shapes, some carved into the rock and some in faded paint on the surface. Shan made out horses, yaks, and deer among the ancient shapes. An angular image he would not have recognized except for the photos Cao had shown him he knew to be a horned eagle.

Tan aimed his light at each of the more detailed images painted above the more primitive shapes. "Demons," he observed.

Shan recognized several of the images. "Apchi, Begtse, red Cumara, and Pehar," he said, pointing to each as he named them. "Protector demons, yes," he confirmed.

Tan's light lingered on a flaming sword held in a hand that extended out of the wall of rubble. "Warriors," he said in an approving tone. "That one died fighting."

Shan gazed forlornly at the debris. Somewhere deep inside it covered the bodies of the two dead archaeologists.

"That's not Buddhist," Tan said. Shan followed his light to a small unobtrusive mark in ochre that was no bigger than his hand. It was the Christian cross Shan had seen in Cao's photo.

"It was the Valley of the Gods," Shan said. "I think all gods were welcomed here." The Jesuit explorer described by Cao had stood in the cave entrance more than three centuries earlier, and had no doubt felt the same excitement that Shan experienced in knowing that devout hands had been at work here for thousands of years. His cross wasn't there to preempt anything. It was just a greeting from the devout of the West.

Tan silently paced along the images. "Why exactly are we here?" he asked at last.

"You heard the director. They are going to finish the job tomorrow."

"There are dead bodies inside," Tan said as Shan produced a cone of incense, then watched in silence as he lit it and laid it on a slab of broken stone. In the dust on an adjacent slab, Shan inscribed the mani mantra with his finger. They backed out of the cave and spoke no more until they reached the truck. Then with the brighter light, Tan located four yellow flags on the slope above the cave that marked the caches of explosives laid for Jiao's demolition of the cave mouth.

When they returned to the parking lot, two of Tan's men were waiting for them. One silently pointed to a truck in the shadows at the back of the parking lot, at the opening that led to the rearmost row of modules. "The truck has a mop hanging off the back. It has two men inside, like an outer guard."

"For the toolshed you mentioned that has more guards beside it," Tan said.

"At the far corner of the equipment yard, yes, sir," the commando reported.

"So consider it a training exercise, Sergeant," Tan said. "Neutralize these two. Nothing fatal. Gag them and tie them to a bulldozer." The soldiers grinned, saluted, and melted into the deeper shadows.

Ten minutes later Shan and the colonel approached the shed. Three of the cleanup crew now stood in front of the door, holding what looked like pick handles. Tan's scouts marched directly up to them. Sharp words were exchanged, a club was raised, and before the man who held it could swing he was on the ground, with the club against his chest. The other two guards backed up, blocking the door. "We have orders!" one of them spat and raised his own club.

"Stand down!" Tan barked as he emerged out of the shadows with Shan. The men at the door hesitated a moment, then recognized the colonel and with fearful gasps lowered their weapons, butt first on the ground, as if standing at attention for an inspecting officer.

"Corporal Cheng?" the commando sergeant asked.

"Sergeant?" came the man's equally surprised reply.

"You know this man?" Tan asked his sergeant.

"We used to be stationed together, sir. Cheng's a prison guard. Or was."

Corporal Cheng seemed to relax. "Still am, at the 404th. Seconded, the warden calls this duty. He even lets us earn wages here too. Hardship pay he calls it."

"I don't recall signing off on that," Tan stated.

"Head of personnel did, sir. Major Xun."

"Earning wages for what exactly?" Tan asked in a simmering voice.

"Whatever Deputy Director Jiao tells us to do, that's our orders. He's in charge of security."

"Then what's Public Security doing here?"

"They were called in to clear the high ground. That's how Jiao puts it. We just keep the troublemakers in line."

"Troublemakers?" Shan asked.

"Nearly two hundred men here, ninety percent of them Tibetans. Like the deputy director says, the bad apples have to be sorted out to avoid spoiling the whole barrel."

"Open this door," Tan ordered. "Now!"

Cheng's companion lifted his club a few inches off the ground. "Don't know about that, sir. The deputy director said—" With a quick nod from Tan, his sergeant slammed a fist into the man's belly. He doubled over, staggering away.

"Open the damned door!" Tan ordered Cheng.

Cheng threw a hasty salute and produced a key. As the door swung open, a fetid stench rushed out.

"Bring them outside, Sergeant," Tan growled.

Each of the four Tibetans had been beaten, though none seemed severely injured.

Tan seemed to force himself to keep his voice level. "What were their offenses?" he demanded.

Corporal Cheng brightened, not realizing that Tan's fury was aimed at the cleanup crew, not the prisoners. He pointed at the nearest man, a compact middle-aged Tibetan who cringed as Cheng moved closer. "This one we caught sneaking around the bulldozers in the middle of the night. The next day we found someone had dropped dirt into one of the fuel tanks. This one—" he indicated another of the frightened Tibetans, but then Tan held up a hand.

"Make notes," Tan said to his sergeant, who produced a pad and began writing.

"This one," Cheng continued, "was ordered to burn those prayer flags that keep dropping from the sky. We discovered that instead he hung them in an unused shed where these two"—he indicated the remaining Tibetans—"had made an illegal altar, complete with a photograph of the Dalai Lama. The deputy director said they should be sent for reeducation, but they are equipment operators and we need them. Said we would just do our own reeducation."

Tan fixed the Tibetans with one of his frigid stares, then gestured Shan forward. "This is work for the civil authority," he announced to Jiao's men. "Inspector Shan will take them into custody." Tan took the notepad from his sergeant and handed it to Shan, then ordered his team to escort the Tibetans to their truck.

The cleanup crew watched uncertainly as Shan assembled the Tibetans in a line, then relaxed when he asked the corporal for hand restraints. He nodded with approval as Cheng ordered the men to place their hands behind their backs and secured them with the plastic ties used by Public Security when making mass arrests. Shan marched his prisoners to the parking lot, where two of Tan's men waited by a pickup truck, supporting Yeshe, the patient from the infirmary, between them.

"Silly cow of a nurse slept the whole time at her desk while her movie kept playing," one of the soldiers reported. "We took his chart and made the bed. She'll have no idea what happened to him."

Yeshe gave Shan a confused smile as he was laid in the back of the truck and the other Tibetans nervously climbed in beside him. Shan drove quickly up the long switchback until reaching the hidden flat where he had intercepted Pike and Cao the week before. He had the four bound Tibetans line up behind the truck and the nearest man groaned as he unfolded his pocketknife, then Shan asked him to turn and he cut off the plastic restraint. After freeing all four, he asked them to help Yeshe out and they sat in a small half-circle of rocks as he passed around his water bottle and told them what he knew about Metok's execution and the deaths of the archaeologists.

"I have an old friend," Shan declared, "who told me about monks from a long-ago time who found a way to travel between the heavens and hells of human existence. They walked between worlds, finding ways to keep the worlds in balance. Right here, right now, that's where you are," Shan said. "You are on the edge of worlds. In the world you just came from men have laid explosives above the ancient cave to obliterate it forever tomorrow morning." He looked at Yeshe the de-molition expert as he spoke. "Four big holes packed with explosives and marked with yellow flags," he said.

"There is another world, above here, where the relics of gods are being recovered and taken to safety. There is also your homes, wherever they may be. It is your choice where you go now, back to the valley, the mountain, or your homes. If you think it safer to take the government's punishment, then go to Yangkar and tell my deputy I said to arrest you. No one from the cleanup crew will reach you in one of my cells."

Yeshe staggered to his feet, pulling off the bandage that covered his head with a defiant expression. "Plastic explosive or just plain TNT?" he asked with a wincing grin.

Another of the Tibetans stood with him. "The mountain is dark and vast. How do we know how to reach the world above?"

"You already have," came a soft voice from the shadows. Jaya, as Shan had hoped, had been keeping watch in the night.

As they began to follow Jaya, one of the Tibetans paused, then ap-proached to press something into Shan's hand. "This was pushed through the window of that shed the first night we were locked in there," he explained. "Bless you, Constable," he said, then turned and disappeared into the shadows. Shan turned his flashlight on the ob-ject in his hand. It was a little blue *tsa tsa*, a crude ceramic image of the god Gekho.

• • •

Tan was sitting outside the module assigned as their quarters with a cigarette when Shan returned to the compound. "I assume all your prisoners are getting what they deserve, Constable," he stated.

"They are grasping the painful lessons of this valley, yes," Shan answered, raising a nod from the colonel.

They sat in silence, the only motion Tan's occasional lifting of his cigarette to his lips and the smoke that seeped out of his nostrils. "Over there," the colonel suddenly said, indicating a patch of sky with the ember of his cigarette.

The meteor was so close they could see a long glowing trail behind it. As it soared overhead, they could hear a whistling sound, then it abruptly crashed on the flat below the pass.

Tan gave a rumbling sound of pleasure.

There was an odd air of familiarity to the scene. Shan realized that this was exactly what he and Lokesh would do on such a night, when the air was impossibly clear and the sky brimming with stars. Years earlier Shan and the colonel could not have been more different. Tan had been the tyrannical, merciless overseer responsible for the prisons where so many died. Shan had been the frightened, suffering gulag inmate who despised men like Tan, who represented all that was bad in Beijing. Now Tan mourned an old Tibetan janitor and sometimes seemed to hate Beijing as much as Shan. With the death of Jampa, Shan suspected he was closer to Tan than anyone other than Amah Jiejie. The grudging respect that had developed between them after so many years of shared ordeals was evolving into something more, although Shan was hesitant to call it friendship.

Neither man acknowledged the bond, but Shan had seen the telltale signs of a transformation in Tan's eyes. The colonel was a hero of the Chinese army, who had immersed himself in the holy cause of taming the heathens and bringing communism to Tibet. He had been a hardened warrior who found glory in training his cannons on monasteries and reducing them to rubble with their chanting monks still inside, or in directing machine guns toward villages, killing even their herds. His had been a sacred cause and he had risen far because he had been the perfect warrior, wrapped in the armor of his perfect cause. They had shared adjoining bedrooms at a conference a few months earlier, and Shan had confirmed what he had long suspected. Tan woke with frequent nightmares. Shan knew Tan was beginning to see the terrified eyes of the innocents who had been shot or bayoneted by his troops. He was hearing the prayers being chanted in the monasteries as his tanks brought the walls down on those inside. The nightmares had come because he had begun to suspect that his cause had been deeply flawed. Without a perfect cause, he could no longer be a perfect warrior.

"My first year in Tibet," Tan said, in a low, contemplative voice, "we stayed on combat alert twenty-four hours a day. I sat in my command seat in the lead tank of my brigade many nights, all night. At first, based on what I heard from Beijing, I was watching for the enemy but after a few weeks we realized there was no enemy, none that would attack a battle line of tanks.

"I started watching the stars instead of the terrain. There were many nights like this, when it seemed you could reach out and grab a handful of the galaxy. At first the vastness scared me, because I was just a little insignificant creature in a uniform, but later the stars calmed me. I wasn't insignificant, I was part of it."

Tan sighed, and Shan heard the rasping that rose in his surviving lung when he was weary. "Hell," he confessed with a forced laugh, "good thing they began ordering us to shell the monasteries, or I might have become a monk."

"*Lha gyal lo,*" Shan said.

Tan gave another laugh. "Victory to the gods, right?"

"Right." After a moment Shan added, "Most forget that it is part of a longer phrase. The 'warrior's cry,' they used to call it, and Tibetans would always offer it at mountain passes, like the one where the dam is being built."

"Why passes?"

"Because that's where the good gods do battle with the evil gods.

They have to hold the passes, or the evil will flood down onto human-ity. *Ki ki so so lha gyal lo*, that's the full cry of the prayer. It means something like *through the strength of your heart and eternal spirit, the gods will be victorious*. There's a second part I learned in prison. *Tak seng khung druk, di yar kye*, which means *Tiger, lion, garuda, dragon. May they all arise here*. They are the allies of the good gods, the pro-tectors on spiritual journeys."

"*Huan, Xun, Jiao*," Tan spat the known names of the Amban Council like a curse. "*Ki ki so so lha gyal lo*," he whispered. "Bring out your dragons, old Gekho." He turned his head toward the pass, where the drone had been defeated that day. "If they wanted this val-ley, they should have asked us first."

Shan was not sure if he was speaking to Shan or to the god.

He slept fitfully on his narrow metal-framed bed in the guest quar-ters, though much better after he got up and reversed the portrait of the Chairman that seemed to be staring down at him. In his dreams he walked along a pilgrim path with Meng and Kami, calling Lokesh's name.

An hour before dawn a terrified scream awakened him. It came from the building next door, the director's quarters. Shan pulled on his trousers and ran outside. Three men jumped from the cleanup crew truck as it skidded to a halt, their clubs ready for action. Tan's sergeant darted out from their quarters, a pistol in his hand.

The director was on his front step, wearing pajamas that clung to his body at several damp patches. "He was here!" Ren cried out. He was near hysteria. "He brought down the skies! He found me in my own bed!"

Shan reached the director at the same moment as the sergeant, who quickly ordered his men to search the building.

"Who found you?" Shan asked. "Who brought down the skies?"

"Who do you think!" Ren's hand trembled as he opened it to reveal several balls of blue ice. "That damned god! The demon! He made it hail on me!"

The sergeant lowered his gun. "Sir," the soldier said, "that isn't possible."

"Don't tell me it isn't possible, you fool! I was there. The hail came pounding down on me! It hit my head!" Ren remembered and began patting his skull as if seeking an indentation. "I could have a concussion!" He seemed near paralysis. Shan twisted his wrist and Ren dumped the ice balls into his own hand. "We'll take care of this, Director," Shan said, then pulled Ren away from the others. He handed the director the little blue tsa tsa god that the Tibetan had given him the night before.

"I . . . I don't know about these Tibetan things." Ren stared at the blue god. He was clearly very shaken. "Some of the men speak about a hail sorcerer who kills people with ice balls."

Shan nodded at the blue figure. "Keep this with you to let the god know you respect him," he suggested. "And I'll light some incense in your room to call in the protective spirits."

The director gave an anxious nod. As he clamped the tsa tsa tightly in his fist, Ren saw that Colonel Tan was staring at him from the step of the guest quarters and nervously retreated inside, Shan a step behind.

Ren led Shan to his bedroom but stayed in the hallway as Shan stepped through the entrance. The bedding lay in a tangled heap. As Shan lifted it, over a dozen ice balls rolled onto the floor. The window at the head of the bed was slightly ajar. Shan leaned toward it to confirm that the sash could easily be lifted from the outside. On the metal sill a ball was melting.

He lit a cone of incense, assuring the director that he would be safe for now. As he left, he heard Ren ordering the sergeant to bring out his clothes. He was too scared to go into his bedroom.

Tan could not contain his amusement when Shan explained the attack on Ren. In the kitchenette of their quarters, Shan laid the blue ice balls on a cutting board and sliced through one. Tan watched him with curiosity as he studied the cross section of ice. "Hail has rings, like a tree," Shan explained. "No rings here. This was made in a freezer."

The colonel laughed out loud. "I like this god!" he exclaimed and tossed one of the ice balls into his mouth.

At breakfast Shan resisted the temptation to go into the kitchen to search the freezer for an ice ball mold. It was probably gone by now, he told himself, then studied the Tibetan workers seated about him with new worry. Dangerous games were being played in the valley of the Five Claws, hopeless, impossible games that could never succeed but could easily result in the deaths or imprisonment of the Tibetans who played them. On the bulletin board by the food line, someone had pinned a new drawing, another caricature. This one was of the Chairman depicted as a five-clawed dragon whose neck had been seized in the talons of a huge garuda.

Tan was engaged in a lively conversation with some of the drivers about the similarities between tanks and bulldozers when the workers looked up then quickly lifted their trays and fled the table. The director and his deputy were approaching, with a Public Security soldier walking behind them. The armed knob took a position behind Ren as they sat across from the colonel and Shan.

"Worried about an attack from another Tibetan demon, Director?" Tan chided Ren, who flushed and kept eating.

The deputy director shot Ren a scathing glance before turning to Tan. "What do you think of our glorious project, Colonel?" Jiao asked. "We are changing the face of your county."

"I admire your willingness to take on such challenges, Comrade Jiao," Tan said.

"Challenges?"

"So remote. So old."

Jiao hesitated. The confusion on his face changed to amusement, and he shrugged. "Moving a pile of rocks is much the same work no matter where you are."

Tan sipped at his tea. "How long have you been in Tibet, Deputy Director?"

Jiao did a poor job of hiding his contempt for the colonel. "Long enough."

Tan returned his gaze with a frigid expression. "Not more than a few months, I suspect," Tan observed. "Took me years to understand how deeply we had underestimated the Tibetans."

"Underestimated pathetic ditch diggers and unwashed sheep herders?"

"Something like that," Tan said. "Nobody asked them about this valley."

Jiao gave an indignant snort as he lifted his mug of tea. "Surely you are joking!"

"Nobody asked me."

Jiao laughed into his mug. "This had been a Beijing project from the very first brilliant suggestion made to the Minister of Public Works. A task force was created. Satellite photos were analyzed, and electrical demand algorithms constructed. They have computer programs calculating peak loads five and ten years from now and how the Five Claws will meet the demand."

"Still, it's my county."

Jiao's eyes flared. "Beijing's county! The Party's county! You haven't even attended a Party meeting in years!"

Tan shot Shan a meaningful glance. Jiao had been investigating Tan. "I found I wasn't learning much at those meetings. I memorized the Chairman's book of quotations decades ago. I have a drawer full of citations and medals for bravery and protection of the socialist imperative."

"Collecting dust! What you know about the socialist imperative is forty years old! This is the twenty-first century!"

"I'll be sure to change my calendar when I return to Lhadrung."

Shan found himself on the edge of his seat, actually worried that Tan might strike the deputy director. Men who knew Tan would be trembling under his icy stare, but Jiao's arrogance blinded him to it. But the director understood and tugged at his deputy's arm as he interrupted. "I have a wonderful video of the Three Gorges Dam, Colonel," he declared. "We can view it in my office. We are planning to use some of their same turbine technology here."

Jiao's mocking stare took in the director as well now.

Tan nodded. "We have an hour before my helicopter returns. We can go straight to your—" he paused, seeing the chief of the cleanup crew darting toward them.

The chief bent and urgently whispered to Ren, whose face slowly drained of color. He abruptly stood, then remembered his guests. "Perhaps you should collect your things first. I will meet you in my office," he said distractedly, then hurried after the crew chief, followed by his new Public Security guard. Jiao muttered under his breath, then drained his tea and hurried after Ren.

Shan and the colonel climbed into their own truck and followed the director as he and Jiao sped toward the southern end of the valley. Half a dozen vehicles were already parked beside a patch of smoldering earth as they approached. The air had a foul, acrid smell, tinged with sulfur and burning rubber. The director and Jiao stood with Lieutenant Huan beside a rapidly expanding crowd of workers staring at a bizarre pattern of objects lying on the ground. Arrayed in two opposing arcs, each about fifty feet long and perhaps thirty feet apart at their tips, were tools and weapons, with a boulder above the arcs that was burning with blue flames.

"I don't understand," Shan heard Director Ren say in a near-frantic voice.

Shan saw that some of those among the workers did understand. Several Tibetans were talking in excited tones, and three or four ran away as if to bring others to witness the miracle. Jiao cursed and picked up one of the tools in the arc, a large hammer with a metal handle. He gasped and dropped it, shaking his hand. The hammer had burned him.

"What the hell is this!" Jiao shouted.

When no one spoke, Shan stepped through the crowd. "Gekho," he announced as he reached Ren's side at the base of the two arcs. "Gekho the Destroyer. Gekho the Mountain God."

"You fool, Shan!" Jiao spat. "Stop spouting nonsense!"

"It was that meteorite last night!" Huan insisted, then hesitated as he gazed at the tools. No one seemed comforted by his explanation. Meteors did not come equipped with the tools of a god.

Shan spoke toward the director and Tan as he recalled the painting of Gekho he had seen in the secret archives. "Gekho has eight arms on each side. In his left hands he holds bow and arrow, lasso, battle hammer, iron chain, iron hook, spear, horn of a ram, and a caldron of boiling water." He pointed to each item that comprised the left arc, which in sequence were an old battered bow with an arrow nocked in it, a coil of rope, the hammer Jiao had dropped, one of the chains used for hauling logs, a large hook that was used with the chains, the handle of a shovel that had been broken off and sharpened to a point, the horn of a sheep, and a brazier filled with a liquid that was also spouting blue flames.

"On the other side," Shan continued, "the ferocious Mountain Warrior God carries a cutting wheel, a maul called the Earth Shatterer, a scimitar, a ball of fire, a thunderbolt arrow, a crushing killing wheel, a battle-axe, and a sword." He pointed to each of the objects on the right side, indicating in turn a large circular saw blade, a heavy sledgehammer painted entirely blue, a mock scimitar that appeared to have been made for the old ritual dances, a tarry black mass that burned with a low blue flame, an arrow with scorch marks on it, a wide smoldering tire that looked like it had been taken off a forklift, an ax painted blue, and a sword that also appeared to be a prop made for dance performances. He paused by the smoldering rock. He doubted it was the actual meteorite, but Jaya and her friends had used the appearance of the meteorite to great advantage. The boulder was cupped at the top, providing a basin for the liquid that burned. "Toys and stolen tools!" Jiao shouted. "Cheap theatrics!"

"The meteor last night?" a voice called out from the crowd of workers. "Like the knob said! We all saw it! It was the arrival of the blue god! He was here! Whatever he touches burns blue!"

"Idiot! It's just some oil or gas!" Jiao snapped. "Get back to work!" he shouted and stepped toward the objects.

"Don't," Shan warned as he picked up the scimitar.

"A sham!" Jiao crowed and bent the old dance prop over his knee. He gestured for the cleanup crew to help clear away the objects. The first man made the mistake of kicking at the burning, tarry object. Flaming black blobs spurted onto his leg and instantly his shoe and trousers ignited. An awed murmur swept through the crowd as he frantically tried to rub out the flames with his hand and blue flames spread onto his fingers. He shouted, then screamed, and as two of his coworkers began pulling off his trousers another ran for a fire extinguisher in their truck.

Shan realized the director had retreated behind Tan to stand among the colonel's soldiers.

"Remove that trash now!" Jiao shouted at the cleanup crew, who now also seemed unwilling to approach the god's implements. Not a man moved. "You ignorant fools! They are props in a game!"

"No," Shan said in a slow, reverent voice. "The objects used in the old rituals like those weapons"—he pointed to the sword and scimitar—"could be called props at first but after the god touches them they have power."

Jiao sneered at Shan and pointed to the ruined cave on the slope above them. "The god is dead! We killed him!"

A worker bravely went forward to the boulder as the flames went out and pushed a tentative finger into the liquid that remained. He lifted his finger to his nose and smelled it. "Not oil or gas!" he announced. He licked his finger. "Water! It's a miracle!"

An excited murmur rippled through the crowd, and despite Jiao's protests, another man went forward, then a third. They each touched the water, then with radiant smiles dabbed it onto their foreheads.

"The god's not dead!" came a voice from the crowd of Tibetans. "Just angry at what you have done! This is his valley!"

Jiao spun about to face the workers. "Who said that?" he thundered. "Arrest that man!" When none of the soldiers or cleanup crew moved, Tibetans surged forward around the boulder, reverently anointing themselves with the blessing water. The deputy director darted to Huan, who produced a small device with an antenna extending from it. Jiao pointed triumphantly up the slope to the yellow flags above the mouth of the cave, then seized the device and pressed a button.

Shan shuddered and took an involuntary step backward. But the caches did not explode. They simply emitted small puffs of white smoke.

"No, no no!" Jiao shouted as he pounded the button again and again.

The explosives were gone. Shan had not been sure if Yeshe the Tibetan demolition expert would have had the strength to work on the slope the night before, but Shan recalled that he had had several strong companions.

The Public Security team seemed confused as they gazed back and forth from Jiao to the drifting plumes of smoke but leapt to action as Jiao turned with a shrill cry. "Those who did this are guilty of sabotage of a national security project!" he shouted to the knobs and pointed back up the slope. "Arrest every Tibetan you find! The charge is treason! If they resist, you must shoot them!"

Choden met them as they landed on the flat outside of Yangkar and drove Shan and the colonel into town, parking behind the station then awkwardly motioning them toward the guest quarters behind the station. A freshly scrubbed and subdued Kami met them inside the door and, with nervous glances at her mother and Amah Jiejie, escorted them toward a neatly laid luncheon table adorned with a vase of mountain heather.

They ate a pleasant meal together, with Amah Jiejie carefully leading the conversation away from criminal conspiracies, and Kami behaved surprisingly well, edging toward mischief only once, when Shan saw her surreptitiously making a small rice ball. He saw her eyeing the colonel across the table, as if gauging the trajectory, and he gently pushed her hand down, knocking the ball from her grip as he did so. She wrinkled her nose at him but then smiled and attacked a pickled radish.

Kami dutifully rose when Meng asked her to help with the dishes, which went back into the box brought from Marpa's café. Shan studied the girl, seeing more than once the intense curiosity behind her defiant eyes, the high cheeks of her mother, and the long fingers that seemed reminiscent of Ko's. Surely this could not be true, an inner voice kept telling him, surely this energetic little creature could not be his own flesh and blood, surely he could not have a family. He was too old, his life was too unstable, his work too dangerous. He had to find a way to tell Meng she must leave, that he would help support Kami but there could be no life for them in Yangkar. He rose and excused himself, saying he had to check the station.

Shan walked through the building and out into the square, which was thankfully empty. He sat on the ground in front of the Buddha, legs crossed under him, and stared into the eyes of the ancient granite statue. He did not know how long he was there, was not aware of a presence beside him until the child's voice broke the silence.

"What are we doing?" Kami asked. She was seated a foot away, mimicking his posture.

"Speaking to the god," Shan said.

"No, we're not," the girl disagreed. "I would have heard you."

Shan tapped his heart. "The god inside me." The child's eyes rose in alarm, and she leaned forward and stared at his chest as if for a glimpse of the deity. "We all have one," Shan said, "but many people refuse to recognize him."

Kami lifted the collar of her shirt and looked down inside it, then back up at the stone Buddha. "Him? You have one of those old things inside you?"

"Her. We can call yours a goddess."

He instantly regretted his words, certain they had frightened the girl.

But Kami seemed more curious than fearful. She put a tentative hand over her heart. "Why would a goddess bother with me?"

"Because you are alive."

"But what does she do?"

"Just witnesses." Shan saw her confusion. "She just watches for now. When you get older she may help you."

Kami was quiet for several breaths, then a bird landed on the Buddha's head, and she laughed.

"Your mother said you saw camels when you came down to visit us."

Kami laughed again. "Like great lumpy horses! I tried to ride one!"

Shan stood and extended a hand, gesturing to a bench. "Let's go sit and you can tell me all about it."

He listened to Kami's excited tales about travel encounters with camels, dogs, soldiers, trucks, and yaks. After a few minutes she stood on the bench and cast a longing eye at one of the trees she liked to climb, but she stayed on the bench, except for a short break spent skipping in a circle in front of him as she described how their car had been trapped by "millions" of sheep one day.

At last Meng and Amah Jiejie appeared and Kami ran to them. Colonel Tan and his commando sergeant met Shan as Choden drove the truck to the front of the station.

"I may be out of touch," Shan said. "I have to go back up the mountain above the Five Claws." They had swooped low over the mountain when flying out, but Shan could not be sure Jaya and the others had understood the warning.

"No," Tan said in a tight voice. "You have to come with us, Shan. I'm sorry."

"But you heard Jiao. The Tibetans up there may—"

"No," Tan interrupted. "The sergeant has something to tell you."

The sergeant grimaced, then fixed Shan with a somber expression.

"I told you, I know some of the men on that cleanup crew, the prison guards on detached duty for Deputy Director Jiao. We got to talking. One of the guards said he heard you called Inspector Shan and asked if you were the one with the son in the 404th."

"I'm hoping we can get him parole in a couple years," Shan said uncertainly.

The guard cocked his head. "No. Your son switched places with a trusty, one of those prisoners allowed to do unsupervised work. The warden said it was so Ko could spy on him." The sergeant shrugged. "It's why I put in for a transfer out of there last year. I'm a soldier, not one of those who likes to torment prisoners. That new warden isn't right. They caught Ko and kept it unofficial, if you know what I mean. Beat him real bad. Blood everywhere. They didn't put him in a bed in the infirmary, just locked him in a closet at the back of the infirmary. More like solitary confinement. No doctors to see him. You know how it goes. Next time they go working high up in the mountains they'll take him with the crew then report that he had a tragic accident."

CHAPTER FOURTEEN

As Shan stared numbly at the landscape below, he was vaguely aware that Tan was snapping out orders into the mouthpiece of his headset. As he regained his senses he realized the colonel was speaking to him.

"I'm sorry, Shan," the colonel said. "I thought the boy had been weaned from his troublemaking ways. You know I don't interfere with prison discipline."

"It wasn't troublemaking. He was helping me, helping us. It's my fault. He was trying to get more information about Xun and Jiao, and what they did at Larung Gar."

"That doesn't involve the 404th. And why would he spy on the warden?"

"How could Jiao recruit guards for the 404th behind your back? The warden and Jiao must have a connection. You heard those seconded soldiers at the Five Claws. They came from the 404th. Xun arranged it with the warden. That warden is new, just arrived last year. It is unusual for you not to promote from within your ranks. Why was he different?"

Tan thought a moment. "Commendations. A record of rapid promotion. And the Commissar sent me a note asking me to, sealed with his chop for emphasis. He hadn't asked a favor for years."

"The retired boss who still gets calls from Beijing," Shan said.

"Who also signed the death warrant for Metok." He did not miss the way Tan's jaw tightened at the mention of the aged Party boss.

"Officially he's been retired for years," the colonel said, "though you wouldn't know from the way people still shudder at his name. Lives on an old estate outside Lhasa. He may have slowed down but his fangs are still sharp."

"Where did the warden come from?"

Tan frowned. "Are you asking me as Ko's father or as my investigator?" Shan did not reply, just returned his steady stare. Tan sighed. "I don't know such details."

"Ask Amah Jiejie. Now."

The colonel muttered under his breath then spoke to the pilot and switched his headphones back to the radio channel. Moments later he was speaking in a low voice to his office. Shan heard him curse, then Tan turned with his hand over the microphone. "Larung Gar. He came from the Larung Gar campaign. Thirteen months ago."

"Meaning just before Huan brought him those six prisoners from Larung Gar. Why would the hail chaser confront that very convoy? Too many coincidences." He recalled Ko's description of the old lama Tsomo who had died on National Day. What had the warden shouted when Tsomo crossed into the forbidden perimeter zone. *Not again, you bastard!* "Who sent those prisoners to the 404th?" Shan answered his own question. "Public Security. Huan and his friends had unfinished business with them. Or," he added, "considered them a threat to their plans."

"There had to be a trial," Tan said, "a tribunal verdict, to send them to hard labor."

"We should get the—" Shan began, but Tan was already back on the radio, asking Amah Jiejie for the records of the six inmates.

"How do we get Ko out of the 404th?" asked Shan when he had finished.

Tan held up a hand then pointed downward. He already had a plan. They were landing at the hospital helipad.

Dr. Anwei, the doctor who had tried to save the old Tibetan janitor, seemed to sense there was some other motive than the unannounced review of the 404th's infirmary that Tan had suggested, but he
seemed to savor the chance to leave the hospital and before they left,
he darted into an office and appeared with a clipboard and a stack of
forms. As one of Tan's utility vehicles drove up with two of his soldiers,
Shan followed the doctor and began to climb inside.

Tan put a restraining hand on his arm. "No. The warden will be
suspicious if you are there. I am going because I am so angry at these
damned medical bureaucrats," he said with a mischievous nod toward
a grinning Anwei, "that I had to go to keep him in line. The comput-
erization of all prison activity is to be completed soon," Tan stated in
a louder, stage voice, "meaning bureaucrats from Beijing will be rou-
tinely reviewing everything we do. I will not have the 404th embarrass
us by poor record keeping." He turned to Shan. "We will find your son.
If he needs medical attention, we will see that he gets it. The helicopter will take you back to Yangkar."

"Not until you return," Shan said. "I will be at your office." He
waited until Tan and the doctor drove away with their escort, then
walked the half mile to the old building in the center of the town. To
his great surprise as he climbed the final flight of stairs to the top floor,
Shan heard Amah Jiejie laughing. He found Tan's assistant in a conference room, having tea with Cato Pike.

The American nodded at Shan, as if expecting him. "I was explaining to this lovely lady about a problem I had once in Beijing. We discovered that a bureaucrat in the Ministry of Foreign Affairs had been
delaying the visas for the family of one of our attachés for nearly a
year, trying to pressure him into sharing secrets about some investment negotiations. So I managed to get a camera installed in his apartment. A few days later I had a video of a little ritual he performed
every day after returning from the office. He propped a portrait of the
Chairman on his kitchen table, took off all his clothes and folded
them neatly on a chair, then put on an old Mao cap and paraded naked in front of the Chairman, calling out criticisms to the portrait. I

showed him ten seconds of the footage and we got the visas in an hour."

Shan offered an uncertain grin. "Why are you here?" he asked Pike as Amah Jiejie poured him tea.

"Call me an American tourist seeking to experience Tibet in all its glory."

"Lhadrung County is off-limits to all tourists," Shan pointed out.

Pike shrugged. "Like I said, all its glory."

Amah Jiejie laughed again.

Shan was not amused. The American seemed more and more like a powder keg with a smoldering fuse. He switched to English. "Why are you are being so reckless?"

"You mean why would a father try to pry open the conspiracy that got his daughter killed?" Pike replied, his voice sharp as a blade.

"The conspiracy is not in Lhadrung town."

Pike didn't reply, just unfolded printouts of more of the emails Cao had intercepted. "I needed a seasoned set of eyes on these records, someone who understands the bureaucracy," he said, gesturing to Amah Jiejie. It was an exchange between an anonymous "Five Claws Project" email address and another address used for the Lhadrung military depot.

Pike read the first out loud. *Checking the order for equipment. Send timetable.*

"Innocuous on its face," Pike said. "But it is only the first of a dozen, and always between midnight and a quarter past midnight, on three successive nights. Special messages at prearranged times between two people using the addresses as cover."

"They were arranging the shipment of the drone," Shan said.

"No, this was weeks before the drone," Pike countered, then pointed to an abbreviation that recurred in each message.

"FAE?" Shan asked.

"Right. They use the American acronym because it was developed in America," Pike ran his finger down the exchange, reading the references in sequence. "*Do you have the FAE yet? Sorry the FAE may come tomorrow. Be patient these things are tightly controlled. I can't be patient, get the FAE.*" And finally, Cato read: "*FAE denied. Just use the conventional explosives I sent.*"

"I don't understand," Shan said. "An FAE?"

"A fuel air explosive. A thermobaric bomb."

"I'm not a soldier, Pike," Shan pointed out.

"It sucks all the air out of an enclosed target. Bunkers, buildings, caves. Made to kill people, not destroy structures." Pike pointed to the dates of the emails. "Not long before my daughter died someone was planning to suffocate everyone in that cave, with help from the army in Lhadrung." Pike switched back to Mandarin and turned to Tan's assistant. "Who has authority to order munitions? Especially such a serious weapon."

"Several staff officers would," Amah Jiejie replied, as Shan handed her the printed page. "All the colonel's direct reports, the headquarters staff, and all of the wardens. But for something unusual, the colonel wants to know about it."

"Except the colonel wasn't up at midnight talking about vacuum bombs with the Five Claws," Shan said.

"Of course not," Amah Jiejie agreed, then asked the dates of the emails. "Major Xun was away that week, at a Party conference."

"But not the warden of the 404th," Shan suggested.

"Not the warden," Amah Jiejie confirmed, then rose as the phone on her desk rang. Shan followed her out of the conference room. When she put down the receiver she looked as if she might weep. "There's a car waiting, Shan. They need you at the hospital," she announced in a brittle voice.

Ko lay unconscious on a hospital gurney outside the surgical chamber when Shan arrived. Dr. Anwei was shouting orders to nurses. Shan ran to his son's side. Blood matted Ko's hair and had dried on his fingers. His prison tunic was torn in several places, and each tear adhered to his flesh with caked blood. A nurse was using scissors to cut his clothing away.

A man was shouting Ko's name in a frantic voice. Only when a nurse began patting his shoulder, did Shan realize the cries were his own. Someone clamped an insistent hand around his arm as he leaned over and tried to shake his son awake.

"He was already unconscious when we found him," Tan explained to Shan as he pulled Shan away. "He had been thrown into a closet with a bunch of brooms and mops. The mop heads were soaked with his blood. The doctor says if he can stabilize Ko, he should recover," Tan explained. "He was beaten so severely his skin was torn open in several places. No bullet wounds but a shallow stab wound on his upper arm where he defended against a blade. He lost a lot of blood. Anwei will close up the wounds and start transfusions. If we hadn't found him . . ." the colonel didn't finish the sentence.

"The broom handles and walls were streaked with blood where he had tried to pull himself up," Tan added as he pulled a phone from his pocket. "This is the doctor's. I told him to take a photo of the back of the closet door."

Ko had drawn something on the door in his own blood, in case he would not live to deliver the message himself. It appeared to be two words, one over the other. Shan studied them, not comprehending, realizing his son would have drawn them while in great pain, in the dark.

"I can make no sense of it," Tan admitted. "It doesn't even look like Mandarin."

Shan realized he too had been looking at the image the wrong way. "It's not," he said. "I almost forgot that he's been studying Tibetan. Writing in Tibetan would make sure the guards or the warden wouldn't understand it." Gradually Shan was able to piece together the rough curving lines. The first word seemed to be *Tara*, the second was *Namdol*. The name of a goddess and the name of the hail chaser.

"Is Zhu back?" Shan asked, his voice cracking.

Tan nodded. "Zhu and his men will guard your son's room. No one but you, me, or the medical staff to go in."

Ko suddenly stirred, responding to the voices. He reached out and grabbed his father's hand, futilely trying to pull himself up. As Shan bent over him, he whispered three words. "Safety in Serenity," he gasped, and passed out.

"I don't understand," Tan said as they watched Ko being wheeled into the surgical unit.

"It's the name of the campaign at Larung Gar that Jiao headed," Shan said. "I think that team became the Amban Council when they moved here."

Shan nodded his gratitude as he stared at the doors of the surgery unit, then reconsidered. "Guards, yes. But I want Zhu with me, in civilian clothes. I'm going back to the mountain. And you need to go kowtow to the Commissar."

Tan's abrupt reaction was unexpected. Shan saw the hardening of the soldier sensing the approach of combat, but there was also an unfamiliar edge of worry. "No," the colonel replied. "You don't know the bastard. A cobra in an old man's body. I've stayed away from him for years."

"You have to go. He's the only one who can give you cover."

"Cover for what?"

"For what needs to be done at the Five Claws."

"Cover? They won't give us cover, they'll just give us two six-foot holes in the ground."

"Then they get away with everything, the murders, the stealing, the lying. And the taking of your county."

Tan shook his head, then lit a cigarette and weighed Shan's words. "I'll make the arrangements," he declared at last. "But I'm not going alone. The old snake only has venom enough to kill one of us."

Shan had called to send Choden out on patrol in a distant sector of the township before the helicopter left for Yangkar the next afternoon. The warden of the 404th had made repeated inquiries about

Ko, insisting to the doctors that his prisoner be returned to the prison infirmary. After the third such call, Tan had muttered a curse and shaken Ko's shoulder.

"Why?" he demanded, ignoring the doctor's protest. "Why is the warden so angry at you?"

Ko, clearly sedated, offered a weak, groggy smile. "He didn't like his death chart."

Tan shot an accusatory glance at Shan.

"But Ko," Shan pointed out, "a death chart is done after death, for those conducting the rituals."

Ko smiled again and asked for some water. It took several minutes to get the full story from his son. First, he reported, Major Xun had arrived for a meeting with the warden and a young Public Security officer, also attended by a tall haughty-looking man who arrived in a car from the Five Claws project. Shan shot Tan a knowing glance. Ko had seen a meeting of the Amban Council. Afterward all the prisoners from Larung Gar were put into solitary confinement.

The next day one of Ko's barrack mates who worked as a kitchen trusty reported to Ko that he had seen the warden sneak out of the back of the administration building and try to burn a rolled-up piece of paper by a toolshed. When it wouldn't burn he retrieved a shovel and buried it, then backed away as if frightened of it. That evening Ko switched places with one of the trusty prisoners who conducted grounds cleanup and retrieved the buried item.

"It was like a Tibetan deity painting," Ko explained, "with symbols I didn't recognize, so I asked one of the old lamas. It made him uneasy too, said I mustn't have it, that someone was playing a bad joke on the warden, because the warden was still alive." One of the new inmates overheard and ratted me out to the warden, to get extra privileges. They dragged me out of my bed at dawn and threw me into solitary.

"They took the chart, but not before I memorized much of it. At the top was the warden's name in Mandarin, then it said he died on October 1 of last year." Ko looked up at his father. "That's the day

the old lama from Larung Gar died," he reminded Shan. It also was
the day, Shan knew, that the ancient holy stones had been demolished
at the Five Claws. "Then below was nothing but Tibetan, mostly images of gods and symbols, with an invocation of the Mother Protectress on the left and on the right the name Namdol. At the bottom
were three inverted V's like hills or mountains, then an arrow pointing to an image of the gate of the 404th."

His son had described what did indeed sound like a death chart,
though death charts were done after the death of the subject to direct
those who conducted the complex, often personalized rites to properly ease the transition of the departed soul. But this had not been
done to comfort a soul, it had been done to torment a soul. And Ko
had nearly been killed for discovering it. Questions leapt to Shan's
tongue, but then he saw Ko was losing consciousness again. His son's
eyes fluttered open. "It's all about the goat," he said, then passed out
again.

It was Tan's suggestion that a more secure location be found for
Ko's recovery. The doctor had reluctantly agreed, but only when Ko
was strong enough to stand after receiving more blood. Hours later
Ko had unsteadily risen then saluted the doctor before shuffling
around the room despite his obvious pain. Shan had taken the oppor-
tunity to ask him why he had spoken of a goat. Ko had winced as he
shrugged. "I tried to speak with one of those prisoners from Larung
Gar about it. I showed him the death chart, then he saw guards coming to separate us, and that's all he said, like it was the most important thing of all. 'It is all about the goat.' But there wasn't even a goat
on the chart."

While confirming arrangements for the helicopter, Amah Jiejie reminded the colonel that she would be away the next day, for she had
agreed to go up into the mountains with Metok's widow. "She is convinced going up to her husband's shrine will help her deal with her
grief so she and her daughter can get on with their lives. She wants to
leave offerings and said she would bring food so we can have lunch

afterward." Tan reluctantly agreed to loan her one of the cars in his pool, only after warning her of the dangerous roads in the mountains.

As they landed by the highway turnoff for Yangkar, Yara and her grandfather waited with Shan's car. They cast nervous glances as Lieutenant Zhu climbed out, carrying two heavy backpacks, but accepted his help in loading Ko into the back and did not object when he joined them in the car. An hour later Ko was lying on a cot in the farmhouse compound, smiling weakly as Yara settled blankets over him and her grandmother pushed a cup of buttered tea into his hand. Shan had already explained that he would have to leave so he and Zhu could be in the mountains above the Five Claws before nightfall, but he made Yara promise she would bring their friend the old Tibetan doctor to examine Ko later that day.

"Meng?" he had asked Yara.

"She had to go to Lhasa," Yara explained. "Seems like she has some sort of regular business there."

"Tell her . . ." Once more Shan felt inadequate when speaking of his lover and mother of his child.

"Tell her when she's back we'll take Kami on a picnic up on a mountain meadow," he said, and rushed away.

As Shan drove, Zhu examined his maps, quickly grasping the significance of the markings that Lhakpa and Shan had added. "So many pilgrim paths," Zhu said. "All converging on the mountain. It must be like one of those sacred mountains."

Shan took a moment to realize the army officer was speaking of sacred mountains in eastern China. Scores of thousands of Chinese still climbed them every year despite the government's effort to discourage anything that hinted of religion.

"It smells like a horse blanket," Zhu protested after Shan parked the car, holding out the tattered coat Shan gave him. The lieutenant looked back down the long gravel road they had just traversed as if thinking of bolting back down it.

"No doubt," Shan said. "When I said come in civilian clothes, I didn't mean your new wardrobe from Hong Kong. We're going into Tibet."

Zhu hesitated. "We're already in Tibet, Inspector."

Shan pointed to the truck, the road, and the highway visible in the distance. "That's China," he said, then pointed in the opposite direction toward the wild, rugged mountains above them where a line of chortens stood like defiant sentinels. "That's Tibet." He handed Zhu a wide-brimmed hat. "They will be watching. If you move like a soldier or carry yourself like someone from the city, they will lose themselves in the stone forests."

Zhu unzipped his new red nylon jacket and reluctantly tossed it in the back of Shan's car, which they were leaving under some trees a half mile below Ice Ball Alley. He choked off a protest as Shan rubbed dirt on his heavy backpack.

"And no guns," Shan said. "It's not our way."

"I'm a soldier," Zhu protested. "You said I was deploying against Public Security."

"No guns," Shan insisted. "And what I said was that you were to be our invisible defense against the knob patrols. They are using electronic devices."

Zhu grinned and hefted his pack. "Good. A field exercise," he said, then unzipped the top compartment of his pack and set his pistol under the seat of the car.

They pressed hard, with Shan setting a grueling pace. Zhu remained silent when Shan knelt at the first pilgrim shrine but followed Shan's action in emptying his canteen and filling it from the pilgrim spring. At the next shrine he copied Shan in placing a stone on top of the old lichen-covered cairn. At the third he joined Shan in kneeling.

As they walked on Zhu whispered something that caused Shan to turn. "*Chaosheng*," Zhu said more loudly. "My grandmother always wanted to take me with her on her *chaosheng* journeys."

Shan hadn't heard the Chinese word for years. It meant *paying respect to the holy mountain*.

"Sometimes I went with my parents to the nearest shrine mountains for a weekend, but never with my grandmother. She would travel for a week or two at a time and sleep on top of the sacred mountain when she got there."

"On your next leave maybe you can go with her."

Something seemed to rattle in the soldier's throat. "She died while I was in officer's training. I couldn't even get back for her funeral. My father took his annual leave so he could scatter her ashes on the top of her favorite mountain."

Shan was about to offer words of comfort when Zhu quickened his pace and pulled away. He did not speak until they reached the shrine before the final steep switchback climb up to the Talons.

"Aren't we supposed to have incense?" Zhu asked as he laid a rock on the final cairn. "My father would light incense when he prayed."

Shan searched his pockets, finding a single cone of incense. "I only have the one," he said, and dropped it into Zhu's hand.

The lieutenant stared at it. "I didn't mean that I . . ." he began, staring at the cone with a troubled expression, then he stuffed it in his pocket and began to climb.

When they reached the camp at the Talons rock formation, Jaya was alone, watching over a kettle of soup. There was no sign of Lhakpa or his four-legged niece. Ko's words still nagged Shan. *It's all about the goat.*

Jaya greeted Shan and eyed Zhu uncertainly. "You brought the army!" she accused Shan after a moment.

"Why would you think that?" Zhu asked.

She pointed to his military boots.

"Maybe I got them at the Shoe Factory," Zhu suggested.

Jaya bent over the pack he had dropped by the fire and brushed away the grime, revealing the small insignia of the People's Liberation Army. She glared at Zhu.

Shan stepped between them. "Yes, Zhu is a soldier. He's been helping me unmask Metok's killers. He went to Hong Kong and found proof that the case against Metok was fabricated. Now he is going to help you with Public Security."

Jaya winced at the announcement.

"Help distract Public Security," Zhu explained.

"Don't be a fool!" Jaya shot back. "They have already arrested over a dozen herders, men and women who knew nothing about what was going on here. No one can defeat them. We just run and hide. And now they have placed those devices on the trails, like they use along the border to detect people crossing over into Nepal."

"Sound and motion detectors?" Zhu asked. "Excellent. Just like we use, only the army has more advanced hardware." He lifted a small laptop computer out of his pack, then quickly set up a small collapsible solar panel and an antenna then began tapping the keyboard. "Just another field exercise," he murmured as he watched the screen. "Confuse the enemy force. Improvise and evade. I've never been beaten." After a few moments he motioned to several blinking lights on what Shan recognized as a map of the surrounding landscape. "Six devices, all within a mile of here. When they pick up sounds or repetitive movement, they will send a team to investigate."

"And then we will have to leave the mountain," Jaya said, despair in her voice.

"Except they don't expect Shan and me," Zhu said with a grin and dumped out the remaining contents of his pack. As Jaya saw the small devices, her eyes went round. She knelt and began examining the little black boxes, firing excited questions at Zhu.

Neither the lieutenant nor Jaya noticed as Shan backed away. He watched the shadows around the camp, and seeing no sign of a watcher, slipped through the felt flaps in front of the rock face.

Only the nearest of the makeshift shelves still held artifacts. Shan paused over them, studying an exquisitely detailed brass figure of six-armed Dorje Phurba, the deification of the ritual dagger, adorned with snakes and skulls. It was many centuries old and very rare. It had not been on the shelves when he had passed them days earlier. Several new objects, not artifacts, leaned against the rearmost shelves. Shan saw a bow and arrow, a bent scimitar, a heavy blue maul, and a sword. Gekho's weapons had been retrieved from the valley.

He ventured past the little cave that served as the hail chaser's quarters, noting the dented helmet lying on a folded blanket, then onto the narrow but well-trodden trail down which the nurse had disappeared on his last visit. He gasped as he realized that the ground had fallen away and he was treading a foot-wide path that clung to the side of the mountain above a chasm several hundred feet deep. His heart pounding, he stared straight ahead and after ten uneasy minutes reached a small tree-lined flat on the other side. The track seemed to follow the scent of burning juniper and incense, and he soon found himself facing a narrow cleft in the wall of the mountain. He followed it into a high-walled cavern that was lit by sunlight leaking through a crack at the top. The chamber was lined with two long altars that seemed to point to a smaller tunnel. Incense burned in bronze pots on the altars, and in a larger brazier juniper smoldered. Someone seemed to be desperately calling the gods.

Shan sensed a vibration in the air, and he recalled the hail chaser's words about hearing the mountain speak, then he realized the sounds were mantras. He followed the sounds down the tunnel and emerged into a spacious chamber whose walls had been squared and plastered in an earlier age. Although the plaster was cracked and falling away in several places, he could make out the primitive, faded images of protector demons painted on them. In the dim light of several butter lamps, he made out four middle-aged Tibetan women sitting in pairs on worn carpets at the opposite side of the chamber. One woman broke off with a surprised cry as she spotted him, but the others continued the cadence of the prayers, though they watched him with alarmed expressions. He exposed his gau and put one hand on it, and they seemed to relax as he offered a respectful nod. The first pair was reciting the Bardo, the death rites. The other two were invoking the aid of the Mother Protector. One of that pair stared pointedly toward a dark patch in the far wall and, following her gaze, Shan discovered another tunnel.

As he passed a sharp curve in the passage, he reached a pool of surprisingly bright light and stepped into a long, wide chamber with a twenty-foot-high ceiling whose plaster walls, more intact, were painted with much more complex and vivid images of the gods. Modern gas lanterns hung from iron brackets in the walls that had been fashioned to hold butter lamps. Supplies were stacked in makeshift half-walls to create a small living space at the near end, where a camp stove was heating a kettle, and also a corridor along a wall painted with prominent Buddhist dieties.

Two figures at the far end stood staring down at a pile of blankets. One turned then approached along the wall painted with gods, his limp accentuated by his hurried gait. "Constable," the hail chaser said in a soft, welcoming tone. "You have come to the mountain. You do indeed never stop investigating." Shan did not miss the hint of caution in his tone.

"It is my burden," Shan replied, studying the next tunnel that led deeper into the mountain at the back of the long chamber.

Yankay gestured to the kettle. "Sit. We will have tea and see if you can finally hear the mountain speak."

Shan complied, looking now at a stone-built shelf full of artifacts nearby. Sitting beside it, his back against the wall of the cave, was Lhakpa, writing in a notebook. The snow monk was archiving the artifacts.

"These are new," Shan said as he approached Lhakpa.

"No, several hundred years old," the snow monk said, misunderstanding.

"Newly recovered," Shan said as he accepted a steaming mug. The two brothers had no reply. His gaze shifted to the black shadow that marked the next tunnel. "Which means," he suggested, "that Gekho's cave is not sealed off. When I was in the valley talking with the workers about the tragedy of the cave's destruction, one said 'if the cave is truly gone,' as if having the entrance closed didn't necessarily mean it was gone. There's a back entrance," he said and pointed to the next tunnel.

The old hail chaser sighed. "We are at your mercy then, Constable. If the government knew, it would come with more explosives and destroy this end as well. More would die, because some of us would not abandon the old god. We have already failed him too often."

"But Shan is not the government," Lhakpa said as he lowered his notebook. He rose and poured himself a mug. "He is the protector of the Yangkar gompa." The snow monk's gaze seemed to challenge Shan. "And the Yangkar gompa has always been the protector of Gekho."

"Yangkar's gompa has been gone for decades," Shan said. As he sipped his tea he saw a large aluminum case in the shadows by the wall. On its side were the words in large black figures. *For Emergency Medical Use.* A medical kit had been stolen from the highway ambulance after all.

Lhakpa saw Shan's gaze and stepped to block his view of the case. But Shan was not interested in pressing him about the theft on the highway, for he now saw that the remaining figure at the end of the chamber was the nurse. "Someone died and didn't die," he said as he recalled his first conversation with Yankay. "Those women are chanting the Bardo for the dead but also invoking mother Tara, who protects the living." He looked toward the nurse. "Impossible!" he whispered as realization struck him. Yankay moved as if to stop him as Shan took a step toward the far end of the cave but Lhakpa put a restraining hand on his brother's shoulder.

The nurse was sitting as Shan approached, singing in a low voice. It wasn't a pile of blankets beside her, it was a pallet. She was holding the hand of her patient. Although much of the prostrate woman's head, including her right eye, was covered with bandages, her long blond hair spilled out over the pallet.

"She has never regained consciousness," the healer said. "I fear her eye is ruined. She seems unable to speak. But most days she accepts the broth we feed her. Her skull was badly fractured. The journey down the mountain would have killed her."

Shan sank to his knees. Yankay had asked Shan about what happened when a soul and body changed their mind after dying. Natalie Pike lay before him, alive and not alive.

CHAPTER FIFTEEN

Lhakpa ignored Shan's queries, making only light conversation as they returned down the treacherous path along the side of the mountain. The nurse too had declined to answer any of his questions, only explaining that they had found Natalie on the day after the explosion, under the debris of a half-collapsed chapel. When they reached the safety of the forested trail Lhakpa finally turned and answered the first of Shan's questions. "How could we tell anyone?" the snow monk asked. "As soon as they learned she was alive those who intended to kill her would come to finish the job, along with all who helped her."

"It's why you and Jaya reacted so strangely when I said her father had come to the valley."

Lhakpa eyed Shan as if searching for something hidden in his choice of words. A heavy weight seemed to descend on the Tibetan. "What could we do for her father, Shan? The hope we might give him would probably be false."

"Surely you know what must be done. Get her to a hospital."

"Some of the old ones say her spirit was separated from her body in the explosion, that it is wandering in the dark and will never find her body if she is moved from that cave. Once I was confident I had learned so much, but now I know how hollow that knowledge is. What if they are right? Yankay insists the best healing place for her is right where she is. And the nurse knows many of the old ways. She

rubs Natalie's pulse points and sings to her, saying if she can just ig-
nite a tiny spark inside her, it will kindle her life fire again. And some
of the old women have been summoning the Mother Protector, never
stopping no matter what the hour." He shrugged. There was anguish
in his voice. "Who are we to say a hospital will be better?"

"But isn't it a lie to keep acting like she died?" Shan asked.

"You saw her. Which is the lie? That she is dead, or that she is
alive? Does it change anything you are doing?"

When Shan had no reply, Lhakpa turned back to the trail and led
him into the gathering shadows.

They were already walking along the empty shelves where the artifacts had been stored when Lhakpa held up his hand in alarm. There
were strange sounds coming from the campsite by the Talons. It took
them a few moments to realize it was laughter.

As they reached the little flat, Jaya was speaking excitedly with
two Tibetan men, some of the herders who were helping her, and
pointed to Zhu, who sat by the fire with a cup of tea.

"Did you find all the devices?" Shan asked as he reached the young
lieutenant.

"I had some devices of my own," Zhu reminded him with a mischievous smile.

"They may never come back!" Jaya said with another laugh.

"You used your own devices?" Shan asked.

It was Jaya who responded. "We found all their listening machines
and moved them to the top of rock spires or down animal burrows.
One went inside an old pilgrim's cairn. We placed one of Zhu's boxes
with each of the listening devices, rigged with a loop, a recording that
will just repeat until the batteries run down in a few days."

"A loop?" Lhakpa asked.

"We got one of the old shepherds to record for us. Whenever Public Security listens to their sentry devices they will hear nothing but
the mani mantra! Lord Gekho will be speaking to them!"

. . .

The Chinese soldier had unexpectedly lifted the spirits of the camp, and as the stars rose, they shared stories of adventures in the mountains. When Zhu began speaking of serving in the Himalayas, Shan feared his tale would relate to intercepting refugees leaving from Tibet, but instead he spoke of encountering a snow leopard with two cubs, which deeply impressed the Tibetans, who considered such encounters good luck. Yankay then offered his own story from his boyhood about an old man who could change shape into a snow leopard. Jaya countered with a tale of a woman who could turn into a mouse, and the Tibetans began a bemused dialogue about the advantages of mousehood versus leopardhood. As Zhu good-naturedly defended the leopard—not because of its claws, but because of its grace and stealth in movement—Shan slipped down the path that led through the labyrinth of the rock outcroppings. He emerged onto a ledge and sat, looking down on the moonlit Valley of the Gods.

Rows of lights marked the workers compound. Here and there twin shafts of light indicated the trucks that worked around the clock. At the far end, a silvery column shimmered where the moonlight touched the tall waterfall. The blanket of night brought a deceiving peacefulness to the valley. How could it be possible that such a placid place, where simple people had touched their gods for centuries, could have attracted so much greed, so many lies, and so many murders? He tried to push the crimes out of his mind and imagine how it had once been. Bold but devout tribesmen had come before history, to erect rows of standing stones. Bonpo pilgrims had arrived in later centuries, to pray and paint the faces of their gods on the walls of the cave. Later Buddhists had come with their own gods, not to attack the older deities, but to find ways to harmonize them, for the sake of the Tibetan soul.

He patted his pockets, looking for incense, then recalled he had given his last piece to Zhu. Instead, he steepled his fingers in a mudra, the Diamond of the Mind sign, and stared at the glistening waterfall in the distance as he tried to fit together the ever-shifting pieces of his puzzle. Despite all he had learned, he could not find the lever, the handle he needed to get inside the conspiracy so he could break it apart. It was as if there were a shadow in its center he could not penetrate. The valley may be a vortex that was causing lives to violently collide, but something else had started events in motion.

But that piece of the puzzle was invisible to him and without it, he was powerless. He had no angle, no explosive piece of evidence, no leverage point he could push to pivot the disastrous events of recent weeks. The forces against him were too powerful. Public Security was against him, the ruthless Amban Council was against him, the governments in Lhasa and Beijing were against him. He was wise enough to know he had lost this time. They would have to claim the miraculous survival of Natalie Pike as their victory and move on. The dam would never be stopped. The Amban Council could not be stopped. Lhadrung County would be swept clean in a few months. He and Tan would be pushed aside, debris of an earlier age. Yangkar would get a new Chinese constable, who would inevitably discover the precious, illegal archives under its streets. Ko would lose Tan's protection at the 404th.

He was about to rise and return to the camp, his heart heavy, when a match flared beside him. Lhakpa lit a cone of incense and set it between them, as if he too needed the gods close.

"An old lama once told me that Tibet is ripe with lives," Lhakpa said after a long silence. "The words nagged at me, and when I later confessed to him that I didn't understand, he said Tibet today forces people to juggle more than one life. Everyone's forced to appear as a loyal citizen who would never publicly acknowledge their faith. But many are also devout followers of the Dalai Lama, who hide illegal images of him in their homes. We can't be faithful without being liars. And then we have lives as productive workers, though seldom in the job we would have chosen for ourselves. We're all actors, with different audiences for each mask we wear, each life we lead."

Shan weighed Lhakpa's words as he gazed out over the moonlit valley. "It is an age of troubled souls," he agreed. "A renowned scientist," Shan observed after another silence. "A professor at a famed Buddist school. A dissident. A prisoner. A snow monk. That's a soul ripe with lives."

Lhakpa went very still. "I'm not sure I follow, Constable."

"My son was nearly beaten to death at the 404th labor brigade because he started asking questions about prisoners who arrived from Larung Gar last year."

"I'm sorry. I will pray for him."

"He'll live. Funny thing, he found out that one of the prisoners who arrived in that convoy didn't seem to know the others, even sometimes didn't seem to recognize his own name." Shan paused, watching the headlights of a patrol car drive along the perimeter road below them. "Understandable, of course, since he had no time to train to become you, Professor Lin. Or Lhakpa. How many other names have you used?"

Lhakpa took a long time to reply. His voice cracked when he finally spoke. "It wasn't my idea. I argued against it, saying I could not subject another man to the suffering of imprisonment intended for me. But they said he had volunteered to switch, to take my place in that prison, that he had no family, that he had been in prison before and could endure it. He was about my age, about my build, so he could pass with those who didn't know me well. They said I was needed on the mountain, that I understand mountains in ways no one else did."

"Meaning the science of mountains," Shan suggested. "Geology. Engineering. Who were they?"

"Those ones who call themselves purba, the resistance. They were here earlier but the old ones sent them away, because they began to suggest violence. Some of them went below, getting hired as workers, and stayed in touch with Jaya." Lhakpa reached into a pocket. "Do you mind?" he asked and produced a pack of cigarettes. Shan had never seen him smoke. "The snow monk doesn't smoke," Lhakpa said with a sheepish tone, "but the professor often did, a habit from university days. I thought I had quit but the last few days of evading Public Security has been nerve-wracking." He lit a cigarette with a book of matches before speaking again. "Yes. Geology and engineering. When I was seventeen, they sent me before what the school called academic commissioners. They were just young Party members who had graduated with degrees in socialist philosophy and such. They never asked me if I wanted to go to university myself, never asked me what I wanted to study. If I had stayed," he shrugged. "If things had been as before, I would have gone to a monastery."

"You would have made a wise lama," Shan said.

Lhakpa gave a grunt that hinted at bitter amusement. "Geology and engineering. They said they were the sciences of progress, for so many mines had to be opened, so many mountains had to be leveled, so many fortifications and dams had to be built.

"Our parents were gone by then and my brother had disappeared with some old unregistered Bonpo monk, so I assumed the worst. I became an engineer then later a professor. They would call me into government service for especially challenging projects. The last one was a dam designed to flood a valley up in Heilongjiang Province by the Russian border. I went out with a survey team and discovered a village of the Oroqen people there, an ancient tribe of which there were only a few thousand left. I went back and told the truth, that there were better dam sites in the region and this one would destroy a village of indigenous people who had lived there for centuries. I was told no, this will be the valley because those people needed to enter the twenty-first century. They were using the dam as cover for their political goals, as a way to justify the destruction of those people. I left the next day. Left the project, left the university, and without a word to anyone, I went to Larung Gar, the school colony, because I had heard people could start over there, could learn to live the life of a monk or nun no matter how old they were, or what their prior life had been."

"You honored your Tibetan roots," Shan said.

"My soul had become a dried, shriveled thing. I honored it for the

first time in my life. I had never forgotten a passage an old lama
showed me when I was young, written by another lama centuries ago.
The man wrote that he was leaving to be a snow monk, that he was
going to go up and sit with the mountain for a few years, until only
the mountain remained. For a while it seemed there was nothing
better in all the world for me to do."

"But you couldn't entirely leave that old life behind," Shan suggested.

Lhakpa nodded. "After a few months my teachers at Larung Gar
discovered my background. They said that I had an obligation to share
my knowledge, that Larung Gar was about understanding the spiritual and natural world. There were Bonpo lamas there who were excited by my published teachings on earth science because, they said, I
was demonstrating the magic of the earth. I had never thought of it
that way but came to realize they were right. The huge anchor mountains they considered sacred were sacred for scientific reasons as well,
because they were the source of so many ecosystems and of the head-
waters for all the great rivers of Asia. The environmental experts with
college degrees were just engaged in a form of worshipful penance,
the lamas said, required because so many for so long had forgotten
how to respect the earth. One of them declared that the earth has
ways of speaking we don't always understand, and my science was
one of the languages of earth magic. I was a bridge, he said, standing
in the middle, connecting those who worshipped the earth in these different ways. Then one day a year and a half ago, that lama came to
me in the night and began whispering of a place called Gekho's Roost."

"So putting on the clothes of a snow monk was an act," Shan said.

"Not at all. I told you, that was my intention when I went to
Larung Gar. Even in Yangkar I was clinging to that dream for a while,
before the business here arose. But that lama Tsomo Rabten changed
my mind with his stories of Gekho's home."

Shan cocked his head. He had heard the name elsewhere. "Tsomo
was the lama who died on October 1."

Lhakpa nodded. "The hour the standing stones came down. His soul was connected to them, Shan, I am convinced of it. He was of the prior generation, who touched wonders that are lost to us now."

"Was your other niece, Tara, at Larung Gar? Is everything you told me about her a lie?"

Lhakpa drew on his cigarette and blew out a long silvery plume of smoke toward the heavens. "I'm sorry, Shan. Jaya says the goat was sent by the gods to keep me honest. Tara was my niece, yes, but she didn't die coming back from her school. She did leave her school but had gone to Larung Gar to seek me out and began attending our secret meetings about the Valley of the Gods. She was fiery, a leader who wasn't shy about declaring that those at Larung Gar owed a broader duty to Tibet."

"Someone on that Institute team that came to Yangkar recognized you from Larung Gar," Shan suggested after a moment.

"The photographer had worked with Jiao there, and one of his assignments was to photograph all those who Jiao branded as troublemakers. Yes, he recognized me. He was confused, because he must have known I had been driven away to prison. Your deputy saved me that day." Lhakpa sighed. "You do know why they were there, don't you, Shan?"

"To begin planning for Yangkar to be the project's administrative headquarters," Shan said.

Lhakpa gave a forlorn nod of his head. "It will be the end of Yangkar as we know it. They poison everything they touch."

In the valley below, Huan's men had mounted a large searchlight on a truck bed and its beam was sweeping the workers compound. Little by little the valley was taking on the air of a prison.

"We can't stop the dam, Professor," Shan said.

"Just Lhakpa. That life is over. And we *must* stop the dam. The young ones are talking about a night of violence, about burning the equipment and the buildings."

"They will be killed," Shan said. "And their families will be punished." New directives had made it a crime to simply have a family member who had engaged in acts of dissent or sabotage.

Lhakpa gave a melancholy nod of agreement. "No one will win," he conceded.

"Sometimes in Tibet," Shan whispered, "winning is just enduring."

They watched the wispy line of smoke from the incense reach up toward the stars. Lives hung by such threads.

"But it *is* the wrong site," Lhakpa said after a long silence. "The geology isn't right, too many fractures in the valley rock structure. There were seismic tests that confirmed that but all those maps have disappeared, all traces of the tests are gone."

"Which is why Sun Lunshi was bringing more maps back on the train," Shan said.

Lhakpa nodded. "Even the economics are wrong. The investment needed for the transmission lines and the loss of power along the lines will make recovery of costs impossible. But this area has nagged the government for decades. Too Tibetan. Too religious. Too suggestive that we are not who we think we are."

"Sorry?"

"Tibetans didn't sprout from seeds planted here. Long ago they came from somewhere to the west and north, from the horse tribes of central Asia, not from China. The cavern and those standing stones were proof of that but . . ." Lhakpa shrugged and stared into the glowing ember of his cigarette. "I tried science. I tried reasoning. I tried compassion. What's left?"

"Prayer?" Shan wondered out loud.

In the moonlight he saw the hint of a smile on the professor's face. "The old herders in the cavern you found, they were praying for months before the explosion in the cave, from the first time those Institute surveyors were spotted in the valley. Now they pray nonstop, all night and all day, in shifts, pray for the valley, pray for Gekho, pray for the American woman. We don't know how long it will be before Public Security discovers them. They won't flee. Public Security will arrest them. That Lieutenant Huan will call them saboteurs and traitors."

"Is that what the others from Larung Gar were charged with?"

Lhakpa sighed. "I hear the 404th is a terrible place."

"There was a meeting at the prison last week. Jiao was there, with Lieutenant Huan and a man named Major Xun, deputy to the governor of the county. Afterward all the Larung Gar prisoners were put in solitary confinement. It means they intend to do individual interrogations of them now, probably brutal interrogations."

The news seemed to strike a painful blow. Lhakpa lowered his head into his hands for a moment. "Our world is such a broken place, Shan. Sometimes I feel like my soul is so withered it will just blow away in the next strong wind. Maybe we should all become snow monks and lose ourselves in the mountains."

"I've tried that. All I got was cold."

Lhakpa gave a grunt of acknowledgment and sighed. "The seeds of this battle didn't sprout in the valley below, but at Larung Gar. It was only the two of them at first, Jiao and Xun. Jiao came in from some high political office in Lhasa, claiming to be the expert at subduing Tibetans. Xun was from some paramilitary unit that targeted social unrest. They showed up one day at our morning prayers, pushing their way through the assembly of monks and nuns, and announced they headed the new Committee of Reconstruction and Safety. The chief lama, our abbot, offered them a blessing and placed prayer scarves around their necks. They laughed, and Jiao blew his nose on the scarf. The next morning they drove up in a limousine in front of a line of cranes and bulldozers. They sounded a siren, though none of us knew what it meant. It became a fixture of our lives for weeks. It was the five-minute warning, after which the bulldozers and wrecking cranes went to work. They ripped right through classroom buildings without even bothering to check if they had been evacuated.

Several of our students suffered terrible injuries. The abbot and I went to Jiao and Xun to complain, and they said we should be thanking them for they were going to create a new, sanitary community where everyone would be much healthier. They even showed us their plans, with new cinder block buildings that looked more like one of those reeducation camps than a Buddhist school. I tried to keep my temper and just remarked that the compound in the drawings was not nearly big enough. They laughed again and said several thousand would be leaving, for their own safety. They even offered us jackets with that ridiculous slogan of theirs."

"Safety in Serenity," Shan said.

Lhakpa nodded. "I said they had no right to attack a peaceful community. They called me by my Chinese name and said I was lucky, that I was a traitor who had been allowed to go into exile instead of prison, but the government could always change its mind.

"I didn't care. What they were doing was wrong, like what was done to those poor people in Heilongjiang Province was wrong, and what they were doing at the Valley of the Gods was wrong. I had to find new places for my classes, but the new Committee always knew and disrupted them no matter where I went, saying they were too crowded, or my classroom had no inspection certificate, or my students were not officially registered. One night when we were gone, they leveled the building I had used that day. The next night, when I was giving a class under the moon, they leveled my home. Then Xun and Jiao came to me and ordered me to leave. I said what they were doing at Larung Gar and the Five Claws was illegal, and that if they persisted I would hold a press conference to announce that none of the proper tests for the new Five Claws dam had been done. We thought putting a spotlight on the dam gave us leverage, that it could be an indirect weapon against them. They backed off for a few days. We formed our own committee, separate from the abbot and managers of the school, who could not risk polarizing their Chinese overseers. We staged sit-ins, surrounding the demolition equipment with hundreds of monks and nuns reciting mantras. We held a prayer vigil with over a thousand people, blocking a key crossroads for forty-eight hours. Metok brought in workers from nearby hotels to join us, shutting down the hotels."

A chill crept down Shan's spine. "Metok? But Metok was here, at the Five Claws."

"Not until eight months ago. He had been working on a highway project west of Lhasa that was abruptly suspended, so he was assigned as engineer for the Committee of Reconstruction and Safety at Larung Gar. He was Jiao's man, or Jiao thought he was. But he changed at Larung Gar. He would come sit with us at prayers. One night he declared that he wanted to help. Tara said he could make maps for us, for retreats and hiding places in the mountains. He became a great friend, and even saved some of our buildings from the bulldozers."

Shan's mind raced. He had to rip apart the puzzle pieces he had thought he had assembled and start over. "But why would Jiao bring him to this valley?"

"Jiao got him the job. A big promotion. But it was because Jiao wanted to keep a close eye on him. I think now it was because Jiao meant to find a way to eliminate him."

"For sympathizing with fellow Tibetans?"

"For seeing Jiao and his accomplices murder my niece Tara."

Shan could not speak for a moment. "You mean she was lost in the demolition of one of the buildings?"

Lhakpa looked at the glowing stub of his cigarette and reached for another, then reconsidered. He reached into a different pocket and produced another cone of incense and lit it with his cigarette. "Their committee published a list of agitators and cautioned them against further activity," he continued. "They used all the favorite terms from the propaganda mills. Antisocialist hooligans. Reactionaries. Hotheads. Outsiders, even, though the gods only know what that meant at Larung Gar. Everyone was an outsider there. Some of those on the lists took the warning and left. But Tara redoubled her efforts, holding more meetings, printing her own notices about freedom of religion and freedom of speech, passing them out in the shelters where more and more people slept at night. She never spoke a harsh word directly about Jiao and Xun, or even their leaders in Beijing. It was always about praying and abiding steadfastly to the Buddhist way of compassion. She encouraged people to distribute flowers to the soldiers, and with each flower people were supposed to say a prayer for the soldier. She developed a following, and her meetings kept growing in size. Jiao loathed her but had to be careful because Beijing officials kept visiting and there were so many tourists coming that new hotels were being built. Larung Gar was becoming a business proposition that just had to be managed responsibly, that's how Jiao put it. There was talk of human rights observers secretly entering the town as well, and they also had to be managed. Public Security started playing a bigger role. Huan arrived.

"Tara heard that some minister from Beijing was coming so she began planning a peaceful demonstration to greet him. She intended to stop his limousine by surrounding it with praying Tibetans and drape prayer scarves over his neck in the hope that the Compassionate Buddha would help him understand. It would have been a deep embarrassment to Jiao, who had told us more than once that when Beijing gave him a task no one was allowed to interfere. He was furious. 'The motherland will not tolerate obstructionism!' he often shouted at her.

"My niece called for a planning meeting on a ledge above the wreckage of a building. Jiao and Xun had an informer inside her group. I was suspicious of one of the nuns who befriended Tara, because she did not seem to know many of the prayers. It was that young nun who told Tara about the ledge that she said was a good meeting place. She led Tara there as we watched from above. We were praying at an old pilgrim shrine with Metok and a friend before going down to join them. Jiao, Xun, Huan, and an army officer came out of hiding when Tara arrived early, alone. It happened so fast. They suddenly started pushing her toward the edge of the cliff, shouting at her. Then there were little flashes and Tara clutched her belly and collapsed. Xun and Huan both had pistols out. They had shot her. Then Jiao kicked her over the edge into the debris of concrete slabs. Bulldozers and trucks began clearing it out minutes later. It took us nearly a day to locate her body at the dump where they took the rubble."

Lhakpa turned at the sound of footsteps. Jaya joined them, sitting beside the snow monk. As she sat the little goat appeared and lay beside the woman, snugging against her leg.

It's all about the goat. The words that had nagged Shan suddenly had meaning. They had misunderstood the death chart. It had not invoked the Mother Protectress, had not set forth the name of a goddess and the hail chaser. The Tibetan names had not been two but one, that of a young vibrant woman who had been named for the Mother Protectress, the niece of Lhakpa and the hail chaser. The inquisitive goat who stayed at Lhakpa's side was Tara. In human form, the one who had been murdered, she had been Tara Namdol, the name written on the haunting death chart given to the fourth man, the army officer who was now the warden of the 404th.

Shan found himself clutching at the gau under his shirt. "So it was the word of a few Tibetans against two senior officials," he whispered.

"Metok and his friend wanted to confront them right away. But the rest of us said no, that we had to wait for the right time, for the right official, for the right leverage."

"But it would always be Tibetan undesirables speaking against two of Beijing's favorite sons."

"Not exactly. We had a video."

Surely Shan had not heard correctly. He turned toward Lhakpa. "You're not suggesting there was a recording of the murder?"

"Not suggesting. It is a fact. Tara had told people that whenever possible we should record all interchanges with the government, because there might be a chance of getting the recording to the outside world, so all the world could then witness the atrocities at Larung Gar. So our visitor had her phone out and had started recording from our vantage point. She thought they might try to beat Tara."

"Visitor?"

"Metok's American friend. A strong woman who smiled a lot, very interested in history."

Shan's head seemed to spin. How could he have missed this? She had written to her father that she had seen something terrible but that she was learning Tibetan ways to fix things. "You mean Natalie Pike."

Lhakpa nodded. "It was her idea, after we convinced the others to hold the video back. There had been an announcement the next day that Jiao was leaving to become deputy director at the Five Claws, based on his success at Larung Gar. She said we might be able to use the video to stop the project somehow. But the six of us were arrested by Huan."

"I had just arrived, with friends from the mountains," Jaya inserted. "I found horses for Natalie and Metok and we fled."

"So where is the video now?"

"Everyone is too frightened to transmit it," Lhakpa explained, "because Public Security monitors most transmissions in Tibet. When we saw her again she said it was safe, in the hands of a nameless friend in Lhasa. She said before they began pouring the foundations for the dam we would confront Jiao with it."

"So Jiao didn't know about it."

"He must know now," Jaya said. "After Metok's arrest they searched his room. Metok wouldn't have willingly given up the information but they use drugs in interrogation."

"They use drugs that wring the last drop of truth from a prisoner," Shan confirmed. "So they must know that the American woman took the video, and that it is in Lhasa somewhere. How long did Metok know Natalie?"

"A few weeks. Before arriving in Larung Gar he had been assigned to that bridge project that was stopped when they found the remains of that Green Standard Army camp she was working on. That's how they met. Metok invited Natalie to Larung Gar so she could see a Buddhist teaching institution, to show her that Buddhism still thrived among Tibetans. Natalie and Professor Gangfen even visited his home in Lhasa."

As the words sank in, a terrible realization struck Shan. An image of the frightened woman with the teenage daughter he had met in Lhasa flashed through his mind. "Then someone has to warn her!" he exclaimed. "The secret Tibetan in Lhasa has to be Metok's wife!"

Lhakpa turned to Shan, then to Jaya, who cocked her head in confusion. "But Metok never had a wife, Shan," she said.

CHAPTER SIXTEEN

The long, winding trail glowed silver in the moonlight as the horses galloped down the mountain. Shan, swallowing his fear that his mount would stumble, pushed the horse harder and harder into the darkness. Zhu crouched low in his saddle at Shan's side. Jaya sang a song to her horse and their khampa guide laughed with joy.

Shan had struggled to sleep when they had returned to the camp, then had suddenly bolted upright. "Amah Jiejie," he gasped, then desperately shook Zhu awake. "We have to go, now!"

"It's the middle of the night," Zhu had protested.

"Amah Jiejie has to be warned! The satellite phone is in the truck!"

"Constable?" Zhu rubbed sleep from his eyes.

"Metok never had a wife! The woman pretending to be his wife is a spy! Metok's wife is a spy. An imposter nun led Tara to be killed. It must be the same woman. The spy is taking Amah Jiejie into the mountains to kill her!"

Lhakpa too had awakened. "You are not making sense," he said.

"Metok's wife asked the colonel's assistant to go with her to a remote shrine. I thought Tan was invulnerable. But there is a way to destroy him. They want to kill Amah Jiejie."

Zhu cursed as he grasped Shan's meaning, and began pulling on his boots. Jaya rose and began poking the embers of the fire.

"You'll never find the trail in the dark," Lhakpa warned.

"The moon is rising," Shan said.

"No, wait," Jaya said. "Get packed and wait here." The Tibetan woman darted up the slope. Ten minutes later she appeared with the khampa and four horses.

They had not reached Amah Jiejie before she had left but the helicopter sent by Tan intercepted her before she met Metok's widow, allowing her to call in with her apology for being ordered to a last-minute meeting and promising to set a date soon for their trek.

Twenty-four hours later Shan paused at the little shrine on the stone ramp he was climbing to once more give thanks that Amah Jiejie had been saved. He always entered the Potala Palace in the traditional manner, the way it had been done for centuries, up the long steep ramp that rose up to the south entrance. As he climbed he considered why Pike had insisted he tell Metok's wife to meet him in the Potala. Halfway up, pausing to catch his breath, he recalled the photograph Pike's daughter had sent to her father. She had visited the Potala with Professor Gangfen, and in the photo she had been smiling with great contentment as she looked out over the huge Buddhist palace. It meant that the Potala wasn't so much a place of beauty for Cato Pike, it was a place of his daughter, perhaps one of the last places on earth where she had been happy.

The roof terrace of the Red Palace, the maroon-colored core of the complex, was nearly empty when he arrived, and he turned to the astounding view over Lhasa and beyond, gazing out toward the river, the train station, and the snow-covered mountains in the far distance. In the few years since Shan had begun visiting Lhasa, the city had become unequivocally Chinese, but here and there a few traditional neighborhoods survived, and the Jokhang Temple in the old Barkhor district stood like a defiant symbol of the Tibetans, surviving the onslaught of the centuries. The Dalai Lamas, whose personal living quarters had been only a few steps from where Shan now stood, doubtlessly had enjoyed this same perspective over a different, simpler world. At least here in the austere stone palace, some of that world endured.

The woman he had known as Metok's wife appeared at his side a quarter-hour after he arrived. Her hair was pinned in a tail behind her neck. She wore makeup and gold earrings. She had become more stylish, even attractive, looking more like the tour guide that was her cover story. It could well be her work when not on special assignment, Shan realized, for appealing young guides were often used to troll for information from Western tourists, sometimes even tempting them into overnight trysts. Shan unexpectedly recalled a tour guide from when he had first arrived in Beijing years earlier as a naive twenty-year-old. She had not really explained anything of historical interest, only spouted scripted observations about the hordes of slaves who died building the structures and the unforgivable, wasteful greed of the aristocrats. Her name had been Jiang, he recalled now, remembered because it was the same as Mao's ruthless wife, who then dominated the government as part of the Gang of Four. Now, staring out at Lhasa, Shan decided to think of the treacherous woman beside him as Madame Jiang.

"The Red Palace was started during the life of the Fifth Dalai Lama in the seventeenth century," Madame Jiang abruptly declared, "though there had been fortresses and temples here for a thousand years before that."

"Spoken like a savvy tour guide," he observed.

The woman nodded and used the push of a crowd of tourists to press against him, apparently following the instincts of her training. "It was still under construction when the Fifth died, but the Regent kept the Fifth's death concealed until the work was completed twelve years later. The fiction was kept up by saying the Dalai Lama was on a retreat or a pilgrimage or in spiritual consultations. A fraud on the Tibetan people, for twelve long years."

Shan considered whether the words were part of an official script, and decided they were because it made the Buddhist leaders sound devious. "I always wondered about the reason for the lie," he said. "A conspiracy by the Regent to maintain power? Perhaps by the builders' union to maintain their contract? And where was his body all that time?"

The woman looked up and summoned the sad smile he had seen at Metok's apartment. "Ever the curious investigator."

"Tibet is built on layers of mysteries," Shan replied. "More so today than ever before." He turned to her. "Did they return your husband's body?" he asked.

"Cremated him," she said. "A box of ashes is all I have."

Shan recalled the crematorium director who had cooperated with Huan. Had she actually been provided with a box of ashes to bolster her cover? He leaned against the half-wall of the terrace to watch as more tour groups arrived on the roof, one of them all Westerners. Cato Pike wore a long coat and had pulled a hat so low Shan barely recognized him among the tourists. Stay in the sun, the American had requested, for the camera's sake.

"The Sixth Dalai Lama lived here as well," Shan said. "The wastrel lama. They say there were brothels at the bottom of the ramp maintained solely for him. One night he disappeared, never to be seen again. Some say the gods took him away for punishment."

Madame Jiang smiled. "My husband would have liked that tale. Except I would say the Sixth was taken to his just reward." She looked out over the crowd, taking no notice of Pike, who now seemed to be very interested in the sculpture of a serpent. "Your message said you know where my husband's things are."

"With a friend he met at work."

"You mean at the Five Claws."

"At the mountain above Gekho's Roost, yes."

She weighed his words. "Are you saying his things are up on that mountain?"

"A backpack of his. With some papers, some engineer's tools, a phone, and a compass. There's a camp where he apparently met with his Tibetan friends, by a stone formation called the Talons."

Shan saw a flicker of victory in the woman's eyes, then she sobered.

"I've been meaning to go see his place of work," she said. "As a way of saying goodbye. Getting his things might give me some degree of comfort. It's been so difficult." Her voice cracked, and she put a hand to her mouth to stifle a sob. "His phone would have his friends' information. Maybe if I could speak with some of them it would ease the pain. I will go."

"You mustn't," Shan said. "Too dangerous. Public Security is on the mountain, including Lieutenant Huan, who framed your husband. Now that I know where the pack is I can retrieve it when I go there next. It's the kind of errand a constable does. Public Security will not suspect, I will just be retrieving the effects of a dead man for his family."

Jiang slowly nodded. "Talons. Like the foot of a hawk."

"Once a great garuda bird protected the mountain and the valley below. When the gods summoned him, he left behind his claws. The Tibetans say it means he is still watching, waiting for the right time to protect them."

"But would you know how to find these bird claws, Inspector? It can be difficult to find your way on those mountain slopes."

"On the western slope of the split mountain, above the big field of outcroppings," he explained.

She repeated his words with a slow nod, then offered the sad smile again before pressing his hand and departing.

Pike waited to approach him until the woman could be seen on the steps below the wall. "Quite the conversationalist, Constable," he muttered, then held up his phone, showing a photograph of the woman he had taken as she stood beside Shan. "Clever bitch. A versatile asset, as they would say in the trade."

Shan shot him a quizzical glance.

"She was on the train that day. Sat beside him and struck up a conversation."

The words slowly sank in. "You're saying she was speaking with Sun before he died?"

"They seemed to hit it off. After a couple hours she went forward and brought back food for them both to eat. I remember because I had been watching from a seat three rows back, hoping the spot beside him would stay vacant so we might chat. But then at the last minute she appeared, just as the train was pulling out. Seats are assigned on the sky train. She had a ticket for that particular seat. So I had to wait until he got up then followed him." Pike scrolled through the photographs he had taken of the woman. "Sun never came back. She stayed in her seat. When I got back to my seat an hour later, she was going through an overnight bag. Only later did I recall that she had arrived without baggage. It was his. She didn't expect him to return."

Shan turned toward the city and gazed out toward the squat fortresslike structure on the far side of the river, then glanced at his watch. "I have lunch with an aging cobra. The train arrives in four hours. Meet me at the station."

The colonel hesitated as they reached the heavy iron gate of the compound on the outskirts of Lhasa. He was more nervous than Shan had ever seen him, and for a moment he thought Tan was going to tell his driver to turn around. But then Tan opened his door and, confirming that no one sat in the decrepit gatehouse, unfastened the latch himself and gestured the car inside as he pushed the gate open.

"There was a time," Tan said when they began driving through a grove of trees, "when people called that a one-way gate, because so many visitors left in a van out the back, either dead or wishing they were dead. The Commissar had one of those wide-brimmed hats the Tibetans wear but he decided it was a cowboy hat, like in the American movies, and he got a long revolver with a leather holster that he liked to use. If you were one of his confidants and he wanted you to get rid of someone for him, he would talk about the intended victim in a disappointed tone then hand you a bullet. That's all. He never said, 'I want him dead' or 'get rid of him.' Just the bullet."

Shan sensed an unusual tension in the colonel's voice.

Tan lit a cigarette, exhaling the smoke with a rasping breath. "Years ago, I went to see him here with the quartermaster from my regiment," the colonel continued. He seemed to think Shan was not sufficiently fearful of the old serpent. "The Commissar had invited us to dinner. We had a good meal, just the Commissar and the two of us. Sat with cigarettes and brandy afterward. We finally rose to go and he walked a few steps from us and said, 'I'm calling you out, you thief!' and drew his pistol. He shot the quartermaster through the heart, right there, in his house. Then he laughed and offered me another drink. 'Better this way,' he said, and then, 'You'll sign a statement that it was a suicide.' It was only the next day that I found out that a special investigative unit had sent him a report proving that the quartermaster had been selling army supplies on the black market for years. He was going to be executed in any event, though I always wondered if his real crime had been not sharing his takings with the Commissar. It was never corruption for him to get a piece. He just called it a gate fee because he was the gatekeeper of Tibet. That was one of his names for himself. The Gatekeeper, or the Avenging Dragon, for a while even Buddha's Fist, when he was purging senior lamas," Tan recounted as life-sized statues of Tibetan gods and saints began appearing on both sides of the driveway.

"He's assimilated," Shan said in a brittle voice. The figures were trophies, looted from temples and monasteries.

"He loves Tibet. They tried to send him to North Vietnam as senior adviser to Ho Chi Minh in the early years, but he chose to stay. He's immersed himself in Tibetan culture, he likes to say." Tan turned to Shan. "What's that word for a senior teacher? Not *lama*, the other."

"Rinpoche."

"That's it. Sometimes he calls himself the 'Rinpoche with a sidearm.'"

Their car emerged onto a small flat plain at the base of a low mountain, with a shooting range on one side of the road and a lake on the other. The small marble pavilion at the base of a dock was badly in need of repair.

"It was built as the summer residence of the Chinese amban in the nineteenth century, then used as a retreat for the Dalai Lama's officials for decades," Tan said. "The Commissar had research done so he could have robes identical to those the amban wore. That's his favorite title. He said the amban never ruled, that the amban's job was just to strike fear in those who did publicly rule so they would obey him at critical times. 'Tremble and obey,' he would tell them, like it said in the decrees from the old emperors. That's what he's done for decades. I think he's what they call in those movies a godfather. Even in Beijing they don't implement a Tibetan policy without speaking to the Amban first."

Suddenly Shan himself was seized with fear. Surely then the Amban Council must be led by the very man they had come to see. It was a terrible mistake. What had Tan said when Shan had first suggested the visit? The old man could only kill one of them. When the car stopped Tan had to pull Shan's arm to get him to leave the car.

The house was built much like the residences Shan had seen at the imperial Summer Palace outside Beijing, with lacquered pillars supporting a portico centered around two enormous enameled doors, and a moongate on one side that appeared to lead into a garden. The slim, well-dressed middle-aged Tibetan woman who greeted them declared that the Commissar was very much looking forward to luncheon with them, then led them down a corridor toward the rear of the house.

The Commissar had been a dark cloud at the edge of Shan's sky for years. During his life in Beijing Shan had known, and reported to, many tyrannical Party operatives who behaved more like members of the imperial court than representatives of the people. His loathing of them had not started immediately, only after he had recognized among a gathering of such Party bosses one of the men who had persecuted his own family and destroyed the gentle intellectuals who had been his parents. The fact that he had gradually withdrawn, declining to kowtow to them, was probably the biggest reason he had been sent into his gulag exile. They had been frightened by him, because he did not tremble and obey. He had thought he had left them all behind, that they could not harm him in remote Tibet. But then he had heard of the godfather of Lhasa and for years had felt the old familiar fear whenever anyone had mentioned his name. The Commissar was seldom visible, but he made his presence known, the phantom planet that affected the orbits of all the others.

Their demure guide led them past several opulently furnished rooms whose walls were hung with antique Chinese paintings. The corridor itself was lined with photographs of the Commissar with nearly every important Beijing official of the past six decades, including more than one with the Great Helmsman himself. They turned down another hall, this one lined with exquisite Tibetan thangka paintings. Some of the furnishings, like the decorations along the driveway, had obviously been provided by the Bureau of Religious Affairs. Shan did not even realize he had stopped before a breathtaking, vibrant image of Yamantaka, Lord of Death, until Tan tugged at his sleeve.

"He got himself appointed the head of Religious Affairs in Tibet for a few years," Tan explained in a low voice, "and sent the best paintings to ministers and Party secretaries. Now he keeps the best for himself. He used to lecture at Party meetings, saying that Religious Affairs was the most important agency in Tibet, that the army might be Beijing's hammer, but Religious Affairs was its precision scalpel." Shan was well aware of how Religious Affairs ruthlessly used its policies to silence all dissent, since by definition any contrary word from a Tibetan was a form of Buddhist impertinence.

They emerged into the gardens enclosed by the high walls Shan had seen from the driveway. Bamboo grew in huge ceramic pots along the inner wall. Shaggy flowering shrubs and hedges, badly in need of maintenance, delineated several smaller enclaves. The closest held a small archery range with shredded targets at the far end and a table close to the entrance with several crossbows and baskets of the sharpened metal bolts used for ammunition. In the center of the row of targets was a post the height of a man. The wood of the post was heavily punctured and showed several dark stains.

They were admitted through a high wooden gate into a garden with a marble swimming pool beside which were a solitary chaise lounge, a bar, and a wooden hot tub on a platform. Two attractive young Tibetan women in nurses' uniforms stood beside the tub with towels at the ready. The figure in the steaming tub had a small towel over his head, keeping his face in shadow. The man stayed seated, not moving the towel as he spoke.

"Fuck me!" His voice was like the cackle of a hen. "You stayed alive, Tan, you stubborn son of a bitch! Bullets, bayonets, cannons, cancer. Nothing can kill you! As indestructible as one of your tanks!"

"Almost as indestructible as you, you scrawny bastard," Tan replied in an even voice.

"People have tried to chew me up for years," the Commissar rejoined. "But they always spit me out."

"Because you're just a sorry sack of gristle," Tan said.

As if to prove Tan right, the old man stood. His naked body was shriveled in every respect. One of the nurses reached out to help him from the tub as the other readied a towel. He pulled off the cloth covering his head as she dried him. He was as bald as an egg. His face was so devoid of flesh it seemed almost skeletal. His skin was like yellowed parchment, stained with age spots.

"You'll stay for lunch of course," he said as a nurse draped a robe over his shoulders.

They dined at a small table in a large chamber that emulated an imperial banquet room, with faux enameled pillars and murals of peacocks and dragons on the walls. The Commissar, now dressed in a stylish version of a Mao suit, with dragons embroidered on the cuffs, studied Shan as he poured wine. He nodded and turned to Tan. "This one's been stomped on a few times," he observed to the colonel.

"Inspector Shan started his career in Beijing and has served under me in Lhadrung for the past several years," Tan replied, as if it explained much.

The Commissar's stern face broke into a grin. "I never trust a man who doesn't show a few scars," he declared and leaned over to pound Shan on the back.

Shan pointed to a short line of raised skin above his eye. "That was the first, from the edge of a metal ruler swung by a teacher in a reeducation camp. I was seven. All downhill from there."

"How did you earn her wrath?" the old man asked.

"I explained that the picture on the wall of the Chairman with a clear face wasn't real, because the real Chairman had moles on his face."

The Commissar burst into cackling laughter, then raised his thin brows, in mock alarm. "Reckless behavior! Stand for the truth at all costs, eh?" he said and raised his glass to Shan. "He'll do," he said to Tan. "He'll do."

More staff silently brought platters of spicy noodles, eggplant fried in pimentos, and chicken in peanut sauce, all dishes of the Commissar's Hunan birthplace. Tan and their host chatted about old times as Shan watched the women who served the food. They were all Tibetan, all very young, very attractive, and very nervous. There was no evidence that the Commissar had a family. The aged tyrant lived alone with at least a dozen Tibetan servants, who seemed to be supervised by the older woman who had met them at the door. Tan had leaned into Shan's ear while they had followed the old man back into the house. "Most of his staff are from transition families," he stated in a low voice. It meant the women had members of their families in a prison and would be well aware of the old man's power to send them to hard labor as well.

Tan had explained that the Commissar was particularly fond of public works projects and was still personally involved in the oversight of half a dozen bridge and highway projects, which the colonel now spoke of as they finished eating.

"Prodigious expenditures," the colonel said. "No doubt a challenge to keep track of those millions."

The Commissar's instincts were still intact. He lowered his glass. "I have a small army of clerks," he said with a question in his tone.

Tan slid an envelope across the table.

"Looking for a piece, Colonel?" the godfather asked. "Not like you."

"Looking for a missing piece. This account," he explained as the Commissar opened the envelope, "had over twenty million transferred to another project over the past ten months."

"The infrastructure budget covers all my projects," the old man said as he scanned the page Pike had printed out. They had been looking for corruption and found no unexpected accounts. Then Amah Jiejie had examined the messages with the eye of a seasoned bureaucrat and declared that a grave sin had been committed. "Sometimes adjustments are made between projects," the Commissar suggested.

"Of course. But this was transferred outside. To the Five Claws project. Or more specifically, to certain contractors of the Five Claws."

"The hydro project? Can't be. That's a Beijing project. Different pocket altogether. No one would shift funds from my projects to pay for that one. It would be stealing."

Tan produced another piece of paper and set it beside the Commissar's plate. "Comrade Ren, the director at the Five Claws, is a figurehead. His deputy does all the work. His project was in a budget squeeze, threatening the schedule for the Chairman's visit in two years."

The Commissar went very still. "What visit?" he asked in a simmering voice.

Tan offered a sympathetic shrug. "They didn't consult me either. My own county." Tan pointed out another page. "Here's an earlier message. He says twenty million is enough out of the bridges, time to tap the highways."

As the old man read the emails one side of his mouth curled up into a snarl. "How?" he demanded. "How do they do this without my knowing?"

Tan nodded to Shan. "We don't know exactly," Shan confessed. "We didn't want to show up with forensic accountants. It would scare them off their game. We do know about a death warrant you signed. They needed to eliminate a man who threatened them, so they made a preemptive strike. Called him corrupt. We know the signature of the governor was forged but your chop appeared authentic."

"Impossible!" the old snake hissed. "I gave no such order!"

"Religious Affairs tried to look into what they were doing at the Five Claws," Tan added. "They seemed to resent the intrusion, so they burned down their warehouse in Lhasa."

The Commissar's breath grew rapid and his throat seemed to creak as he tried to form words. "That fire on Kunming Road?" he demanded. When Shan nodded, he seized a wineglass and shattered it against the wall.

Shan did not react, even though it felt as though a great weight had been lifted from his shoulders. "They are very clever, very sure of themselves," Tan continued. "They scored a big victory at Larung Gar then moved on to the Five Claws. They call themselves the Amban Council."

Another low hiss escaped the Commissar's lips. He was the Amban, and Shan knew now that he had no council. His eyes narrowed as he looked at the copy of Metok's death warrant. He stared at his chop on it for several long, rattling breaths. Murder and corruption were routine aspects of the political chess game the Commissar had played for decades. Far more grievous would be the sin of forging his personal chop. "Larung Gar, you say," the old man said. "Give me the names on this so-called Council," he ordered, then turned the envelope over and pushed a fountain pen toward Shan.

The staff began to retreat, as if sensing an imminent eruption. The older woman produced a bottle of pills and set it beside the Commissar, who swatted it to the floor. His lips curled and his hands began to shake. "Larung Gar!" he repeated. The woman began to rub his neck. He seized a fork and made a vicious swing toward her, but she easily dodged the blow, as if expecting it, and snapped at him to behave.

The Commissar took the list of four names. As he read it his face flushed and his entire body began shaking. "I have two men who take care of problems for me," he said in a venomous whisper. "But they are away just now." He pointed with a trembling finger at a wooden box on a sideboard, which the woman brought him with a despairing expression. He reached inside it and withdrew several objects, which he kept clasped in his hand. Two of the nurses appeared with a wheelchair. As they reached out to help him into it, he shook them off and extended his hand to Tan, who took its contents without a word.

As the nurses pushed the Commissar away, the woman lifted the list of names Shan had written, read it, and gave a long sigh before dropping it on the table. "He was with the Commissar for two years. A wicked boy. He was a bad influence on the Commissar. I finally convinced the master to send him away."

"Who?" Shan asked.

"The Commissar finally agreed, but only if he could find him a good position. He was sent to run that campaign at Larung Gar," she said as she pointed to the last name on the list. "Jiao Wonzhou."

The woman spun about and disappeared in the direction of the wheelchair, leaving Shan and the colonel alone. Shan realized Tan was staring into his cupped hand at whatever the Commissar had placed there. After a long moment he turned his palm and the objects rolled out onto the table. The Commissar had given Tan four bullets.

The long sleek train was just pulling into the station as Shan met Pike at the entrance. Shan positioned Pike at a table of the tea shop where he had first seen the American, then, borrowing his phone, waited for the last passengers to clear the platform before approaching the knot of staff assembled by the dining car. The conductor sagged as he spotted Shan, then finished his instructions to the staff and motioned them toward the cartons of food being loaded at the other end of the car.

"I'm fairly certain no one died today, Inspector," he said as Shan reached him. "No passengers who failed to rise up out of their seats, no corpse in the cargo car."

"Congratulations, comrade," Shan said. "But I'm interested in an old corpse, not a new one."

The conductor frowned. "That was an accidental death, the doctor confirmed it."

"There's many kinds of accidents." Shan held up the phone with the image of Madame Jiang. "Do you recognize her?"

The conductor stared at the photo, too long, before looking up. "I see hundreds of people a week, sometimes thousands. How would I remember one face?"

"Try harder. She was on your train. She's quite attractive, the kind of woman who stands out."

"Inspector, please. I can't say."

"Try harder. Or we can get a lie detector test. Yes, on second thought, let's do that. I can probably have you back here by midnight or so."

"Impossible!" the conductor protested. "I must ready the train for the return! We have a very tight schedule."

"Perhaps you can make the return train tomorrow or the next day. Should I go find your boss and tell him the news? It would seem the courteous thing to do."

"I don't know her name!"

"Look it up. I can tell you the seat number. Right beside Sun Lunshi, the man who died."

"I can't look it up. She never bought a ticket."

Shan saw how the conductor nervously watched a Public Security patrol walking down the platform. "Surely you don't allow stowaways, even beautiful ones."

"Surely we don't say no to Public Security." The conductor closed his eyes and shook his head. "Look, she ran into the station in Golmud and demanded we hold the train. She made me search my computer for Sun Lunshi and asked his seat number, then just darted on board."

"And they stayed together the entire trip?"

"She read a magazine at first, and took a nap, or at least seemed to. I remember because it seemed odd that she seemed to have urgent business with the man but didn't speak to him right away."

She was working hard at doing nothing, Shan knew. It was a technique taught at police academies for not spooking informers. Show no aggressive attention, just be disinterested and casual, giving the target a chance to speak first. "But eventually they spoke."

"I wasn't there the entire time, but yes, about halfway through the trip. A lot of passengers were asleep by then but those two began talking."

"Did they eat together?"

"Is that important? No idea." The conductor took off his hat and ran his hand over his thinning hair as he tried to recollect. "Yes, something from the snack bar. Sandwiches and sodas, I think. The dining car was all booked, blocked out by tour groups."

"You didn't notice he was missing later?"

The conductor shrugged. "We dim the lights. People huddle down in their seats and sleep."

"And she never asked you about him, never acted as though she might be concerned about his whereabouts when he disappeared?"

The conductor hesitated as he grasped Shan's question. "No," came his nervous response.

"As if she did not expect him to return."

The conductor's face clouded. "I'm not the detective here." He retreated a step then paused. "She looked in his baggage when he left. The overnight bag and the tube."

"Tube?"

"A long black tube with a handle on it, nearly as long as your arm. One of those cases used for charts and blueprints."

"And maps," Shan suggested. "It was not with the baggage collected after he died."

"Because she took it."

"And you didn't stop her?"

"I was at the end of the car when she passed me with it on the way out. I said, 'Maybe you should leave a receipt or something.' She laughed and showed me her badge again," he explained, turning to look down the platform. The engineer was shouting for him from beside the locomotive. Obviously relieved for the excuse, the conductor mumbled an apology and hurried away.

As Shan watched him retreat, a lanky figure stepped off the train. The conductor apparently muttered something to the man as he passed him, for his head snapped around in Shan's direction. He seemed to groan as Shan held up a hand for him to wait.

"What good fortune to see you, Doctor," Shan said in greeting.

The doctor did not share the sentiment. "I have to report to the office," he said impatiently.

"Fine, we can go there together and I can speak to the train master, so I can explain that you can't make the next train because law enforcement needs you."

The doctor sighed. "What is it you want, Inspector?"

"The autopsy report for Sun Lunshi. You never sent it to me."

"I gave it to the Public Security officer who followed up for you. Lieutenant Huan, Lhasa Division. He said he would get it to you. Hardly worth the trouble. It just confirmed my initial findings. We hand out warning brochures to every passenger. We can't be responsible when people don't read them."

"I don't follow."

"He inadvertently killed himself. His levels of benzodiazepine were off the chart."

"A drug?"

"A sleeping aid. It's a long trip, a stressful and restless night for many. We tell passengers to never take such drugs on the sky train. It inhibits breathing, lowers blood pressure. Combine that with even a moderate case of altitude sickness and the results can be fatal. You saw his blue fingers, his cyanosis. The fool didn't have a chance. He took too many pills, fell asleep, and never knew he was shutting his eyes forever."

"Tell me something, Doctor. Could a few pills like that be mixed in with soda and swallowed?"

"Of course. They're small pills, hardly noticeable in a swallow of soda. Or if given a few moments to dissolve, not noticeable at all."

Shan glanced at a passing knob patrol and thanked the doctor. He willed the doctor to walk away, then gazed with new understanding at the shiny, serpent-like machine beside him. The sky train was a murderer's paradise.

"It's not your fault, Shan," Pike said. They had been sharing a pot of tea as Shan explained what he had learned.

Shan looked up from his cup. "What do you mean?"

"Look at you, like you just came back from a funeral. I've seen it before. The investigator syndrome, the psychiatrists call it. My Irish grandmother had another name for it: 'sin eating.' But there's so much sin here you'll choke to death."

Shan could not push the forlorn tone from his voice. "They were laughing together, you said. Then she gave him a soda knowing it would kill him. I should have known the first time I met her. I should have known before, when I saw that the front data sheet on the file about Metok had been replaced. I blinded myself. I saw her as a victim and only wanted to protect her. She helped kill Lhakpa's niece. She single-handedly killed Sun."

"They were both already dead when you met her," Pike pointed out.

"But not Jampa, the old janitor. I told her, Pike. I told her Metok had got a message out from the jail. I was trying to comfort a grieving widow. Instead I gave the Amban Council the information it needed to find and kill Jampa. I should have known right away because all the framed photos in his apartment only showed Metok, no family shots. I was blinded by her grief. I responded with my heart and not my brain and it got Jampa killed. And I pushed my son under their boots. He could have been killed. Then they nearly killed Amah Jiejie."

"You astound me, Shan. You have lived all your life in this fucked-up country, even survived a gulag prison camp, but you still have such naivete. It might be charming elsewhere, but here it is poison. Is it because you don't see the evil or because you just don't want to believe it?"

"You don't understand, Pike. They don't sense evil in anything they do. They tell themselves they are just doing their job, serving the motherland."

Pike frowned in disappointment. "Then you are becoming one of them."

"No. After all these years, I am finally becoming one of their victims."

The American did not reply but withdrew several index cards from his pocket. They had small punctures in the top corners, as if they had been pinned to the wall. "The members of the Amban Council. Jiao is in charge. He spent his first ten years in Public Security, then went to a job with the Party. A troubleshooter. A fixer. He did a term as special assistant to some retired Party kingmaker here then was sent to Larung Gar, but not to construct new housing. He created a palatable plan to eliminate the politically unreliable crowds gathering there and snare a few of the more vocal dissidents in the process."

The American tossed out another card. "Major Xun. Before Larung Gar he was in Kashgar, devising ways to smoke out Muslim rebels. For a year he was assigned to work with Jiao there, when Jiao was in Public Security. They created a team that dressed in black, with black ski masks. They snatched suspected dissident leaders out of their beds in the night, never to be seen again."

"How could you possibly know this?" Shan asked, then after a moment answered his own question. "Amah Jiejie."

Pike nodded. "Amah Jiejie may seem a sweet old aunt. But she is quite the cunning operative herself and knows people in key offices all over China. When she calls someone, it is as if the colonel himself is calling." He tossed out another card. "Huan. He showed up in Larung Gar and made quite an impression on Jiao and Xun. After they destroyed the main classrooms, the teachers kept their students together for classes in makeshift locations. But Huan always knew where they were, to strike next."

Pike tossed down another card. It didn't have a name on it, only the numbers 404. "The Amban Council likes to meet in obscure places. Cao and Tink triangulated emails to fix several of their locations. A safe house run by Public Security. Once at a club reserved for senior Party members. Once at the arsenal in Lhadrung. That one surprised me, but then they found another location. The 404th hard labor prison."

Shan took the card and wrote a name on it, the fourth name he had given the Commissar. "Captain Wenlu. The warden. He nearly beat my son to death. The Tibetans already knew," he added and explained that the warden had received a Tibetan death chart. "Those from Larung Gar knew and never told us."

"Christ, Shan, you work for Colonel Tan. It's a wonder you haven't received a death chart."

Shan gave a bitter grin. "The astrologer who made the chart is a friend of mine. I think."

"It all started at Larung Gar," Pike said. "They had their female spy there. In emails Xun and Huan call her their 'robed eyes.'"

"She was the nun," Shan said.

Pike nodded. "A nun, a widow, a flirtatious train passenger. Like I said, a versatile asset."

"And a tour guide," Shan added. "A woman of many talents."

They watched in silence as passengers began to board the next train.

"I keep watching that video that Zhu brought back from Hong Kong," Pike said. "That knob officer said he had orders from Colonel Tan. He said it tentatively, like he wasn't sure he believed it. Then he shrugged and said, 'Too hard to resist.' I keep asking myself why he added that. Did you see her today, I mean really see her? You had described a forlorn widow desperate to protect her family and restore her husband's good name."

"It was the same woman," Shan said.

"Yes and no," replied the American. "That's not the woman I saw today. I saw the woman from the train. She was wearing a loose jacket today, but underneath were tight jeans, makeup, and manicured nails. She knows how to deliver the goods."

"Goods?"

Pike rolled his eyes. "She's trained to use her body, Shan. She was in Hong Kong, I am sure of it. She took that man to her hotel room, and in a few hours he was ready to give her anything she asked for."

Shan looked with despair over the queue of eager passengers waiting for the next train. "Every time we think we have a lead, we slam into a stone wall. We don't have the maps. We have no proof that this woman killed Sun. We have no proof that she was in Hong Kong. We don't even know her real name or where she really lives."

"Not for a couple more hours anyway," Pike said with a dangerous grin. "Tink is tailing her."

Shan was early for his rendezvous at the Jokhang Temple with Meng and so took advantage of the thinning crowds to get reacquainted with the thousand-year-old structure. He paused inside the entry to buy incense from a toothless old woman then walked slowly inside, letting his senses adjust to the dim light and the acrid scent of incense and butter lamps. A few pilgrims were still completing the interior circuit, pausing at each of the little low-doored chapels that lined the passageways. Shan ascended the nearly empty stairs to the second floor, where a more condensed ring of chapels encircled the hall. Shan sat on a bench near a shrine to a protector deity and closed his eyes, sensing the air of ancient devotion that seemed to permeate the temple. Here the afflicted and other seekers had come for centuries, lighting incense and lamps to converse with the gods. Lokesh said that if you tuned your soul just right, you could hear the echoes of the devout from across time. Shan looked down at a stick of incense in his hand

and wondered if it would provide the cleansing he needed after spending two hours with the Commissar. The different mantras of the few pilgrims and monks still in the chapels flowed out into the hall and seemed to combine into one rhythmic prayer. He let the sound wash over him, let it become the salve he needed for his aching spirit.

After a few minutes, he rose and walked along the chapels, exchanging greetings with the monks and nuns who were beginning to sweep the floors, and pausing in a chapel to light his stick before the Historical Buddha. As he passed a chapel on the way to the stairs, he recognized the images of the Medicine Buddhas over an altar on which a solitary incense stick burned. The only occupants were two women murmuring in the corner beside the altar. He extracted another stick, intending to light it for Ko. He bent to pass through the low entry then froze and abruptly backed away. The two women were a nun and Meng.

Neither had seen him, and Shan edged into a shadow where he could study them without being conspicuous. They were facing each other, not the gods, and the nun was holding one of Meng's hands while working the beads of a rosary, a mala, with her other hand. Shan found himself inching closer, trying to understand, then he saw the glass of water sitting between them. Meng wasn't there as a tourist, wasn't there because she had struck up a casual conversation with the nun. They were reciting a Medicine Buddha mantra, slowly, because Meng stumbled over the words. The mantra was considered to be a powerful antidote to disease, provided it was recited the traditional one hundred eight times over a glass of water, which the patient then had to drink. Shan watched until the nun squeezed Meng's hand and gestured for her to lift the glass.

He left the temple, then the temple grounds, and walked around the adjoining block before reentering the courtyard a few minutes past their appointed hour. Meng waited for him on a bench. He sat beside her. They both looked up as a chorus broke out above them.

"From one of the roof chapels," Shan said.

"It sounds like blessings drifting down from the heavens," Meng observed, then after a moment pointed to the main gate. "There's a strange fossil in the flagstones," she said.

"It's called the Amolongkha," Shan explained. "The old ones have many different stories about it. Some say it was a demon trapped in stone by the earth gods. Some say it is a protector, sleeping there until it is needed."

"It's not needed now?" Meng asked after a moment.

Shan did not reply. "We should walk the pilgrim's path around the temple," he said instead.

"I have a long drive back," she said. Her voice was weary.

"The Nangkhor Kora is the name of the path," he said, and rose, extending a hand. "It's been redeeming souls for over a thousand years. Lokesh says pilgrims leave tiny traces of spiritual energy along their paths, in which case this one must have the most energized air in all of Tibet."

Meng hesitated, cocking her head toward a *clip-clop* sound at the main gate. An old woman was progressing along the path in traditional prostrations, rising, advancing a step then dropping her body to full length on the ground. The sound came from the worn wooden blocks strapped to her hands to protect them.

"The two-legged horse, some of the old Tibetans call it," Shan said of the rhythmic sound made by the wooden blocks. "I was in a cell once with some old monks. It had a narrow window near the ceiling that allowed in a little light and sound. There was a shrine nearby, and every few days their faces would light up with joy when they heard that sound. Clip-clop, clip-clop. Some pilgrims travel like that for weeks, even months. Good for the soul, terrible for the knees."

Meng gazed at the ragged, stick-thin woman. For a moment Shan thought he saw envy in her eyes.

They walked along images of deer and dharma wheels that adorned the outer wall then reached the long line of prayer wheels mounted along the kora path, huge brass drums embossed with auspicious signs and the mani mantra, which was offered to the gods with each spin of the wheel. Shan showed Meng the best grip for spinning

the wheels, and they advanced down the line like eager pilgrims, setting each one in motion. Meng laughed as they spun the first one,
Shan's hand on hers, but her smile faded, and as they reached the last
one it was replaced with a somber, almost desperate expression.

In the shadows behind the temple they sat on a bench and watched
in silence as the old woman caught up and passed them, her passage
marked by the fading, hollow sound of her wooden blocks.

When Meng's eyes came back to him Shan turned over her hand
and dropped something in it.

"What's this?" she asked as she lifted her hand.

"My rosary, my mala. The beads are carved sandalwood. Lokesh
thinks it may be two or three hundred years old, making it saturated
with spiritual power."

"I don't understand."

"I want you to use it, not one of the cheap plastic ones I expect
you bought here."

Meng stared at the old beads. "Why would I need beads?" she
asked in a tight voice.

"For your mantra. There's more than one for the Medicine Buddhas. *Om bhaisajy bhaisajye bhaisajye samugate svaha*, that's probably the one you were taught in their chapel. Once you start you need
to finish all the beads, all one hundred eight."

Meng seemed to sag. "Can't we just pretend for a while longer?"
she whispered. "Not everything in life has to be investigated."

"Pretend?"

"Pretend that we would raise a beautiful young woman together."
Meng's voice cracked as she spoke. "Pretend you and I would sit in
her university graduation and laugh about being taken for her grandparents."

"That day in the square when you told me about Kami, you said,
'I know she will do well with you,'" Shan said. "It was only later that
I realized it sounded like you meant you would not be there." Meng
did not respond. "That woman, the caretaker who always hangs back.
She's not with you for Kami's sake."

"Care for Kami is part of our arrangement. But yes, she is a nurse. There are days when I need special medicines, days when I can't really function. I used up almost all my savings on the trip down here and to pay for her and my medicines. I'm sorry. The money was supposed to be for Kami."

Shan found he could not speak. He took her hand and gripped it tightly.

"I was supposed to go for another treatment today, but they aren't really doing any good." Meng lifted the beads in her other hand. "I came here instead and found another kind of treatment."

"There's always other doctors," Shan murmured.

"No. It's too advanced. They said if we had caught it a year earlier, when the pains first started, I may have had a chance. But the nearest doctors to my station were a hundred miles away, and I couldn't leave Kami by herself." Meng shrugged. "But I got her to her father. Like one of those pilgrim journeys in a way."

"How long?" he asked after a long silence.

"Five or six months, maybe as much as a year." Meng leaned her head into Shan's shoulder and gripped his hand tightly. Tears were streaming down her face. "I'm so sorry, Shan."

"I'm so sorry," he echoed.

A new *clip-clop* rhythm rose from the corner of the temple. Neither spoke, neither moved, as another pilgrim made her way along the ancient path in front of them and slowly disappeared around the next corner.

CHAPTER SEVENTEEN

The nondescript building Tink led them to was at the edge of the Nor-bulingka, the park of the elegant old Summer Palace once used as a residence by the Dalai Lamas during the warm months, a perfect location for a clandestine safe house. Shan guessed the plain-looking structure had been built during the years of Tibetan modernization in the 1950s when yak trains had hauled European furnishings over the Himalayas, including the old record player and stacks of 78 rpm records Shan had once seen in the young Dalai Lama's residence. Housing had been built for senior officials close to the palace, and this house would have been only a few minutes walk from where the Dalai Lama had lived.

The building, with walls of tan stucco and a red-tiled roof, was a duplex, but Tink had reported that the second unit was empty, without any furnishings. After sitting in the darkened street for nearly an hour, Pike muttered impatiently and opened the door of Shan's car. "I'll just reconnoiter a bit."

"There could be a security system," Shan warned.

"Doubt it. The security of a safe house is based on it being unknown." The American rummaged in his backpack and extracted a pair of pliers, a screwdriver, a flashlight, and a small flat metal bar. "Just do your job, Constable," Pike said in a tone meant to preempt any questions. Then he slipped into the shadows.

The woman appeared a quarter-hour later, carrying a shopping bag from the bus stop down the street. Shan waited a few minutes then knocked on the door. He stood to one side so as not to be seen through the window, then planted a foot inside as she opened the door. She gasped as she recognized him and retreated several steps.

"Bastard!" she hissed.

"A pleasant evening," he observed as he closed the door behind him. "You can smell the flowers in the Dalai Lama's gardens."

"You have no idea what you're dealing with, Constable," she said when she found her voice. "You should just go. I don't have to tell anyone that you breached state security. Not yet."

In contrast to its simple exterior, the house was expensively furnished, in Western style, with a large flat-screen television on one wall and photographs of European cities on another. Shan motioned her to the overstuffed sofa. "State security," he repeated. "Is that what you call it? Assembling false evidence for the murder by execution of Metok. The murder of Sun Lunshi on the sky train. Demeaning yourself to play the widow of Metok in order to find and destroy the evidence of murder by your handlers. You were their spy among the nuns at Larung Gar, the one who arranged the death of Tara Namdol. So busy. So many faces. How do you keep them all straight?"

She sneered at him. "Huan wanted me to shave my hair off. I said wearing a robe and taking off all my jewelry was as far as I would go. I learned that novices don't shave until they take their vows, so it worked fine."

"What an abundance of names you use. Do you even recall your real one?"

The woman's eyes flared. "Just call me a loyal soldier in the service of her government."

"Try Kim Nakai," came an amused voice in English. Pike stepped out of a darkened doorway, holding a badge on a lanyard. "Kim. Sounds Korean," he added, then fanned three passports in his other hand. "The one in front shows entry into Hong Kong six weeks ago."

The woman's fingers curled, and she tensed for a moment as if about to leap at Pike, then she calmed and decided to speak to Shan. "My father was from North Korea. He provided many services to Beijing and was allowed to emigrate."

"Intriguing," Pike said. "A spy for the Chinese in North Korea. Following in daddy's footsteps?"

Kim slid along the sofa as if to distance herself from the American as he approached. She twisted as she reached the end, pushing her hand into the cushions.

"Looking for this?" Pike asked, suddenly aiming a pistol at her. "First place I looked, since I realized you must do a lot of your work on your back." He hefted the weapon in his hand. "Wonderful gun. A German Walther. So cosmopolitan of you."

Kim seemed genuinely frightened of Pike. She rose to stand behind Shan.

"It isn't the bullet you need to worry about, sister," Pike said, heat rising in his voice. "It's who we're going to tell about your misadventures."

"Your Colonel Tan is a worthless relic!" she spat. "He is powerless in Beijing. His hour is over!"

Pike ignored her. "Tan is just one possibility. There's the Hong Kong authorities for the bank fraud you committed. The Ministry of Justice in Beijing for arranging a murder by execution—something like that undermines the people's faith in government. How about the Ministry of Tourism for committing a murder on their precious train? Or perhaps one of the American newspapers with the tale of how you helped to kill my daughter?"

Kim's sneer slowly faded.

"I was thinking more of the Party disciplinarians," Shan said, "about the conspiracy of the Amban Council to take over Lhadrung County. But, of course, my first choice is the Commissar. Or do you just consider him another old relic too?"

The words caused her to sag, and she lowered herself onto the sofa. "I am just a soldier. I obey orders."

Pike began opening the drawers and doors of cabinets, pocketing two extra magazines for the pistol, then smiling as he extracted several pieces of paper from a desk drawer and scanned them. "Boarding passes to and from Hong Kong," he declared. "A taxi receipt from Golmud on the day you boarded that train. Cab fares to and from Metok's apartment. Behind on your expense reporting, Miss Kim? What's next, a receipt for the sleeping pills that killed Sun Lunshi? Using soda as a murder weapon, how original."

"We are taught to improvise," she snapped back. Her gaze hardened. "And a foreigner acting against the People's government will not simply be deported. There's evidence that could indicate that *you* killed that man on the train. I would be happy to supplement it. That would mean hard labor for the rest of your life. Perhaps in one of the prisons that we will soon be overseeing?"

Pike emitted a low growl. His lust for vengeance for his daughter's death had been like a slow smoldering fire, and the flames seemed closer than ever to eruption.

"We just want to chat a few minutes, Kim," Shan said, "then we can leave. Tell the truth and you can forget all about us."

"For a starter, where are the maps you took from Sun?" Pike interjected. "In Huan's office?"

Kim stared at both men in silence, then gestured toward the closet by the door. "No one cared about the maps, other than to keep them out of the hands of Metok and his foolish friends."

Pike opened the door and pulled out a black plastic tube from the closet.

"Good," Shan said, "an encouraging start. Now let's chat about Hong Kong."

She asked for a drink and laughed when Shan brought her a glass of water, then she stepped to a cabinet and retrieved a bottle of whiskey. She looked at them expectantly. Pike nodded, but Shan just took a sip of the water.

They spoke for nearly an hour, during which Kim warmed to her task. She seemed not to consider their questions a serious threat and was not shy about boasting about her undercover accomplishments, since she clearly expected that Pike would be deported soon and Shan would be arrested. She confirmed that she had gone to Hong Kong to suborn testimony about Metok. She laughed when Shan asked where the money was and, in a taunting tone, explained that she had stolen account records and forms from a bank clerk and created a false account document as supplemental evidence. "Right there, in the second drawer," she said, nodding toward the desk. "I brought more forms back, just in case."

After finishing her glass of whiskey, she enthusiastically declared her relief to be finished with the boring role of Metok's wife, for which she had borrowed the daughter of a Public Security secretary, bribing her with a new computer in order to have her report to the apartment for two hours each day. Kim proudly recounted the details of her mission on the sky train, which she claimed to have executed flawlessly. "He might have saved himself if he had called for the doctor," she added with a shrug, as if it assuaged her conscience.

Finally, she yawned and stood. "I'm tired. We're done."

"No," Shan said, "sit at the desk. You have some writing to do. Just some supplemental evidence, as you say."

Half an hour later she threw her pen down. "I've done what you want. Leave," she snapped, and stepped toward her bedroom.

"One more thing," Pike said with a grin, and before Shan could stop him he slapped the woman with the back of his hand, so hard the blow sent her sprawling back onto the sofa.

She glared at the American as she rubbed her cheek. "You have my gun," she said through clenched teeth.

"My gun now," Pike growled.

"If I reported that a foreigner had stolen a gun from a Public Security officer, you would be the most wanted man in all of Tibet."

"Please do," Pike shot back. "The press conference with all the American reporters will be stunning."

"*Wo cao ni!*" Kim spat.

"Unladylike," Pike chided, and stuffed the pistol into his belt.

Shan stepped in front of the American to shield the woman from him. "When does Lieutenant Huan leave for the mountains?"

A satisfied sneer grew on Kim's face. "He left hours ago to take the news to Jiao. I called him as soon as I left the Potala."

Shan and Pike exchanged an alarmed glance. She had played them, dragging out their interrogation.

"Huan and Jiao won't just take that phone with the video when they reach that camp whose location you so helpfully provided, they will eliminate all witnesses to his doing so. By the time you get there, all those Tibetans will be dead!"

CHAPTER EIGHTEEN

The Talons had a new image painted on the flat rock face above them, a garuda, the ever-watchful bird protector. "No one here," Tan said as he, Shan, and Pike approached the campsite. Shan glanced at his watch. "Two more hours," he pointed out. They had bought time by calling Major Xun and telling him Tan and Shan wanted to meet with the leaders of the Amban Council to negotiate the custody of the phone they sought and resolve their mutual problems. Xun, though confused at first, had quickly warmed to the suggestion. "You're sure this is the place?" Tan asked then Shan pointed to the shadowed juncture between two of the stone claws, where a figure in a gray cloak stood up. Tan held up a hand as Shan was about to introduce Lhakpa. The colonel didn't want to know the Tibetan's name. He had readily agreed to loan Shan a helicopter but only if he joined the expedition. The vengeance he sought was not against Tibetans.

In the gnarled trees just beyond the stone claws, a fire burned in a ring of stones, with rolled blankets beside it. As Shan stepped to the campfire he made out Jaya and the hail chaser in the shadows of the trees, the latter working his mala, his staff leaning on the tree beside him. The ragged old weather wizard took no notice of them, other than pulling his staff closer.

Jaya gestured to the little spring that wound through the shadows of the trees, then saw Ko limp into the clearing and helped him to a flat rock, handing him her own water bottle as he sat. Shan's son had also stubbornly insisted on joining. He had been slowed not by his injuries, which were rapidly healing, but by the complex horoscope chart Shiva had given him before their departure. Every few minutes on the hike up from the flat where the helicopter dropped them he had paused to study it.

"I was getting worried that they would stop you," Jaya said, nodding toward the nearby cliff. Shan look down and with a sinking heart saw ten figures walking up the steep switchback trail that led to the Talons from the dam site. Three wore the uniform of Public Security, the others the coveralls of Jiao's cleanup crew, now with rifles slung on their shoulders.

A cold fist seemed to close around Shan's heart as he saw Pike extract the pistol he had taken from the woman in Lhasa. The American's fury smoldered more intensely with each passing day, and now he gazed down at their new opponents with the eye of the starving predator who had finally found his meal.

"It's not our way," Shan said to him.

"Your way? You mean let them get away with it all and live a long life because they will be punished in their next incarnation? I don't have time to wait forty years so I can step on the bugs they become, Shan. Not my timetable. Not my way. It wasn't *your* daughter they killed."

"There's been too many bullets fired already," Shan said. "If we use guns on our side, the Tibetans believe the gods will abandon us. It's not the Buddhist way."

"Tell them my god abandoned me a long time ago. They won't need to touch a gun." Pike popped out the magazine and checked its load. "Tell them to have their gods turn their backs. I'll only need a few minutes."

"You'll never survive."

"Survival isn't all it's cracked up to be."

"We have two hours before the young ambans arrive."

"I'll take a nap."

"No. You'll come with me to see the work of the Tibetan gods. You owe the Tibetans that much."

The shelves past the black felt wall held no artifacts when Shan led Pike past them, but the American lingered at the array of weapons and tools at the rearmost shelf. Pike lifted the heavy maul and hefted it with an approving nod. "Blue?" he asked.

Shan explained how the objects had been used.

"Hammer of justice then," Pike said of the tool. His tone was still grim but his curiosity was roused. "You sure your Gekho doesn't have some Viking blood?"

"The Earth-Shattering Maul, they call it. For crumbling the walls of deception."

"Exactly," Pike mused as he leaned the maul against the shelf again. "Hammer of justice," he repeated.

"There was a boulder spouting blue flame from its top when we arrived at the scene," Shan recalled. "When the flames went out we discovered only water. It was taken as a miracle. I still don't understand."

Pike grinned. "Dirty hands. They must have someone who studied a little chemistry."

"Dirty hands?" Shan asked.

"Hand sanitizer. It's just water and ethanol. Light it on fire and it burns blue until all the ethanol is consumed. Nothing left but water. Buddhist chemists. Very clever."

The air was strangely still as they emerged from the trees, and the American paused, though Shan was not sure if it was because he had seen the narrow, treacherous path that edged along the cliff face or if he had heard the faint echo of the mantras from the far side.

They followed the sound across the face of the mountain. Pike did not hesitate on the tiny goat track but slowed as they reached the cave. The mantras were much louder now. Wisps of juniper-scented smoke wafted from the opening.

"Taking me to some smoky shrine won't change anything," the American growled. "No wild-eyed deity is going to change my mind."

"I honestly don't know what to call what is inside."

"I'm not going to fall on my knees and sob for repentance of my evil intentions," the American said, glancing back and forth from the cave to Shan. "I don't want to be saved, Shan. But I don't want to be disrespectful to them."

"Are you arguing with yourself?" Shan asked.

Pike grimaced. "I'm so far beyond saving I don't even know what saving is."

Pike stared in the direction of the chanted prayers. "You're asking me to go inside her mountain," he said, pressing his hand against his face for a moment. "Every night I have the same nightmare. I have buried her and later I come back to the grave with flowers and her hand is out of the ground, like she has been clawing back from death. I'm weary of burying her every night, Shan. But I know I will be doing so every night until those bastards are brought to justice. You have to let me make my justice, Shan," Pike said, then turned as an old *dropka* woman with a heavily wrinkled face arrived, balancing a bundle of juniper boughs on her shoulder. She stared silently at them, then resolved Pike's dilemma by thrusting the bundle into his arms and entering the cave. Without another word, the American followed her inside.

The number of Tibetans inside the chamber had more than doubled. They sat on odd carpets and blankets, all chanting the same mantra now, the invocation of the red Tara, the fierce goddess Metok had invoked. The old woman led Pike along the smoldering braziers, pausing at each to recharge it with new boughs. Pike mutely complied, holding the juniper until he stood at the last brazier, his task complete, and stared at the tunnel that led deeper into the mountain. He did not look back at Shan, just proceeded into the darkness.

Shan caught up with him by the little gas stove in the long chamber, where the kettle simmered. Yankay sat nearby, on a stack of folded blankets, nursing a cup of tea.

"Nothing is more patient than a mountain," the hail chaser proclaimed, then gestured to the kettle. "Have some tea."

Pike accepted a cup as Shan poured and drank in silence, gazing first at the pool of light at the far end of the chamber then the murals of demons on the wall, given movement by a long row of flickering butter lamps. He seemed to have grown exhausted when he finally spoke. "Who are they?" he whispered.

"There were a lot of names for them," Shan said. "The faith testers, the enforcers of the straight path, the protectors of right conduct. I've even heard them called the conscience demons. Pilgrims came for hundreds of years to walk along that line."

Shan saw that Pike's hand had gone to the gun on his belt.

"Now it is your turn to walk it," Shan said.

Pike did not take his eyes from the demons as he replied. "That's why you brought me here, to be mocked by a bunch of Tibetan gremlins?"

"If that's what you wish to call it," Shan said, "then yes. They reflect whatever the pilgrim brings to them."

Pike did not react as Shan took the mug from his hand, just kept staring at the frightening images. "I'm tired, Shan," he finally said, "so damned tired of this world. I thought I would spend my life in the military, but the politicians gutted the role of the soldier. I thought I would spend the rest of my life in the FBI bringing criminals to justice but only discovered that the line between sinner and saint was too blurred for me. I thought I might be a scholar and help a younger generation understand the world, but then I realized that maybe if I left them alone they might have a chance at creating a better world. I lost my heart when my wife died. I lost my soul when my daughter died. If I could be certain you would be able to give those bastards what they deserve, I think I might kill myself right here."

"But you won't," Shan said.

Pike's voice had grown hoarse. "Why?"

"This is Gekho's cave."

Pike twisted to look at him in confusion. "No. Gekho's cave is on the other side of the mountain. They destroyed it."

"This is Gekho's cave," Shan repeated, then extended a hand to help the American to his feet. "This side offers a way out."

Emotion roiled the American's face. His confusion lingered but took on a hint of fear, then dread. Pike took a step forward, then another, walking along the demon gods as if his feet had grown leaden. He halted, then bent to set his gun on the floor of the cave before continuing. As Shan followed a few steps behind, he could hear Pike murmuring something and quickened his pace to listen. "Hail Mary, Mother of Grace," he heard, then with the next breath, "*Om mani padme hum.*" Shan realized that he should not be surprised that such a complicated man should have a complicated mantra.

Halfway down the long chamber Pike paused to look at the Tibetan nurse, now visible as she sat in the light at the far end, but he quickly looked away. He was greeting each of the demons with a respectful nod now and lingered long enough to study the flayed human skins, skull necklaces, and wrathful serpents that adorned the images. At the painting of the particularly demonic black Makhala, Pike bent to set his two ammunition magazines on the floor. His anger had burned away, replaced by despair. He stood like a devout pilgrim before the wrathful demon, who clutched tiny broken humans in his eight hands, then went on to the final image, that of Yamantaka, Lord of Death, whose image was surrounded by flaming skulls.

Finally, he gazed at the nurse, who still sat bent over her work, heedless of her onlookers. The little area where she worked was partially obscured by boulders and stacks of the rugs and blankets that were used for sleeping.

Shan stepped past Pike and turned to study him. The American looked sapped of strength, as if he had been physically fighting with the gods.

"I read that the old pilgrims came to this cave to bury their particular demons," Shan said.

Pike's brow furrowed, as if he had heard a troubling question in Shan's words. Then Shan stepped backward, leading him into the little alcove. The query on Pike's face seemed to intensify, then Shan stepped aside and the American froze. The prostrate form on the blankets against the wall was turned away from them but its long blond hair was conspicuous.

The big man's voice cracked as he spoke. "You . . . you found her body."

"We found more than that," Shan said as Pike approached the blankets.

The woman rolled over. One eye was still bandaged but the other was bright. "Hello, Papa," Natalie said with a smile.

The American was paralyzed. "I never . . ." he sputtered, "I couldn't . . . how could I even hope . . ."

Natalie's words were slurred, and her single eye seemed to have difficulty focusing. "Until you're here," she said, "there's no way to get here."

Pike sank to his knees and wept.

When they returned to the camp, Ko was lying in the shadows, still studying the perplexing horoscope chart Shiva had given him. Lhakpa was sitting beside him, helping to decipher it.

"There's auspicious events ahead," Lhakpa observed. "And joy and death, but that's only the first part. Shiva likes to tantalize with the old signs. There's a barrel, and a blue wavy line like a stream, and two birds. I've never seen the like." He did not mention one of the most obvious of the images, a set of manacles. The snow monk professor pointed to another image. "And a bowl of something white. Milk. Why milk? I can't see—" He was interrupted by a sharp whistle from above. A young Tibetan sentinel, whom none of them had seen, waved his hands from a perch in the rocks above. Jaya and Ko stepped deeper into the shadows of the trees.

Shan stood with Tan and Lhakpa between the high spines of stone as Jiao, Xun, and Huan finally entered the camp. Huan, his pistol in his hand, kicked at the blankets by the firepit, then raised his gun as Xun peered into the shadows between the rock claws.

The surprise on their faces quickly changed to smug satisfaction as Shan and his companions stepped into the open. "Three old dinosaurs all in one place," cackled Huan. "We should call a museum."

Jiao, clearly in charge, shot Huan a peeved glance and ordered him to holster his gun. The deputy director studied Shan and each of his friends then decided to speak with Shan. "You know why we are here, Constable."

"To conclude all this business," Shan replied as he returned Jiao's cool gaze.

"Exactly. You've made it all so convenient. Give us the phone with the video. If we later discover you have duplicated it, then all those Tibetans we sent for reeducation will find themselves transferred to the 404th hard labor prison with ten-year sentences."

"You have no authority over my prisons," Tan hissed.

"Fifteen years then. And they won't be your prisons for long, old man." Jiao looked at his watch, then extended his hand for the phone.

"You misunderstand," Shan said. "We are terminating your conspiracy." He extracted several pieces of folded paper from his pocket. "Your Miss Kim was very cooperative." He unfolded the papers. "First, a signed confession that she lied to a Public Security officer in Hong Kong, wrongfully telling him that Colonel Tan ordered him to bear false witness, with enough detail to prove that the three of you fabricated a case against Metok to commit murder under cover of the law. Then these," he fanned out three sheets. "Apparently you all have bank accounts in Hong Kong that cannot be explained. Corruption often carries worse punishment than murder in the motherland. If you try to explain them away by saying Miss Kim made false account records, then you only implicate yourselves more fully in Metok's murder." Pike had offered an expression for the tactic which Shan suspected was out of Shakespeare. *Hoist on their petard.*

Jiao laughed. Huan put his hand back on his pistol. "So resource-

ful, to the very end. I respect that, Constable," Jiao said. "You have a
tenacity of spirit that I admire, really I do. Twenty years younger, and
you could have joined us. Was it you who attacked the director with
ice balls?"

"Sorry. Everyone said the mountain god flung that hail, including
the director himself."

It was Major Xun who spoke next. "You do understand that you
are surrounded by our men, all of them armed. I fear we may be
looking at another one of those terrible road accidents in the mountains. Do you drive? I foolishly forgot to ask whether Professor Gangfen did."

"A real one or another fake one?" Lhakpa asked.

Xun grinned. "Good. You understand. Can you all fit in one car?"

"How many times have we said it in training, Major?" Tan said in
a disappointed tone. "Never assume you have the upper hand until
you have actually seized it." The colonel motioned Xun to follow him
to the cliff edge. It was over two hundred feet to the bottom, but they
could clearly see the file of men in coveralls being marched off by Zhu's
men. Zhu, standing on a boulder, waved at Xun and the colonel.

"In her statement," Shan continued, "Agent Kim states that you had
her reserve three tickets on tonight's flight to Katmandu. You actually
do have tickets waiting for you, though they were reserved out of Colonel Tan's office. Leave now and you can still make it. From there you
can fly on to India or Hong Kong. A new life in the same body."

Jiao seemed amused. "Same body?"

"Stay here and you will be put against a wall and shot. For corruption. For murder. But most of all for lying to Beijing. The Tibetans
would expect you to be reincarnated. Something very lowly, I should
think. A squirrel perhaps?" he asked, turning to Lhakpa.

"Moles," the snow monk replied. "The mountain god needs workers below the ground."

Suddenly Huan recognized Lhakpa. "You! The damned professor!
I suspected you had escaped, damn you, but only confirmed it in our
recent interrogations at the 404th. You're the bastard who slipped

from my custody in that hail storm!" He lifted his pistol, aiming at Lhakpa's chest.

Jiao pushed down Huan's gun. "You know nothing about our relations with Beijing," he said to Shan.

"Of course we do. We had to think like Public Security. Watch when your subject least expects it. Intercept emails. Emails sent over many weeks, with glowing reports of progress. Never a mention of all the accidents, and wholesale lies about foundations being poured and the control room being almost complete. Sounded like an entirely different project when I read them. There was even one about a parade of grateful Tibetans showering you and the director with flowers on May Day. I doubt even Beijing believed that one."

"Shut up!" Huan shouted. "You are finished! No one will listen to you! You will all be gone! You're as good as dead already!"

Shan ignored him and kept speaking to Jiao. "I didn't mean to confuse you," he said. "The evidence won't be presented by me or the colonel. We have collected all the proof of your crimes in one file, so it reads like a story. All except that of your murder of Tara in Larung Gar. We'll keep that among us. The proof will be presented by another old relic. He was most unhappy to find you had forged his chop and used it on several critical documents. And to usurp the name of the amban—that was sacrilege. Just how accurate is the Commissar with his crossbow?"

Jiao went very still.

Huan stepped closer to Lhakpa, aiming the gun at his head now. "Give us the phone!" he screeched.

Jiao ignored the Public Security officer. "The Commissar understands the need to cut corners from time to time, in the interest of the motherland."

"Too late. He probably would have taken a bribe if you had offered one." Shan shrugged. "But you hurt his feelings. You may not believe in the mountain god, Comrade Jiao, but the Commissar is a god of the Party. As old as the hills but revered almost as much as the

Great Helmsman. There is no one in Beijing who will not take his call, no one who will not accede to his wishes."

"How could you have known about the signatures?" Jiao growled.

"The governor wasn't even in Tibet when he supposedly signed Metok's death warrant. And why would the Commissar put his chop on it when the project wasn't his?" Shan asked. "Major Xun didn't realize that when he started stealing glances at Colonel Tan's mail that the colonel's assistant would start stealing glances at his. You were using faxes because the email service was unreliable. You probably shredded yours. Xun did not."

Shan's gaze shifted to Major Xun. "Amah Jiejie found them in a file taped to the bottom of a drawer in your desk. What was your phrasing? Oh yes, 'The smelly old ass won't know the difference.' I thought you meant the colonel at first but then you replied that he was half-blind anyway. We were confused about that until we intercepted the earlier emails. Your arrogance blinded you to the fact that the Commissar and Colonel Tan are old compatriots. The Commissar didn't know he had signed off on switching twenty million to your control, not to mention a diversion of heavy equipment from his highway project. Twenty million is a lot. You probably do have secret accounts in Hong Kong, come to think of it. And imagine when we confront those contractors who worked at the dam when they were supposed to be on other projects. They will be scrambling all over each other to make confessions, hoping for leniency. Beijing's enforcement policy against corruption is very effective. You know how it works. First one in gets immunity, everyone else a bullet. Or maybe they will just go with murder charges, that might be more politically palatable." He shifted his gaze to Xun. "Of course, things will go more quickly for you, Major. A military court doesn't get bogged down in bureaucracy. How long do you suppose, Colonel, before a bullet is reserved for Xun's head?"

"Did you kill Jampa?" Tan demanded of his chief of staff.

"Not exactly." Xun sneered. "He was still alive when I left him in that alley. He didn't resist, just started one of those damned mantras."

"Less than a month," Tan replied to Shan. "And I will reserve for myself the honor of pulling that particular trigger."

"Then there is the warden at the 404th," Shan added. "He will sing for his life when we tell him that you have all confessed."

"Never!" Huan shouted. "This changes nothing! We will just advance our plans. None of you leaves the mountain alive!" He stepped toward Tan, who fixed him with a cool, level gaze. "Including you, old man. Xun will step into your office. I will become head of Public Security in Lhadrung County. We will have plenty of time to clean up all the loose ends, like that old hag of a secretary you have." He raised the pistol at Tan, ten feet away. Tan reacted only with a taunting grin. Huan fired.

Tan shuddered and clamped his hand over his upper arm. Blood oozed out around his fingers. Huan laughed and raised his gun again but as he fired, a figure speeding out of the trees crashed into him. The pistol fired twice as Huan and his assailant hit the ground.

"Ko!" With a wrench of his gut Shan realized his son had deflected the shot that was meant to kill Tan. The two men wrestled on the ground. Blood spurted from the tangle of limbs. The gun fired again, and Huan went limp.

Shan ran to his son, but Tan was there first, pressing his palm against a bloody spot on Ko's upper chest as he lifted him to examine his back. "A clean shot, out the shoulder," the colonel explained as Shan desperately confirmed his son's pulse remained strong. "Nowhere near a vital organ. That's good. Not much blood coming out of his mouth. Looks like it only grazed his lung, mostly through muscle. A battlefield wound, not a death blow." The colonel stared at Ko, who had passed out, and Shan realized the colonel was almost as stunned as Shan. The prisoner of the 404th had saved the life of the tyrant of the Lhadrung gulag.

Jaya reached down and with Tan's help carried Ko into the camp, where she leaned him up against a tree then draped a blanket over his legs as she began tearing off the bottom of her shirt to bind the wound.

Tan stripped off his own tunic and took off his shirt for her to use. Lhakpa lit a stick of incense and stuck it in the ground beside Ko.

Jiao gave an exaggerated sigh as he gazed at Huan's body. "Always too excitable," he declared, and made a gesture to Xun, who silently dragged the dead Public Security officer to the edge of the cliff and pushed the body over.

"You should go now," Shan said to the remaining conspirators.

"We are not finished," Xun spat, raising his own gun.

"You can still make that plane," Shan pointed out.

"Or what?" Xun sneered. "You'll try another cheap trick and call it the magic of the mountain god?"

"Cheap?" Shan replied.

As Xun looked over Shan's shoulder the color drained from his face. He seemed to shudder, and then stepped backward. Natalie Pike, supported by Jaya, had stepped out of the shadows.

"Impossible!" Xun gasped. "I laid the final charges myself! She's dead! She has to be dead!"

"This is Tibet," Shan said. "The dead always live again."

The American woman, the bandage still covering her eye, said nothing and extended the cell phone Xun so desperately sought. As Cato Pike emerged from the shadows, Shan's heart sank. He had left Pike alone with his daughter, giving him the chance to retrieve his pistol where he had dropped it on the cave floor.

But then Shan saw he was not holding the pistol, but instead had the blue sledgehammer that had been adapted as a ritual weapon. As the American took a step toward Xun, the major raised his pistol. Shan inched forward.

Tara the goat appeared beside Pike. She cocked her head at Xun, then gave a bleat as if in recognition. She lowered her head and charged the man who had killed the human Tara. Xun, clearly frightened of the small animal, shot twice at her as he retreated, missing both times. She gained speed to ram him but then suddenly skidded to a stop. Xun was gone.

"Pull me up!" the major shouted in a voice that held more anger than fear. He had fallen over the edge but had grabbed the thin ledge of rock that extended outward from the cliff. "Damn you, pull me up!" Xun dangled over the void, cursing and calling Jiao's name. Jiao took a hesitant step toward him then halted as he saw Pike striding forward with a treacherous grin. Pike's gaze lingered for a moment on Xun's pistol, lying on the ledge a few feet away, then the American turned to Shan. "What did you say this was called, Professor?"

"The Earth-Shattering Maul," Shan replied.

"Right." Pike looked at his daughter, then at Shan, before he swung the maul high over his head and slammed it onto the ledge rock. The thin lip of the ledge made a cracking noise but remained intact.

"Pull me up, you fools!" Xun shouted. "I will sign a confession!"

The words stopped Jiao, who had been slowly moving toward the major.

The cracking sound continued. "Wolchen Gekho, Sangwa Dragchen!" Pike shouted, invoking the old names for the fierce mountain deity, and slammed the god's maul onto the rock again. One of Xun's hands reached up over the edge, clawing for purchase, then the outer two feet of the ledge cap broke away and he was gone.

Pike looked back at his companions with a solemn expression. "Earth-shattering," he declared, then shouldered the maul and faced Jiao.

The pistol was in the deputy director's hand, but he slowly lowered it as he stared at the empty space where Xun had been.

"You should go, Jiao," Shan said again. "Catch that plane. Get out of China. Lose yourself somewhere. India might be easiest, or Vietnam. We will give you a twenty-four-hour head start. If you are lucky, you might even evade the men that the Commissar will send." He looked at Tan, who still sat beside Ko, and then Lhakpa. Both just returned his gaze with grim expressions. Neither objected. Huan and Xun had been the killers. Jiao had been the mastermind, the dreamer, like so many in China's recent history, who inspired the killers. Shan gestured to Lieutenant Zhu, who had appeared by the Talons.

"The cleanup crew is being recalled," Shan said to Zhu, "back to their army duties. Have one of your men escort Deputy Director Jiao back to his quarters to pack his bags, then to the airport. He has urgent business elsewhere." Zhu whistled and one of his commandos stepped out of the shadows behind him.

Jiao gazed forlornly at the soldier, then back at Shan, shaking his head. "You're nobody," he said, his voice cracking. "I was going to fire you when I moved to Yangkar."

"You're nobody," Shan echoed. With a dazed expression Jiao followed the soldier out of the camp.

Tan signaled for Zhu to wait, then scribbled a note. "See that the warden of the 404th gets this. He is to report to me first thing tomorrow. And radio for my helicopter. Tell them to bring Dr. Anwei. He has two patients for the hospital."

CHAPTER NINETEEN

The foundation for the control building on the upper slope had been laid, and a small arbor laced with flowers erected over a podium in its center. The ceremony for the chiseling of the pass, as the deputy director had described it in the invitations sent out weeks earlier, had been designed by Jiao long before his disappearance. The scene looked as if it had been staged for a Party poster. Young Tibetan women in colorful traditional garb and freshly scrubbed workers in helmets stood on either side of a four-foot-high model of a transmission tower. A public-address system played favorite hymns of the proletariat. The Commissar, wearing a once-stylish Mao suit, sat in a place of honor in the front row of chairs, tended by two of his nurses.

The director had protested loudly when Shan and the colonel had visited his office to report that they had sent Jiao away. His complaints had quickly faded, however, as Shan had begun explaining the conspiracy of the Amban Council.

"I didn't know," Ren had mumbled at first, but soon he was feverishly disassociating himself from the deputy director, calling Jiao "that arrogant young cub from Beijing." He clutched his belly when Tan sternly described the misuse of army resources, and for a moment Shan thought he was going to be sick. "These issues were all about operations," Ren nervously pointed out. "He was in charge of operations, not me."

"Except" Tan said, "you were the director. Surely you knew something. The chain of command always bears responsibility."

"This is a national project!" Ren cried. "We abbreviated procedures, yes, but for the good of the nation. Jiao had the full support of the bosses in Beijing!"

"Did you know that Xun and Huan blew up the cavern to kill the people inside?"

"Of course not! The demolition seemed the correct thing to do, from the engineering perspective."

"They arranged the death of one of your engineers," Tan pointed out.

"Metok was executed for corruption. A Public Security matter. There's always a few bad apples on such big projects."

"Metok was a good man, an honest man, killed by dishonest criminals," Shan stated.

"It would seem logical to add you as a suspect to that investigation," Tan suggested.

Ren was a man of few strengths, but one of them was recognizing the subtleties in the words of powerful men. He seemed to collect himself and squared his shoulders. "It would be a blow to the integrity of the government to have the head of the project accused as well," he ventured. "Perhaps we could find another way. For the good of the people."

"I can see you are a man of sound practical judgment," Tan replied in a wooden voice. Shan had had difficulty talking him out of offering Ren up on a skewer to Beijing. The Amban Council had all been dealt with, the warden having been demoted and sent to a desert outpost. The Tibetans who had been detained by Huan had all been released from the Shoe Factory and transported back to their mountain homes. Tan had even reluctantly accepted Shan's recommendation that each family be given a mule out of the prison stables. The Larung Gar prisoners at the 404th had also been given their freedom, and made a tearful reunion with Lhakpa, who had waited outside the gate for them.

Now, as his ceremony began, Director Ren motioned for his

companions to stand as a banner was unfurled on two long stakes held by workers. *Modern Tibet is a Chinese Tibet*, it read, only in Chinese characters. Gathered all around them were Tibetans, from the work crews and from the surrounding countryside. Ren gave a short, tentative speech, followed by words from managers from each of the companies involved in the glorious endeavor. As they spoke, Ren looked forlornly at the little detonator switch mounted on the podium. Chiseling the pass, imploding the overhanging cliff walls, was to be the final step in preparing the dam foundations.

Colonel Tan sat on one of the folding chairs near the director, with Shan on one side and the aged Commissar on the other, nurses hovering behind him. Shan ventured a glance over his shoulder. On a ledge above them were more spectators, including Cato Pike, Jaya, Lhakpa, and the hail chaser who, true to reputation, was doing one of his strange dances, shaking a bundle of twigs toward the narrow mountain pass. A murmur went through the crowd as they saw him, and workers pointed upward to a long line of prayer flags fluttering down from the sky toward the opposite slope.

As the last of the speeches ended, Director Ren rose and placed his hand over the switch. "I present to you the culmination of all our work," he announced, then hesitated. He fumbled in his pockets, then withdrew the little blue tsa tsa of the mountain god which Shan had given him. He positioned it on the podium, facing the mountain, and pushed the switch.

The massive four-hundred-foot-high ridge of jutting rock that was the final impediment to shaping the dam seemed to shudder as the buried charges detonated. It began to slide down the face of the mountain. Then suddenly there were more detonations, much larger, spewing rock fragments high over the valley, and a line of smoke and dust appeared along the upper slope opposite them. The entire face of the mountain bulged, groaned, and began to slide into the valley. The Commissar cackled with glee and clapped his hands. Director Ren stared stricken, clutching the podium as if he were in danger of falling.

Lhakpa and his friends had already known about the hidden fissures that had been part of the ancient shrine complex, but the seismic maps Sun Lunshi had died for had allowed Yeshe the demolition expert to lay more charges much deeper and higher than he could otherwise have done.

The ground under their platform began to shake. Two of the honored guests fell as they tried to step off the foundation. The slope along the foot of the valley began to collapse, then the destruction was lost in a massive cloud of dust. Tan turned and nodded to Zhu, who raised a hand to his chin and spoke into a small transmitter.

Less than a minute later Tan's helicopter landed on the road above them and a soldier ran to the colonel with an envelope. The colonel solemnly read the contents then handed the yellowed paper to the Commissar, who read it, nodding. Propped up by his nurses, he stood and stepped to Director Ren, who still stood as if paralyzed, staring at the vast cloud of dust.

"A damned shame, Ren," the Commissar declared in a dry, amused voice, then handed the paper to the director. "Beijing should have known better than to ignore us. We could have told them. Damned shame," he repeated and looked back at Tan with a mischievous sparkle in his eyes.

The challenge in their plan had been to find a way to detonate the fissures without having it blamed on the Tibetans. Cato Pike had at first refused to leave his daughter's side, just as Shan would not leave Ko's, but after two days the doctor had declared his patients out of danger. Ko would have an impaired but functioning lung and Natalie Pike, with therapy, was expected to regain full use of her limbs. Dr. Anwei was not as sanguine about her eye but was hopeful that doctors in America could find a treatment. Both patients had urged their fathers to go rest, and Cato Pike and Shan had joined Tan and Amah Jiejie at a dinner where Pike and Tan had finished a bottle of vodka, during which the American had learned of Tan's own bitter attitudes about Beijing. It had been near the end, when Tan had poured fiery *bai jin* whiskey for all, that Pike had offered the suggestion that would put all the blame on Beijing.

It was, Shan had to admit, a brilliant strategy. The fabricated note, dated nearly forty years before, was a report from a quartermaster that addressed the problem of excess and aging munitions left from prior hostilities. He recommended that they be dropped into a fissure in a distant uninhabited place called by the Tibetans the Valley of the Gods. Amah Jiejie had artfully affixed old stamps reflecting its authenticity and had verified that the quartermaster had conveniently died years earlier. The finishing touch had been Pike's inspiration as well. They had baked the paper in Amah Jiejie's oven to age it, with Tan hovering over the oven with ebullient anticipation, clapping the American on the back as they waited. The unexpected explosion had not been the work of Tibetans, it had resulted from the arrogance of Jiao and his patrons in Beijing, who could now readily blame the fugitive deputy director for the catastrophe.

The wind on their backs began to rise, slowly clearing the dust cloud. The high V-shaped pass was no more, replaced by a wide, jagged opening with a gaping crevasse below it. There would never be a dam across the valley.

Shan went to the director's side, who stood alone, still staring at his ruined project.

"There was no way for you to have known," Shan said. It had the sound of a suggestion. "You were brought in after the project was conceived and its plans laid."

"No way I could have known," Ren repeated in a dull voice. "I was . . ." he seemed to have trouble speaking, "I was brought in later."

"Jiao was a criminal who committed a fraud on the state. His friends Lieutenant Huan and Major Xun have also disappeared. No doubt they were part of the conspiracy."

"A conspiracy against the state," Ren mumbled.

"Against the people and their blessed motherland," Shan suggested. "I will say you cooperated fully with my investigation, that we couldn't have exposed them without your help. The colonel will confirm that. Everyone will soon recognize that as bad as this news is, it is better to receive it now than after billions are spent on a project that was always going to fail. Which means they will applaud your courage in speaking up."

As Shan's words sank in Ren seemed to regain some strength, though his voice cracked as he spoke. "You would do that?"

"You need to start clearing out the equipment and the buildings, immediately," Shan said. "But yes, I will do that. It will be a secret report, of course, sent through Tan and the Commissar. But your superiors in Beijing will see it."

Ren sighed. "They're building lots of bridges in Manchuria. I like bridges. I'll find a bridge project."

"Excellent. The people of Manchuria will be the better for it."

Ren nodded and began to step away, then turned and stared at the little blue god on the podium. He retrieved the figure and put it in his pocket, then left to return the valley to the gods. High above, a new line of prayer flags was drifting downward to settle over the debris field. Gekho's mountain had been wounded but still survived.

When Shan reached them, Tan and Zhu were studying the far slope with binoculars. A small crowd of Tibetans were excitedly pointing to a shadow halfway up the mountain, beyond the new rubble field. "That Gekho is one cunning rascal," Tan said with a grin as he handed Shan his binoculars. Shan aimed them in the direction the Tibetans pointed then grinned. A new cavern had opened on the side of the sacred mountain.

EPILOGUE

"Ah yi! Save me from this foreign devil!" Lhamo crowed, throwing up her hands in frustration as she aimed her cry at Shan and Meng, who sat on a bench on the opposite side of the farmhouse courtyard. The old Tibetan woman turned back to Cato Pike and renewed her animated discussion, jabbing her finger into the American's chest with each syllable.

Lhamo's husband, Trinle, and Lokesh watched from the doorway of the smaller house where they now lived, each of the old men casting anxious glances at Shan. Pike threw up his own arms in exasperation and Lokesh groaned, but then the American leaned close to the old Tibetan woman and spoke in a lower voice, as if confiding a secret. Lhamo reacted with surprise, then after Pike unfolded a piece of paper from his pocket she listened to him closely, then nodded. She shook Pike's hand vigorously, pinched the American's cheek with her other hand, then gave him a cigar, which she lit from the end of the cigar stub she clenched in her own mouth. As the American walked away, she stuffed the paper into her gau.

Pike grinned, puffing on the cigar, as he reported to Shan. "A tough old vulture," he proclaimed, "but I like her. An astute observer of the human condition. She said the constable has the most stubborn spirit of any person she has ever known."

"We knew that," Meng said. "And?"

"She will accept Shan's boots and binoculars. And a hundred dollars."

"A hundred dollars?" Shan gasped in alarm. "I don't have a hundred dollars."

"My gift to you. She's never had American currency, it seems. Not sure she knows what a dollar's value is, but it was worth the gleam in her eyes when she saw the bill. I'm afraid," Pike sheepishly admitted, "that she may have the impression that Benjamin Franklin is the American Dalai Lama." He shrugged. "I had to close the deal." He glanced over at the old woman, who stared at them expectantly. "Oh, and the merchandise is to be delivered immediately."

Shan called over Yara's son, who was playing with a much-subdued Kami, and whispered in his ear. The boy grabbed Kami's hand and they ran toward the big house. The two were back moments later, laughing, and clutching Shan's boots and binoculars. Meng took the worn boots and the battered binoculars and, with a ceremonial air, set them in a basket that had been adorned with red yarn. As the makeshift matchmaker, Pike escorted them with the gifts to Lhamo, who watched with a wary air until she confirmed the contents of the basket. With a whoop of joy, she pulled out the boots.

"I don't know if they are Trinle's size," Shan cautioned.

"Trinle? Who said anything about my husband?" the old woman asked, then kicked off one of her own shoes and pulled the boot on. She stomped her foot down with a satisfied gleam. "Milk price is paid!" she shouted for all in the courtyard to hear. She had not noticed that her granddaughter and Ko had been listening from a second-story window, and Shan watched as they joyfully embraced.

Lhakpa the snow monk had watched from the stable, where he sat on a keg with his goat at his side, sharing a hearty laugh with his brother the hail chaser. Shan had wondered more than once if it had really been the old hail chaser, not the doctor, who had saved his son.

He had feared for Ko's life as they had waited for the helicopter with Dr. Anwei. But then Yankay had seen Shiva's astrology chart and pointed with excitement at the bottom row of figures, which none of them had been able to decipher. "You have to live now, boy," the hail chaser had exhorted. Ko had weakly shrugged his shoulders. "You have to, son, because this says you will be getting married!"

Thus they had embarked on a double wedding ceremony, subject to Shan paying the customary milk price to Yara's grandmother, to compensate her household for the loss of a strong young woman. Shan had chosen not to point out that since they were all going to be living in the same compound Lhamo was not in fact going to suffer the loss of Yara.

Meng had agreed to marry Shan the day he had returned from monitoring the dismantling of the Five Claws compound. He had actually been doing research on whether Choden had authority to conduct a simple civil ceremony when Marpa and Shiva had descended on his office, insisting that the event deserved a grander and more traditional celebration. Shan had seen the shy anticipation in Meng's eyes and agreed, provided that some old Chinese traditions might be added to the Tibetan affair. The next day he had driven Meng to Lhasa, where they bought traditional clothing and boxes of small sweet cakes.

He had waited to break the news to Meng that Tibetan weddings were essentially three days of drinking and feasting. Meng and Ko had both understood the importance of acting quickly, though no one would speak of the reasons. Ko's medical parole lasted only so long as it took him to regain enough strength for hard labor, and Meng's own health on any given day was unpredictable. Tserung the mechanic had reluctantly accepted that he would not have time to brew the special wedding beer of Tibetan tradition and Shiva had dropped all her other work so that she could produce elaborate astrological charts for the marriages, which had, to Shan's great relief, identified a propitious date that provided for a short weeklong engagement for both couples.

The guests began arriving by early afternoon. Marpa, assisted by several townspeople, had arrived to set up large braziers scattered around the courtyard, several for cooking and one by the freshly painted gate for burning fragrant juniper. As they began cooking traditional dishes Tserung arrived with a truckload of tables and chairs. Lines of brightly colored prayer flags were strung across the courtyard and more juniper boughs were stacked by the gate. Tara the goat scampered about happily, though more than once she had to be guided away from the tub of beer that Trinle began dispensing.

Shan had stood in the window of his new second-story bedroom, watching the activity in the courtyard with an unfamiliar contentment. Not since his childhood had he felt the joy of family, and he had long ago given up any hope of ever again finding that happiness. Lhamo, Trinle, and Lokesh had already begun to enthusiastically play the role of grandparents to the other residents of their new home. He was well aware that Ko would soon be back in prison and Meng would succumb to her disease, but this joy would live forever in all of them, in this life and the next.

From the adjoining room where the women were preparing for the ceremony he made out Meng's throaty laugh, then Yara's giggles, and thought once more of the transformation the three of them had been undergoing. When Shan had finally returned with the rapidly recovering Ko, Meng and the others had already rehabilitated much of the old house, scrubbing and painting and even bringing back two large rugs donated by the carpet factory. Only later had Shan realized that the paint-stained tunic Meng wore was in fact her old Public Security uniform, stripped of insignia. With Lokesh's help, she had made a little altar in their bedchamber and joined in the construction of a larger one by the main entry below. With the aid of local herders and two yaks, they had even brought down from the hills a weather-beaten, centuries-old figure of a Buddhist saint they had found toppled and half-buried on the slope above the house and erected it outside the gate, to protect the household. Kami's campaigns of terror had largely subsided, and she had developed an odd rapport with Tara, who stayed at the farmhouse with the girl while Lhakpa helped Tserung and Lokesh with their daily work in the secret archive.

Out in the courtyard, Shan found Lokesh chatting with Shiva by the row of auspicious signs the astrologer had painted on the courtyard wall. As Shan approached, Lokesh cocked his head toward the gate. Squeals of laughter could be heard down the dirt track, and Shan hurried to the entry to see Tink in a beautiful, if overtight, silk dress, holding a cane as she walked beside Cao, who carried Natalie Pike on his back. Cato Pike rushed past Shan.

"What are you thinking?" the American called to his daughter. "You can't possibly—"

"Can't possibly miss this grand event," his daughter interrupted. Her words were still slightly slurred but her speech had much improved since Shan had last seen her in the hospital.

Pike darted forward to steady Natalie as she slid off Cao. "The doctor said—"

The American woman held up her hand to cut off her father, then accepted the cane from Tink and adjusted the red silk patch over her eye. "The doctor said I am ready for travel to America. If I can go to Baltimore, then surely I can go to Yangkar," she declared and limped forward.

At last the assembly quieted and Kami appeared in the doorway of the main house, wearing a simple red dress and holding a bouquet of fresh heather. The coral and turquoise beads that had been woven into her hair rattled as she scampered to Shan's side. She reached up and took her father's hand as the brides, with excited murmurs from the onlookers, stepped into the courtyard.

Both of the women had beads in their hair. Yara's long black tresses had been gathered into the traditional one hundred and eight tiny braids, most anchored with beads of turquoise and amber, although several were of silver, borrowed from friends all over the township. Over her richly embroidered blouse hung the silver gau of her grandfather, set off by a necklace of large amber and agate beads. From her belt hung an ornate silver hook, a symbol of the milk pail hook that nomadic women traditionally wore at their waists. On her head above the braids was a khampa-style fox fur cap.

Meng, in the red dress they had bought in Lhasa, had beads woven into a dozen small braids. Around her neck she wore a silver-and-turquoise prayer amulet, loaned by Shiva. All signs of the pain she increasingly experienced were banished by her radiant smile.

As the wedding party gathered in the center of the courtyard, Tserung, who had disappeared an hour earlier, arrived with a herder, carrying a cask of fresh water between them which he set on the cobbles. Shan glanced at Shiva, marveling at the magic that had caused her to include the traditional wedding cask in the horoscope for Ko. Under Lhamo's careful instruction, the two couples joined hands and walked around the cask three times. Lokesh, wearing a shirt embroidered with auspicious signs, had proclaimed that all was ready for the formal blessing when the ominous *thump-thump-thump* of a helicopter suddenly rose from the south. Every smile faded as it settled onto the flat hilltop above the farmhouse. Colonel Tan climbed out, then gave a hand to Amah Jiejie. Both of them were wearing long coats, which fluttered in the rotor wash as Dr. Anwei jumped out.

The joy in the courtyard had disappeared by the time Tan entered the gate. The colonel solemnly eyed the assembly. With rising dread Shan realized that if he had brought the doctor, then it must mean they intended to clear Ko for return to his prison. He glanced at his son, whose crestfallen expression showed that he understood. Yara clutched Ko's arm tightly, as if to prevent him from being dragged away.

"You, you, and you," Tan snapped, pointing to Yara's son and two teenagers from the herding families Lhamo had invited. "Go help the pilot bring down the liquor and cakes." A mischievous glint rose in the colonel's eyes. "This is a wedding, isn't it?" he asked, then helped Amah Jiejie out of her coat. She was wearing a surprisingly elegant dress, with a Tibetan comb of silver and turquoise in her hair. Tan took off his own coat, revealing a dress uniform resplendent with medals. He hesitated as he saw the uncertain expressions of the Tibetans, then Amah Jiejie tugged his arm and whispered in his ear. He considered her words, studying the Tibetans again, then unbuttoned his tunic and tossed it on the front rail of the stable, leaving him in a simple blue dress shirt.

Choden broke the tension by bringing the colonel a mug of beer, and the smiles began returning, which grew wider as the pilot led in the procession carrying cartons of vodka, arack, sweet rice cakes, sacks of uncooked rice, fresh fruit, and a surprising array of Chinese foodstuffs.

"Eight dishes for the married couples," Tan declared, referring to the traditional Chinese wedding feast. Several of the courses appeared to be in cans, but Shan appreciated the effort. "Eight," Meng explained to the curious Tibetans, "is the lucky number for weddings, because the number eight also sounds like the Chinese word for good fortune." Marpa ventured forward and Amah Jiejie began explaining how the food should be prepared.

Shan watched silently as Dr. Anwei approached Ko, bending with an ear to his son's chest to listen to his breathing. Ko stood still as a statue, his countenance hardening as if he were already bracing himself to reenter the razor wire compound of the 404th. Anwei lifted Ko's arms and probed the flesh over his wound, nodding and murmuring words of approval. Yara hovered close by, reminding the doctor that Ko was still very weak and greatly in need of rest. The doctor smiled and vaguely nodded, as if not understanding the worry his presence had caused, then stepped away as the helicopter pilot held up a glass of beer for him.

Tibetan weddings, Shan had learned years earlier, were much more about celebrating than ceremony. Eventually, after the tub of beer was refilled, Lhamo began directing the guests into a line along the edge of the cobbled yard so they could pass by a small table before moving to the benches in the center. On the table was an aged, foot-high bronze figurine of the Mother Protectress and a small bronze brazier in which incense burned. A stack of white silk prayer scarves lay on the table beside a wooden bowl filled with yak milk. Lhamo insisted Tan stand at the front of the line but the colonel stood awkwardly immobile, not understanding. Lhamo laughed, then draped a prayer scarf around his neck and demonstrated how everyone was to dip their fingers in the milk and flick drops in the air, a gift to the gods.

At last the couples stood before Lokesh. The gentle old Tibetan had been excited when Shan had asked him to give the marriage vows, but he had grown increasingly nervous about his role, saying he did not know what to say or, to Shan's surprise, what to wear. Lhamo had at first insisted he wear a monk's maroon robe, but the old man had adamantly refused, stating he had never been properly ordained. At last Shiva and Yara had fashioned an old gown into something resembling the vestment of a senior Tibetan official and had somehow even managed to find one of the squared caps worn by such officials. It was faded and tattered, but the old man had seemed to grow taller as Shiva had set it on his head.

When the assembly finally quieted, Lokesh extended his arms and each couple closed their hands around one of his. "Let us bear witness to the wholeness of our existence," he declared. "Let us bear witness to the triumph of love and compassion over the uncertainty of all life." A tear of joy rolled down the old man's cheek, and for a moment he seemed unable to speak. Then he cleared his throat and nodded. "It is done," he announced with a nod to each couple. "You are one."

Lhamo stepped forward with fresh bowls of milk, which each bride drank, to the cheers of the Tibetans. Gifts were then announced, beginning with the elegant astrological chart that Shiva presented to each couple. At the top of each was a pair of leaping fish, the symbol of conjugal happiness. As the bottom was a carefully inscribed verse from a traditional wedding song. *The man is like the sun, the girl is like the full moon*, it said. *When the sun and the moon meet, there is happiness in the village.*

Shan shot a grateful glance toward Shiva. She had not included the full wording, which referred to the young man and young girl. Her horoscope, moreover, simply predicted great happiness for Shan and Meng instead of the traditional prediction of many years of happiness. He knew Meng had been feeling spasms of pain during the ceremony, but she had simply gripped his hand more tightly and with obvious effort kept the smile on her face.

Amah Jiejie gave each couple a bottle of rice wine and before pouring, she linked each of the pairs of glasses with red thread, another tradition of old China. Tan too had a gift for Shan and insisted Choden come forward to listen. "You must help me with this one, Deputy," Tan stated to Choden, who nervously saluted the colonel. "Your boss has gotten married."

"Yes, sir."

"He has even more responsibilities now."

"Yes, sir," Choden repeated.

"Which means you have more responsibilities."

"Sir?"

"Constable Shan is being given three months' paid leave," Tan announced, and turned to Meng. "That is, if you can stand to have him around for so long."

Meng squeezed Shan's hand again. "I will try my best to endure him," she said, then completely unsettled the colonel by giving him an embrace.

The sun had set and several tubs of beer had been emptied before guests began to drift away. The pilot approached Tan, pointing to clouds that were beginning to cover the moon. Tan nodded and retrieved his uniform tunic, which Amah Jiejie helped him into. He stepped to the gate then paused, growing more sober, and Shan followed his gaze toward Dr. Anwei, who was escorting Ko through the crowd. The colonel studied Ko as he finished buttoning his uniform. "You know you are on medical parole, prisoner Ko," he declared.

"It's his wedding night, Colonel," Shan inserted.

Tan ignored him. "The prison system is responsible for your medical attention until your doctor releases you."

"And then my parole ends," Ko replied in a brittle voice. Yara appeared at his side, desperately gripping his arm.

Tan turned to Anwei. "I release him," the doctor stated.

The words stabbed at Shan. Tan meant to take his son back to the gulag.

Amah Jiejie pushed a thick file into the colonel's hand. Tan hefted it. "Everything the government knows about you is right here. To the bureaucrats this file is more real than the flesh and blood Ko." He held it in front of him and looked at it, shaking his head. "A chronic offender. Hooligan gang leader. You were arrested once for knocking down streetlights. A very difficult prisoner in those early years. Mess hall fights, escape attempts, assaults on guards. It's all there. One of the old files, not yet entered into the new computer systems. This file makes you more real to the government than your own flesh and blood, son. Now that Amah Jiejie has adjusted certain other records, it is the only evidence of your existence as an inmate. Everything about you, up to this night." Tan corrected himself, "Or rather, up to the day you nearly died saving my life." The colonel gave an exaggerated sigh. "This is Tibet. To live again you have to die," he said, and dropped the file into the brazier.

Shan and his son stared in stunned disbelief as the papers began to curl and burst into flame.

"As of this afternoon there is no longer a record of you at the 404th. You are dead to them. If ever asked, the doctor and I will confirm that you died of injuries received on that mountain. We shredded your hospital file before we left Lhadrung."

Ko leaned on Yara as if he might fall. "You're not taking me back to the 404th, Colonel?" he asked.

"Never again," Tan replied. "But you will have to persuade your constable to issue you a residency permit," he added. The colonel began to follow the pilot up the darkened hill, then paused and turned. "*Lha gyal lo*," he said, and disappeared into the shadows.

AUTHOR'S NOTE

If anywhere on our planet could be described as the landscape of the soul, it must be Tibet. This remote, rugged land, closer to the heavens than any place on earth, became the home to scores of thousands of temples, shrines, monasteries, and convents, with a culture and social structure uniquely focused on spiritual pursuits. It has long been a treasure unappreciated by the world that still offers lessons for us today.

Some of those lessons relate to respect for the earth and the extraordinary sustained efforts by Tibetans to populate their land with structures of reverence. While Gekho's Roost is the product of a novelist's imagination, Gekho was an important earth deity worshipped long before Buddhism arrived in Tibet, and his Roost is an amalgam of many authentic sites, encompassing even the fields of standing stones left by the devout forebears of modern Tibetans. Many of these prehistoric patterns of stones have been identified, mostly in western Tibet, and have intriguing links to the ancient horse warrior cultures of central Asia, as further examined in John Vincent Bellezza's valuable book *The Dawn of Tibet*. What was it about these high ranges that caused so many to linger and build monuments to that which they held sacred? What was the process by which the devotion of fierce warriors evolved into the complex cosmology of compassion that became Tibetan Buddhism?

Such questions led me to suggest in this tale that these lands might be characterized as the Rosetta Stone of the soul. If so, then perhaps it is inevitable that they encompass extremes of the human journey. The Tibetans spent several centuries reverently constructing their temples, eschewing technological advancement and economic progress so they might focus on the mysteries of the human spirit. The Chinese have spent several decades dismantling those buildings and the peaceful society that erected them so they might advance a more secular, intolerant political agenda. Over ninety percent of Tibet's holy buildings, numbering in the tens of thousands, have been destroyed over the past sixty years in a relentless campaign of cultural annihilation. Another lesson of Tibet, often reflected in Inspector Shan's saga, has been that it is darkness that defines the light, and suffering that gives meaning to compassion.

The roots of the Tibetans still run deep, and from time to time significant new Buddhist institutions do emerge, such as the teaching center of Larung Gar. While I overlaid a novel's plotline upon that academy, it is a real-life microcosm of Tibet's struggle. Larung Gar remains a rare ray of hope for Tibetans, despite Beijing's wrenching initiative to reduce its size and importance to the Buddhist community. As reflected in these pages, thousands of monks and nuns were abruptly expelled from the school and forced to abandon their monastic careers by officials who seemed to equate spiritual pursuits with acts of political rebellion. Larung Gar endures, however, keeping ancient traditions alive.

One of those venerable traditions that have always fascinated me is that of the hailchasers. For centuries these weather charmers, who were often trained as rigorously as Tibet's acclaimed medical doctors, roamed the land, consulting and placating the earth deities to protect farmers and herders. Elaborate festivals, with roots in pre-Buddhist Tibet, were often staged in monastic centers to honor those deities in the hope of avoiding the land's violent, sometimes fatal, hailstorms and earthquakes. Some in Tibet suggest that the failure to keep harmony with such deities is why its landscape has been so ravaged in recent decades. Mountain ranges have been stripped of their fertile forests, huge mines have depleted their minerals, and the land's unique wildlife decimated. Major new dams are being built at a frantic pace to power Chinese cities in the east, without meaningful environmental assessment. Some Tibetans in remote regions have been abruptly introduced to the twenty-first century by the arrival of clearcutting timber crews and bulldozers that scrape away the mountain that had always been home to their protective deity.

As I immersed myself in these modern Tibetan realities while writing the Inspector Shan series I came to see Tibet as a vital barometer of our own humanity. The rest of the world too often turns a blind eye to the oppression that occurs there and in neighboring Xinjiang Province, preferring to focus its moral outrage on issues that pale in comparison to the abject human rights abuses of this struggling region. Those abuses diminish all of us. We can't fight for human rights in one place, in one political context, and not fight for them everywhere. The most profound lesson of all from Inspector Shan is that the Tibetan journey has become our journey too.

:Lha gyal lo,
Eliot Pattison